IN ROBIN'S NEST

Elizabeth Sumner Wafler

E L I Z A B E T H   S U M N E R   W A F L E R

authorHOUSE®

AuthorHouse™
1663 Liberty Drive
Bloomington, IN 47403
www.authorhouse.com
Phone: 1 (800) 839-8640

Published by AuthorHouse 02/12/2016

ISBN: 978-1-5049-7906-1 (sc)
ISBN: 978-1-5049-7907-8 (hc)
ISBN: 978-1-5049-7908-5 (e)

Library of Congress Control Number: 2016902228

Print information available on the last page.

Any people depicted in stock imagery provided by Thinkstock are models, and such images are being used for illustrative purposes only. Certain stock imagery © Thinkstock.

This book is printed on acid-free paper.

For Porter
And in memory of my mother
Sibyl Eskew Sumner

PROLOGUE

Robin Hamilton

2013

Lessons learned are like bridges burned: you only need cross them once. Yet there are those of us who learn those lessons only after crossing our bridges over and over, retracing our footsteps as if looking for a mislaid pen or pair of glasses.

One late February evening while the wind probed and rattled the shutters of my brownstone, I read that my favorite band had filmed a documentary about the band's history. The television premiere was scheduled for that Friday night. Delighted, I called Theresa in Paris, wishing it were possible for the two of us to watch the show together. I knew that my daughter's boyfriend would be away, so I called her and asked if she would come and watch with me. I heard the grin in her voice, "I'd love to, Mom."

And then the night arrived. Was it meant to be that the producer had chosen to include film footage from the very concert I had attended that fateful night in 1977? It had been a long time since I'd thought about the night I'd met Dean Falconer. I sat in stunned reverie for a space of time, my daughter, Lark, beside me nonplussed.

All the rationalizations with which I'd built my careful house of cards shimmered before me. Could I somehow manage to pick my way back across those charred bridges for the sake of my only daughter? I wanted to tell her the truth.

Maybe it wasn't too late.

CHAPTER

1

Lark Hamilton

2013

Despite a wind that threatened to freeze my lips to my teeth, I had to grin at the thought of my mother: beneath the sophisticated surface of Robin Hamilton, New York professional, simmered the soul of a seventies rocker. Swaddled from head to toe, I plodded the last block to her home on the Upper West Side to watch a documentary about her favorite band with her. As I mounted the steps of the brownstone my grandparents had bought for a song in 1961, Mom abruptly pulled open the great door. "Lark! Did you *walk*? Are you not frozen?"

"Hi, Mom. No cabs," I said, kissing her warm cheek and tugging at the layers of scarves around my neck.

"I made a fire for us. Go get warm! I'm just opening the wine and putting a snack together." Uncommonly pretty at fifty-four, my mother, wearing a white tunic blouse and jeans, disappeared into the kitchen.

Shrugging from my coat, I extricated the laptop from my bag and made a nest in the Indian-patterned pillows tossed about the sectional. I would catch up on work while keeping one supportive eye on the TV. My phone sounded from my pocket, a pissed-off wasp against my hip. A text from Ben: "Hey, beautiful. Can't wait to see you tomorrow."

Ben. I had met Ben Holland one sultry summer night at the West Village rooftop party of one of my yoga students, Kimberly Kist. Swathed in whispering raspberry silk and sporting an armful of gold bangles, Kimberly had handed me a glass of sauvignon blanc in the kitchen and whispered breathlessly, "Lark, I have *the* man for you. Kirk invited him."

"Kimberly. You know I don't …"

"He's *gorgeous*, Lark," she purred confidentially. "His mother was a Brazilian *model* in the sixties!" To my skeptical expression she said, "At least *meet* the man … and talk to him."

"What does he do?" I asked grudgingly. Kimberly had fixed me up before with a Wall Street broker who, although witty and attractive, had a regrettable penchant for cocaine.

"He's a coffee buyer!" Kim said over her shoulder, fairly pulling me by the hand. I followed her onto the roof fragrant with the potted gardenia trees her husband Kirk grew.

Kirk and Ben stood under a string of industrial twinkle lights holding bottles of beer. That night I wore my long blond hair in a loose ponytail over the shoulder of a short indigo sheath embroidered with silver thread. Kirk introduced me to Ben, whose eyes, as dark as the beans he bought, lingered on mine. His teeth were very white, and the lights glinted off shiny black hair that needed cutting.

"Lark?" He tasted my name for the first time. "Like the songbird."

"It's a nickname. My name is Laurel," I said, extending my hand. "Apparently, I was a very happy baby."

Two days later, the two of us met for coffee. Ben introduced me to the art of cupping through importer samples and his milieu of green buying in verdant Latin America for Coloma Cup Coffee. An inveterate teacher, I talked of trends in twenty-first century education. Later that night, we taught each other what we liked in bed.

Ben and I had been happy in our love for more than two years. But lately, a gaggle of unsettling thoughts about our relationship had been springing up like mushrooms after days of rain. It was time to talk to him. I would do it tomorrow.

A metallic clang from the kitchen intruded on my reverie; I knew Mom was pulling out a pretty tray. Presentation was a big thing with Robin.

I noticed the program had started and called, "Mom, it's on!" I glanced from my laptop to the television screen and did an incredulous double take. I stared at the face of a girl in the swaying throng perched on the shoulders of a very happy-looking young man. *Is that my mother?* Riveted, I called, "Mom, are you coming? There's a girl who looks an *awful* lot like *you*."

"Be right there, darling!" Her voice was light, amused.

Since she was sixteen years old, Mom had been crazy about the Eagles, who had rocked the country and chronicled the high-flying seventies. I'd cut my teeth on that music. And now that vinyl was back, it was pretty cool that Mom still had her old records. I liked the scritch-whish of the needle as it rippled over the grooves. I would swear Mom would want me to toss her original copy of *Hotel California* into her coffin before I closed its mahogany lid for the last time.

My mother rounded the corner with the tray of appetizers: quinoa crackers, our favorite truffle cheese, fresh berries, and two glasses of wine. She peered through her distinctive tortoiseshell frames at the screen and lowered the tray to the cocktail table. The Eagles strummed their guitars and tossed their rock-star tresses—young, tight-jeaned, newly minted gods. "Oh, there's concert footage too … and from the Hotel California Tour! Lord, Lark," she breathed, fingering the chunky strands of turquoise beads at her throat, "look how *sexy!*"

"Mom. Watch the audience." I located the pause button just as the camera panned toward the girl again. "Look. *There!* The girl on the blond dude's shoulders. It *is* you, isn't it?"

Mom sank to the sofa as we stared at the close-up of the impossibly young and luminous Robin Hamilton, size six, chestnut hair falling in Farrah Fawcett waves around her face.

"Mo-om?"

She nodded almost imperceptibly. "I'm fine, Lark. Just ... surprised."

"Where was this? Did you know you were being filmed? This is so cool!"

My mother clutched the stem of her glass and took a liberal gulp. "That was the DC performance," she added as if it made everything clear. I unmuted the TV.

"So who's the cute guy? Did you know him?" I asked. A prickle of concern began along the edge of my scalp, and I slipped my hand around hers. She was trembling. "Mom, what is it?" I asked softly.

Her lined eyes closed. The song "Victim of Love" spun up and out of the television. As the drummer sang, "Tell me your secrets; I'll tell you mine. This ain't no time to be cool," pain and something else, something inscrutable, settled over her face like a cloud shadow on a mountain. Beyond my grandpa Hank's andirons, the fire snickered and blazed.

After a long moment, my mother opened her eyes. She turned to me, her smile open, loving. "An old friend," she said evenly. "Someone it's time you met."

CHAPTER

2

Robin

1977

From the moment I registered at NYU, I insisted on an authentic dorm experience, with benefits: I would bump my laundry bag home once a week to Mom's squeaky-clean washing machine and enjoy some home cooking and a little pampering.

"Mom, I'm home!" I dropped my things in the foyer of the brownstone to which my parents had brought me home from the hospital as a baby and stooped to pet our capricious cairn terrier, Atticus. The little dog loved people but could be vicious with other dogs, as if to disaffiliate himself from the canine camp.

A lilting voice greeted me from the kitchen. "C'mon back, darling! I left the shop early today." Since I was ten, my mother, Olivia Hamilton (née Courtwright), from whom I'd inherited my green eyes, had managed the bookstore Speak Volumes on Fifty-Third Street for an eccentric gentleman who lived in red-velvet seclusion in a penthouse on Central Park West. With a degree in library science from Hunter College and a passion for American literature, Mom dreamed of owning the bookstore herself one day.

"What smells so *divine?*" I asked, my stomach grumbling.

"Pineapple chicken." She hugged me. Her familiar lemon-sugar smell settled around me. "It's a new recipe from *McCall's* magazine. Your dad's on his way."

"I have some news that will make his day." I grinned and opened the refrigerator to inspect its contents. Snaring a block of cheddar in a baggie, I pinched off a hunk and popped it into my mouth. My first word, rather than *Da* or *Ma* like most kids, had been *cheese* or a close approximation: I'd toddled to grasp the handle of the fridge demanding, "Deese!"

The solid slip-thunk of the front door announced my father's arrival. "Robin!" I could hear his broad grin. "Didn't expect you until *tomorrow* night. What a treat!" Chestnut hair the color of my own tumbling over his forehead, tie askew from the day, Henry Anderson Hamilton strode into the kitchen with the laundry bag I'd dropped. As he bussed my cheek I winced at the six o'clock whisker rasp against my skin. "I've missed you, sweet pea!" My dad was the happiest person I knew; his initials, HAH, fit him to a tee.

"Robin, why don't you go ahead and put your wash in while we have a drink?" Mom said, covering the rolls on top of the stove with foil. "Then we won't have to listen to the machine while we eat." She turned to my father. "Robin has news." She gave my father a big smooch. I averted my eyes as his hand cupped her backside. I loathed the thought that my parents might still be having sex.

Dad went to the wet bar in the living room and poured three glasses of Lancers. "I declared a major today … a *double* major," I said, tipping a wink to my mother and settling into my chair. I paused a beat. "English and philosophy."

With those words, I revealed my intention to follow my father down the road paved by the great minds of his heroes Thomas Jefferson, Thurgood Marshall, and Gloria Allred (whom he admired for her savvy, chutzpah, and shapely legs). He collapsed into his chair and the throes of ecstasy. "You little minx!"

Hank Dad had eschewed the practice of litigation with its often chaotic, long hours and latent deadlines that could interfere with the positive work-life balance he craved. His residential real estate practice afforded him a comfortable living with a home-for-dinner practice. He and Mom enjoyed cooking dinner together and bantering over the evening news from the little black-and-white set in the kitchen.

"What field are you thinking?" My father was beaming so brightly you could have read by him.

"I have plenty of time to decide that, Dad," I said laughing.

As the washing machine ground through its old gears in the kitchen, Dad said, "There are two kinds of lawyers, Robin: those who make love and those who make war. If you're not the warring type, you won't enjoy litigation. Now *real estate* law, on the other hand, is a *family* practice of sorts … with real rewards." Atticus crouched in front of Dad, his preferred human, poised to spring into his lap. Dad patted his chest with both hands, Atticus's green light, and continued, "You're dealing with mostly happy people, usually taking a step up in life." I had heard it all before but indulged my father his passion that night.

At the table Mom passed a platter of chicken, golden robed in pineapple syrup, my way. She had loosened her dark hair from the french twist she wore for work, and it moved softly about her shoulders. She asked about my most recent problem. "How goes it with Darlene?"

Being the only one from my circle of private-girls'-school friends to choose NYU, I'd applied for dorm life hoping to be assigned a compatible roommate. I'd received a letter informing me I would be rooming with Darlene Blount from Queens. On move-in day we'd met for the first time. Darlene's kohl-rimmed eyes, jet-black hair, and Ramones T-shirt were anomalies in the days when most girls resembled the silky-tressed, squeaky-clean models of the Gee, Your Hair Smells Terrific ads in *Seventeen Magazine*. I'd never met anyone like her. But it wasn't Darlene's appearance that had quelled the possibility of friendship. I found her interesting, faintly mysterious. And I knew she was smart. But as soon as our parents had left us to get settled, Darlene had been inexplicably hostile. "Keep this preppie crap on your side," she'd snarled, raising her lip like Elvis. After two weeks, I'd had my fill of her darkness and music that could inspire suicide.

"It's impossible," I said around a bite of salad. "I'm just hanging in there, trying to stay out of her way."

"I admire you for sticking it out, sweet pea," Dad said, anointing a second roll with butter. "These things build character."

Sated by the delicious meal, I gathered my clean laundry (tenderly folded by my mother). Dad walked me out into the twilight. "See you next week, counselor," he said, tipping me a two-fingered salute.

Three days later, I met Theresa Cleary at a reception the English honors college held for those who had earned the distinction of National Merit Scholar their senior year of high school. (Theresa always maintained that her test performance was a mere fluke, though a practical and self-promoting one, while I was authentically brilliant, deserving of the feather in my cap.)

A few minutes past fashionably late, I shook the soft academic hands of the honors college faculty and found the name tag table, spotting my preprinted one. Only two other tags remained, Catherine Cabot and Theresa Cleary. Nearby, a shambling bear of a professor in a flapping navy blazer clapped a bug-eyed runt of a boy in my English class heartily on the back. I feared the little dude would take a header into the punch bowl.

I stood alone sipping from a Styrofoam cup of tea and wondering what I should do with the tea bag when a slight girl slipped through the doorway. She was as boyish of figure as I was curvy with masses of Titian hair tumbling down her narrow back. I watched her move through the reception line, her manner as vibrant as her hair. This girl had what my dad called moxie. Mouth tugging into a grin, I reached for the name tag as she approached the table. "You are Theresa Cleary from Chicago, Illinois."

11

"I am." There was music in the two syllables as her eyes searched mine. Theresa's eyes weren't the light hue of most redheads but a rich, deep brown that made for an arresting contrast with her pale skin.

I handed her the tag and indicated my own with a forefinger. "I'm Robin Hamilton, New York, New York."

She wrapped my hand in both of hers. "Congratulations on your scholarship, my dear," she said, mimicking the faculty members.

We laughed together for the first time and soon decided to go to lunch together. In our first hour we discovered that we both liked chef salads with blue cheese dressing and cold Tab from the bottle; found sororities pretentious, catty, and exclusive; loved the band the Eagles; were terrible at math; had a taste for marijuana; were Francophiles, dreaming of living in Paris; and were miserable with our current roommate situations.

I told Theresa about Darlene, and she told me about her roommate, Donna, who sneaked guys into their room (with Theresa right across the partition dividing the small space). "Talk about awkward! She actually tried to introduce one of them to me when I walked in on them. The dude wanted to shake my hand!" she shrieked in disgust. I hooted with laughter.

The poster child for darkness was reassigned and moved out of my room three weeks later, and Theresa moved in, though she had moved into my heart much sooner. We became the sisters we had wished for as two only children, trusted confidantes. The fall of our sophomore year our parents helped us rent a down-at-the-heels but surprisingly spacious one-bedroom unit in a student apartment building. Theresa's mom cleaned out her Chicago basement and drove a U-Haul trailer filled with an assortment of odds and ends all the way to New York. The prize was a pocked but pretty antique armoire (though it never quite lost the peculiar fusty smell of Theresa's aunt Pauline) in which we installed our little TV, turntable, and speakers. My parents invited Mrs. Cleary to stay at the brownstone while in the city, and she accepted. My father made spaghetti bolognese and garlic bread for us all that Saturday night. Theresa was a near replica of her mother: Colleen Cleary was a gung ho middle-aged cheerleader, her own mop of riotous red hair threaded with gray.

In our first pad Tee, as I quickly began to call her, and I hung Eagles posters, made Chef Boyardee pizzas from the bright-yellow boxes, and watched *The Love Boat* and *Saturday Night Live* in its heyday with John Belushi and Gilda Radnor. We exercised and danced to Fleetwood Mac and Supertramp and cried with Dan Fogelberg, but the Eagles were our perennial favorite. We studied and talked late into the nights from twin beds with matching, braille-like chenille spreads.

Late one May afternoon at the end of junior year, during my turn to clean, Tee came home from an exam as I was scrubbing away at the little sink in our kitchen. She was nervous about something, drumming the fingers of her right hand against her hip, as was her way. I snapped the yellow rubber glove from my hand and turned off the faucet. "What's going on, Tee? Did the math not go well?"

She leaned against the counter and said sheepishly, "Rob, I've been waiting for the right time to tell you something." I waited as she revealed that she had applied for a study-abroad program a month before. We'd both received the same glossy brochure and letter in our mailboxes, but I'd thoughtlessly tossed mine.

"It was just a lark in the beginning. I didn't really think Mom was going to go for it, but then I got accepted." Avoiding my gaze, she began toying with the salt and pepper shakers. "And she said she could swing the extra dough." Finally she reached for my hand and peered into my crestfallen face. "It's *Paris,* Rob … What if it's my only opportunity? The only chance I ever get?"

"You're doing this then," I said. I looked at my best friend, to whom I was closer than my own parents. She bit her bottom lip and pushed the salt she'd spilled into a little pile. I opened the fridge and grabbed a beer, popped the metal tab, took a big swig, and pitched the metal tab into the sink.

"Robin, you can come visit while I'm there. You're practically fluent in French, much better than I am." I burp-hiccupped against the back of my hand. "The croissants! The Left Bank! The Louvre! French *guys*! C'mon, Rob … you *know* we'd have a blast!"

As Tee rhapsodized on about the program, I slid down the refrigerator door to sit on the scarred old linoleum. A kaleidoscope of memories of the last three years flashed before my eyes and splintered into random images: the two of us schlepping loads of stuff up the stairs of our building, breathless with laughter; a meatball slipping from my ill-advised meatball sandwich and rolling across the restaurant floor while we were on a double date;

14

us pulling all-night study sessions with Tab and bags of Oreos; me throwing up on a sexy bass player's shoes at the Bottom Line. *What will I do without my best friend? She's embarking on this adventure without me. And senior year!*

Selfishly considering the implications, tears stung my nose. "But, Tee, you butt rash, what will I do without you? I'll have to get a new roommate," I wailed.

"Maybe Darlene's still available!" Theresa said brightly. We giggled then, both sniffling, and the tension broke. Tee extended a hand to help me up. "Let's don't think about it anymore tonight. We have *plenty* of time until I have to go."

I pulled another beer from the fridge and handed it to her, a conciliatory gesture. We sat on the sofa and began to talk of the summer that shimmered ahead of us like a meadow, its fence in the far distance. With our summer jobs, we'd have more spending money. We punctuated sips of beer with talk of summer festivals, shopping in the village, parties we would throw. We spoke of summer flings. Tee and I had had our share of boyfriends, but neither of us felt we'd ever been in love. I had a chemistry experiment in mind: to find out if the spark that had leaped between our friend Nick and me would lead anywhere. Theresa had just met a foxy law student with a blue MG convertible and the improbable name of Tink. Now she flashed the mischievous grin I loved. "Let's see what trouble we can get into tonight."

CHAPTER

3

Robin

Summer 1977

"We *have* to get ourselves out of this city!" Theresa groaned and jumped to her feet. She batted ants from the seat of her white shorts. "You and I, my fine-feathered friend, are going to DC for the Hotel California concert." It was our day off from work, mine from Speak Volumes and Tee's from typing and filing in the university admissions office. We'd spent the afternoon in the park browning our legs and then reading in the shade, watching desultory games of volleyball and the inveterate joggers trudging along in the heat. Even the foliage seemed listless, the congenitally exuberant dogs dispirited.

We'd attended several good parties in June and even hosted a pretty wild one at our small place, dancing until two in the morning, Nick playing DJ with our albums and his. There was just something about Nick. He was playful and spontaneous, as un-self-conscious as a child. I found him very alluring. We had made out a little that night just before he'd told me he had taken a summer internship in his hometown of Ithaca. Theresa had learned that Tink, a.k.a. Theodore Tallent Treadwell IV, had a fiancée on whom he was industriously cheating. Almost all our other friends had left the city. It was shaping up to be one bummer of a summer.

Twining my chestnut mane up from my sweaty neck, I responded from my seat on a wedding quilt made by my grandmother Courtwright, "Well, hell *yes,* we should. How much are tickets?"

"Eh, a minor detail." Tee twitched a shoulder and helped me fold the quilt. "Don't worry; we'll pool our resources."

My mind ticked ahead to early August. "I suppose we could take the bus … but let's see if Carol Anne wants to go." Carol Anne was our one friend still in NYC with a car.

A sweaty, extraordinarily red, hairy-chested guy bounced up to us, an orangutan in blue nylon shorts and tube socks. "You ladies wanna play some volleyball?" he asked happily, bouncing on the balls of his feet.

Tee narrowed her eyes. "No. Thanks." She made a gagging face at his hirsute and quickly retreating back.

The weather in Manhattan had been sweltering, but there was another deterrent to outdoor activities. A serial killer, armed with a .44-caliber pistol, had begun stalking women with long dark hair, casting a pall over the city like a net. Incredibly, he penned letters to the newspaper about his exploits, calling himself "Son of Sam." Women thought twice about going out alone at night, some even going as far as wearing wigs or bleaching their dark hair blonde. While I maintained only a peripheral interest in the headlines, Tee read all the grisly stories about Son of Sam, engrossed in the details. "Theresa, stop reading that stuff!" I warned one morning as I discovered her on the living room floor, the paper spread around her, a black-and-white puddle of foreboding. "You'll have bad dreams."

Theresa had been a highly imaginative child. Her father had been killed in a plane crash on her eighth birthday, her mother just thirty-one years old. The morning after the funeral, little Theresa had been sent to school as usual. Colleen had showed up on time at Drs. Shapiro and Rosenblatt's dental office where she'd worked as a hygienist to improve the smiles of others. Despite Theresa's recurring dreams—her father's face framed by a window in a fiery, plummeting plane—Colleen had insisted they carry on as before. And to all outward appearances they had.

"It's *fascinating*, Rob," Theresa answered now, not looking up from the story. A newsprint smudge tipped her upturned nose.

We were psyched about the Eagles' new album, so the timing was perfect for a road trip. We had never seen the band in concert and were over the moon at the prospect. Not only was Carol Anne on board, as the pièce de résistance, she had a discreet older cousin in Baltimore who had offered to put us up for the weekend.

On the thirteenth of July, Tee and I were in for the evening. Ours was the only occupied flat in the building for the remainder of the summer. We'd stood on line for an hour that afternoon to see the movie *Star Wars* and then had picked up good, cheap takeout from Mamoun's Falafel for dinner. The phone rang about eight o'clock. I answered; it was my mother. "Hi, darling. Anita Roth just called and said there are a lot of power outages in the boroughs and into Manhattan. Is Theresa there with you?"

"Yep, she's right here, Mom." I inclined my head to peer at Tee on the floor painting her toenails a candy-apple red, white cotton balls blossoming between her toes.

"Bonjour, Madame H.," she called.

"Bonjour, Theresa," Mom sang out. "You girls stay cool and lock up. I've just taken a beautiful roast chicken out of the oven and made a cold salad, so if our power goes, at least Dad and I have something nice for dinner. Do you have candles in case you lose power? Have you eaten?"

"Yes, we've eaten, and … we have lots of candles actually." I regarded the assorted candle stubs on hodgepodge saucers placed about the room. "We're cool. See you soon, Mom. Love you."

As I replaced the receiver, Tee grinned. "Not only do we have candles, *but* … the last one of those amazing doobies Nick left us!" She tightened the cap on the bottle of polish and reached for the little carved wooden box on the trunk coffee table where we kept our stash. Wiggling her dark brows, she placed the joint across her top lip like a mustache, a flame-haired Groucho Marx. It was *Mork & Mindy* and *Three's Company* night on TV. We settled in and lit the joint, talking and giggling about the bizarre *Star Wars* characters, Tee trying to mimic the voice of C-3PO.

It was about ten thirty when everything went as dark as the inside of a boot. We had raised the living room window of our third floor flat to allow the smoke to escape but now forced open the stubborn one in the kitchen. We squinted out at the blackness; not a single pinprick of light shone from the buildings across the way. No moon lit the scene. The absence of taxi horns or haranguing sirens left an eerie vacuum of silence. "Holy shit," Theresa breathed. It was as if we were the lone survivors of some futuristic Rapture.

"I wish Nick or Gino and Ty ... or *somebody* was here tonight," I said, the prickle of chill on my flesh, and bumped toward the kitchen to grab a couple of Tabs while they were still cold. We sat, popping the bottles open with a church key, and opened a bag of Doritos. We waited by candlelight in a vague aura of apprehension. The apartment was growing warmer. The weed had made us stupid with sleep, and we dozed.

I startled awake and peered owlishly at my watch in the dimness. It was ten minutes after three, and the candles were guttering low. I had a foul taste in my mouth and a gloating headache. Theresa at the other end of the sofa woke as a terrific *ka-blam* reverberated from somewhere close by. We jerked to attention, completely sober. "What the *hell*?" we said together. Someone had kicked in the street door and was in the building. The reckless sound of battering began below.

Panicked, we realized the candles were giving a slice of light to the hallway beyond, and we crept around the room snuffing them out. "Do you think it could be Son of Sam?" Tee's voice quavered in the hot room.

"Oh my Lord!" I hissed, heart trip-hammering in my chest. Our eyes accustomed to the darkness, we regarded each other: the whites of Tee's eyes showed all the way around. The clamor grew louder and closer. Whoever was in the building was making his way upward.

"The chain isn't enough!" Tee seemed near hysteria.

"We'll block the door," I said, springing into action. "*Help me, Theresa!*" Pure adrenaline must have enabled us to push the unwieldy armoire in front of the door. Surely the groaning and protesting of the old piece could be heard in Far Rockaway.

Breath ragged in her throat, Tee said, "We have to hide!" A single pair of footfalls echoed from the stairwell on our floor. The only weapon in the apartment was the old baseball bat that had belonged to her father. Theresa kept it like a talisman under her bed. She moved toward it.

"The closet," I hissed. But Tee first scrabbled under her bed, fingers closing around the bat. Then she crab-crawled toward me, her lips pulling back from her teeth. I nudged her through the jungle of clothing in the closet and followed, crouching low. With shaking hands, I slid the door along its track. We were as still as flatware in a drawer for a time.

As the minutes dragged by, I began to smell my own acrid body odor. A runner of sweat made its way down my back and into the cleft of my bottom. Someone gave our apartment's outer doorknob a twist-turn-pull just as a belt slithered from the shelf above us. The buckle struck the closet door like a tuning fork. I stifled a scream and closed my eyes so tightly white spots appeared behind my lids. I became aware of the sharp, hot ammonia smell of urine. My heart contracted with sympathy for my friend, but I didn't dare speak.

The intruder must have moved on, for there was no other sound from the door but then came the tear of splintering wood and crashing from far below. We sat transfixed for perhaps another excruciating hour. Finally I slid the closet door open. Strobing blue lights from the street below illuminated the space. Theresa sat in the corner, hair plastered to her forehead, eyes dark as plums, still clutching the bat to her chest. "I think it's over," I said. I reached for my friend, gently unwrapped her hands from the bat and pulled her to her feet. We staggered rubber-legged to the front windows. In the pale yellow light of early dawn we could see cops and Tim, a campus security guard, on the sidewalk. At our screams for help they turned, craning their necks at the two of us practically hanging out the window.

Later as the punishing sun climbed high on another day, Tim told us the intruder had to have been a looter acting under the cover of the blackout. The Con Edison power system had completely failed the night before. It would be late that night before all service was restored to the city. The damage to our building indicated to police the looter had made his way upward checking to see how many people might be in the building and then had ransacked the unattended apartments on the way back down.

We guessed Son of Sam had stayed in for the night. Three weeks later, on August 10, we learned the monster had been apprehended. He had murdered his sixth victim and left seven others with injuries they would carry to their graves. Theresa and I drank a celebratory glass of champagne with my parents that night. It would be years before I would learn what the awful experience had cost my friend.

CHAPTER

4

Robin

August 1977

An early-autumn breeze heralded the morning of the road trip, and the cloudless sky was cerulean, a balm on Theresa's and my shock-worn souls. Carol Ann pulled her mother's grating Ford wagon to the curb, and Theresa and I swung our bags into the back. Snub nosed and freckled with white-blonde hair long enough to sit on, Carol Ann was one crazy, fun girl. We headed out of the city in high spirits, blasting the Eagles from the eight-track, windows down, Medusa hair whipping around our heads.

In the passenger seat I helped Carol Ann navigate, the road map as complicated to fold as an origami bird. Theresa in the backseat was rolling joints for later from the small baggie of Acapulco gold that Carol Ann had scored for the trip. "Woo-hoo!!!!" I yelled above the wind. "Are we getting fired up, girls?"

A busload of jocks passed us on the left honking and blowing kisses. Ignoring them, Carol Anne sighed, "Isn't Björn Borg gorgeous?" We spoke of Borg's Wimbledon tennis victory in July and of sexy bad-boy Burt Reynolds in the comedy hit *Smokey and the Bandit*. We talked and laughed about any and everything, the way you do in the uncensored company of close friends.

In Maryland by five o'clock, we had more than enough time to relax and primp for the concert. Tee, at the wheel as the wagon bumped into the driveway of Carol Ann's cousin Debbie's home, uttered a barely audible, "Wow." A small stone craftsman cottage was surrounded by roaring green, orange, and pink foliage and a host of gewgaws—gazing balls, gargoyles, and impish gnomes. We climbed out, stretching our limbs and gawking, to retrieve our bags. A tall, blue-eyed woman trotted out to the porch on bare feet to embrace Carol Ann, her aunt Colleen's only daughter. Her gray-blonde braids tied with yarn seemed to have a life of their own the way they bobbed and danced. "Welcome, gals, I'm Debbie!" she said. "Bathroom, refreshments, or showers first?"

If our first glimpse of Debbie wasn't enough to confirm her level of cool, our appraisal of her place instantly did. In a poster above a Victorian sofa made of carved wood and purple velvet, Janis Joplin clutched a microphone in both hands and squinted blearily down at us. A great black tomcat uncurled itself from the depths of an armchair and approached us, mewling, twining around our legs. As Tee reached to pet the cat, it leaped to the coffee table, where a tarnished octopus of a bong reached out its tentacles in welcome. Any lingering doubts we had about Debbie's discretion were dispelled like smoke. Pun intended. Debbie reappeared through a beaded curtain, bearing a tray of Tabs, chips, and dip. "Shoo!" she said to the cat and lowered the tray to the table. "That's Jimi Hendrix, Jimi for short," she said fondly.

Tee, Carol Anne, and I pulled on tight, wide-legged jeans, the hems hanging long over tall platform heels. My jeans laced sexily up the back with a brown leather cord. Carol Anne and I dressed in ruched tube tops with big shirts tied at the waist, and Theresa pulled on a low-cut long-sleeve tee, looping a fascinator around her neck. We rolled our tresses and sprayed them with Aqua Net and anointed ourselves with Debbie's patchouli oil. Merrily instructing Debbie not to wait up for us, we pranced out to the car and were on our way.

We shared a joint in the parked car at the arena giggling at the fishbowl cars around us of people doing the same, and then got out and threaded our way through the crowd. Channeled through a ticket line like minnows through a sluice, we pocketed our stubs and pressed on through the throng. Tee spotted our seats— numbers 8, 9, and 10—in the orchestra section about midway back from the stage. We settled in, buzzing with pot and anticipation. A bearded manager materialized from the depths of the darkened stage to ask if the crowd was ready for the band. On our feet in seconds, we screamed and clapped until the stage was illuminated. We squinted up at a neon image—the cover of the *Hotel California* album—at the rear of the stage. The band members strode onto the stage, hipshot and grinning. Glenn Frey, in a University of Colorado T-shirt and tight jeans, said deprecatingly, "We're the Eagles, from Los Angeles?" as if there might be a single soul in the auditorium with half a doubt. As the band led off with the eponymous song from the album, we were swept away, the bass vibrating through the soles of our shoes. The skunky-sweet, weed-infused air began to grow warmer. I peeled off my outer shirt and stuffed it into my suede hobo bag.

The low-tide crowd began its surge toward the stage. Everyone danced with abandon. Girls began scaling their boyfriends' shoulders. I felt a tug at the leather lacing of my jeans and looked for Theresa—my number one suspect—but both she and Carol Ann were clapping high above their heads. The undulating bodies were packed so closely it was difficult to turn. But when I did, I came face-to-face—more precisely, face-to-collarbone—with the best-looking guy I'd ever seen. I felt my pupils expand as the moment spun out. A spotlight that seemed to single out the two of us revealed the perfect cupid's bow of his lips, a white smile in tanned skin, clear gray eyes, a strong chin with a little cleft. His shaggy, longish hair was crayon-box maize.

Communicating to me through gestures, my mystery man offered a position astride his broad shoulders. He hoisted me up as the band launched into the encore, everyone's favorite song, "Take It Easy." My cavalier bore me closer to the stage, where the two of us were unwittingly immortalized on film our daughter would see thirty-five years later.

As the band left the stage to thunderous applause, he lowered me to my feet again. He gently held my upper arms, lowered his head, and paused, searching my eyes. The air around us felt charged somehow, full of portent. He kissed me lightly once. I ran my tongue across my top lip, tasting salt from his skin. He laughed softly. Carol Anne and Theresa appeared, both of them grinning like fools. I recovered enough to say, "I'm Robin Hamilton. These are my friends Theresa and Carol Ann."

"Dean Falconer," he said, smiling from me to my friends. "What are you ladies doing after?" He turned to a well-muscled jock and a petite brunette with an orange silk hibiscus blossom behind one ear. Dean introduced them as his friends Clay and Suzanne. They were headed to a party back in Georgetown, where they were students at Georgetown University. "You could follow us. I mean, if you'd feel more comfortable," Dean said.

Though instinctively cautious about taking off with a guy I'd literally just met, I couldn't deny the connection I'd felt with Dean Falconer. Theresa and Carol Anne were game. "There's safety in numbers," Tee murmured into my ear. "Besides, with our own car we could split anytime we want." And so we were off, chattering and reliving the concert, our wagon following Clay's stylish Cutlass Supreme through the darkness.

The main drag at GU was congested with late-night revelers who spilled from restaurants and stood on line in front of rollicking pizza joints and bars. Now I could see Dean's head in silhouette in the backseat; my stomach did a funny little flip in response. Four blocks over the Cutlass slowed in front of a brick building on the corner. There was a crowd of people in front, Styrofoam cups screwed into their hands. "This must be the place, chickies!" Carol Ann sang out.

We reapplied lip gloss, and Theresa opened a roll of peppermint Certs. "Ooh, I need one of those!" Carol Anne said.

Momentarily serious, Theresa asked me around a mint, "Do you want to be left alone with this guy, or should I stay close?"

"That remains to be seen," I said, taking a mint for myself. I raised one eyebrow at myself in the rearview mirror and inspected my mascara. "Let me talk to him for a while." Dean stepped to open our car doors. "A southern gentleman too!" I whispered.

Inside Dean's friend Dave's place, twenty or thirty people were smoking, drinking beer, and dancing to Boston's "More Than a Feeling" booming from a set of expensive speakers. Dean offered me a beer from one of the battered kegs lined up against one wall. We sat together on a blue-carpeted stair step and regarded the scene. From the loudest corner a skinny guy in a Keep on Truckin' T-shirt yelled, "Dude, quit bogarting that doobie!" Another guy in a rubber wolf mask with wild silver hair sticking up was blowing shotguns to a couple of giggly, wasted girls. Theresa and Carol Ann stood nearby, cups in hand, talking with Clay and Suzanne and another good-looking guy who was eyeing Theresa appreciatively. I sipped at my beer, hearing scraps of their conversation—good-natured arguing about which Eagles' album was the best.

"So where are you from Robin Hamilton?" Dean's eyes scanned my face as though it were a treasure map.

"My family lives in Manhattan. I'm a rising senior at NYU." I tilted my head to my friends. "Theresa's my roommate. She and Carol Ann and I drove down today for the concert." I grinned. "I know you're from the south. Where do you live?"

Dean lifted his chin and returned the grin. "Virginia. Home's just two and a half hours from here." The party was throbbing and so loud that Dean was practically shouting the last part. "Let's go outside," he said close to my ear. He stood and took my hand so naturally it was as if we were under the spell of some ancient alchemy. Theresa was dancing with the good-looking guy—who was grinning as though he couldn't believe his good fortune—at the center of a web of people. As Dean and I threaded our way to the door, I caught her eye and tipped her our okay wink.

Dean and I sat alone on a crumbling brick wall. Most of the others had drifted away or back inside. Dean told me he was a first-year grad student at GU, an aspiring architect. He loved baseball and was as big an Eagles fan as I was. As he spoke, I regarded the well-muscled forearms below his rolled-up flannel shirtsleeves, the hands with the short-clipped nails I preferred on a guy. The man was purely male, sexy as hell, but there was a gentle quality about him.

"You ready for another beer?" he asked.

"Not just yet." I was buzzing on his grin by then.

"You're a really beautiful girl, Robin. I couldn't stop looking at you at the concert."

Cheeks pinking, I bent over my cup and finished the last swallow of beer. The party was winding down, and people were beginning to leave in pairs. Tacitly Dean and I rose to move back inside. The Eagles' "Victim of Love" pulsed from the speakers. Tee and Carol Anne sat talking with Suzanne, Clay, the good-looking guy, and the dude in the Keep on Trucking T-shirt, who now wore the wolf mask, an unlit cigarette stuck between its grinning black lips. Dean poured beers for the two of us, and we took seats on a denim sofa stained with beer (and God knew what else). Though we joined the others in conversation, our eyes kept sliding to each other's faces.

When Theresa and Carol Anne were ready to leave, Dean's lips brushed my hair, and he said, "If you want to stay, I can drive you back later. I wish you would … stay."

I met his clear gray gaze, my heart pounding, and made a quick decision. "I'm going to stay on a little longer," I told the girls, trying to sound casual. "Dean can drive me back."

Carol Anne, her tongue wedged into the corner of her lips, wrote Debbie's phone number on the palm of my hand with a ballpoint pen.

Dave went upstairs with one of the giggly girls. We could all see her panties beneath her short dress as she tripped up the stairs. Clay and Suzanne and the good-looking guy, who looked decidedly morose, left for their apartments in the same building. Dean and I were alone. While he went to the bathroom, I popped a Cert and knelt in front of Dave's collection of albums. I sat back on my heels and flipped through them, looking to find something to fit my mood. As I lowered the needle on Fleetwood Mac's eponymous album, Dean reappeared. He pulled me to my feet, kissed me again, and led me in a slow dance to Christine McVie's "Warm Ways." Back on the sofa again, I slipped off my shoes and curled my feet beneath me. Much higher on Dean than on the weed and beer by that time, I pulled his face to mine. He slipped his hands into my hair, to cradle the back of my head, and kissed me, open-mouthed now. His mouth was delicious. I felt I would drown in the purest lust I'd ever experienced. We drifted between making out and talking for hours, getting up only to change records and once to eat fruit from Dave's fridge. Dean never touched me below the neck except to trace my collarbones with the pad of his thumb.

I woke and felt Dean's solid presence behind me, his breath, his chin in my hair. My lips stretched into a lazy smile. The clock on the sound system read 9:13. Unwilling to share my nasty morning mouth, I gingerly rose and stood looking down at him. The light from the window fell in stripes across his handsome face, his gold hair. Dean stirred but was still again.

I slipped into the bathroom, found a crumpled tube of Dave's Ultra Brite, and stood brushing my teeth with a finger. I had been right to trust Dean: the night could've been stamped with a PG rating. I finger-combed my hair, washed my face, and wiped the night's mascara from my eyes with a tissue. I opened the door and heard Dean in the kitchen. Suddenly shy as a geisha, I padded in. "Hi," I said and leaned against the counter.

He scored with "I knew you would still look pretty in the morning. Do you drink coffee?" At Dave's little glass-topped table we sipped coffee and ate glazed donuts from a box of Krispy Kremes we found on top of the refrigerator.

"You know, I'll be here all weekend," I said, my hands cradling a blue GU mug. "I'd *really* like to go back to Debbie's and take a shower."

When Dean went to shave and shower, I called Debbie's house from the phone on the kitchen wall. I'd neither seen nor heard any sign of Dave or the girl upstairs. I heard the drumming of Dean's shower, and spoke to Tee. "So what *happened*?" she begged. I could hear her happy-for-me smile. I told Tee Dean and I were headed out to Debbie's. "Take it easy, baby!" she said breezily.

CHAPTER

5

Dean

August 1977

The morning after the concert, Robin and I walked to my building around the corner from Dave's to pick up my Jeep. I regarded her long hair and asked, "Would you mind if I put the top down?" *Man, she was beautiful in the mellow morning light.*

From her bag Robin pulled a pair of aviator sunglasses and one of those ponytail holders with the plastic balls on it like my sister Leslie wore. "Weren't you ever a Boy Scout? *Always* be prepared," she said primly, pulling her hair back. Silver earrings hung from the sweet little ears I'd kissed the night before and held the sunlight. *I am such a schmuck.*

"Actually," I said with a grin, "I was an Eagle Scout, *am* an Eagle Scout. Once you achieve Eagle, you have it for life."

"Ah, of course you are."

"Growing up in a small town, that's what you did." I shrugged. Together, we put the top down on the Jeep. The day was going to be warm and sunny, and I had a pretty girl next to me. I aimed for Baltimore and pushed the Eagles' *On The Border* into the eight-track. Robin and I smiled at each other over the wind and the music. *Pretty as hell and an Eagles' fan to boot.*

As I swung the Jeep into Debbie's driveway, Robin invited me inside to wait. She'd told me Debbie was cool, but the bong on the woman's coffee table was a surprise. Debbie looked like a hippie past her expiration date, but she was nice. Sitting on the edge of a big ugly chair upholstered with cat hair, I chatted with Theresa and Carol Ann, liking Theresa immediately. Robin had told me that Theresa was like a sister to her and that she was torn apart about her leaving for Paris.

What the hell am I doing? I asked myself in that strange place, for about the fifth time in the last—I looked at my watch—thirteen hours. *Had it only been that long?* I was getting involved. I'd dated plenty of great girls in high school and college, but none had had such an instantaneous effect on me. I felt as if I had been struck by lightning or hit by a Mack truck or some damned thing.

I'd had an oblique view of Robin the last hour of the concert, and she had one foxy body: generous breasts, waist I could probably fit my hands around, long legs from canted hips though she wasn't tall, and one of those heart-shaped bottoms. The leather laces on the back of her jeans had taunted me. I'd known she'd be a prize astride my shoulders, and I hadn't been able to resist closing the gap between us to get her attention.

And the way she'd responded to *me*; it blew my mind. She seemed utterly fascinated by everything I said. And intelligence shone in her intense green eyes. She was classy Manhattan, private girls' school educated and headed for law school. But I had graduated magna cum laude from the University of Virginia, had a rich old man with a two-hundred-year-old horse farm, and was on my way to becoming an architect. So it wasn't her credentials that undid me.

I felt protective of this girl, as if she were one of those painted eggs my mother kept locked in a cabinet in the dining room, a Fabergé. I wanted to tuck Robin in my pocket for safekeeping. She reminded me of my youngest sister, Mary, who was fifteen and smart as hell and aspired to be an equine veterinarian. But at the same time, Robin had me so torqued up I wanted to nail her standing up. And she was clearly into me. She gazed at me as if I were a hot fudge sundae and she'd been on a diet for a year.

When she reappeared fresh and glowing from the shower, shiny hair spilling over her breasts, I swear my heart leaped. She was dressed casually in a different pair of jeans, a soft-looking mossy-green sweater, and little brown boots. Grace Slick was belting out "White Rabbit" from Debbie's speakers, which were the size of chifforobes. The imagery hit home: a potion labeled Robin Hamilton had cajoled, *"Drink me."* Damned if I wasn't falling in love.

I found myself utterly happy about the day. I wanted to take Robin to lunch at my favorite burger place, introduce her to my good friend James, show her the campus. I hadn't had a girlfriend since I'd been in DC. Robin made me realize I'd been lonely. I wanted to walk and talk with her. I wanted to spend every minute of the weekend with her.

I wanted her.

CHAPTER

6

Robin

1977

Dean and I were positively ravenous by the time we left
Debbie's, so he made straight for the Tombs restaurant, a block
from the historic GU campus gates. I took off my sunglasses and
admired the exposed brick walls and rowing decor. My stomach
rumbled loudly in response to the smell of grilling meat from the
kitchen. "James is working," Dean said. He smiled and nodded in
the direction of the bar. The room was noisy, packed with late-
lunching students and locals as we made our way to the bar. James
wore wire-rimmed glasses, his hair in a long blond ponytail. He
was tall like Dean with the posture of a palace guard.

"Dude! How was the concert?" he asked, high-fiving Dean.
James's grin was unaffected despite a sizable gap between his two
front teeth. He noticed me then and smiled, lifting his chin in my
direction. Dean introduced me. "This is Robin Hamilton from
New York. We met at the concert last night." The words hung in

the air like those in a cartoon bubble. Dean and I shared a look, realizing how they had sounded, and tacitly agreed to say no more. From the overhead speakers, Carly Simon's voice soared. "Nobody does it better."

James said, "Well, welcome, Robin from New York. What did you guys think about the show?" James was friendly, joking around with Dean while he filled drink orders with aplomb. We sat at a table with an unlit hurricane candle and red checked tablecloth and ordered cheeseburgers. Two more of Dean's friends came over to speak to us. I could tell he was proud to introduce me. When James had a break, he turned a chair around backward, straddled it, and asked me what I did in New York. Dean plucked two fries from the basket, dunked them in catsup, and nudged the basket toward his buddy. James was energetic and interesting; you just had to like him. We shared a chocolate brownie with ice cream and talked of the buzz of the times: President Carter's pardoning of the Vietnam draft dodgers, the *Star Wars* craze, the untimely death of Elvis Presley in Memphis.

Afterward with the Jeep's top down, the sun warm on our heads and shoulders, Dean pointed out special spots in Georgetown. He showed me the *Exorcist* steps at Prospect and Canal where scenes from *The Exorcist* had been filmed. We talked of other scary movies—we had both jumped a foot at the end of *Carrie* with Sissy Spacek, the part where the hand comes up out of the grave—and other favorite movies. We quoted lines from the movies *Jaws* and *One Flew Over the Cuckoo's Nest* and challenged each other to finish lines of dialogue, laughing in amazed pleasure.

"Do you want to see where I play baseball?" Dean asked shyly. I could tell he really wanted to show it to me. He had been on the baseball team in public school in Virginia but played just for fun now, pickup games with friends. At the field, which was as groomed and manicured as a Westminster hound, we drifted toward the metal bleachers. "What a great day," Dean said, looking around happily. He slipped an arm around my waist and pulled me to him for a kiss. I smiled up at him, and he kissed me again, lingeringly, and then a bunch of guys strode onto the field, laughing and calling to each other.

"Tell me about your family," I said in the dappled sunlight, twining my hair up into a ponytail again.

"Well, our home is a farm in Keswick near Charlottesville."

"You live *on a farm?*" I said, astonished.

"Yeah. It's over two hundred years old. My great-grandparents named it Villeneuve, French for—"

"New colony or … settlement," I interrupted saucily. "I've had seven years of French, actually."

"Ah, of course you have." Dean grinned.

"Touché. Just good ole Miss Pruitt's School training." I put my hand on his back. "Sorry. Tell me more about Villeneuve."

"Well, it's not pretentious like it sounds," he said. "My mom mucks around the barn in rubber boots half the time. She's a peach, a great horsewoman. Villeneuve's a horse farm," he

41

explained. "My dad works as hard as the help. He loves it. He even does some of the bush hogging. There's always plenty to do on fifty acres." I interrupted to ask what in the world bush hogging was. Dean explained how they mowed the grass with a specialized cutter pulled by a tractor.

As the game on the field picked up, Dean leaned forward to watch, elbows on his knees, hands loosely clasped. "We usually have around fifteen horses, broodmares and a stallion, and there are always young foals that we sell off as weanlings or keep and train. Everybody in the family helps take care of the horses." He turned back to me with a grin. "If you ride a horse, you're expected to bathe and groom it yourself afterward, or woe be unto you."

I laughed, and he continued, "I've ridden all my life, my sisters too. We learned to ride before we learned to swim … or ride bikes."

"I've never been on a horse in my life." I shook my head, marveling.

"*City* girl." Dean grinned. He took off his sunglasses and gazed at me. His eyes, the color of slate, dallied at my lips. He leaned in and kissed me again. The guy could kiss.

"The horses?" I reminded him with a grin.

He replaced his sunglasses. "Well, my dad and I foxhunt with our retired event horses." He began to run his hand through my hair from crown to ends. "There's a cool tradition every Thanksgiving morning called the Blessing of the Hounds. It's at a beautiful old gothic-style church right down the road from the farm." Dean's eyes behind his shades followed the baseball as it flew into foul territory.

"Shi-it, man!" the hitter, a fat guy in a Dodgers jersey yelled.

"They bless *the dogs*?" I asked.

"They do. The priest blesses the hunters, the hounds, and even the fox before the day's hunt. Hundreds of people come—it's quite the spectacle. Everybody's in full color dress."

"Do you wear one of those cute red coats?" I asked, picturing Dean looking prince-like on a horse, like in one of those hunting prints.

"They're actually called pinks."

I was fascinated. Dean's home sounded like the set of a movie. "What's the house on Villeneuve like?" I asked. I liked the taste of the pretty name Villeneuve and the images it conjured.

"It's a hundred-year-old Georgian, a two-story box. Mom has a lot of her mother's and my dad's mother's English antiques ... so it has a lot of authenticity about it."

"How far out in the country are you? Are you really ... isolated?"

"Nah, Charlottesville is only fifteen miles away. It's a college town but with a lot of history ... and culture, opportunity as they say. You know Thomas Jefferson's home Monticello is there."

"I didn't know that," I said thoughtfully.

"Folks say Charlottesville's the best of both worlds." His eyes lit up. "I'm going to have my own firm there. The countryside's beautiful—we're in the foothills of the Blue Ridge Mountains. They really do look blue—all different shades of blue—at different times of day." He fell silent again at the crack of a bat. Our eyes followed the fly ball, each of us lost in our own thoughts.

A gaggle of girls had come to watch the game (or maybe just the guys) and moved toward the bleachers. The baseball groupies, short shorts barely peeking below long jerseys, languidly flipping their hair, were making their presence known. Covertly I studied Dean's profile. The angle of the afternoon sun, more oblique now, gave it a chiseled elegance. He slipped an easy arm around me again and squeezed my shoulder. "I should have asked you what *you'd* like to do while you're in town."

"Well," I said after a moment, "there's a gallery in DC that I've always wanted to go to … if we have time." I looked up at the sun. "The Phillips Collection. But I'm not sure where it is. My favorite painting in the world is there, the most important Renoir."

Dean furrowed his brow in concentration, nodding his head. "That sounds familiar. We can find a phone booth and look up the address. Want to get some dinner in DC, too?"

"Sure! Sounds cool," I said.

Dean stood and dug into his pocket for his keys. "Let's boogie."

We found the address and headed to the museum. Dean slipped the Jeep easily through the congested afternoon traffic. I loved to watch him drive, the wind playing through his golden hair. *He is so gorgeous!* I noted a pack of gum and some crumpled receipts in the cubbyhole and a roach clip and lanyard tassel hanging from his key chain. I wanted to know everything about Dean Falconer. The song "Green-Eyed Lady" came on the radio. "Hey, it's your song," Dean said with a grin and turned it up. I laughed, pleased and knowing I'd never hear the song again without thinking of that moment. We found a spot on the street near Dupont Circle, and I fished my purse for quarters for the meter.

"This is an unexpected bonus to an already awesome day," I said as we walked down Rhode Island Street. Dean grinned and reached for my hand. We stopped to look at a *Star Wars* display in a colorful bookstore window. I told Dean about my mom and the book shop in New York.

"I'm diggin' that name. Speak Volumes," he said. "It's really creative."

"My mom suggested the name to the owner; she's clever that way."

Around the corner we found the three-story Greek Revival townhome that housed the Phillips Collection. Putting the pieces together in his mind, Dean said, "Man, now I know … I've read about the architects, Hornblower and Marshall. They began this project at the turn of the century. This was the first museum of modern art in America."

We weaved our way through the galleries of the collection. I'd never met a guy who was sophisticated enough to even pretend to enjoy a museum for my sake. I'd had dates who had taken me to the Met only to look furtively at their watches or stand jingling the coins in their pockets, but Dean really seemed to enjoy himself and discussed the art appreciatively.

"Here it is!" I breathed as we faced the painting we had come to see. "Renoir's *The Luncheon of the Boating Party.*"

"Oh, *yeah*. Sure. I remember learning about this one in an art history class. It's real pretty ... the colors and the light."

"I *know*. That's the thing I love most about it. See how he used the white paint on the glasses to make them appear to shine? He was *such* a genius."

We stood soaking in the vibrant colors and the angle of the light. I wanted to run my fingers over the lifelike figure of Aline Charigot (later Madame Renoir) seated in the foreground and the brushstroked fur of her little dog perched before her on the table. Years later at the Musée D'Orsay in Paris I would gaze at a mortar bust of Madame Renoir sculpted by her husband. And Tee beside me would murmur, "Now *that's love.*"

After a moment Dean spoke again. He sounded like an excited boy. "I'm going to backpack through Europe one day, see all the best museums, the ancient architecture in France and Italy ... Germany and Czechoslovakia. The buildings over there—the cathedrals, monoliths—make ours look like they were made of Tinkertoys. You know what I mean?"

I nodded, picturing the two of us holding hands across a sidewalk café table in Paris, a red beret topping my hair like a cherry.

Back outside the museum, I said, "That was *far out*, Dean. Thank you!" I did a little skip-jump up to high-five him on the sidewalk.

He smiled down at me. "I've never met a girl like you, Robin. You make me feel ... just ... happy ... all the time. I know that sounds sappy as shit. But it's true."

"I'm pretty happy too," I said quietly, my heart pounding.

It was approaching the dinner hour. Dean had offered to take me out, but I suggested now that we pick up a bake-it-yourself pizza and take it back to his place. I didn't want to share Dean anymore. In the Jeep at the next light he turned to regard me solemnly. Moonstone eyes clear, both hands on the wheel, he asked, "Do you want to stay with me tonight, Robin?" The air around us felt effervescent.

"Yeah," the new brazen me answered.

And *that* was *that*.

Back at Dean's place, while Dean was in the bathroom, I placed a call to Debbie's house from the kitchen, which was as clean as a new paper bag except for a couple of reddish Rorschach splotches on the stove. *Did guys never wipe down stovetops or counters?* Dean returned and moved behind me. He raised my hank of hair as I ended my conversation with Carol Ann and kissed the back of my neck. He had brushed his teeth. He opened the fridge and pulled out a couple of beers. Inside I glimpsed what looked like a half case of beer, an open package of hotdogs, an egg carton, sticky condiment bottles, and little else. I was glad we'd gotten the pizza. Dean preheated the oven.

I nodded my agreement and headed to the bathroom. I thanked God Dean had an extra toothbrush. Surrounded by the masculine smells of shaving lotions and deodorant soap, I was relieved the fixtures appeared to be pretty clean. I perched on the toilet, winding tissue around my hand, and glimpsed a blue bar of soap on a rope in the shower. I grinned, thinking every guy must have an aunt who gave him soap on a rope for Christmas. I appraised a stack of green and brown towels on a shelf and the forest-green robe hanging on the back of the door.

I washed my hands and pulled the terry robe to my face to see if it smelled like Dean. Breathing the scent of him, I pretended to swoon, vamping for my reflection in the mirror. "How is this real?" I breathed aloud. Two days ago I'd had no idea that a guy named Dean Falconer existed, and already I felt I was in love with him.

The object of my desire sat cross-legged on the front room floor, thumbing through albums. "Hey, beautiful," he said and handed me a beer. "Make yourself at home."

"I really like your place," I said softly and took a measured sip. "It looks like you." Dean grinned and slid *Frampton Comes Alive* from its jacket. He dusted the album with his sleeve.

"I'm putting the pizza in, okay?" Dean asked.

"Yes, please." I sat down on the tasteful green plaid sofa and crossed my legs in a practiced fetching way. I sat my beer down on the one scarred end table lit by an attractive brass lamp and wondered if Dean's mother had helped with his decor. To my right an enormous drafting table regimented a full quadrant of the room. I smiled at a brigade of sharpened drawing pencils and white erasers lined up with perfect precision. An M. C. Escher poster I recognized, the one with the convoluted staircases, was pinned simply to the wall above. I got up and wandered over for a closer look at the lines on a large pad of paper atop the table. "Will you show me your work?" I asked.

Dean handed me up onto the stool and leaned over my shoulder, smelling like a handful of tender green leaves. He pointed to details, telling me about his current residential design project. "It's been a killer, mostly finished, all due on Tuesday. I'm glad I'll have something to keep me busy tomorrow." We looked at each other. "After you're gone I mean." Until then, we hadn't spoken of the inevitability of Sunday.

We moved to the sofa. Frampton crooned, "I'm in you, you're in me ..."

"There's a reason we met each other, you know, Dean? But it's impossible for now, isn't it?" I searched his eyes.

"We seem so right together, sweetheart. We'll just ... find a way to see each other as often as we can ... We'll figure it out," he said firmly. As he leaned in to kiss me, the oven timer beeped. "What timing," he said.

"No pun intended." I grinned. We rose to see about dinner. I found the plates and napkins and laid them out on the coffee table.

"Do you have any candles?" I asked.

"My sister Leslie gave me one of those big scented ones … It's around here somewhere." He scavenged through cabinets and came up with a chunky gold column. He fished a book of matches from a drawer. We sat on the carpet, legs beneath the table, to eat.

"Would you mind if I turned on the Yankees game?" he asked. "We can turn the sound off and still listen to the music." I nodded, mouth full of cheese and sauce. "They're headed for the World Series this year. I wanna see 'em win it." He grinned. I wiped a smear of sauce from his cheek with my napkin. I liked watching the man talk about the things he loved.

After dinner, he cleared the plates and insisted he would wash them the next day. He snared fresh beers for us, and we moved back to the sofa. He rolled his sleeves down and placed an arm around me. I nuzzled my head on his chest in the sweet hollow between his neck and one shoulder and listened to the music, the Doobie Brothers now. I was as content as a cat with a bowl of sweet cream. The Yankees with a comfortable lead, Dean turned the game off and grinned. "Want to get high?"

"I hoped you had some," I said. Dean swung down the hall to his bedroom and came back with a joint. He tipped it into the candle's flame, and we passed it back and forth, nodding our heads to the music. A red-and-black dartboard hung above a tiny recessed dry bar topped with an ice bucket and a few dusty UVA beer glasses. "Can we play darts? I bet I can take you."

Dean laughed. "Competitive, are we, Robin? I'll take you on." We horsed around throwing darts and laughing, and I beat him, two games to one. The games were over then.

"A hot shower with that soap on a rope I saw in there would feel great," I murmured and pushed my lips into a sexy pout.

Dean looked down at me, eyes lazy-lidded, head cocked, and smiled. "Would you like some company?"

"That might be nice," I said silkily and pulled him toward the back. We brushed our teeth again, together, and it didn't even feel awkward.

"Let me warm it up for us." Dean reached to turn on the water, unbuttoned his shirt, and pulled his arms from the long sleeves.

Oh, my. He had just the right amount of chest hair for my liking, golden like the rest of him. A curling swath of it crept low over his hard young belly, a narrow strip disappearing below the waistband of his Levi's. My heart thudded in my throat as I stood captivated, watching his every move. Dean unzipped his jeans and let them and his boxers drop in one motion, never taking his eyes from mine. He was as beautiful as Michelangelo's *David* and clearly aroused for me. He stepped into the shower and called over his shoulder, "Come on in when you're ready."

Gulping, I stripped to my bra and panties and paused and then peeled them off as well. I followed him into the steamy enclosure. Dean pivoted us so the warm water was on my back and shoulders and slid the door closed. He looked me slowly up and down. "You have a gorgeous body." My chest rose and fell heavily with my breathing. He made a big show of placing the soap on a rope around his neck, raised one dark eyebrow, and wiggled it. I laughed, a throaty laugh that sounded like Barbara Stanwyck's in the movies. Dean's skin was pure velvet under the pads of my fingers. I grew weak-kneed with desire as we began to kiss more deeply. He nibbled my bottom lip, my ears, and the hollow of my throat as the warm water cascaded over us. When I began squeezing my hair, Dean turned off the water and shepherded me out. He dried me gently with one of the green towels. I felt cosseted and smoothed, though the core of me pulsed with anticipation. He wrapped me in the big green robe, himself in a towel. "That was the hall of fame of showers," he said, his beautiful mouth, rosier from kissing, stretching into a grin.

"Indeed." I reached for his blow-dryer to give my mane a perfunctory drying. I turned off the dryer and heard the opening notes of *Hotel California*. Dean padded back to me and led me to his room.

I was dying to see his most intimate space and what it would reveal about him. I pretended not to notice the bed at once, looking pointedly to the chest of drawers. On its top was a baseball in the palm of a well-oiled leather glove, a handsome tortoiseshell box, and a small pewter tray of coins and pockety things, the coins stacked by size in orderly quarter towers and nickel and dime skyscrapers, a tiny minted city. I looked more closely at an engraved brass square atop the box that bore the initials DTF in block-style letters. "What does the *T* stand for?"

"You'll have to guess," he said.

Then I turned to the elephant in the middle of the floor—the massive bed, a water bed, the first I'd ever seen. But it was not at all sleazy looking as I'd imagined. It was tastefully framed in wood veneer. A striped spread cloaked the expanse. Stacks of books lay on the floor against the walls around its perimeter—school texts, design and architectural volumes, some classic novels, and sports magazines—no *Playboys*. About a week's worth of clothing was draped over a butler's rack in one corner, but otherwise the room was neat. I was gratified to see no dirty underwear on the floor or plates of fossilized food, as Tee and I had seen in some our friends' apartments. A goosenecked reading lamp on the headboard lit a soft, warm circle on the bed.

A box of tissues, a UVA mascot figure, and a framed picture sat on the shelf of the headboard, the picture like one of those family Christmas-card photos. I sat down on the bed and reached for the frame, giggling and righting myself as a wave rolled away from me and back again. "Your family!" I said.

Dean sat down beside me. "Yeah, that was two years ago." He pointed to the tall, blond man. "That's my dad, Tom—"

"Thomas!" I interrupted, triumphant.

"Close, but wrong." He grinned. "It's Thompson actually; I'm a junior." He indicated the striking petite, dark-haired woman. "My mom, Laurel." And indicating each of the smiling Falconer girls, he said, "My sisters, Leslie and Mary."

I looked at each of them closely. "It's a good family, a happy one I can tell. You and Leslie look like your dad."

"We do." He replaced the frame. "What's *your* full name?"

"Robin Courtwright Hamilton from head to toe," I said creamily.

"Are you on the pill, Robin Courtwright Hamilton?"

"Absolutely," she said in my voice.

Dean leaned back against the pillows, watching me speculatively. He looked thoroughly edible. Lazily he reached to untie the robe's sash, and I wriggled my shoulders to let it fall around my hips. He pulled me down and over him, to lie along his length. The robe and towel fell away like smoldering cinders. "Robin, I want you so much."

I wasn't a virgin, but I wasn't accomplished in bed. I sensed that with Dean it wouldn't matter. I met his gaze. "I want you too," I breathed. "I think I'm in love with you."

"It's crazy," he said, his hands moving the length of my back to caress my bottom, "but I feel the same way."

It began then. I was lost and found, both at the same time. We made love once, twice, and a third time that night—well, five times total if the next morning counts—the water bed rocking us like a single small craft as we moved together. We got up to change the music and drink water at intervals, holding each other at the kitchen sink. Toward morning we drifted as a chiming rain began.

A while later, Dean sat down beside me, forming a swell of wave that bumped me upward. I woke and blinked at the morning light around his head, a nimbus of gold. He had showered again and smelled of soap and coffee. He wore a freshly laundered gray GU baseball T-shirt over his jeans. He bent to kiss me. "Good morning, gorgeous."

"Let me catch up with you first," I said, ducking away and drawing on a robe. I climbed from the bed—climbing from the middle of a water bed is neither an easy nor graceful venture—to brush my teeth and shower. Dean laughed and called after me, "I'm going to go make us some eggs; they're my specialty."

Wrapped in the green robe once more, I joined Dean in the kitchen, and we ate wobbly scrambled eggs out of the pan like starved animals. "These are *delicious*," I moaned.

"Good, 'cause they're about the only thing I'm really good at."

"Oh, I could name a few other things," I said coyly.

He grinned, stretching his arms, and scratched his head. "I could use a nap already ... don't know *why* I'm so beat."

"Would you like some company?" Laughing, we moved back to the bedroom, made love, and talked quietly, limbs entwined, until it was time to go.

We were bummed then, climbing into the Jeep for the last time. We talked of the fall to come and made tentative plans for Dean to take the train to New York for a long weekend in three weeks' time. He tried on a cheerful expression for me: "We'll figure it out."

Dean came into Debbie's house to say good-bye to the others and then walked me back out onto the porch. We gravely regarded the mailbox, shaped like a Volkswagen bus, beside the front door. A rolled-up circular stuck out its back door.

"It was amazing," I said, "all of it."

We kissed and kissed, and then Dean stepped away. "We'll figure it out," he said. "I love you. See you in three weeks." I stood there hugging myself, trying not to cry, and waved until the green Jeep turned the corner and out of sight.

CHAPTER

7

Robin

1978

I spent my senior year of college hermit-like, nurturing hurt from twin betrayals: my best friend's departure and the loss of my first love. My longing was a smarting sting no ointment could assuage. Colorful postcards with excited scrawls of the things Tee had seen and done in Paris appeared regularly in the brownstone's mail slot. In the first weeks Theresa had fallen in love with the city of lights. In three months' time, she had fallen for Laurent Pelletier, a sexy painter she'd met at a café in Montmartre. Laurent was twice Theresa's age with two daughters. I wondered if Tee's upbringing sans father had drawn her to Laurent. Theresa's mother wrote to me concerned that the man would permanently tie her daughter to France. We both waited to see. Theresa transferred to a small university to finish her last quarter credits and married her Frenchman in a simple civil ceremony. *Oh, Tee.*

I had returned to live at home. My intuitive parents gave me a wide berth. I studied prodigiously. As a result, my final GPA was so stellar I applied to several law schools in the northeast, including Georgetown's prestigious school of law. I was accepted for the fall semester of 1978. I was well aware Dean might be in DC but didn't permit myself to think about him or our time together.

He had never written. He had never called.

If I saw Dean Falconer again, I didn't know how I would react.

"I think Georgetown would be a good choice," my mother innocently enthused. "The change of scenery and an exciting new city to explore will do you good. You have a wonderful life ahead of you, darling." I knew my parents had been concerned about me, but they had said little until then, their faith in my good sense and resiliency unflagging.

But I had written to Theresa, a long, tear-stained, angst-infused letter. She wrote back immediately and, like Mom, encouraged me to go to Georgetown. "If it's meant to be, you and Dean will get together again," she said. "If not, at least you'll be getting on with your life. Don't let this knock the wheels off your law-school plans."

Georgetown beckoned to me like the outstretched hand of God on the ceiling of the Sistine Chapel. There was really no choice about going. My year of self-pity had come to an end. A pragmatic plan in place, I found a one-room studio apartment in a pretty nice building near the school of law.

The Capitol Hill area of Washington, DC, where energetic young movers and shakers lived and worked was exciting. It was common to see politicians striding along Pennsylvania Avenue discussing legislation, arguing with lobbyists or reporters, staffers scurrying like tugboats in their wakes. I was in awe of the female representatives and legislative correspondents who populated the bustling lunch-hour spots. They were elegant in their tailored suits, high heels tapping briskly on to the next meeting. The superambitious shopped the same well-stocked markets on 7th Street that I did.

I walked past colorful old row houses nestled among grand early-nineteenth-century manor houses and came to know the city. Each vista seemed so expansive. It hadn't occurred to me before how vertical my New York City perspective had been. One Saturday I took the bus to Arlington Cemetery and wandered the immaculate grounds beneath great shade trees—chestnut, oak, linden. I sat before the Tomb of the Unknown Soldier amid tourists from the four corners of the world to wait for the changing-of-the-guard ceremony, the smoothed marble steps cool beneath my bottom. Stoic guards in pristine uniforms marched, rifles on their shoulders, before the tomb. Most of them didn't look old enough to shave. My dad would be pleased that I'd witnessed the moving event.

In a tangle of Asian tourists I regarded the grave of President John F. Kennedy, the poignant eternal flame. The shutter clicks of a dozen cameras punctuated the tourists' brisk conversation. And then in front I saw a flash of shaggy gold hair on a head that towered above the others. I felt as if I'd mainlined adrenaline, my heart beating crazily. I stood motionless as the figure turned from

59

the graves. In the circle of the guy's arm was a lovely young Asian woman. They chatted softly, intent on each other, her bright face turned up to his. It was not Dean. I wound my way back down the hill to the visitor center on trembling legs.

The next afternoon some wistful internal compass guided me back to the Phillips Collection. Feeling the old familiar stab of pain, I took a deep breath and propelled myself inside. I sat alone on the padded leather bench in the gallery of *Luncheon of the Boating Party* and allowed the painting's luminous beauty to wash over me. It was a small victory in my recovery from Dean Falconer.

I met my first friend. Stepping into the elevator of my building one evening after a class, I met a girl I'd seen around the building. "Hello, I'm Robin," I said at the same time she spoke in a Cincinnati accent: "Hi. I'm Cindy." We laughed, and I complimented her on her striking outfit.

"I'm meeting some people at Feathers. I'd invite you to come," she said, regarding my nonparty clothes, jeans and loafers, "but I'm late as hell already."

"Oh, that's okay, but I'd love to go sometime," I said and realized it was true.

Thursday afternoon, Cindy, who was also a first-year law student, knocked on my door. She had been out until three that morning but looked as fresh and smoothed as rising dough. In the time I knew Cindy I never once heard her mention studying. She was tall, with a chest as flat as a boy's and legs as bowed as a career bull rider's, but she had learned how to dress and always looked terrific. Cindy's carefree attitude was what I needed to get back out again.

Dressed carefully in slinky dresses, Bare Trap platform shoes, and often a silk flower pinned behind an ear, we made the disco scene with regularity. I drank in every minute as if it were a potion for forgetfulness. One Saturday night Cindy and I pranced into Spin!, a disco as rowdy as a circus and favored by thirsty Georgetown law students. The music met us like the blast from a passing subway car. I felt the reverberating beat from KC and the Sunshine Band's "I'm Your Boogie Man" through the soles of my shoes as we waited to be seated. I knew I looked good. In the crow's nest that night was the popular DJ Felix "FM" Moore whose outrageous banter made us blush. Under the mirror balls my dress shimmered like a mermaid's tail. Aware of the pairs of male eyes tracking our movements, we ordered drinks and sat moving our shoulders to the music. "Who will the lucky ones be?" Cindy asked with a grin. Her black hair was pulled so tightly back she looked exotic, like a geisha in the dim light. A bored candy-and-cigarette girl in a spandex jumpsuit languidly threaded her way through the tables peddling Salems, Marlboros, and enough Junior Mints and Cracker Jacks to satisfy any case of the munchies.

Talk from tables drifted like the bruise-colored haze of smoke. John Giannangelo, Democratic Congressman from New York and minor celebrity, and his entourage were partying in one of the side niches. A tidal wave of Aramis made it to our table before two interchangeable guys did: Fred and Frank. I wondered who wore all the cologne, maybe both of them. In big-collared shirts, tight jeans, and platform shoes, they looked like extras for the film *Saturday Night Fever*. We hit the teeming floor to Chic's "Le

Freak" and danced two more numbers. When a slow song began, my partner, Fred, grinned and pulled me to him. I stepped away as though he had popped the top on a grenade and broke away for the ladies' room. Cindy giggled hysterically at my heels.

"You can't smell it on me, can you?" I shrieked, scrubbing at my hands and arms at the restroom sink.

"No, but I can see it! It's like a tattoo!" Cindy howled.

We slunk out hoping Fred and Frank wouldn't be waiting. A pale young man in a suit so severely conservative he was either a mortician or an earnest young aide approached. A bloody square of tissue stuck to a nick under his chin. "Hello, ladies," he said. "Congressman Giannangelo would like you to join him at his table." Cindy and I looked at each other with big eyes and then shrugged *why not?* We would at least score free drinks.

John Giannangelo was a commanding presence, powerfully built with a big-featured face, not conventionally handsome but arresting. He rose and motioned Cindy and me over. Hooded black eyes under a head of obsidian curls lingered on my face. He said he had noticed our grace and beauty on the dance floor. *Okay, he's hokey,* I thought. But the man was funny and charming, his manners unimpeachable. John spread his hands. "I can get you into any disco in DC, even the members-only clubs," he said, as though his address was 1600 Pennsylvania.

I had a hard time pretending not to see the tissue on the young aide Curtis's face and finally pointed meaningfully at my own chin. As his fingers brushed the spot, he flushed a deep plum and furtively dipped a paper napkin in his drink to dab at it. I smiled at him reassuringly. After a few minutes, his equanimity restored, he asked Cindy to dance. John moved to sit next to me. "Do you have plans for dinner tomorrow evening, Robin?" Recently divorced, he explained he needed a beautiful date for a business dinner. "It will be a nice affair at the Herald Inn on N Street. Do you know it? As a fellow New Yorker, I would be honored if you would accompany me." I knew the hurt I had suffered the last year made me vulnerable to the attention. Being made to feel special, singled out by such a powerful man, was a heady feeling. I had no intention of getting involved with a much-older man, let alone a congressman, but could I turn down such a fancy dinner date? I accepted but sidestepped giving him my address, instead suggesting we meet at the inn.

I dressed in the pearls my parents had given me for my eighteenth birthday and a soft brown wrap dress. I wound my chestnut mane into a sophisticated French twist. I splurged on a taxi and arrived just as John's elegant black limousine pulled to double-park at the door. He launched his big frame from the car, dismissed the driver with a single thump of his fist on the trunk, and joined me on the sidewalk. Exclaiming over my dress and hairstyle, he inclined his arm, and we mounted the front steps.

A large jade Buddha in a niche over a Victorian sofa greeted us just inside. Amused, I regarded the funky decor as we moved through the lobby: warm wood paneling, colonial prints, splashy French bar posters, silk flowers, marble fireplaces, and smoothed oak-planked floors. John took my wrap and handed it off to a tiny coat-check woman who blinked at him in recognition from behind enormous blue eyeglasses. "Shall we?" John said, pocketing the claim tag, his hand at the small of my back. The second-floor dining room was roped off from the eyes of curious uninvited guests with a braided gold cord like you would see in a theater. A silent waiter ushered us inside a mahogany-paneled room set about with candles and flowers on heavy Victorian sideboards and the center of a round table for twelve. Several well-heeled people were already gathered. John introduced me to his friends, one a French diplomat on my right, the first native Frenchman I'd ever met. John smiled in surprised appreciation as I conversed with the man in French over cocktails. The Frenchman had not been to America before and found it loud and brash, the food perplexing. A stout diplomat and his wife, who appeared to have been spray starched, ignored me completely. I looked around brightly, listening to the casual conversation. Apparently I wouldn't be hearing any earth-shattering political business. I talked mainly with John, on my left, about New York City. We were served a four-course meal, oysters Florentine and beef tournedos, with champagne and several expensive wine selections.

When I felt John's thigh press against mine under the table, I pushed back from my dish of bananas Foster and asked to be excused. In the powder room I chatted with the exquisitely beautiful black woman who had smiled at me a couple of times across the table. As we inspected our makeup, she introduced herself as Felicia, the date of Senator Hopkins from Maryland. The way she said it made me suspect she was a professional. I was rinsing with mouthwash from a little paper cup when Felicia asked, "Are you seeing Congressman Giannangelo?"

"Oh, no!" I almost inhaled the stuff before spitting it in the sink. "Just tonight," I added and then felt like a complete idiot. I backpedaled, dabbing at my face with a towel. "I mean ..."

"Don't worry, baby," Felicia laughed softly. She pursed her mouth and reapplied red, red lipstick.

After coffee, the party moved to the dark paneled bar downstairs for brandy. I had had several glasses of wine and wanted to keep my wits about me. I eschewed the proffered brandy and asked for a glass of water. *Aha*, I thought as I glimpsed Felicia and the senator mounting a back staircase.

John murmured in my ear, his breath hot and heavy with liquor, asking if I would like to join him in his room for a nightcap. I was on my feet in a heartbeat, looking down at him. I managed a gracious smile and thanked him for the evening, claiming an early-morning class. "Okay, honey," he said and rose, swaying slightly on his feet, his big hands raised in mock surrender. "Another time." But I thought I detected a glint of anger in his black eyes.

I buckled my seatbelt in the back of the taxi and realized what a fool I'd been. I should have known that the man's motives couldn't have been pure. But flattery can be its own master, one of my grandmother's aphorisms. I was a little afraid of John now and resolved to have nothing further to do with him. Two afternoons later I turned the corner to my apartment and, burdened with grocery bags, fumbled for my key. I almost tripped over the long white box propped against my door. I sat the bags down and curiously opened the box labeled with the Georgetown Blooms branding. Nestled in tissue was a sheaf of dewy, long-stemmed yellow roses. The simple white card inside gave only the name John and a phone number. How naive I had been to believe he couldn't find my address! I crammed the box, tissue, and pungent flowers into the garbage chute, thorns tearing at my shaking hands. Fleeing to the safety of my apartment, I brushed past two neighbors coming down the hall. They stopped a heated argument about the phone bill long enough to stare at me as if I had snakes for hair.

I ventured to classes that week almost furtively, expecting to see the man around every corner, like the leering ghoul he'd become in my imagination. By the middle of the next week, I'd heard nothing further from Giannangelo and began to relax.

CHAPTER

⌒

8

Robin

1978

Despite everything, I yearned for Dean Falconer. I recalled in
vivid detail the magical weekend and replayed over and over the
words we had spoken to each other. No promises had been made,
but nothing about Dean had given me reason to suspect he was
insincere or a user. I'd been in DC for three weeks, and our paths
had not crossed.

The first week of October, the air crisp and tinged with
autumn, I walked to the law library to return casebooks. It was
the sweater weather I loved best, the breeze intoxicating. I was
wearing my favorite cobalt-and-mustard-striped sweater with a pair
of denim gauchos and brown riding boots. I wandered into a small
park and claimed an empty bench. I had been reading for hours
and lay my head back to gaze into the arching limbs of a maple
tree. Its green and gold-going-tangerine leaves swayed gently,
dappling the sunlight that fell around me. I closed my eyes.

"Robin? I thought it was you," Dean said stiffly. Only he could say my name in a way that made my entire body respond. The man I'd tried to will away from my subconscious stood before me, the sun gilding his wavy hair, which was shorter now. My heart bobbed into my throat like an apple in a tub of water. Dean's face was as lean as a blade, tight with apprehension. Two guys bisected the grass, yukking it up about mustache rides. Dean scowled at them and filled the awkwardness. "How are you? Are you in law school here?" He had remembered my plans. Torn between telling him to go straight to hell and humbling myself long enough to get an explanation, I decided I wouldn't cut off my nose to spite my face. I had to know the truth. I would hear what he had to say.

"I'm at GU law, yes," I said, cool, defensive.

"Can I sit down?" he asked miserably. I moved my purse, indicating the bench with a flip of a trembling hand.

He sat heavily, his expression miserable. "I fucked it up, Robin."

"You certainly did," I said, not looking at him. "*Royally.*"

"The week after the concert last year, my dad was in an accident. He was *killed*, Robin," he said, his face like wax before a fire.

"Oh, Dean," I cried, horrified. I turned to him, my efforts to be aloof forgotten.

"He was shot ... by one of his best friends. They were out hunting. It was ... horrible. We were afraid Bill—his friend—was going to commit suicide over it." Blinded by tears, I groped to place a supportive hand on Dean's shoulder. "My uncle called me home. My mom was devastated, just lost, and the girls ..."

"I'm so sorry, Dean."

He swiped at his eyes with the knuckles of one tanned hand. "I stayed home for a semester and took over Dad's work on the farm." He dragged his eyes to mine. "I was too freaked out to call you at first ... holding Mom and the girls together was ... the hardest thing I've ever done in my life. Then as the weeks went by, it just got ... harder ... and then too much time had gone by."

I looked at him.

"I know that's no excuse! But when I did call you, your number was disconnected. I figured you had ... moved on," he said. My heart felt like a sponge squeezed of its water.

His eyes captured mine. "Robin, I ... our time together ... it was unreal."

"Yeah. It was, Dean." We watched a pair of agate-eyed pigeons—blue gray and purple speckled above, pink legs below— bob and stagger in search of crumbs. The breeze lifted and teased at our hair. I gathered my thoughts like an armful of straw. "I knew it wasn't like you to just ... drop me like that. But I felt almost ... buried ... with hurt all this time. My senior year of college alone, Theresa in Paris." I paused, fighting a fresh onslaught of tears. "It was ... so hard getting over you. I moved home with my parents. I applied to law schools, and I came here."

"I'm so sorry ... what I put you through." His voice sounded as though his throat had been sanded.

We sat without words for a suspended time. Finally, I looked at him again, the corners of my lips rising into the semblance of a smile. Dean twisted on the bench to face me and sought my eyes. "Robin, will you forgive me?" he pleaded, his face naked, exposed.

After a moment, I answered gently, "I can."

Dean breathed out a titanic breath of relief. I laid my hand palm up between us on the bench. He covered it with his. We sat for a moment palms together, as if drawing strength.

"Are you seeing anyone now, Robin?" he asked then. I heard the soft edge of hope in his words.

"I'm not seeing anyone ... haven't seen anyone actually since you. Since you left. Are you? Seeing someone?" A military helicopter chopped overhead, flying low, scattering the pigeons. We followed it with our eyes.

"Actually, I've been up to my neck in women," he said, a hand flat under his chin, "my mother and sisters." We laughed a little. Dean looked at his watch, the one I remembered, the one I'd seen on the tanned wrist in my dreams. "I have a class at five fifteen. May I call you sometime, Robin?"

"I hope you will," I said quietly. Hope bloomed like a mushroom cloud in my chest. I wrote my number on the back page of one of his textbooks.

The very next day, a Thursday, he did call. The beautiful patch of weather had held; the sky was cerulean. We met at the same park to study.

Dean and I spread my old patchwork quilt beneath a yellow-leaved walnut tree, its sprawling limbs a canopy. We lay back reading, balled-up-jacket pillows beneath our heads.

Dean's voice floated on the breeze; he sounded shy. "This kind of reminds me of the afternoon that weekend … at the ball field, before we went to the art gallery. Do you remember?" The wind played through the dark, dark branches of the tree overhead. A yellow leaf drifted to my chest. With Dean's proximity, red-and-blue checked shirtsleeve rolled up a brown forearm, the meter of his breath, I found I had read the same passage on constitutional law about four times. "But I was kissing you then," he said.

"I was thinking the same thing," I said. Tears pricked behind my lids. He rolled onto his elbow and gazed down at me. I looked into his clear gray eyes. Dean traced my lips with one finger. Top lip. Bottom lip. It had been so long. I twined my arms around his neck, steel to magnet. Again.

The next morning the skies were leaden, pregnant with rain, a marked contrast from the day before. Dean and I had planned to meet at my place after our classes and make plans. But he arrived at my apartment in a deluge, and history repeated itself. We spent the afternoon in my bed, Dean's shirt and pants dripping down the side of my shower curtain.

Making love with Dean was even better than before, sweeter and more intense because of the time we'd lost. As I moved above him, my hair fell around his neck and shoulders. He murmured, "My gorgeous girl … I love you."

My throat caught, full of joy. "I love you too."

Saturday night we went dancing for the first time together, with Cindy; her new boyfriend, Kurt; Dean's friend Clay; and Clay's girlfriend, Helen. I was thrilled to be out as a couple with gorgeous Dean. We still loved rock and roll, the Eagles best, but disco music was made for dancing: the Latin influences and synthesized beat made you want to move. At Cagney's we waited fifteen minutes for a table near the dance floor. I watched Dean walk over and call something to the DJ.

"What are you up to?" I asked with a grin.

He pointed toward a mock innocent expression. "Who me?"

When the song "Fly, Robin, Fly" began, I jumped up and pulled him to the dance floor, tossing my skirt like a flamenco dancer. Later, we drifted into Spin! Frank "FM" Moore was off that night. The crowd was thinner, and we easily found a good table. We sipped drinks and enjoyed the night's more-soulful black bands, like the Gap Band. Dean and I sat close together, holding hands and kissing.

I glanced at the dance floor and did a double take at a large, well-dressed man doing a barely passable hustle with several young women. John Giannangelo was a distinctive presence, his head like that on a Roman coin. My heart in my throat, I excused myself to go to the ladies' room. I stood over the sink nauseated and trembling and allowed the cold water to pool between my wrists. Cindy came to check on me. "Robin, you okay? Dean and I were worried about you."

"I'm fine ... but Cindy! I saw John Giannangelo on the dance floor!"

"Oh no! Really?" Her head jerked to the back of the door as if the congressman would be peering in. "But surely he won't bother you tonight; you're with Dean." She handed me some paper towels. "C'mon, honey, let's go back."

As we approached the table, Dean looked up, concerned, but Cindy mouthed to him, "She's okay." No sign of the congressman.

Dean regarded me. "Where were you, sweetheart? You okay?"

"Fine." I smiled. "I was just feeling a little ... light-headed."

"Well, let's get you home and into bed," he murmured close to my ear. "I'll be just what the doctor ordered." And he was. Just.

October passed into November, the weather sharp-edged and beautiful. The trees released their tenuous hold on their leaves. The leaves drifted down, becoming a crunchy carpet for our feet. The days Dean and I spent together passed idyllically. Both our workloads ramped up, and we studied long hours together. On the nights we spent at his new apartment, this one closer to mine, Dean was often late at his drafting table, drinking coffee, a windfall of crumpled paper around his stool.

One cold night, I awoke to find him missing from bed and padded into the living room in one of his button-down shirts and a pair of black panties. Dean, in a pair of UVA boxers, was bent over his table, his beautiful shoulders knotted and hunched. I moved behind him and wrapped my arms around him. He reached to hold my forearms and asked, "Hi, sweetheart, did I wake you?"

"No, I was just chilly," I said, scrubbing my cold nose into his neck. I began to massage the knots from his shoulders. He stretched his neck like a satisfied tomcat. "Am I distracting you?" I breathed into his ear.

"You, my love, are a welcome distraction," he said and pulled me into his lap. We kissed, his mouth tasting sweet, of coffee. Greedy and impatient, I pushed our clothes aside and lowered myself to him.

Dean clicked off the gooseneck lamp clipped to the table. I slipped into the bathroom. My cheeks were flushed and rosy in the mirror. I grinned at myself and padded to the bedroom for seconds.

Dean was everything I dreamed he would be in a boyfriend. I began to think more about our future. I knew I wanted to marry him someday, but we talked of the future only in nebulous terms. As the Thanksgiving holidays approached, we made separate travel plans.

Dean was needed in Virginia. Mrs. Falconer had not made the progress the family had hoped, and Dean needed to check on his sisters. His aunt Martha and uncle John had been godsends— Martha cooking and ferrying the girls and John running the farm.

74

But John was barely managing to keep up with his own work and responsibilities.

I wanted to meet Dean's family but understood it wasn't the right time. And I missed my parents. We would have a lovely Thanksgiving in New York. Mom always invited neighbors, friends, and acquaintances that had no family gathering to attend to come to the sumptuous dinner my parents worked days to prepare. I pictured the brownstone decorated in an explosion of fall color—lime, Kelly green, orange, persimmon—with gourds, pumpkins, chrysanthemums, and fall foliage, with yet more pumpkins on the front steps. Good wine would be plentiful, the conversation lively and interesting. There would be other Thanksgivings to spend with Dean.

Dean and I returned the Saturday after Thanksgiving to a blustery, frigid Georgetown. He reported that his mother had been depressed and distant, his sisters troubled. But as they were young and resilient, he prayed they would adjust. Spending time with Dean had been good for them. I knew it was difficult for him to focus on his course work with family concerns. But I also knew our love was to him the safe and warm place it was for me.

CHAPTER

⌐~⌐

9

Robin

Christmas 1978

The streets of Georgetown rang with the sights and sounds of Christmas. A light snow fell overnight, a dusting of confectioner's sugar. Exams were over. Dean and I were ready to party hardy with our friends. I slipped into a scarlet dress and silver wedge-heeled shoes and brushed a shimmery shadow onto my lids. While waiting for Dean's knock, I put on the fluffy brown-and-white rabbit coat that had been a gift from my parents, tied its leather belt, and appraised myself in the mirror.

We stopped first at a party at James's apartment that was rock-and-roll rowdy with students blowing off steam. Helen took a picture of Dean and me, Dean laughing and handsome in a dark-green pullover, his arm encircling my waist. We didn't have a picture of the two of us yet, and I hoped the photo would turn out well. James had some great weed. He invited Dean, Clay, Helen, and me up to his room for a smoke.

We piled into a taxi for Spin! and arrived at the club laughing. We toasted each other at a table so far in the back of the room the couples on the dance floor looked like gyrating pygmies. When the Bee Gees' "How Deep Is Your Love" began, Dean and I grinned at each other and made the journey to the roiling floor.

Back at the table, Clay told us they'd learned a group of Arab sheikhs were partying in the club that night. Apparently they were in one of the side rooms blowing cocaine. Helen grabbed my hand. "Less go take a lil peek at the sshheikhs," she slurred. Among suit-clad businessmen in the second alcove sat four saturnine, bearded men in white head wraps. We regarded them from about ten feet away. Their silky robes were the color of fresh butter, elaborately embellished with embroidered trim. The men were drinking and flirting with well-dressed women, but we saw nothing illicit about their movements.

Then jolted, as if struck with a cattle prod, I recognized John Giannangelo in their midst. I stood mesmerized, breath held. I followed his dark curls as he bent over a small mirror on the table. Helen elbowed me. "They'rrre doin' coke!"

"Shhhhhh, it's Giannangelo!" I whispered, my heart racing.

Helen's dark brows furrowed. "Who'sss that?"

The congressman couldn't possibly have heard, but he raised his head and looked directly into my face. His eyes glittered crazily. A flare of recognition appeared to register in his big-featured face. I did an abrupt turnabout, propelling Helen forward, and made for our table as if the hounds of hell were at our heels. Dean and Clay stood talking with two guys at the next table. I had a moment to compose myself and clutched a glass of water. Dean turned to me and grinned. "Did you get a good look at your sheikhs?"

"Their robes were prettier than our dresses," Helen said. She twined her hard arms around Clay's neck. I sipped demurely at my water, willing myself to appear calm. When the beginning beats of Marvin Gaye's "Got to Give It Up" reverberated through the club, we all bounded up to dance.

Dean and I were about to head for our own celebration at his place when heads began turning toward some activity behind us. The group of sheikhs, exotic as giraffes, drifted toward the door.

John Giannangelo appeared at my side. My heart plummeted toward my stomach. He said in his deep, cultured voice, "Merry Christmas, Robin." He squeezed my elbow lightly and moved on with his group, nodding and smiling into the crowd as he made his way to the door.

Dean turned to gape at me. "Who the hell was that?" he growled.

"It's a long story," I said.

"I'd like to hear it, Robin." The others tensed, the back of the night broken.

The four of us were subdued on the ride back, Helen nodding off on Clay's shoulder with her mouth open slightly. Dean had been deathly quiet. The taxi took us as far as Clay's apartment. The temperature had dropped significantly, and few people were on the streets. As Dean and I started down the sidewalk, he said, "You have something to tell me, Robin?"

"Dean, in September … we were broken up. I had just moved here … I felt really lonely. And I guess it made me vulnerable. Cindy and I met that man at Spin! one night. His name is John Giannangelo. He's a congressman from New York."

Dean stopped to look at me, nonplussed.

"He was very charming," I continued. "He asked me to a fancy dinner at the Herald Inn."

"My God, Robin. Did you sleep with him?"

"No!" I shouted. "It was all respectable … but I know, have known, it was stupid and impulsive to go."

We started walking again; my feet were freezing. "Why would you go out with a smarmy old bastard like that … and a congressman, Robin! I can't believe this. You lied when you said you hadn't been seeing anyone!" he ranted.

"I wasn't *seeing* him, Dean; it was just the one night. But there's more," I said miserably. Dean stopped again, glaring at me under a streetlamp. A huge tinsel candy cane thwacked against the metal in the wind. "I met him at the inn that night … took a taxi. I didn't tell him where I lived … but two days later when I got home from school, there were flowers at my door."

Dean's hands were deep in his pockets, his shoulders hunched in his coat as if to ward off a blow. "What happened then?"

"I never heard from him or saw him again. Until tonight."

"Robin, I thought I knew you. I just didn't think you would do something like that." He shook his head as if to clear it.

"You do know me!"

We were in front of his building then. "I'll drive you home," Dean said shortly. I began to cry. "I need to think about this," he said.

He handed me into the Jeep, his face shuttered. He flipped the heat on and blew into his cupped hands. Slowly the two blocks of ice at the end of my legs began to thaw. Dean never took his eyes from the road. I was anguished. He walked me into my building and kissed my forehead briefly. "I'll call you later."

I climbed the stairs to my apartment like an old woman. I brushed my teeth; stripped, my clothes littering a path; and put on a long cotton gown. I drank a huge glass of water and drew the curtain. I looked dismally out at the twisting snowflakes that had begun to fall.

I missed Theresa desperately. I wanted to pour it all out to her, to cry on her shoulder; a letter wouldn't suffice. I did cry then, great hiccupping sobs; hot salt tears and mascara ran down the front of my white gown. After a space of time, I calmed and sat down on my upholstered chair in silence. I laid my head back, scrubbing my cheek against the fabric, and nodded off.

I jerked awake to a knock at my door. I was on my feet, heart thudding, disoriented. My bedside light was on. The little silver clock on the nightstand read 1:19. The knocking came again. I called, "Who is it?"

"It's Dean." My apprehension was replaced with a rush of sweet hope.

I unchained the door and opened it, my heart thudding. Dean began first. "Robin, I'm sorry. About that Giannangelo guy … I went a little nuts. I felt betrayed … concerned, and damned jealous at the same time. I've been driving around and sitting out front in the Jeep. It's cold out there."

"Come in, Dean," I said gently. I held my arms out to him, stained nightgown, red swollen eyes, and all. Dean came into them and embraced me tightly. "Let's just get some sleep," I said into his chest. I reached to extinguish the lamp. We lay on my bed and slept like stones until nine o'clock the next morning.

We woke hungry and bundled up to go to brunch, a woolly toboggan over my wild hair. We ate like starving refugees at our favorite diner—eggs, pancakes with butter and syrup, bacon, and hash browns. But our conversation was subdued. The swags of tinsel, waxy flakes of fake snow, and "Holly Jolly Christmas" on the jukebox didn't dispel the tension that stretched between us like hot wire. But Dean asked if I wanted to go to the movie *Superman* starring Christopher Reeve and Gene Hackman the next night. We went our separate ways to do errands and our laundry.

The next morning Cindy called me, breathless. "Robin! Have you seen the news?" Her ominous tone told me it couldn't be good.

"No. What's going on?"

As she gave me the scoop, my flesh crept with chill. A high buzz began in my ears. The *Washington Post* and television networks were reporting that New York congressman John Giannangelo had been indicted in a scandal they were calling Operation Abscam. Giannangelo had accepted a bribe from an FBI agent posing as an Arab sheikh. He had been offered money in exchange for helping the Arabs overcome certain immigration laws. "Oh my God!" I said. "Dean and I saw him in Spin! Friday night with some sheikhs … some Arab men!"

I had to talk to Dean, to tell him about Giannangelo in person. Had he already heard the news?

I spent an anxious afternoon nauseated and shaky. Dean knocked at the door twenty minutes before I expected him. I was wearing only my underwear, my hair wrapped in a towel. I draped the damp towel around my torso and opened the door. "Dean, you're way early." I managed a warm smile. *How I love this man; everything has to be okay.*

"I wanted to talk before we went to the movies," he said.

He knows. But he's calm. A measure of relief rang in my chest as I pulled on my bathrobe.

We sat down on the bed, and Dean said, "Robin, I've been really messed up about this Giannangelo thing … You've heard the news today?"

"Yes," I replied quietly, waiting.

"What if you had gotten more involved with this man?"

"I know," I said wretchedly. "But I wouldn't have!"

"Look, I've done some stupid things in my life too. I'm sorry I overreacted. I love you, Robin. I do know you, and I want to be with you. Forever."

My eyes filled, tears sliding down my cheeks. Dean leaned over to kiss me. "Don't cry, sweetheart," he said. He took the towel, dabbed at my tears, and began squeezing at my hair.

"Make love to me, Dean?"

"I think I could manage that," he said with a flicker of the adorable grin I hadn't seen for a couple of days. He raised his hand to pull at the robe's sash. Neither of us ever saw *Superman* at the theater. Years later, catching it on cable TV, I would recall poignantly the night Dean and I made up after our first fight.

Christmas was just around the corner. We planned an intimate celebration before leaving for our homes as we had at Thanksgiving. I wanted to take Dean to New York with me. There was no place like New York City at Christmastime. It was decorated so festively with the towering blaze of the Rockefeller Center tree, the enchanting department store windows, the fairylike twinkling lights, and the brightly festooned horses and hansom cabs in Central Park.

And I was dying to introduce Dean to my parents. But as before, I understood the responsibility he felt toward his family. I truly admired him for his loyalty. I packed my bag, making sure I had stationary and a pen in my purse. I would write Theresa a nice long letter on the train to New York.

I met Helen for a quick lunch at the diner. She shook her head in disbelief as I explained the "Giannangelo debacle"—as I would always remember it—to her over club sandwiches and cold Tabs. "Thank God it had a happy ending," she said. Helen had had her film developed and handed me the picture of Dean and me from the party at James's place. She'd had double prints made so I had a copy to give to Dean. I grinned at the photos and carefully tucked them into my purse as if they were treasure. Helen was headed to Maryland for the Christmas break. I hugged her good-bye, and we wished each other Merry Christmas. I would never see Helen again.

My mind ticked ahead to the evening; excitement rippled through my midsection. I was cooking my first meal for Dean. I hummed Christmas tunes and smiled at people on the street. I went to the market for the dinner ingredients, a pair of elegant red tapers, inexpensive champagne flutes, and a small bouquet of spicy white carnations for the table. Dean was splurging on a celebratory bottle of champagne.

I'd helped in the kitchen and certainly watched my parents cook often enough, but I had never prepared an entire meal. I called my mom at Speak Volumes to ask how she would cook a roast the butcher said was the right size for two people. A roasting pan had come with my tiny furnished kitchen, and I tugged it noisily from the oven drawer. I plopped the roast into the pan and nestled chopped carrots, potatoes, and onion quarters around it. I sprinkled it with onion soup mix and water and covered it with a tenting of aluminum foil before sliding it into the oven. I made a green salad and then began to prepare the most challenging dish: my mother's famous scalloped potatoes. I peeled and sliced the potatoes—very thin, Mom had cautioned—and made a white sauce of butter, flour, and milk, next stirring cheddar cheese, salt, pepper, and a pinch of nutmeg into it. I poured the sauce over the potatoes—slopping a good bit of it over the sides of the dish—and sprinkled it with more cheese and breadcrumbs I'd made from my morning toast. Then I set it on top of the stove until the roast was done. It was quarter to five, and Dean was due at six. I had to clean up, set the little table, shower, and dress. As I showered, I thought about the first shower Dean and I had taken together and giggled to myself. "An-tic-ipation, an-tic-i-pa-a-tion is making me wait," I sang, my voice reverberating against the tile.

I wore a silky green dress I had found at a consignment shop. It accentuated my green eyes, and I knew Dean would love it. He arrived promptly wearing a white shirt and red pullover sweater and jeans, his suitcase in one hand and the paper-bagged champagne in the other. "You look good enough to eat," he said, shucking out of his coat. "It's not the finest," he said, brandishing the bottle, "but I got us an extra surprise." He grinned and pulled a joint from his pocket. "Your table looks great," he said, moving into the little dining alcove. "Is that roast beef? Man, that smells *good*!"

"It will be ready in about an hour," I said. Then I confessed I'd called my mom three times that afternoon. As we laughed together, I placed the champagne into the refrigerator. Then I remembered the photograph. "Oh! Guess what I have!" We regarded ourselves in the picture. The camera had captured our happiness, the love between us.

Dean slipped his copy into his suitcase to take home with him. "I'll show it to my mom. She'll have a fit over how pretty you are."

Dean lit the joint and raised the window just a bit—the wind outside was positively glacial—and we sat leaning against my large floor pillows, laughing and talking, the Eagles' *One of These Nights* on the stereo. Dean pinched the joint at midpoint and smiled shyly. He looked completely adorable. "I have something for you, sweetheart." From his shirt pocket he withdrew a tiny white cardboard box.

"Dean ..." I murmured as he held the box out to me. On a bed of cotton inside was a delicate pair of silver earrings. As I laid them in my palm, I saw they were little birds.

"I decided they were robins," he said.

"I love them. Thank you, sweetheart! I'm putting them on." Jumping up, I moved to stand in front of my mirrored dresser and worked the wires through my lobes. Dean came to stand behind me. We stood gazing at our reflection. He pulled my hair aside and bent to kiss an ear and then my neck. Entranced, I watched his gilded head and the hand he raised to slip into the V-neck of my dress. "Not so fast, Mister," I giggled. "I have a gift for you too."

"You *know* what *I* want," he said lasciviously, drawing my earlobe between his teeth.

Squirming from his grasp, I went to my bedside table and took out a small red box cinched with green ribbon. "Merry Christmas, Dean," I said. He opened the box and lifted the silver medal up by its slender chain. "It's Saint Thomas," I said, "the patron saint of architects."

"It's great, Robin," he said sincerely and then grinned. "I didn't know architects had their very own saint."

"Turn it over," I urged. I'd had the jewelry store engrave the back with "Forever, Robin."

"Put it on me," he said, turning his back. I clasped the chain around his neck, and we kissed and wished each other merry Christmas again.

I went back into the kitchen, threw my apron on, took the roast out of the oven to rest, and put the potatoes in. I lit the candles while he opened the champagne. "I've never done this before," he said, "but the dude at the package store told me how." He pulled the wire hood, grimaced, and popped the cork, spattering the carpet and the front of his jeans. We sat down to the meal hooting with laughter.

"This is delicious, sweetheart," he said, sliding his fork under a second bite of potatoes. "You can cook for me *anytime*."

"Guess who's doing the dishes?" I grinned.

In the end, we washed them together and left them to dry on the drain board. We flipped on a radio station playing Christmas music and slow danced, sipping our champagne in the glow of the candles.

After a while Dean said huskily, "As good as you look in that dress, I'm about ready to get naked." That was all it took for me. We carried the candles into the bathroom and placed them on the back of the toilet. We showered by candlelight, making love there, the water eddying around us. "Merry Christmas!" we shouted, laughing like loons as we finished.

Later in bed Dean raised himself on his elbows, regarding me intently. "You are so beautiful, sweetheart. The earrings look just like I knew they would."

I reached for the medal that dangled from his neck and brought it to my lips. I whispered, "I hope you'll wear this always, especially while we're apart."

"Robin … you're the best … thing in my life," he said, his voice husky with emotion.

"I love you, Dean," I whispered, my eyes filling again. *I seem to cry so easily these days.* Twin tears slid into my ears as my lids closed in rapture. *Must be what love does to you.* We spent the rest of that wonderful night together, cuddling and making plans for our New Year's Eve celebration. The next morning we bundled up against the cold, got our bags together, and were off to Union Station in Dean's Jeep. My train was called first, and I boarded.

From my window seat, I watched Dean on the platform. As the train lurched away, he waved, and then he plunged his hands deep into his coat pockets and bounced on the balls of his sneakers. He hadn't bothered to shave that morning; his face was shadowy and pink with chill. I leaned my head against the window, fingering one of the new earrings, and gazed at my love until his figure grew smaller and smaller and then disappeared entirely.

My heart swelled with excitement when I saw the familiar street decorations in Manhattan. My parents met my train, and we rode home in my father's black BMW. Mom was full of the plans they had made for my time at home. They had bought tickets to see the Rockettes at Radio City Music Hall, as was our annual tradition, and this year we were going to see the newest Broadway play, *The Importance of Being Earnest.* Another night we were going to a dinner party at the Roths' and to *The Nutcracker* at Lincoln Center. Dad piped up, "I also want to take my girls for cocktails atop the Empire Hotel."

I had told my mother about Dean. She asked me careful questions about him on the way home. I gushed about how wonderful he was until my dad rolled his eyes at me in the rearview mirror. Dad sat quietly behind the wheel, but he hung on every word. Both of them were shocked and sympathetic about Dean's dad's death and family situation.

Mom had decorated beautifully: small boxwood wreaths with red velvet bows and a larger wreath for the great front door graced the house. (Dad brought the door wreath in at bedtime each night to keep it from being stolen; after all, it *was* New York City.) Garlands of fresh white pine crested the bannister and mantle. The beloved needlepoint stockings stitched with our names—Hank, Olivia, and Robin—that our friend Anita had made for us when I was a baby hung from the mantle. The regiment of nutcracker soldiers we had had since my early childhood stood guard along the front windowsills. An enormous tree glimmering with gold and silver orbs spread its limbs to preside over the living room. Even Atticus looked festive in his red-and-green jester collar with tiny red bells, but the little dog wore a pissed-off expression and planted himself often to scratch at the collar with a back foot.

In my room a small, fresh arrangement of crimson-berried holly sprigs and white spider mums greeted me on my bedside table. I smiled and sat down on the double bed to take off my shoes, rubbing my cold toes. On my pillow were a few of my favorite little chocolates. *My sweet mom.*

My thoughts turned to Dean; I wondered what was happening in Virginia. *Dean.* I reached for a decorative pillow on my bed and hugged it to my chest. I hoped things were going well with his family and they would be able to enjoy this Christmas. *Next year Dean and I will spend Christmas together,* I thought. I would bring him home with me to New York. *Or maybe we will go to Virginia,* I thought with a swell of excitement.

The air redolent with the smell of Hamilton Christmases drew me downstairs. Mom had made a simple crab quiche and salad. I knew she had probably been on her feet all day at Speak Volumes, helping frantic last-minute Christmas shoppers. Impulsively, I kissed her cheek. The three of us had a quiet dinner with wine, and they caught me up on the latest news. The Rosenblums next door had installed a hot tub in their garden, and my parents were pretty sure they got in it naked at night. And down the block, the Capellis's son was "on dope." I felt my face redden at that last remark and studied my salad, painstakingly loading the perfect bite of lettuce, celery, tomato, and carrot on my fork.

One of our family traditions was to read Truman Capote's bittersweet memoir of a particular childhood Christmas, *A Christmas Memory.* "Let's start it tonight," I said. We moved into the living room; Dad banked the fire and ousted Atticus from the center of the sofa. Mom reached for her reading glasses, but I said, "Let me read tonight, Mom."

"Okay, Rob!" She smiled, propping her feet atop the veteran ottoman I had lain across on my tummy to watch *Captain Kangaroo*. Atticus, minus the festive collar he had managed to remove, jumped onto my chair. He turned three times before settling against my hip. I'd read just two chapters when Dad nodded off on the sofa. Mom looked at him with fond indulgence. She whispered, "Let's finish it tomorrow night." She reached for a throw with Santa and his eight tiny reindeer on it and smoothed it over his big torso. I rose and checked the fire, poking at the orange-blue embers until they were settled. Mom and I turned out the lamps and ascended the stairs quietly. I could hear the ticking of the old mantle clock that had been a wedding gift to my Courtwright grandparents.

"Do you think Dean's the one, darling?" Mom asked.

"Mom, we're too young to get married. I've just started law school, and Dean has another year in his program … but I am *crazy* in love, Mom, and he loves me too."

"It's lovely to see you so happy, darling. I can't wait to meet this fellow. Night, night, sleep tight; see you in the morning's light."

While Mom worked the final day before the holiday, Dad and I set out for a little shopping and lunch. He wanted to know all about the classes I had taken that semester. We enjoyed the time together, completing our shopping lists, and then collected his car and drove to pick Mom up and take her to dinner. We went to her favorite restaurant, Gabriella's, for Italian, where I stuffed myself with spaghetti carbonara and a luscious, fluffy tiramisu. I had probably gained a couple of pounds already. *I'll dance them off when I get back to DC,* I thought complacently.

The days were passing quickly. The shows we went to were terrific, but we had differing opinions about the casting of *The Importance of Being Earnest* and argued heatedly about it on the way home. "Wilde would never have casted a woman in that role," my father had said.

"That's just sexist. You're impossibly conservative." I said from the backseat. I'd reached the point in the visit where my parents were starting to get on my nerves.

On Christmas morning we awoke like incredulous children to a lovely eleven-inch blanket of snow, the first white Christmas in six years. We didn't poke a toe out, instead reading and lazing by the fire most of the day. I ate most of the box of the Russell Stover Rosebud Mints that Dad unfailingly placed in my stocking every year. (Inveterately, I nibbled the pastel mint parts from around the icing rosebuds first before sucking the rosebuds until they dissolved on my tongue.) We dressed warmly and walked the glittering blocks to St. Michael's for the annual candlelight service. We spoke to the Roths and the Capellis seated behind us. Jeff Capelli did look a little stoned, and I grinned to myself. On the way back, our arms linked, we called "Merry Christmas!" to neighbors and strangers alike. We stamped the snow from our boots on the stoop, and Mom said, "Why don't you call Theresa? For a Christmas treat."

"*Allo?*" Tee answered, sounding very French. It was so good to hear her happy voice.

"*Joyeux Noel,* Madame Pelletier!" I caroled across the ocean that separated us. The sibilant long-distance tone even sounded like the scrubbing of shells across sand.

"*Zut alors,* Rob! How are you? Merry Christmas, *cherie!*"

"I'm fine," I laughed. "Merry Christmas! How are you and Laurent?"

"We're fine. Tabby and Michelle are here with their husbands. Tabby told us she's pregnant, and we've actually had fun with them for a change. But me a grandmother! Are you kidding me?" She laughed, chagrined.

"Only by marriage," I said.

"*Tu est …* you are in New York?"

"I'm at home. I don't have much time, but there's so much I want to tell you. I am so in love! But, Tee! Dean and I almost broke up a couple of weeks ago." I told of the Giannangelo debacle with Tee asserting "Oh no!" and "*Pauvre bebe!*" in the pauses. "But man, Dean and I had fun getting back together!"

"Rob. I'm so happy for you!"

"So what's it like sleeping with an old guy like Laurent?" I teased. Tee had sent a photo of her husband. He was striking—tall, dark, and handsome at forty-four.

"Rob, you have *no idea!*" She was whispering now, afraid of being overheard. "The boys I went to bed with in New York knew nothing about a woman's geography. Laurent had a vasectomy when his girls were small, so we don't have to worry about using anything. And maybe it's because he's French, but … *si fantastique!*" she sighed. Tee told me she had taken a position as a copy editor for a publishing company and would begin working right after New Year's. She was excited about starting a career.

We knew the long distance was costing my parents a fortune, so Tee said she could call me back on New Year's Day. We wished each other Merry Christmas once more, and I hung up the extension in my parents' room. I lay back on the bed for a few minutes, wishing for the hundredth time that Theresa didn't have to live so far away.

I would be going back to DC in two days and spent them taking long walks and reading a novel by the fire, Atticus often curled into my side. One day I had lunch with my best friend from high school who was in town, Beth. Beth had graduated from Davidson College in North Carolina and was engaged to her college sweetheart, Kent.

The last night my parents hosted their annual holiday dinner party. Mom had been working on the menu and cooking for days. She took great pleasure in entertaining, and it was fun to hang out in the kitchen with her. We dressed to the nines for the party. I greeted the guests at the door and hung up their coats while Dad served the hors d'oeuvres. We enjoyed expensive wine and talked and laughed with old family friends—the Roths, Hicks, LeVacas, Boucks, and Gibbs. The meal was superb—stuffed crown pork roast, (my now special) scalloped potatoes, lemon green bean bundles, yeast rolls, and a rich chocolate-mocha cheesecake. I cleaned up the kitchen afterward and went to bed early.

I awoke refreshed and felt excited butterflies in my tummy as I remembered, *Today I see my love!* Then I sat bolt upright, suffused with nausea, and ran to the bathroom, my mouth streaming saliva into the toilet. I retched, but my stomach was empty. I grabbed a washcloth from the shelf, ran it under cold water, and held its coolness against my jaw the way my mother had when I was a little girl. When the feeling subsided, I showered and packed and joined my parents downstairs. I refused breakfast. "I think I might have a bug," I said.

"Well, at least take a banana," my mother said. I snagged one from the pottery bowl on the counter for the train. I hugged my parents at the station, told them I loved them, and thanked them for the wonderful Christmas. I couldn't wait to get back for New Year's in DC.

My train was late. Hours later I turned the key in my apartment lock. I looked about my cozy one-room home and noticed the carnations on the table. The white flowers were dead. The petals lay on the tablecloth like litter on snow. I turned to pick up my suitcase and noticed a folded piece of notebook paper just inside the door.

Dean has already been here! As I read the note, my hand lifted involuntarily to press against my mouth. I read it again … and a third time. I sat down on my bed in grief and disbelief.

Dear Robin,

    Uncle John and I drove his truck down today just long enough to pick up my things. I'd hoped you would be back so I could tell you all of this in person.

    My mom had a breakdown, and we've hospitalized her. The girls are a mess. I may have to stay at home for another semester to help. I can't believe this. I can't believe I have to leave you again. I'm so sorry, sweetheart. But at least this time, you'll know where I am.

    My address and phone number at Villeneuve are on the back. I hope you had a good Christmas with your folks. I'm sorry about New Year's. I can't believe I'm writing this. I'm wearing my medal and thinking of you.

Love forever,

Dean

I lurched back into the bathroom, looked at the red candles sat on the tank, and threw up again. I crumpled and sat on the cold porcelain tile. Like an oscillating fan, my thoughts turned back and forth between pity for Dean and his family and the tyranny of our circumstances. *Dear God, why can't things work out for us?*

I had Dean's number but was afraid I might call at a bad time. Of course he had mine too. He would call soon. Exhausted, I clicked off my lamp and fell onto the bed in my clothes. Sometime during the night, I slipped out of them and beneath the covers. I slept fitfully, waking at the slam of my neighbor's door. Remembrance of the night rose as if it had been submerged in deep

97

water. When it did, I boohooed for a while and then rose to go to the bathroom.

The nausea hit me again. I barely made it before I vomited. Standing shakily, the truth swamped me like white water. I scrabbled through my unpacked travel case for the pink sleeve of birth control pills and counted back the punched-out plastic bubbles. I had missed three pills (three!) somehow in the last month. "Oh my Lord," I said aloud. My period had not come over Christmas. I counted the pills again. I was six days late. In the street a fire engine blasted by, the cacophonous siren intruding on my disbelief. I showered, tried to wash away the growing certainty, and stepped out before the mirror. I wiped the condensation from the surface with a trembling hand and inspected myself. My breasts were fuller, my pink nipples a darker mauve, and the veins across my chest darker and more prominent. Hands against my flat stomach, I said to the pale, green-eyed woman in the mirror, "You're pregnant."

CHAPTER

⌒

10

Robin

1979

I spent a few virtually sleepless nights, limbs leaden as though I had slogged through a field of sucking mud. I wrote a letter to Dean in support of his decision: "You did what you had to do, what a good son would do. My thoughts and prayers are with your family."

Dean called on a Saturday morning, sounding loving and preoccupied. He thanked me for being patient and understanding and said he missed me badly. He had told his aunt and uncle about me and showed them our picture. They were sympathetic and encouraged him to make time to come and see me.

My classes would resume in five days. I called the university health center and made an appointment. The rumpled young doctor was kind as he confirmed the pregnancy. "Forgetting pills especially at the beginning or end of your pack can increase the rate of pregnancy. Now, if you have this baby, you can expect him or her to be born about August fifth." He pushed his John Lennon glasses up his nose and regarded me solemnly. I had been pregnant the whole month of December then. I couldn't articulate a single response. "Have you thought about what you want to do, Miss Hamilton?"

I had thought of nothing but.

I didn't have the heart to burden Dean with this front-page headline. On the other hand, I needed him to help make the decision. We had both tangoed. The timing was as poor to enter into marriage as it was to have an abortion. Either scenario would be difficult. My Catholic parents would never support an abortion. Utterly consumed with Dean, I'd given no thought to any conceivable (no pun intended) negative consequences. I had been on the pill! This speck of life, just a blastocyst of cells at four weeks the doctor said, was a life nevertheless, a life conceived in love. Part Hamilton and part Falconer. My parents—I loathed the thought of telling them. And Dean's mother—what would the news do to her?

And so I waited.

I received a letter from Dean and read it a dozen times, keeping it in my pocket, fingering it often, as though it were a talisman. I mailed him cheery little thinking-of-you cards, the words light, and once a deeply emotional love letter. On New Year's Eve, Dean called again, the news grim. The eldest sister, Leslie, eighteen and the more sensitive of the two, had essentially stopped eating when her father had been killed. Their aunt Martha had forced a hostile Leslie to mount the scales. At five feet seven, Leslie had weighed in at 104 pounds. An excellent student and bookworm since childhood, Leslie had dropped out of her first semester at UVA as if leaving a shop she'd been browsing. She had begun seeing a boy with a reputation for trouble and was breaking curfew and coming home smelling of booze and cigarettes.

Sixteen-year-old Mary had become fearful and skittish. Though she'd been looking forward to getting her driver's license for months, she refused to discuss it now. Mary went about her after-school chores, taking care of the animals, but did so dispassionately, as though folding laundry. Dean was deeply concerned about his sisters, especially Mary, with whom he was closest.

Laurel Falconer sat in the psychiatric wing of Martha Jefferson Hospital, her head like a wilted balloon flower on her slender stem of a neck. Both girls wanted to be with their mother, now their only parent, but faced with her silent stares, they found their time with her gut-wrenching. Often Leslie wept all the way back to the farm, Mary holding her sister's hand and gazing dry-eyed out the window. Dean, the eldest at twenty-four, was the head of the family whether he liked it or not. Exhausted, he said, "I wish I could teleport myself to you for the night. Beam me up, Robin!"

"Me too." I covered the receiver and stifled a sob.

"I'm going to ask Aunt Martha to stay with the girls for a weekend—a whole weekend," Dean said, his voice muffled. I pictured him stretching his long frame across the bed, scrubbing his face back and forth into a pillow, as was his habit. "I need to see you. I need to be in your arms." My stomach flipped, and I pressed a hand against my mouth. I wanted to tell him so badly then.

In the next days I became aware of my decision the way your eyes get used to the dark. Plunged into blackness, your pupils contract, and silhouetted edges begin to appear. One by one shapes begin to bloom—a counter, a chair, the floor, a door—until you can navigate. Dean and I were in love. Though our time together had been short, a season, it was the real thing. I could not end the life of this baby.

But I could not tell Dean now.

With hindsight a smug and sure twenty-twenty, I could have found a way around it, a way to tell him without compounding his problems, but I was barely twenty-two years old. I did what I thought was right at the time.

On the first day of classes, I went to the dean's office and withdrew from law school. I was going home.

I stepped from the train at Penn Station in New York City, my heart as heavy as the two suitcases of necessities I carried. The rest of my things would just have to be sent for later. The streets were bleak with detritus, gray snow piled at the curbs, but the sky was clear and bright as I plodded to the subway.

I let myself into the house knowing neither of my parents would be home from work. Atticus met me in the foyer, enraptured. *You're back already?* I fed him and, hoping we didn't meet another dog, took him for a quick spin down the block. The familiar smell of our house—beeswax, lemon, Atticus's kibble, nutmeg, and fresh laundry—smoothed my jangled nerves. As I wandered the well-loved and tended rooms, it struck me that the house had become a niche for two—two place mats on the kitchen table, two rumpled chair cushions, two pairs of shoes by the back door. I knew my parents had grown accustomed to their empty nest. My stay would be as brief as I could manage.

"What in the world? Robin!" Mom cried, entering the foyer ahead of Dad. "What a happy surprise!"

"Hello, sweet pea! What are you doing back?" Dad boomed.

I rose to greet them and let them smother me with hugs. Mom noticed the suitcases by the stairs and looked from them to my face. "Are you all right, darling?" she asked, her face tight with apprehension.

"Yes, I'm all right," I said and moved to a chair by the fireplace. "May we sit down and talk?"

I told them everything. As my mother wept for me, I moved to sit at her feet. She stroked my hair. My father said all the things I had known he would: "You were right to come home. We will take care of you. It will all work out."

But in the following long winter days, each of them asked if I would reconsider telling Dean about the baby. They felt keenly that Dean deserved to know. But I was adamant. Not then, not yet.

I couldn't visualize myself as a mother, that I would be holding a child of my own in eight months. My Madame Alexander dolls still looked down from their places on my bedroom bookshelves, and my bulletin board held high school invitations, tickets, photographs. Resolutely, I made an adult nest of my room, boxing my childhood belongings for the basement.

I knew my parents' hearts ached for me. They had never considered that I wouldn't finish college and marry before making them grandparents. They kept up brave faces for me, and if they cried as they held each other in the night, I never heard them.

Of course I called Tee. Though she listened and cried with me over the literal sea of distance, it was not the same. She vowed to come and be with me when the baby was born.

I was not ready to think that far ahead. I couldn't think beyond the next week when Mom would go with me to my first obstetrician's appointment. It was some small measure of consolation that proficient and jovial Doctor Taliaferro had delivered me when I was born. In my coat and boots I walked for miles. I thought of little but Dean. My love and desire for him was undiminished, as present and familiar as the scent of my hair blowing around my face. I remained suspended in the present, like the wintry slate clouds above the city.

CHAPTER

11

Robin

1979–1980

Awaiting the baby that winter and spring, my father and I sat up late one night in his study talking softly. It was my dear dad, in his cozy cinnamon Mr. Rogers sweater with the elbow patches, Atticus snoring like a human at his side, who helped me find my plan B.

"Rob, what do you think about doing paralegal work? You'd have more time to spend with the baby." He nipped at a short tumbler of scotch. "You'd still be making a contribution to the profession. Most lawyers rely heavily on their paralegals."

"I don't know what to do, Dad." I blew across the surface of my chamomile tea, peering into the steaming cup as if an answer might be found there. I knew my baby deserved a mother who would be there to make breakfast, pick him or her up from school, and spend time with him or her in the evenings. I owed my child … everything. While I'd cut my teeth on the law, I couldn't continue the path I'd begun at Georgetown.

"I've been asking around, sweet pea. *Hypothetically*," he added quickly at my raised brows. "You know I'm connected. Pace College has a respected paralegal certificate program. With the credits you've already earned and your diligence, you could complete it in five or six months."

I sipped my tea pondering. "Dad, I hope you know how grateful I am to you guys for supporting me and taking this whole thing on," I said, indicating my small swell of belly. "But I want to be independent as soon as I can."

He patted my hand. "Well, the paralegal program would certainly help you do that. By this time next year you'd be able to take a job. Earning the certificate would give you a leg up on paralegal candidates who *don't* have it." We heard water running through the old pipes in the master bath. Dad looked toward the door. "You should know your mom has been kicking around leaving the shop to take care of the baby for you."

"Oh no! Dad!" I reacted, spilling my tea a little. "I would *never* ask her to do that! She *loves* her work!"

"Are you kidding, Rob? You know your mother. She loves *you* more, and she can't wait to get her hands on the baby." He grinned. "It will be like having a little *you* around here again. Mom can always go back to the shop later on."

"Well, you guys are too much," I said around a lump in my throat. I rose to give him a hug. "I'll talk to Mom in the morning, and I will think about it."

* * * * *

Tucking my unwieldy form into a college desk was a surreal experience. I did my best to ignore the covert stares from other students. Much to my chagrin, my center of gravity compromised, I'd begun to waddle. That I was carrying an actual child just didn't seem real. One day in the middle of contracts class, everything changed. Winter was hanging on with the persistence of a badger, and the humming of the radiators in the old classrooms made me drowsy. Dr. Napolitano was droning on about illusory contracts when I felt a stirring, like the flick of a goldfish tail just above my pubic bone. Rapt, I sat as still as a stare. I felt it again. An incredulous smile stretched itself across my lips. I dropped my pen to my notebook and cradled my lower belly. I felt the sensation again and then once more. Fathoms deep from the less-than-desirable circumstances, this inchoate life was making itself known. The baby was real, part of me forever.

My parents noticed the change. At dinner that evening, Dad said, "Sweet pea, I believe you are glowing as they say."

Mom had been late at the shop, supervising inventory, and had been distracted since she'd gotten home. She stopped and studied me now and put her fork down. "Oh, darling, you really are."

I studiously cut my meat into uniform little pieces. It still felt awkward talking about being pregnant with my parents, even though they had been nothing but loving and natural with me. "I felt the baby move for the first time today. In class," I said, still averting my eyes.

"Robin, how *wonderful*," she breathed. "I *still* remember the first time I felt you. I was sitting on a bus in Chinatown."

I smiled and wiped my mouth, replacing the napkin over my lap. I watched as it rose like an ocean swell. Mom followed my gaze and asked, "Is she moving now?"

I nodded.

"May I?" her eyes asked. She rose and stooped beside my chair, placing her hand over my belly. The obedient baby rolled again. Mom grinned as if she'd won the church raffle.

"Dad, do we still have my baby cradle in the basement?" I asked.

"Of course we do," he answered, "and all your other baby things."

Mom was starting the coffee in the kitchen. "Wouldn't you like to have some new things especially for this baby?"

"I'd like to use my old things; no sense spending money on things we already have."

Dad grinned at my pragmatism and winked at me over a last sip of wine.

* * * * *

For the first time since I found out I was pregnant, I began to think more about the baby than about Dean. I was beginning to get excited about the sweet little outfits and blankets we were making ready for the baby. Anita Roth and the parish ladies had showered me with a layette. I doodled names for boys and girls in the margins of my notebooks. Usually I wrote the surname Hamilton and a few times Falconer. By mid-July my belly was the size and tautness of one of the soccer balls I'd played with at Miss Pruitt's School.

One day in the library I saw a guy that looked incredibly like Dean from the back. I froze, heart trip-hammering until he turned around, his face hawk-like and pitted with acne scars. I found that my hands had moved to cover my stomach as if to protect the baby. I wondered what unexamined subconscious notion had prompted such a reflex.

And though I willed myself not to, I dreamed about Dean again at night, about us making love, Dean curling around my belly, stroking my breasts. Waking from those illusions, tears drying on my face, I wondered what Dean would think if he could see me. In the space of a single week I picked up the phone to call him twice, but frustrated with my convoluted thoughts, I replaced the receiver before dialing.

I finished my first semester of classwork on July 15 and attended Lamaze technique classes at the hospital with Mom. I wasn't the youngest mother-to-be, but I was the only without a wedding ring. I felt the others speculated about me, and not one of them spoke to me the entire course. At my eighth-month checkup, Dr. Taliaferro had suggested a new pain-blocking procedure for labor called an epidural. But when he'd described how they would (simply!) thread a needle into the spaces of my spine, I'd shuddered. I wanted to have the baby naturally. I didn't want to wake when it was all over the way my mom had when I was born. It seemed anticlimactic, like showing up at the end of a surprise party, having missed the best part, the big moment when the guests shout surprise.

On August 3, a cloyingly humid night only a fern could love, Mom knocked on my door. I lay on top of the covers in my lightest gown, my belly a small heaving mountain. "Do you feel like talking, darling?" she said.

I laid aside an old, worn copy of Dr. Spock. "Sure, Mom, come on in." I scooted my girth over for her to sit down and winced. "Ooooh, I think she's playing soccer tonight." A little monkey foot jabbed against my lowest rib again.

"May I feel?" Mom asked. She placed her hand over my abdomen. I hated it when strangers touched me without asking but welcomed my mother's touch. "Do you think it's a girl?"

"I do think she's a girl," I said. I'd sensed it for a while but hadn't articulated it before that moment.

"I dreamed it was a girl," she said. After a moment she grew solemn. "Robin, I want to talk to you. About Dean again."

Oh, shit, here it comes. I waited, knowing what she would say.

110

"Robin, your dad can't imagine not having known about you and missing being there when you were born. Dean has already missed the entire pregnancy. It's his child too."

"You're right, Mom," I replied shortly.

"You haven't contacted him, have you?" she asked, beginning to stroke my hand as you would an animal that might bite you.

"No."

"Well," she said and gave my hand a final pat, "if you change your mind, or if a times comes that you want us to call him, I am prepared to do so." She placed her palms together as in prayer and pressed her fingers against her lips. She was quiet for a while, and then she said, "You're an adult now, Robin, almost a mother yourself, and we will respect your wishes. But will you pack Dean's phone number in your suitcase just in case?"

"Okay, okay, I will," I groaned, rolling my eyes to the ceiling. "But keep away from that suitcase!" She stood and sighed. I felt churlish then and contrite and put my hand on her arm. "Mom, I'm sorry. I love you. I feel really bitchy tonight."

"I understand." She stood again and smoothed my brow. "I felt like tucking you in tonight. It could be the last night you go to sleep as *my* little girl. You have that look about you."

"Do I? Well, I'm past ready to get this show on the road." My eyes fell on the bag in the corner that awaited the trip to the hospital. I had packed my things and two of the doll-sized gowns I'd received from Anita, the soft yellow one with Peter Rabbit hand-embroidered on a tiny pocket and a pink smocked one with tiny rosebuds. I was dying to know which one of them would be worn home from the hospital and who would be wearing it. I wanted so much to see the baby's face.

"Night, night, sleep tight; see you in the morning's light," Mom called softly, closing the door behind her.

Her intuition was right. I woke at four thirty with a dull, deep, deep backache. The baby was very still. I changed positions and tried to drift again, but the sensation returned a few minutes later. I got up to pee. My belly had dropped low, low into my pelvis, and for a week I'd had to hold it up off my bladder to go. I crawled back between my sheets and pushed a pillow behind my back. Minutes later a searing pain banded my abdomen. I gasped and sat to turn on the lamp. I looked down at my belly as if expecting to see the Triple Creek Ranch logo burned into my nightgown. Tremulous and gasping, I called, "Mom! Can you come?" My voice rang high in my ears. There was no mistaking this punishing pain.

Mom padded in wide-eyed, hands fumbling to cinch the sash of her robe. I was on my feet beside the bed. I followed her eyes toward my feet where three drops of blood spattered the cream wool rug. More spots crept across my white gown. "Ohhh, Mom, I'm bleeding! Is that supposed to happen?" I cried and then doubled over again as a new surge of agony traveled the equator of my belly.

"It's normal to spot a little. You're okay," she said, hurrying to my bathroom and returning with a towel. She pressed it tightly

112

against me. "Can you get dressed?" She yelled, "Hank! Please get the car; Robin's in labor."

Down the hall, Dad bumped around and then poked his head in the door, his hair wild. "Showtime, sweet pea?" Seeing the blood, he blanched. "Hang in there; I'll have the car down in front in a minute."

I gasped as another pain swamped me and panted to my mother, "This is happening really fast, isn't it?"

"It seems to be. I need to time the pains now. Try to remember the breathing, deep and slow." In a big shirt now, I pulled on panties over the towel and maternity jeans and stuffed my feet into sneakers. Mom bent to tie the laces for me as she had when I was four years old. How very far we'd come.

Rain was falling in great sheets. Dad had double-parked at the curb and sprinted from the sedan with a large umbrella. Cringing at a spraying squall, I gingerly stepped into the backseat, Mom close behind. A cabbie momentarily delayed honked and hurled curses at us through the rain. We caromed away as another contraction rounded home plate. Mom said, "That was six and a half minutes. We were right to head to the hospital. Breathe, Robin. That's right ... that's it."

At the hospital, the nurses had their way with me, stripping me of my clothes and any notion of modesty I'd ever known. Comfortable for the moment, I lay tucked into the starch-sheeted hospital bed. My parents sat as stiffly as ventriloquist's dummies on the room's plastic sofa. Dr. Taliaferro strode into the room, hair sticking up in the back as though he had bolted from a cot, to confirm the labor. It was six-thirty by then; just a sliver of sun peeked through the blinds at the window.

"Mr. Hamilton, do you want to go get a cup of coffee while I check Robin's progress?" Dr. Taliaferro asked.

Dad paled, uncrossed his legs, and sprang to his feet. "I'll be right outside."

Mom's grin flickered for a moment. "He's so cute."

I changed positions and felt a hot whoosh of liquid as forceful as that from a garden hose rushing from my body. I shouted, losing control, "I'm hemorrhaging! Help me! Oh, God ..." I began shaking violently. Mom pressed her hands against her heart. I was counting on her to keep her composure as she always had.

Dr. Taliaferro quickly assessed me. "Relax now, Robin ... You're not bleeding; your water just broke." He smiled reassuringly. "That means you're a keeper—this baby's coming soon." In my pain and panic I had forgotten about the water-breaking part. "I'll see you shortly."

The stout nurse who looked sort of like Ethel on *I Love Lucy* briskly rearranged my coverings and gave me a sip of water through a bendy straw. "Not too much now; we'll get you a big cup of whatever you want after the baby comes." Mom came to stand on the other side of the bed and breathed with me again.

And then one of the best surprises I could have hoped for showed up: Theresa Cleary Pelletier perfunctorily rapped on the big wooden door and breezed into the room. Her molten hair was cropped short. Elegantly dressed in layers of dark knit and black high-heeled boots, every inch the Parisian, she grinned her familiar grin. "Tee?" I breathed. "Oh, Tee! I can't believe it!" My eyes flooded as she approached the bed and kissed me on both damp cheeks.

"I *told* you I would come. How are you? I see I barely made it in time. She and Mom exchanged hugs and greetings, apparently coconspirators. Theresa had shown up at the house and, finding no one at home, headed to the hospital. Dr. Taliaferro came in again to check my progress. As another contraction came, Theresa sat down on the sofa, twisting the straps of her purse, her eyes practically out on stems. Neither she nor I had ever even been around anything like that.

"Let's get her to the OR," Dr. T. said to Ethel, and then to me he said, "Are you ready to meet your baby? It shouldn't be long now. When you go into labor, you don't mess around."

I smiled up at him gratefully and then raised my head to feast my eyes on my friend again. *Theresa.* Dad loped back in. I was glad Tee would be there to wait with him. Now I had almost all those I loved best in the world with me. Almost.

In the operating room minutes later, fear leapt like a trout in my chest. I remembered the epidural and pleaded for it as if asking a judge to spare my life. "The window of opportunity for that has closed, my dear. You were blessed with one of those record-short labors. This baby is coming now," Dr. Taliaferro said. "Mrs.

Hamilton, breathe with her through these last contractions? Fast, hard puffs now. That's the girl."

As I breathed and gripped my mother's hands, I closed my eyes. Unwittingly Dean's face materialized behind my lids. The sun played in his hair. He was grinning at me, his gorgeous face open and relaxed. *Oh, Dean. Oh my. Dean. Oh …* "Dean," I groaned aloud, wanting him terribly. I could smell the leafy scent of his hair, feel his hands reaching for me.

"Do you want me to call Dean, darling?" Mom loomed over me, her dark eyes anxiously searching mine.

"No, Mom," I moaned. Then the worst agony yet seemed to rip me in two. I let out a throat-scouring yowl. I sounded like a wounded animal in a trap, my misery complete.

"Okay, Robin, I want you to push, bear down now … That's it. And one more time. Your baby's head is coming. One more time …" said the doctor. I was squeezing Mom's hand so tightly our hands seemed to have melded. She was breathing hard and crooning to me at the same time.

And then I felt the most tremendous flood of relief as my body expelled the baby. "*She's* here … She's just fine," Dr. T. announced.

"She!" Mom and I said at the same time and burst into tears of joy.

A new nurse bustled around making the baby ready and presented her to me bundled in one of those pink-and-blue-bunny blankets in every hospital in America. A little pink cap framed her face. "You have a very healthy and *beautiful* baby girl," the nurse said.

Finally, her face. I devoured it gratefully. Petal-soft, pudgy cheeks. Fine artist's- brush sweep of dark brows. Itty-bitty round nose. How could nostrils be so tiny? Her darkish, gray-green eyes were alert and seemed focused on mine. I touched the tiny comma of cleft in her chin. She was unmistakably her father's daughter. "She's amazing," I whispered with the greatest rapture I would ever experience.

My mother looked from the baby's face to mine. "Darling, I'm so proud of you. She's perfectly healthy and so lovely. You're a mother. God has blessed you."

"Oh, Mom," I sobbed, "I didn't know I'd be so happy." We were quiet for a moment. "She looks like *him*. The best of him."

Mom pressed her lips together and nodded twice in acceptance. "She looks like you too, I think. Like you did when you were born," she said.

Kind Dr. Taliaferro, who we'd virtually forgotten—though he'd been busily finishing up at the business end—said, "Let's get you back to your room so the others can see this perfect specimen. She's almost as pretty as you were when you came squalling into my hands."

"Thank you so much, Dr. Taliaferro," I said, suffused with gratitude. As the nurse took the baby to weigh and measure her, my girl began to cry for the first time. "Oh, listen to her!" I said amazed. The nurse said the baby was six pounds, nine ounces, and twenty inches long.

"She's a *long* sip of water," Mom said with a grin. A bolus-like lump formed in my throat. *She'll be tall like her father*, I realized. *Oh, Dean.* I reclined, peering down at my own bloomy Renoir. I brushed the downy fuzz along her jawline, like that of the white peaches I'd loved as a child. An orderly wheeled us back to my private room where Dad and Theresa waited. They stood and exclaimed over the baby and me. My father kissed my forehead, his eyes filling. "What do we call this divine dumpling, sweet pea?"

For weeks I'd thought of many pretty girl names, of the most popular names of the day, and of classmates' names from Miss Pruitt's School that I'd admired. Now I announced the name I had decided the most fitting. "Her name is Laurel Olivia Hamilton." I paused. "After both her grandmothers."

Mom swallowed, her lips turning up into a smile. "There's a nice symmetry to that, darling. I'm honored." But her eyes told me she was thinking of the three-hundred-pound gorilla in the room: Dean, his mother, and their unwitting role in the event. I passed Laurel to Dad. The three of them took turns holding the baby as gingerly as if they were inspecting antique porcelain.

The nurse returned and handed me a little paper cup with a pain pill in it. I drank deeply from an icy cup of Sprite, my thirst unquenchable. I marveled at the relative flat feel of my belly and breathed deeply into the tug of the stitches I was beginning to feel, though they seemed to be at a great distance. I was drowsy, as content as a grazing cow. A skinny nurse who introduced herself as Laurette—"How good of you to name your baby after me!" she cackled—came to take Laurel to the nursery. I told Tee I couldn't wait to talk and talk and talk with her. They all left then, insisting I sleep and closing the door softly behind them. I plunged into a layered velvet sleep.

I awoke disoriented, the room fully dark. With a rush of sweetness accompanied by a pulsing throb between my legs, I remembered. I heard a nurse making her way down the hall, opening and closing the doors of the other patients. The clock on the wall said it was five after seven in the evening. I scrabbled under the blankets for the call button and asked a nurse to bring me the baby and another pain pill. Impatient, I called home from the phone beside the bed and was surprised when Anita Roth answered. "Robin, I'm so thrilled for you, dear! I hear baby Laurel is beautiful!" Anita said the family was on their way back to the hospital. She had brought a tray of sandwiches to the house and started a load of laundry for us.

"I can't *wait* for you to see Laurel. You're such a good friend, Nita. I know they'll appreciate your help." I hung up as a new nurse, Kathleen, came into the room with my swaddled little love. When I saw Laurel's face again, my breasts ached in response. Kathleen gave me an injection that would dry up my milk. I was so entranced with the baby I scarcely felt the needle's prick. Kathleen showed me how to tickle the baby's cheek to get her started sucking on a plastic bottle of formula. My daughter was a natural. I chuckled when she burped like a gunshot over my shoulder after drinking only a few ounces. I thought of Dean again, of how we would have laughed together.

119

When Kathleen left, I propped the baby against my knees and gently unwrapped the swaddling to examine her. She was a petit four of a baby, delicately pink and white. She had my mom's and my finely shaped hands; the fingers seemed carved by a clever miniaturist. But her little feet were Dean's. *Genetics don't lie, unlike me.* Dean's narrow heels, the crescent-moon sliver of toenail on his pinkie toes. "That little piggy nail will be a pain to polish one day," I said to her. Laurel's skin was soft and butter sweet. I couldn't believe that inside her were tiny little ovaries, a womb of her own. I rewrapped the blanket and held my daughter's face level with mine. Enigmatic gray-green eyes regarded me solemnly. "Guess it's you and me, my darling. I promise to do the best I can." I wondered if her eyes would be gray like Dean's or become the green of my own. Laurel closed her eyes as I planted little kisses over her face. I laughed when she fussed in earnest for the first time, fists the size of cherry tomatoes flailing. I reached for the bottle again. "Here you are, my darling." She squeaked and grunted, a greedy piglet.

Room 3512 became a verdant, fragrant paradise. My parents' friends sent glossy green-leafed plants and lavish arrangements of pink-and-white flowers: peonies, lady's slipper orchids, roses, snapdragons, and sweetly curled tulips. Pink and white balloons tethered by ribbons floated above serene-faced stuffed animals and dolls.

The following morning a woman who introduced herself as Genny from hospital records came to collect information for the birth certificate. Laurel was in my arms sucking noisily on another bottle. "What a little beauty!" Genny exclaimed. "She's sure to grow up as pretty as her mother." She smiled, pen poised, and recorded my full name on the form. "And her father's name?"

"Dean Thompson Falconer, F-a-l-c-o-n-e-r," I stated without hesitation.

"And what's the little angel's name?" she continued.

"Laurel Olivia Hamilton. L-a-u-r-e-l," I said.

"The baby's last name will be Hamilton?"

"Yes, Hamilton," I said firmly, just making the decision. "Her father is not in my life."

A day later, I was home again, feeling wonderful, totally enamored with the baby who slept in my old cradle next to my bed. I was thrilled to have Tee with me again. As I rested and healed, Tee and I lay on my bed with Laurel between us, holding her dimpled doll fingers and gazing at her as she slept. We talked for hours every day, catching-up talk, the sort that wasn't possible during long-distance calls or letters.

Neither Theresa nor I had ever even been around a newborn baby. Everything she did amazed us. "Rob, you're somebody's *mother*," Tee marveled again and again. I knew it would be awful when she had to leave, but for the present we were old roomies, best friends in the world. "I'm bummed I didn't get to see you walking around *plus grande* ... big and fat!" Tee said.

Of course we talked of Dean and our untenable circumstances. I told Theresa I still intended to contact him but wanted to wait until it felt right to me. "Don't I have the right to decide?" I said.

"I guess, Rob," she said.

I made Theresa change a dirty diaper just for the experience. I gleefully watched her clean Laurel's bottom with a cloth, grimacing, swearing in French, and exaggeratedly averting her nose. The last day of Tee's stay, we took the baby to Bryant Park in the new carriage my parents had given us. Her first time al fresco, the baby lay wide-eyed, entranced by the trees, the expanse of blue sky, the cotton ball clouds. "She's so alert," Tee said. "I can tell she's going to be smart like you, Rob. And not unlike a wise little Yoda she does look." I hooted and swatted at Tee in mock horror.

As Laurel grew older, she would accompany me to Chicago while Theresa was in the city. Laurel loved her cosmopolitan and exotic "Tante Tee," who, without children of her own, spoke French endearments and doted on Lark. And Tee would send little presents from afar—charming anachronistic toys and puppets at first, then little treasure boxes, and later intricate flea market baubles.

Dad and I drove Theresa to the airport, leaving Laurel home in her grandmother's arms; it would have been hard to say who was more contented. I walked Theresa to her gate. It had been a wonderful reunion, but it was always hard for us to say good-bye.

With her cropped hair, Tee's eyes were enormous. "Robin, I hope you're doing the right thing—about Dean, I mean. You know I want what's best for you—and for Laurel."

"Tee," I said, brushing aside her comment as I would a fly, "it meant the whole world to me that you came all that way and were here for Laurel's birth." We hugged again. "Will you and Laurent be her godparents?"

She placed both hands over her heart. "Awwww, Rob," she said. "I know I speak for Laurent; we would be honored."

"I love you, Tee," I said, wiping aside a tear. "Hey, I just this minute realized the L-a-u connection … Laurent and Laurel."

Tee laughed. "And I love you. Now mind you stay healthy, or else I may come back and whisk that little darling away." We smiled at each other for a last moment as her flight was called a second time. "May the force be with you *and my goddaughter*," she said with her old grin and bent to pick up her carry-on bag. My throat clogging with tears, I watched her red head bob down the Jetway until it disappeared.

* * * * *

At two months of age, Laurel chuckled aloud. The house rang with her musical peeps and trills. One Sunday afternoon, she lay on her tummy on a floor pallet in a pink-and-orange-striped sleeper. She waved her arms and legs, as though dog-paddling, her taffy-blonde head held above the water. Atticus cocked his head with interest from his perch on the ottoman. The dog had been surprisingly tolerant with Laurel. He seemed to regard with fascination her noisy, miniature humanity. Dad stretched out beside Laurel and made goofy faces and a general fool of himself. Mom and I looked on indulgently from our chairs as we read. Laurel crowed, bobbing her head, the taffy hair whorling neatly at the crown. "This baby is as happy as a lark!" Dad said. She truly was. And at that moment she was Lark.

I was astonished and humbled by the fierce bond between my daughter and me. The love of my child had eclipsed my yearning for Dean.

CHAPTER

12

Robin

1980–1981

Lark was ten months old and the apple of our eyes. I would change, feed, and dress her in one of her cute doll-sized outfits in the mornings before I went to class, and then I'd hand her off to Mom. In the afternoons, Lark greeted me with exuberant squeals and grins that showed off her top and bottom Chiclet teeth. The new recipient of the Courtwright women's thighs, Lark was chubby. She was not yet trying to stand but content to crawl and scoot from room to room in her walker.

The weather was warm in May with the promise of summer. I took Lark to the park often. Though I was a single mother, I knew I was incredibly fortunate to have my parents to help take care of Lark. Many women did not. And how Mom and Dad loved their grandchild. By that time I was a week away from earning my legal-assistant certification.

One Wednesday evening, I attended a group study session at the library and afterward got stuck on the train for forty-five minutes. I found my parents and Lark already at the dinner table when I got home. Lark industriously smeared applesauce across the tray of my old high chair. As the phone rang, I snagged the receiver from the wall phone. "Hello?" I answered, inclining my head to give Lark exaggerated air kisses.

The long-distance operator's voice captured my attention at once. "Allo?" she said around clicks and cracklings. "Is this Miss Robin Hamilton?" *Theresa!*

"Yes," I said happily.

"Go ahead, Monsieur."

Monsieur? "Robin, Laurent Pelletier here ... from Paris." Like most Parisians, Laurent spoke flawless English.

"Hello, Laurent. How are you? Is everything all right?"

"Robin, I'm calling about Theresa." His voice was grave. A chill began to creep along my arms.

"What is it, Laurent?" The harvest-gold phone cord was long enough that I could move to a kitchen chair. I sat down heavily. My parents studied me, Dad spooning applesauce into Lark's open baby-bird mouth.

"Ma-ma!" Lark said.

"Theresa is experiencing panic attacks," Laurent said. "She ... hasn't left the apartment voluntarily in more than a month. She has taken a sabbatical from her work. She is sleeping now. You see, she was *mugged* one evening on her way home. She was physically unhurt, but *le connard* held a knife to her throat as he stripped her of her handbag."

Oh, Theresa. I listened with mounting concern as Laurent described taking a reluctant and silent Tee to a psychologist who had diagnosed her condition as post-traumatic stress disorder. Theresa had managed to subjugate a shrouded fear stemming from as far back as her father's death and including the blackout episode in college. Apparently the recent event had brought the terror back, had triggered it, he said.

"Robin, I've done everything I can to help her ... I'm calling to ask if you could come. I feel badly asking ... I know you have your little baby to care for—"

I interrupted without hesitation, "I will come. I can arrange things with my parents." Both my parents were nodding their heads in confirmation. My mind ticked to the days ahead. I could arrange to take my finals early; I was ready for them. Laurent would make my travel arrangements.

"Please give Tee my love and tell her I'll be with her soon," I said. I hung up the phone, plucked my cherub from the high chair, and told my parents the grim news.

Twisting my long hair in her sticky little fingers, Lark regarded me soberly. "I don't know how I can do without this monkey," I said, putting her over my shoulder and holding her close. I'd never spent a night apart from Lark. But I would do anything for Tee.

In the luxe first-class seat Laurent had booked, I pushed the window shade up to study the vivid early sky over the wing and pensively sipped at a cup of tea. I had risen at four in the morning, and it would be evening before I arrived in Paris. With no annoyingly chatty seatmate, I was free to reflect.

Theresa had become a moderately successful journalist for the political magazine in Paris. We'd not spoken in three months, I realized. Tee had been consumed with the busyness of her career, with playing hostess at Laurent's gallery, and with the myriad issues of her demanding stepdaughters.

Why had the traumatic night we'd suffered three years ago affected Theresa this way? Why her and not me? *The mind is incredibly complex.* Theresa's doctor and Laurent believed that because I'd been with Tee the night of the blackout, I could help her talk through it and begin purging the fear from her mind.

A horse-faced stewardess offered me more tea, a pair of disposable slippers, and a blanket. I accepted all gratefully, slipped from my heels into the slippers, and pulled the light blanket over me. With a thumb, I slid the snapshot of Lark from my wallet and peered at her precious face. "Absence makes the heart grow fonder," my grandmother Courtwright had said, but I knew I couldn't love my child more.

My old Judas thoughts turned to Dean. How right I had been to keep our baby! What if I hadn't? Would Dean love her as I did?

He would if he could see her and hold her in his arms. His arms. I turned toward the window as tears oozed. Watching Lark grow the last months, I'd considered calling Dean again. I was reclaiming the grace and courage I had lacked during the pregnancy and Lark's infancy. When I returned from France, I would serve the ball into Dean's court and see how he played it. The stewardess brought warm towels around. I bathed my face and hands as the breakfast trays were served. I nibbled on a buttery croissant, a ham-and-cheese omelette, cheese, and fruit. Eventually the roar of the engine lulled me to sleep.

Hours later, Laurent Pelletier, whom I recognized from his picture, met me at Charles de Gaulle Airport's bustling baggage claim. He kissed both my cheeks in greeting. His photograph had not done him justice. I could see how Theresa had fallen for him so quickly. Laurent was warm and gracious, but his dark eyes were rimmed with sadness. I spotted my voluminous bag, and Laurent carried it to the trunk of his black Mercedes.

I couldn't help but feel excited about seeing Paris for the first time. On the dusky drive to the Pelletiers' boulevard Saint-Germain apartment, Laurent pointed out the lights of Notre Dame on the right bank of the Seine. The lights reflected off the rippling night water like a casting of gold coins. Through the moonroof of the car the gray-blue evening sky deepened. I lowered my window, and a fresh, cool, faintly salt-scented breeze teased my face and hair. Seeing Notre Dame brought Dean to mind again. I hoped he would see it one day. Maybe he already had. I shook myself, willing away torturous thoughts.

"Are you chilled, Robin?" Laurent's accent was silken. He reached toward the heat dial.

"No, no, I'm fine; the air feels wonderful." I managed a smile.

The Eiffel Tower wasn't visible from the route, but Laurent promised to show me the sights another day. My thoughts turned to Theresa. Laurent began to detail the therapy her doctor had proposed. The three of us would meet with Madame Desrosiers the following morning. Tonight I would shower my friend with love.

A sturdy and florid female domestic opened the door of the apartment and greeted us in lilting French. "Bonsoir, Monsieur Laurent, Madamoiselle Hamilton." I realized she must have been briefed on me. The French were formal and apparently as thorough as their neighbors to the east.

Laurent said to the woman in French, "Madame Heloise, may I present Mademoiselle Hamilton?" And to me he said, "Robin, this is our devoted Madame Heloise; we couldn't do without her. Know that she speaks little English." He smiled. "She can't be bothered to learn." He asked Heloise to show me to my room.

"Oui, monsieur," Heloise piped briskly. She lifted my weighty bag as though it were made of straw and led me toward a long hall lined with more art.

"I'll tell Theresa you've arrived," Laurent called after us.

The spacious apartment was elegant and bright and decorated with clean contemporary pieces. Stark white walls provided the perfect backdrop for Laurent's vibrant paintings. I loved his still-life work—eclectic arrangements of fruit and flowers and found objects—and the life-sized portrait of Theresa, hair aflame, wearing a plum dress and sapphires, over the mantle in the living room. My room echoed the rest of the apartment, spare except for a brightly hued rug in the middle of the floor. An antique sleigh bed beckoned, the linens crisp and turned invitingly down. And on the expanse of wall above it was a series of three of Laurent's botanical studies.

Theresa had told me that Laurent's family money had allowed him to paint until he had established a place for himself in the community of commissioned artists. I realized his work must fetch large sums. I unpacked and freshened up a bit and then ventured out to find Theresa. The apartment was redolent with what smelled like roast lamb. My stomach grumbled in anticipation. I hadn't eaten in six hours. Theresa sat at the edge of one of the white leather living room sofas. I saw her before she saw me, and my heart stabbed as I registered her thinness, her haunted eyes. Theresa stood and burst into tears. "Rob!" she said and held her arms out to me. As we embraced, I noticed her hair lacked its former luster. It didn't smell fresh. Tee's wraithlike appearance contrasted sharply with the vivid portrait behind her on the wall.

"Darling, Tee, everything will be okay. We're going to get to the bottom of this thing, I promise," I said as if soothing a frightened child.

"Je suis désolé ... You came all this way and without Lark." She clutched her hands nervously. I realized we had our work cut out for us.

The three of us sat down to dinner in the dining room. Madame Heloise's succulent lamb chops and fresh vegetable risotto, followed by piquant goat cheese and fresh, crisp salad greens, was incomparably delicious. I ate every morsel of my chocolate profiterole dessert, while Tee only picked at her plate.

Laurent was clearly crazy about his young wife. After coffee in the living room, he kissed her good night, murmured something into her ear, and retired to his own room. I went to bathe away the day of travel. As I filled the luxuriously appointed bath, I regarded my first bidet with amusement.

Refreshed and comfy, I padded to Theresa's room, where she was reclining on a great gilded bed, her pretty face as pale as the linens behind her. Though shattered, this was still my best friend in the world. I grinned and jumped onto the bed. I told Tee about Lark and how fast she was growing, spreading the sheath of photographs I had brought with me across the duvet. Theresa exclaimed over the baby, her face lighting for the first time. *"L'ange! Tu est belle!"*

Madame Heloise knocked to ask if we would like a nightcap. Wide-eyed, I accepted a heavy crystal tumbler of scotch. "Tee, you live like a queen!"

"I realize that," she said simply. "Too bad money can't buy peace of mind. But I feel better just having you here, Rob, I do! But I feel terribly guilty about taking you away from Lark."

Looking intently into the face I loved, I said, "I don't want to hear you say that again, darling. I am here because I want to be."

132

Theresa closed her eyes and nodded, a single tear coasting down one wan cheek. And then jet lag began to claim me. "Rest well," I said, kissing Tee's forehead. I closed the door softly behind me.

As Theresa, Laurent, and I pulled away from the apartment the next morning, Theresa's mouth trembled below large, dark sunglasses. She pulled a large silk scarf closely around her shoulders. She said little in the car as Laurent and I chatted brightly. Laurent held the wheel with his left hand; his right firmly held Theresa's.

Handsome with cherry paneling, fresh flowers, and overstuffed chintz chairs, Madame Desrosiers's office could almost lull you into believing you were there to have tea with royalty. Indeed the doctor's carriage was regal, but her open manner put me at ease immediately. For ninety minutes (in which a silent, blue- eyed woman brought a tray of tea and coffee) I spoke until my throat was scratchy of Theresa's obsession with the Son of Sam story and described the night of the blackout, tasting words I hadn't spoken in years.

As details emerged, the doctor would interrupt and ask Theresa's perspective. For the first time Laurent learned the whole story. Madame Desrosiers concluded the session and asked if she could speak to Laurent alone. Tee and I waited in the exit room. Laurent later told me the doctor felt the session had been productive and an integral part of Tee's recovery.

I attended the next three sessions with Tee. Laurent would drop us off and drive to his studio. I had been nowhere except the doctor's office and the apartment since I had arrived. On the third day Theresa said as casually as if commenting on the weather, "Let's go *out* to lunch today."

In the backseat my heart leaped. Laurent turned to stare at his wife. The hope in his eyes was so naked I had to look away. And then he asked with a tremulous smile, "Where to, cherie?"

"I'd like to go to Bistro Beaubourg," Tee said evenly. "Robin will like it, and it's nice enough to sit outside."

We were seated at a quiet corner table in the sunny courtyard under a red umbrella. Theresa ate from her plate of perch with fennel, tomatoes, and wine and a potato galette. But she looked as if she should be stamped with a "Fragile" sticker. The three of us shared a nice bottle of white wine, a Vouvray from the Loire Valley.

Each night when I went to bed, I prayed for Tee and for my baby at home. I missed Lark terribly and couldn't wait to hold her again, to kiss her cheeks, and to smell my favorite spots beneath her chin and at the tender nape of her neck.

Theresa and I participated in two more sessions together, and after each the three of us lunched at Tee's favorite spots. Laurent drove me to see the Eiffel Tower and the Arc de Triomphe and down the historic Champs-Élysées. He parked near Ladurée and returned with a beautiful assortment of airy, pastel macaroons.

One afternoon in a spot rowdy and clotted with tourists, Theresa had a panic attack, the first I'd seen. "My heart, Laurent!" she gasped. She held her chest and trembled. Laurent's arms tightly around her, Tee closed her eyes. I saw her lips move with the calming mantras Madame Desrosiers had taught her. She breathed slowly and deeply, fighting the panic. I stroked her hair. "That's it. You're so brave, Tee."

Each day my friend's face regained color. Madame Heloise prepared all her favorite meals to tempt her appetite. We enjoyed them with robust glasses of good French wine. At last the lines around Theresa's eyes and mouth began to smooth, her cheeks to take on the former curves.

On Saturday, though the clouds were pregnant with rain, we went to the world's largest flea market, Les Puces de Saint-Ouen. I loved the funkiness of it—the antique luggage, jewelry, architectural pieces, books, and garden pots. I bought a pretty antique alphabet poster for Lark's room and a handsome antique wooden box for my parents. The air rang with of the sounds of hawking vendors and twitters from the tall cages of parrots and parakeets as flashy as a marching band. Theresa laughed easily that day, though she continued to cling to Laurent's hand or arm.

On Sunday the three of us headed south into the quiet countryside. We passed through quaint villages, farms with vivid fields of lavender and poppies. We stopped at a small family market for a fresh baguette, a sampler of cheeses and sausages, fruit and bottled water, and two bottles of wine—a dry white Sancerre and light red Beaujolais. Laurent was enjoying teaching me about wine.

The sun high, we spread our picnic in a grove of trees. We laughed a great deal. Tee lay gazing at clouds, her mass of Titian hair like a ring of fire on the grass. "Wouldn't a joint be perfect about now, Rob?" she said. Laurent shook his head with an indulgent smirk. He said recreational drugs had never appealed to him.

"I guess those days are behind us, Madame Pelletier." I hadn't smoked in over two years. It was a tranquil, healing afternoon for us all.

An easy alliance had sprung between Laurent and me. I was coming to love him, to think of him as I would a brother-in-law. His love for my truest friend was strong and lasting. This simple fact filled me with gratitude for his solid presence.

The next week Madame Desrosiers asked that Theresa attend her sessions alone. Those mornings I drove Tee to the doctor's office, parked the sedan, and wandered into a different café each day for a decadent, flaky chocolate croissant or crepe and a café crème. I was surprised to hear so many different tongues in the conversations around me—German, Chinese, Dutch, and once what I thought must be Portuguese. The last day of appointments as I enjoyed the last of my rich coffee, the woman at the next table whom I'd seen before, with the Brillo Pad hair and nostrils so elongated you could have inserted a couple of nickels into them, moved on, leaving a French tabloid on her table. I picked it up, amused at the universal love of gossip.

I glanced at this or that overweight, stretch-marked cinema star in a bikini and then did a double take at a photograph on the second page. It was the Eagles. I read the article with interest and learned the band had broken up. The paper reported that the band members had developed a conflict of interests and that collaboration on the last album had been miserable. I was shocked and wanted to confirm the story from another source. I couldn't wait to tell Tee about it when I picked her up.

Tuesday afternoon Theresa and I walked to the Musée D'Orsay in a cool, slanting rain. She explained I would see more of the impressionist work I loved there, rather than the Louvre. I savored the Renoir masterworks and told Tee the stories of the two very different experiences I had had at the Phillips Collection in DC. In a gallery of late-nineteenth-century sculpture, we found the bust of Madame Renoir in a case. Her husband, then almost crippled from unrelenting rheumatism in his hands, had created the piece shortly after her death. "Now that's love," Theresa murmured, her eyes shining.

On Wednesday afternoon Tee took me to her favorite place in Paris, the Luxembourg Gardens. "Robin," she said, taking my arm as we strolled through the old iron gates, "I can't believe I was trapped in that … shell … of my own fear for so long." Madame Desrosiers had said that fear was at the root of Theresa's problem. The sessions were helping my friend to excise the fear like a rotten tooth. "And I have missed this place. Isn't it beautiful?" she said, gesturing with a sweep of one small, expressive hand. "I used to come here once a week to write."

"It is spectacular! Now you can do that again," I said, smiling at my friend. We stood at the edge of a round, shallow pool dotted with jaunty wooden sailboats of yellow and blue. Young children industriously prodded the boats along with long sticks. I wished for Lark as we watched little boys in short pants and T-strap shoes at play. Artists perched at easels around the perimeter of the promenade painted vistas of the park in the light. Wide, old stone stairs, their steps worn into silky troughs by millions of feet, were flanked with columns topped with centuries-old statuary. Weatherworn cherubs held aloft urns filled with riotous flowers and trailing vines. The steps led to upper terraces and paths surrounded by dense green foliage. Tee and I could have been extras in a movie as we sat in a pair of painted metal chairs, a row of nodding summer flowers at our feet, Marie de Medici's former palace magnificent behind us.

I had waited to bring up the subject of Theresa's therapy, but the moment felt tranquil, ripe for disclosure. "Tee," I said carefully, "I wish I'd known how deeply that night in New York affected you. And I've wondered if there was ... something I could have done ... but you seemed fine after those first few days."

"I compartmentalized it, Robin. That's how my mind copes with fear. My pattern has been to bury shit ... trauma ... deep within myself. I'm afraid my mother encouraged that. After I was mugged, the new fear was too much to add to what was already there. It was like ... you know when you try to cram too much into a suitcase? You can force the lid down, but when you let go, it pops back up; the contents are too full to compress. Does that make sense?"

"It makes perfect sense," I said, watching her face. A rubber ball rolled toward us, chased by a darling little boy. I bent down and caught the ball in one hand and grinned at him. "Voilà," I said, offering it to him. He took it in both pudgy hands, smiling shyly, and ran away on sturdy legs.

Theresa's eyes followed him. "I have to deal with the fear head on … fight it from now on, now that I can see it for what it is. It's real, and it can feel … just crushing, but it's just fear. It will get easier with time." She looked at me again.

"Tee, I'm so proud of you. It has taken a lot of courage to do what you've done." I leaned over to hug her thin shoulders.

"Thank you, my friend." She smiled. "I know I couldn't have done it without you. I'm going to continue to see Madame Desrosiers. And I'll have Laurent—he's been amazing—and *you*, you've been *incredible*, Robin! You'll be pulling for me from across the ocean, right?"

"You can count on it, baby." We smiled at each other in the sunlight.

That evening, my last in Paris, Laurent drove us through a fine mist to the elegant old restaurant Lasserre on avenue Franklin D. Roosevelt. The street was still, the streetlamps haloed in mist, as Theresa and I walked beneath Laurent's huge black umbrella. I regarded with awe the Louis XVI furnishings, the brocaded walls, and the tables set with fine porcelain and crystal glasses edged in gold. And the ceiling! Painted with clouds and an azure sky, it could be retracted in fair weather to allow moonlight or sunlight to pour into the room.

My mouth twisted as the steward ceremoniously decanted our wine into a silver pitcher. Laurent smiled at me as if I were Marie Antoinette, laughing and feasting on Belon oysters, fillets of sole with asparagus cream sauce, and a salad of truffles. After a soufflé

Grand Marnier, I was practically woozy from the decadent excess. I couldn't imagine *l'addition* in the leather binder Laurent held. I sensed the extravagance was his final way of thanking me for coming to Paris.

The last night Theresa and I sat up in her bed again talking of the future. I told her I was determined to tell Dean the truth about Lark. Her eyes fervent with passion, she said, "It's time, Robin. You owe it to Dean. To Lark. And even to yourself, although you may not yet realize it."

Early the next morning we left for the airport. Both Pelletiers embraced me. Theresa promised to call me with updates on her progress. Laurent said simply, "Thank you, Robin," his throat constricted with emotion.

"Give *mon alouette* a kiss from Tante Tee!" Theresa called as I moved down the Jetway.

* * * * *

I was grateful Lark hadn't taken her first steps without me. It had been only twelve days, but it seemed a month since I'd seen her. The child seemed to have grown an inch. I put her in bed with me the first night. Snuggling with her, I tumbled into a miles-deep sleep. My mother tiptoed in and plucked the baby from the bed without waking me the next morning. I slept for ten straight hours.

My excellent grades and certificate in paralegal studies arrived in the next afternoon's mail. Mentally I checked off another benchmark toward my independence. It was time to draft my first résumé and begin to search for a job. Once again for a time, I forgot my commitment to call Dean.

I knew Dad's contacts in the legal community would be invaluable. We discussed the fields of law again, and I spent several mornings in the library pouring over information about the fields that interested me. In the end I decided to apply with a firm specializing in trusts and estates. That lawyers in these fields usually built long-standing personal relationships with their clients appealed to me. An acquaintance of Dad's, Stephen Adams (who looked like Gary Cooper) of the firm of Wickersham, Collins, and Adams, was adding a paralegal to their growing practice. At my interview I found Mr. Adams a thoroughly nice man, and he hired me on the spot. I had my first job.

My parents and I agreed Lark and I should stay with them until I was on my financial feet. Mom and I shopped for business attire. She bought me two tailored suits and three blouses. I dug in at the firm, working prodigiously, but at the end of the day the sight of my child always reinvigorated me. I loved giving Lark her bath and snuggling as we read *Pat the Bunny* or *Goodnight Moon* at bedtime. She babbled and drooled and patted the books, completely absorbed in them. "Night, night, sleep tight; see you in the morning's light," I would say as I put her down.

Lark would be a year old in a few days and looked more like Dean than ever. The early taffy tuft of hair had become Dean's darker gold. She was beginning to use real words now—Ma-ma, Gam-ma, Gam-pa, bye-bye, quack, moo, and Ack-cus. After dinner one evening she pulled herself to a standing position at the old ottoman. We laughed at her astonished face.

It was time to call her father. It took me two days to make the call after I'd made the decision. On a Saturday afternoon, Lark down for a nap and my parents out of the house, I dialed the number, my heart thudding with anticipation. I heard the phone ringing in Virginia, my palm slick with sweat on the receiver. "Hello?" an out-of-breath, feminine voice answered on the sixth ring.

"Hello," I responded in my best Miss Pruitt's School voice and a bravado I didn't feel. "This is Robin Hamilton calling. With whom am I speaking please?"

"This is Laurel Falconer." Her voice was friendly. "Robin." She paused, searching her memory. "Hello, my dear, I'm glad that you called. Dean's not here right now." She paused again, and I felt a prickling disquiet. "Robin ... Dean tried for months to find you." My heart flipped in my chest as she added, "He was very much in love with you, but ... I'm afraid I was quite ill at the time and needed my son. Dean was wonderful to take the family in hand. It has taken me ... a long time to pull myself together after my husband's death."

I managed to murmur something that sounded like "I'm-so-sorry-but-pleased-to-hear-you-have-recovered" while my thoughts spiraled crazily.

"Dean is engaged to be married in June," she said quietly. Eight words and my legs threatened to fold like a battered lawn chair. I sat heavily on the floor, a death grip on the receiver in my fist. "I hope this news isn't painful for you." Only like a rusty hatchet in my sternum. But this kind, southern-voiced woman, Dean's mother, was only the unfortunate messenger. "Would you like me to have him call you?"

I collected myself with effort. "No, thank you, Mrs. Falconer. And please, will you keep this conversation between the two of us? Please. I don't want to interfere."

"Well … yes, of course, if you want me to," she said slowly. "I understand. I'm sorry I won't get to know you, Robin," she continued gently. "If Dean loved you, I know you are a special woman."

I couldn't remain on the line another second. "Thank you. Good-bye, Mrs. Falconer." I sat looking at the receiver until a shrill tone began. Then I walked ponderously up the stairs to my room where Dean's beautiful, rosy-cheeked baby lay sleeping peacefully, a yellow cloth duck peeping from beneath one plump arm. I sat beside the crib and watched her in a void of stillness until the room grew shadowy and she woke. "Hi, sweet Lark," I said. She grinned from ear to ear, her face flushed, sheet creased, so vulnerable. She pulled up to stand, her chubby tummy pushing against the rail of the crib and held her arms up to me, "Ma-ma!" I picked her up and held her against me, closing my eyes. Her diaper was wet and heavy. She squirmed to be changed. I took care of my daughter's needs.

I would not be undone by this. Not again. I had Lark, and she was enough. I headed down the stairs again, my blissfully oblivious child chattering happily on my hip, to the kitchen to start dinner.

CHAPTER
13

Dean

1980–1982

Missing Robin like hell, I wrote her two mushy letters I knew she'd like—just days apart. Within ten days, both of them reappeared in the mailbox at Villeneuve. Someone had scrawled "No longer at this address" across both of them. Bush-hogging all afternoon, I thought, *Why would she move?*

I took a long, hot shower, my muscles tired and sore, and stretched out across my bed. At least hard work kept me from thinking too much about sex. I reached for the phone and scrap of paper with Robin's number. The phone rang once in DC, and then, following three shrill tones, an automated voice said, "The number that you have dialed is no longer in service." I hung up, nonplussed, checked the number again, and redialed with the same result. *What is going on?*

The next morning I called directory assistance and got the number for the law school registrar's office. "I'm sorry, sir; I'm not allowed to give out personal student information," a woman said.

"Please. I have to find her. I'm … concerned about her."

"I'm sorry, sir." But then her voiced softened. "Actually, I see here that Miss Hamilton withdrew from school … at semester."

What? Robin quit law school? "Is there a forwarding address?" I asked the woman.

"I really am sorry. I can't provide that information." I thanked the woman and held the receiver to my chest for several minutes. *What now?*

I worked hard the next few days replacing sections of fence, hoping to hear from Robin. But as another week went by, there was no word. If she had quit school, something was very wrong. Maybe she had gone home to New York. I called directory assistance for the Hamiltons' number. I remembered her father's name was Hank. I tried Hank, and there was no listing. Then I tried Henry. The operator told me that Henry A. Hamilton's number was an unlisted one. I had no idea what the name of his firm was.

I'd been a fool not to get Robin's New York number. I knew her parents lived in an old brownstone on the Upper West Side, but what was I supposed to do? Go knock on a hundred doors? I had about as much chance of finding Robin as I did of signing a free agent contract with the Yankees.

Friday night I waited up for Leslie to come in. I'd spent the evening watching TV and playing backgammon with Mary. My little sister had finally lost the wide-eyed, perpetually startled look she had developed after Dad had died. Tonight she had laughed aloud at my corniest jokes. But I had sent Mary to bed at midnight. I felt like an indignant father sitting there fuming about Leslie until two thirty, wishing I had a joint to smoke.

Leslie crept in then, and I asked from the shadows, "Where the hell have *you* been?" startling her. In the lamplight I saw my sister had a kissing chin and messed-up hair. She waved her hand in dismissal. "I've been at a party, with Tony, at the place of some friends' of his." Tony Childs, no doubt.

"Listen, Leslie, I don't like having to act like a parent, but it's not safe out driving around this late."

"You are not Dad!" she spat, venom in her gray eyes.

"Well, I'm the closest thing you've got to it right now. Get upstairs!" I growled, rising from the chair as if to do something we would both regret.

"Gladly, Mr. Prison Warden!" she yelled, but I detected a prickle of fear in her eyes.

"We'll talk about this in the morning," I said through clenched teeth, breathing hard. Leslie stormed up the stairs and slammed her door. I hated myself then for scaring her. Wearily, I moved to the liquor cabinet, poured myself a hefty scotch, and took it upstairs. I lay back against the pillows on my bed, sipping from the glass and thinking about Robin, how much I wanted and needed her. *Where the hell is she?* I thought for the hundredth time.

On a whim one Saturday I drove to Georgetown. It had been a long time. I realized I had no idea how I would find or contact any of Robin's friends there, but I went to the apartment building and knocked on door 129 with a lump in my throat. A tall—Amazonian-tall—girl with oily black hair answered the door and scowled at me. She said yes, it was she who had gotten my letters and put them back into the mail chute. She knew nothing of Robin. Looking past the girl, I glimpsed the apartment where Robin and I had loved each other, and a flood of memories just about took me down. With effort, I thanked the girl and walked away.

I went by the Tombs and found James in. "It's great to see you, buddy!" I said, squeezing his shoulder. "How've you been?"

"Dean, I've missed you, man! How is your mom?" I sat and ordered a beer, and James and I caught up with each other. I told him I was looking for Robin. "Dude, I'm sorry," he said. "I never saw her again after that night at my party."

Two beers later, I rose to pay my tab. James waved my open wallet away. "It's on me, Dean. Good luck, man. I hope you find her; girls like Robin don't come along every day."

"No, they don't," I said, my throat constricted. "Later, man." I had to get out of there before I started bawling. I climbed in my Jeep and aimed it for the farm. The only girl I had really loved had disappeared like the sweet smoke from a doobie. All I could do was pray and hope that Robin would get back in touch with me.

By summer there was still no word or trace. The situation was like a ball game that had gone into extra innings, tied at zero inning after inning, and finally called because of rain or dark or who knows what … but in the end it didn't count.

The farm and helping with the girls consumed all my time. I had the barn help, Harry and Justin, to take care of the horses but still could use more manpower. Uncle John helped me on weekends, but I carried the bulk of the load myself.

I *had* to get back to school. With just a few more courses in my master's program, I knew I could finish it at UVA in no time. What I really needed was a farm manager, to fill Dad's shoes.

My mother had made nice progress. The doctor had started her on a new medication that seemed to be making the difference. Mom was more animated and spoke of coming home to us, of the farm and her animals. The attending physician planned to release her in two weeks' time, when the antidepressant had reached its full effectiveness. He said she would need to stay on the medication for at least six months.

The girls were guardedly excited about the homecoming. Mom's depression had frightened and confused them. Both of them had been happier since I'd come home, although the truce between Leslie and me had been strained since the night of our fight. But Leslie's clothes no longer hung on her tall frame. Her cheeks were gently rounded again. I took her fishing one Saturday

as our dad had done. On the pond we had learned to swim in as
children, the opportunity to talk presented itself. Leslie spoke of
her eating problem. I listened casually but was duct-taped to every
word. I alternately baited our hooks with crickets and cast my line.

"I know about anorexia, Dean; I've read the magazine stories
and seen all those movies." A huge catfish jumped from the water
across the lake, making a loud clattering smack as it plunged
again below the surface. Her gray eyes on the rippling water,
Leslie continued, "When Dad died, I just couldn't eat, and then
when Mom went off the deep end, I felt like the only thing I
could control in my life was what I put in my body. It was just like
the girls you hear about on TV. But it's very ... I don't know ...
seductive ... when you're in the middle of it."

I looked at my sister. Her lashes were dark with unshed tears.
"You were lucky to be able to see it, Les, and ... stop it before it
killed you. There are people who don't, and they *die*. This has
been ... a total nightmare for everybody, but you're better now.
We all are ... and life will go on." We watched our floats drift and
bob silently with the boat's wake, the only sounds the drone of
horseflies and the water lapping lazily at the sides of the aluminum
boat.

"Oh, and yeah," Leslie said, startling me from a reverie, "you'll
be happy to know, big brother, that wild Tony Childs has headed
west, left for Colorado last week, to work on a cattle ranch. His
old man laid down the law." Leslie watched me from the corner of
her eyes, gauging my reaction. I just nodded my head. "He wasn't
my type anyway," she added a minute later, wrinkling her nose
and sniffing. She reeled in her line, swatting at a horsefly, and cast

again. "I got one!" she called excitedly as her cork plunged beneath the surface. I cheered her on as she reeled in a thrashing bream as big as my hand.

"Nice one! Way to go, Sis." I grinned. We caught a nice mess of fish that afternoon and gave them to Justin, who took them home for his wife, Stacey, to fry for supper. The trip had been a success.

I also spent time with Mary, driving her to and from school every day until summer vacation started. I quizzed her for tests on the morning drives, and some afternoons we'd get frozen slushies for the ride home. We fed the horses early in the mornings when the barn was cool. One afternoon we took the three hunting hounds out into the fields to run. I almost crapped my pants when she asked me out of the blue, "Does everybody have oral sex, Dean?"

My thoughts ricocheted like bats in a box. "What do you mean, honey?" I asked, buying time.

"I hear people talking about it at school, and I just ... wondered if it's something that you *have* to do when you have sex."

"Are you having sex, honey?" I asked, a pain beginning behind my right eye.

"Dean! No! I don't even have a boyfriend!"

I wracked my brain trying to come up with a decent answer for my sweet little sister. "Well, when you make love ... with ... someone you truly love ... you do what you feel comfortable doing." The dogs came bounding back, weaving through the tall grass, hassling, great tongues lolling, Buddy with the ball. I wrestled it from his mouth, wound up like Catfish Hunter, and threw the ball again.

"Okay," Mary said studiously, rubbing at a scratch on her boot with a thumb.

"And if you think about having sex before you're married ... and I hope you don't ... only do what makes you feel respected. And make sure you are protected. Do you know what I mean by that?" That was all I could stand to say.

"Yeah." She looked up at me again and punched me in the bicep.

"Oww! Damn, you pack a punch!" I said, holding my arm. Mary grinned and took off after the dogs. While she had floored me, I was humbled to know how much she trusted me, that she would ask her brother about something of that nature rather than Leslie.

One morning in the barn as I squeezed a sponge over Tartan's broad haunches, I heard Mary talking to her horse Missy as she tended to a sore spot on the mare's leg. Missy was all stillness ... completely captivated by Mary's tone. It was the intro I had been looking for. "Hey, little sister, how 'bout I call Dr. Doss, to see if he could use a teenage helper this summer?" I knew the clinical experience would be good for Mary, and she would be terrific with the animals, a win-win situation.

"I guess so. Are you trying to get rid of me?"

I laid my thumb across the hose nozzle and sprayed water up and over the stall wall between us.

"Crap, Dean, you got my hair wet! I'll get you back double."

"I'll get you back triple." I grinned at our old routine.

Mary loved riding in my Jeep with the top down. One afternoon the first week of June, the two of us were driving home from the farm supply store together. I pulled into the drive from the main road and stopped the Jeep. "I've got a charley horse," I said, reaching down to rub my calf. "You drive us to the house."

"Dean, I can't drive!" Mary said, looking at me as if a third nostril had spontaneously appeared in my face.

"The gas is on the right, the brake in the middle, and the clutch is on the left. If you can use the pedals on the piano, you can work the pedals in a car. Then, little sister, all you have to do is steer."

"I don't know, Dean. I'm scared. What if I wreck us?" There were two hectic spots of color on her cheeks.

"Do you think I would let you drive *my Jeep* if I was worried?" I said, tipping her a wink. I got out and strolled around to her side of the car and then made her scoot across the console and into the driver's seat.

Mary did drive that day—after a lot of jerking and bucking and grinding of my gears—all around our property, and loved it. I took her out every afternoon that week. And when she was comfortable, bordering on cocky, I took her to some parking lots in town to practice parking. We picked up a driver's manual from the DMV, and Mary studied for the Virginia driver's test.

Majestic Oak Hill, the next farm over, was home to the Babbitt family. Mr. and Mrs. Babbitt had socialized quite a bit with my parents through the years. They were generationally wealthy but good, down-to-earth folks. I had grown up with their kids, Billy and Victoria. Billy and I were the same age and had gone through junior high and high school together. We'd played on the baseball team in high school, he the shortstop and me the first baseman. Billy had been a helluva hitter, the star player. An all-around good guy, he had been voted by our senior class Most Friendly *and* Most Sportsmanlike. Billy had been headed for the University of North Carolina, handpicked by selective recruiters for a scholarship, but the summer before we were to leave for college he'd wrapped his truck around a hundred-year-old oak tree one night on the way home from a party. Suffering two compound fractures and slight brain damage from a concussion, Billy hadn't been able to go to college after all. I knew Billy worked for a homebuilder in Charlottesville now. Though he had regained most of the short-term memory function he had lost, the limp that remained after a year of intense physical therapy would be with him until the day they closed his coffin.

I had Billy in mind for the position of farm manager. If he was interested, I knew he would do a good job and earn more money than he was at present. I was counting on Mom to go back to keeping the books when she got home and was strong again. On the tractor one Thursday afternoon in July, the sun biting my neck as if it had teeth, a baby-blue Mercedes Benz 500SL rolled up the gravel drive, its tires gathering dust and scattering it into the air. *Shit, I just washed my Jeep,* I thought. It was Victoria Babbitt's car.

Victoria was thirteen months younger than Billy and me and had gone through junior high with us. Before ninth grade she'd transferred from public school to the swanky girls' school in Ivy. I hadn't seen her much after that, though she'd asked me to take her to a school dance once when she had been in eleventh grade. I'd known she had a crush on me; Billy had told me so. I'd taken her to the dance and had even made out with her a little in the driveway when I'd taken her home that night. She'd looked hungrily at me all that evening and had asked me to call her, but shortly after, I'd met Katie Sumner, a petite blonde and a talented violinist with a dry wit. Katie and I had dated until she'd gone off to study at Indiana University's prestigious school of music. After that, I'd never seen her again.

Sweating like a pig, I climbed down from the tractor and walked across the grass to greet Victoria. "Dean Falconer!" she said, smiling and stepping out of her car in a pink Sweet Briar College T-shirt, coltish legs in Daisy Duke cutoffs. "I heard you were home." She took off her sunglasses. "I'm so sorry about your father; He was a sweet man," she added kindly.

"Thank you, Victoria. How are you?" I said, pulling a bandana from my back pocket and wiping my face streaming under a UVA baseball cap.

"Well, I'm just fine, Dean. I'm home this summer and wondered if you wanted to take me out to dinner," she said with a toss of her blonde head and a saucy smile. I knew Victoria had studied for a semester in Italy and then earned her master's in teaching at Sweet Briar. Victoria's quiet, dark-eyed beauty had ripened since I'd seen her last.

I smiled at her. "A dinner out would be pretty nice actually. I've done nothing but work and crash every night since I've been home."

"Well, how 'bout tomorrow night?" Victoria suggested. "There's a new Italian place downtown that's supposed to be fantastic."

"It would be my pleasure ... on one condition," I said.

She laughed, tossing her hair again. "And what's that, Dean Falconer?"

"That you let me drive that sweet car." I gestured to the sleek coupe. It was mighty sweet, the sun glinting off its blue paint and immaculate chrome.

"Well, okay, but I have a condition too," she said, opening the car door and stepping in. "That you smell a little better than you do right now." *Shit.* Victoria laughed at me, put her sunglasses on again, and started the engine. She spurted away, kicking up the dust again, and called out the window, "Pick you up at seven."

I went inside to cool off, thinking about what had just happened. I stood over the kitchen sink, drinking water and looking east toward the Babbitt place. I'd unwittingly stumbled into a date with the girl next door.

A week later my mother finally came home to Villeneuve. The girls had cleaned the house thoroughly, putting crisp sheets on Mom's bed and armloads of fresh-cut summer flowers in her room. Aunt Martha had cooked all afternoon, Mom's pot roast recipe. She and Uncle John would stay for dinner with us. Before her breakdown and with Martha's help, Mom had stoically and silently boxed all of Dad's clothes and taken them to Goodwill. (When she gave me Dad's watch, I almost started bawling.) We were all a little nervous about how Mom would reacclimate, my father's ghost in every room.

Uncle John and I drove Mom home from the hospital. She was timid and seemed fragile at first in the hubbub of hugs and greetings, but by the time we sat down to the big oak table, the girls chattering like magpies at her elbows, Mom was laughing at all of our news.

When Uncle John asked the blessing, we all echoed, "Amen." Then Mom cleared her throat and surprised us with a little speech that I thought was pretty eloquent. "I want to thank you all so much for your love … for being so … strong, giving me the time I needed to recover. I know it couldn't have been easy around here, without … your father *and* without your mother." She looked around the table at each one of us, her eyes bright with tears, though she kept her composure. "I am so proud of you … the way you have rallied together and kept Villeneuve going. Your father would be very proud." She looked back at me. "Dean, I am beyond proud of the man you have become. I know about all you've done," she said and winked at Martha. "You've sacrificed a great deal for your family. I want you to know that I intend to make it up to you."

"No, Mom. I did what I did because it was the right thing to do. It's what Dad would have expected." I reached across the table for her hand. "I love you very much. We all do. We're proud of your courage, Mom."

Smiling broadly, Uncle John lifted his glass of red wine. "To Laurel Falconer ... and to family."

"To Laurel Falconer and to family," we all responded.

The evening was a success, a benediction to the last two and a half years of pain, of fear and uncertainty. I couldn't help breathing a huge sigh of relief as I climbed the stairs to my room that night. I felt like a grand piano had been lifted from my twenty-five-year-old shoulders. My mother had made a damned miraculous recovery, and I was free to get on with my life.

But as I crawled into bed that night, the sheets cool on my body, my thoughts turned to Robin again. I reached for the book I'd been reading, Ayn Rand's *The Fountainhead*, and slid out the fingerprinted photo of Robin and me at James's Christmas party. I stared at the picture for a long time, running my finger over Robin's face. She was so beautiful in that red dress; she actually glowed. With love for *me*. It seemed like such a long time ago.

Taking Victoria out felt strange at first, as though I were cheating on Robin, and then it was as if I was on automatic pilot: hold the door for her, smile, look interested when she's talking about girl stuff, pull out her chair. But Victoria was a nice girl. She arrived like a breath of cool air on that sultry summer night, wearing a pretty white sundress and sandals that contrasted with her golden summer tan. And that sweet ride: the coupe hugged the curves of the country roads like a lover. James Taylor's *JT* spilled from her in-dash cassette player. I couldn't have stood it if Victoria had been a big Eagles' fan.

I ceremoniously parked the Benz a block away from the pedestrian mall for the benefit of a clump of frat boys who were gaping like fools at the car. Victoria and I entered the restaurant, my hand automatically at the small of her back. We placed our wine order, and I regarded Victoria across the table. I liked the combination of Virginia drawl, intelligence, and dark eyes you don't usually see in blondes. We took our time getting reacquainted over spaghetti carbonara, salad, and crusty bread. After dinner we walked out onto the outdoor mall where musicians were playing outside the shops, their guitar cases strewn with dollar bills. I was curious about Victoria's experience in Italy and what she had seen. She told me about it as we strolled.

And that night as I pulled up in front of my house again, she leaned over and gave me one light, sweet kiss on the lips. After she'd caromed away again, I stood listening to the haranguing cicadas in the trees. What I didn't feel was real chemistry with Victoria. What I felt was relief. I would be safe with this girl. I wouldn't lose my heart and soul to her.

* * * * *

Mary was champing at the bit like her spirited mare Missy, like any happy teenager, to get her driver's license. Mom and I decided to surprise her with a Jeep for her seventeenth birthday. I drove her to the DMV on her birthday, and she passed the test. She came out acting all cool and asked for the keys to my Jeep. She drove home, a shit-eating grin splitting her face the whole way.

We crunched down the drive at Villeneuve and rounded the curve to the house. The family and barn help were gathered around a shiny blue Jeep. Leslie had decorated the windshield with a huge white bow. Mary hopped down, her mouth an astonished O, to cries of, "Congratulations!"

"Really?" she said over and over, walking around the car and shaking her head in thrilled astonishment. The next Monday morning my little sister started work at the veterinary clinic.

Mom had wholeheartedly agreed with my choice of Billy Babbitt as farm manager. I took him to lunch in town and offered him the job with a good salary. Surprised by the offer, Billy asked if I was sure he could handle the job. I reassured my old friend I had faith in him and knew he would do a good job. "How about a six-month trial run?" I said. Billy accepted gratefully and began work at Villeneuve two weeks later.

Leslie, in the meantime, had applied to the University of Virginia for the fall semester and had bought her books and a bunch of new clothes. She was fired up about going to college and living in the dorm with a roommate from Richmond whom she had met and liked. Hope shone in her eyes again.

I would finally be going to grad school myself and took an apartment in town where I could work on projects and plans in peace. I left Villeneuve in late August. Victoria and I went out three more times, to the movies and to the wedding of one of her friends from Sweet Briar. By then everyone had begun to think of us as a couple. I guess it was inevitable. Victoria helped me move into my new apartment and decorated it for me. She came over to cook dinner for me a couple of nights a week. Victoria loved and got on well with my family, and I took her to Villeneuve on Sundays for Mom's big noon meal.

I kissed and hugged Victoria affectionately the way a boyfriend would, but I still didn't feel the heat … the passion … I'd felt for Robin. *Robin.* I wanted to get married and have a family. I didn't have my first choice of woman—maybe someone like Robin was a once-in-a-lifetime shot. But Victoria was a good catch; the blending of our families would be a good one. I couldn't go on living in the shadows of the things that might have been. I slipped out of the man that belonged to Robin like a snake shedding its skin.

In my bedroom at Villeneuve on Thanksgiving night, I reached behind my neck and released the clasp on the St. Thomas medal. It was warm in my palm from lying against my heart. For a moment I pictured Robin's face again, seeing her as she'd looked as she'd given it to me. My heart squeezed with a long-familiar pang. I went through my chest of drawers and found the things I was looking for. I put them in a shoe box and taped around it with masking tape. With a Magic Marker I labeled it DEAN'S and slipped out to hide it in my secret boyhood cubbyhole in the barn.

At Christmastime, Leslie helped me pick out a sparkly half-carat diamond ring, and I asked Victoria Babbitt to marry me.

CHAPTER

14

Robin

1980–1988

Lark had her first messy cold and spiked a fever. I took her to the pediatrician hoping to get a prescription, but the doctor said the cold was a virus; it was best to let it run its course. The fever was productive, she explained, helping Lark's body fight the virus. *Easy for you to say, when I'm the one walking the floor with her at night.* I was irritable and exhausted in the mornings but grateful I had my mom to take care of Lark at home while I worked, unlike many mothers who had to schlepp their kids out to day care.

We were two birds together, a robin and a lark, certain now that Dean would never share our nest. I tried not to show my sadness around Lark. She was a preternaturally perceptive child; her little face mirrored mine when I was feeling blue. One of our favorite books to read in those days was *Are You My Mother?* The mother bird in the story leaves an egg in the nest and goes in search of food. While she is away, the baby bird hatches, and

163

because it cannot fly, it walks to find its mother. It encounters a kitten, a hen, a dog, a cow, a boat, a plane, and finally a power shovel and asks each, "Are you my mother?" The power shovel eventually drops the baby bird back in its nest, and mother and baby are reunited. Lark wanted to read the story again and again. I taught her to say "Mama Robin and Baby Lark" as we looked in the mirror. At thirteen months Lark was ready to walk, wander, and explore, as curious as *The Poky Little Puppy*. Grandpa Hank quickly went about childproofing the house with gates and locks.

I did the family grocery shopping on Saturday mornings, Lark in the cart in front of me. People were drawn to her rosy prettiness and bright chatter. Each time, I bought her a little red-and-yellow box of Barnum's Animal Crackers. Lark would ask for them as soon as we entered the store, so I always headed for aisle eight first. She would eat a cookie or two from a gummy fist and mimic the animal sounds. "Ooh, ooh!" she'd cry as she pulled out a monkey, or "Gurrrr!" for a tiger.

In those days Mom would say to Lark, "How did you get to be so smart?" She taught Lark to answer, "I was born that way!" The best part was that as Lark parroted the phrase, she'd stick out a dimpled arm and point her finger, *that way*. We made her say it over and over.

At eighteen months Lark loved to go out to the front steps of the brownstone to sit and talk. "'Teps and talk, Mama," she'd say, pulling me by the hand. One day on the steps she looked at me, her face astonished. "I've got fingernails on my toes, Mama!"

Though Theresa and I wrote to each other regularly, I missed her more than ever. I felt an ineffable sadness about our likely lifetime separation. And then one drizzly April Sunday night she called from Paris. She was coming to Chicago for two weeks to visit her mother. Overjoyed, I arranged to make a weekend trip with twenty-two-month-old Lark in tow. I was dying for Tee to see the baby again. Theresa sounded strong and happy, scoured clean of fear. She would be starting a new job, a nice promotion, when she returned to France, as a staff writer for the magazine.

I took a personal day the next Friday. Lark and I excitedly boarded the train for Chicago. Theresa met us at the station wearing a broad grin and a knitted black beret over her flaming hair, longer again. It thrilled her when Lark greeted her with "Tante Tee!" as I had taught her.

"Rob, your *alouette*! She is so beautiful!" Tee took Lark from me to hug and kiss her. She looked wistful and then gazed at Lark's face. "And looks ... exactly like her father," she added quietly.

"I know. I think about it all the time. She even has some of his expressions. But I'm okay, Tee. I really am. I'm over him. I'm getting on with my life."

"*Bonne fille*," Theresa said, nodding once firmly and taking my arm. We began to walk. "Let's take this little angel to meet her grandma Cleary." I spotted an idling taxi, and we headed for Colleen's new apartment in the old Gold Coast section of the city.

On Saturday night, Colleen, who was clearly enamored with Lark, urged Tee and me to go out and leave the baby in her care.

Theresa and I jumped at the chance. Lark had developed a degree of stranger anxiety at home, and I worried about leaving her, but as we slipped out, she was busily smearing Colleen's caramel custard across the tray of the high chair we'd unearthed from the basement, crowing and kicking her legs with delight. Tee and I set out to find a neighborhood happy hour. Though we'd been through a great deal of adult drama in the last two years, we felt very young that night in jumpsuits and geometric jewelry. At the Tavern on Rush, we might have been two college girls. The music was good and loud, the place packed. We sipped scotch and waters and enjoyed the appreciative looks from men, although no one bothered us. Later, we walked just down the street to Bistro Zinc for dinner. We studied the menu on the glass, Theresa twitching a shoulder, pouting, and looking very French. "Let's see if they know how to prepare authentic French cuisine," she said over her shoulder as we entered. We ordered a bottle of wine, and Theresa ordered cassoulet with white beans, sausage, and duck confit in flawless French. I moaned over a plate of Norwegian wolffish with glazed mushrooms and potato-leek ragout. We savored just one bite each of warm clafoutis. Thoroughly sated, Tee leaned back and sipped a café crème. She sighed and conceded to the waiter, *"Mes félicitations au chef."*

We strolled ponderously back to Colleen's, stopping at a package store for a bottle of Scotch. I was happy to see my cherub sleeping surrounded by pillows on Theresa's bed. We said good night to Colleen, who was ready for bed. "I'd forgotten how exhausting it is keeping up with a toddler," she marveled. Tee and I took two glasses of scotch upstairs. As before, we sat on the bed talking with Lark between us. Apparently Theresa's stepdaughter

Tabby wouldn't allow Tee to babysit for her new baby, Jacque Charles. "He's so cute! But Tabby doesn't trust me, the little bitch."

"Give her time. She'll come around." I smiled and regarded my best friend. It was preposterous to think of Tee as a grandmother at twenty-four. "Do you ever wish you could have a baby? Have Laurent's child?" I asked and pulled at a strand of my hair wedged between my melting ice cubes.

"You know, I really don't," she said pensively. After a moment, she said, "I used to say that we could always adopt a baby someday. Laurent would if I wanted it. But our life is pretty perfect the way it is. I don't feel the need for a baby of my own to complete me. Maybe I'm not the maternal type." She looked at me for confirmation. "Everyone doesn't have to be, right?"

"Of course," I answered. "I didn't get much of a chance to decide whether I was or not." I gazed down at Lark. "But now I can't imagine not having her, a life without her. Life's funny, isn't it, Tee?"

"Stranger than fiction, my friend," Tee said with a wry smile. She raised her glass to clink against mine. "Have you thought about dating, Rob?"

"You know, I honestly haven't," I said, amazed. "I'm so busy with this little monkey." I smoothed Lark's damp hair. She was too warm for the sleeper Colleen had put her in. I took the blanket off her and unsnapped the sleeper's legs. "And with work. I'm so exhausted I fall asleep when my head hits the pillow." I sipped again at my drink. "I don't really *go* anywhere to meet men, just back and forth from home and work." I grinned. "There is one guy at work, Porter, who's attractive ... but you know dating work associates is ill-advised.

When the phone rang, we both jumped. The baby fussed at the shrill sound, scrubbing her nose into the mattress, and was still again. Theresa reached for it, cringing in Lark's direction, and then she whispered, full of joy, *"Allo, cherie!"*

"Bonsoir, Laurent. I miss you!" I stage-whispered toward the receiver. I went to wash my face and brush my teeth while Tee was on the phone. When I came out in my pajamas, Theresa was standing in a pair of aqua panties, rummaging through her suitcase. She pulled out a matching aqua nightgown and pulled it over her head. *French women and their fancy, sexy lingerie,* I thought, fleetingly envious, and then rushed to say, "I'm glad you and Laurent are so happy, darling. You're wonderful together."

Tee appraised me. "You're a beautiful woman, Rob. You look even better than you did in college. You should meet someone. You deserve some romantic ... tending."

"I know you're right," I said, readjusting the pillows behind my back. "But I'm *constantly* busy." I sipped at my drink. "There *are* times I feel lonesome. But you know, Tee, I don't pine after Dean the way I used to," I said and realized I spoke the truth.

"I cannot *believe* he's married," she sighed, closing her eyes and shaking her head.

"I know. Yet another tragic development in the Robin-and-Dean saga." We drank in silence for a few minutes. "I don't think

I'm ready … to *date* yet. But I *am* fired up about moving into my own place." I smiled. "Don't get me wrong; my parents have loved having us there, and they've been completely wonderful, but it's time for me to fly on my own."

"What about sex, Rob! Don't you miss it?" Tee insisted, frowning.

I smiled a little half smile, remembering for a moment. "I sure miss it with Dean. But with things the way they are right now, I guess every sexual impulse has just been purged out of me."

"Well, promise me you'll at least start looking at men again," Tee said. She yawned hugely.

"Okay, okay! I promise." I laughed and yawned at the same time. "Ha-ha-ahh-hahhh." I stuck a finger into Lark's diaper. It could wait till morning. Tee and I turned out the lamps and tumbled through sleep on either side of my daughter.

Sunday morning we went to brunch with Colleen and Tee's aunt Bridey—possibly the world's loudest-talking human in this teeny-tiny Chanel suit—and they drove us to the train station. Theresa had brought Lark a Madeleine doll from Paris, dressed in a bright-blue coat and yellow straw hat. Lark clutched the doll in one chubby fist and waved it. "Bye-bye, Tante-Tee!" she piped at my prompting.

"Bye-bye, *mon petit alouette!*" Theresa said, her eyes filling.

"Thanks for everything, Colleen," I said warmly. "Write soon, Tee!" Missing her already, I swayed on the platform, Lark on one hip, my diaper bag and purse slung over a shoulder, and my heavy suitcase in one hand. "Bye-bye!" We all smiled and waved.

For Lark's second birthday, a few of the neighbors came to the brownstone for cake and ice cream. Even Atticus tolerated the pointy paper party hat Lark placed on his head, one of his ears comically crimped by the elastic band. Dad captured on camera the moment the birthday girl sang "Happy Birthday" to herself along with us and then planted a hand into her grandmother's buttercream icing.

Through his generous real estate contacts, my dad helped me find a decent apartment just four blocks from the brownstone. It was a two-bedroom, second-floor walk-up, badly in need of airing and fresh paint. It came complete with a dead mouse in a kitchen corner. The tiny bathroom had no shower, but a surprisingly luxurious claw-foot tub separated the bedrooms. I wanted to do the work myself. It would be my first adult home, and I was thrilled with it.

The October late nights I peeled, scraped, scrubbed, and painted were some of the best nights I'd had in a long time. I brought my little cassette player over, sat it on the kitchen counter, and listened to Hall and Oates, Journey, and the Eagles while I worked. I could finally listen to the Eagles without drowning in a puddle of tears and self-pity. With the apartment's four windows open wide, I listened to the sounds of my new neighborhood as I slapped the paintbrush up and down the walls. Someone in the next building played a record of Puccini's *La Bohème* at the same time every night. *That should be soothing for my new little New York native*, I thought with a grin.

I worked at the office all day, went to Mom and Dad's for dinner to see Lark, and then headed back to the apartment to paint. We would move over Thanksgiving weekend. I took Lark to the new apartment when I had finished the work to show her where we would live. I flipped on the light. The paint job was strictly amateurish, but it was a soft, sunny yellow that pleased me, and "yeh-yoh" was Lark's favorite color. Lark looked around curiously, her little brow furrowed. "Why is dare no tunniter?" she asked.

"Oh, darling," I laughed, "we'll bring the furniture *with us* when we move."

Dad contracted for a moving truck and two men to help us move. As an early Christmas present, Mom bought us a pretty yellow-and-blue floral sofa bed and a chair in a blue companion fabric. I shopped at a thrift store for other things. Anita Roth, who luckily for me was on yet another of her redecorating binges, gave me a pair of matching chairs for my bedroom and a soft blue rug for the front room.

The movers showed up two hours late and dropped and broke my little kitchen table. I shrieked as one of the wooden legs rolled into oncoming traffic. Dad hurt his back moving the sofa. A nasty neighbor popped in demanding to know if I had noisy children. The toilet refused to flush. I discovered a pair of big nasty roaches frantically mating—at least somebody was having sex—in one of my freshly papered kitchen drawers. When Lark arrived with my mother late that afternoon, her little pink suitcase in one hand, she promptly vomited across Anita's rug. The poor baby had a stomach bug and cried and cried to "go home." After everyone had left, I put Lark in the claw-foot tub with me, shampooing her golden hair and soothing her with spills of warm water. We spent the next couple of hours in the rocking chair in her little bedroom until she finally fell asleep. We were home.

Just before her fourth birthday, I enrolled Lark in a preschool near my office. I was concerned about how she would fit in with other children as an only child and the epicenter of a tight-knit clan of adults. I walked her into the sunny classroom with some trepidation. In a crisp jumper and red Mary Jane shoes, her bright pigtails tied with blue ribbons, my daughter marched over to a tangle of kids at a sand-and-water table and never looked back. I slipped out gratefully but hovered over the telephone on my desk all day, afraid to take a lunch break. But Lark took to school like an intrepid little spelunker in a treasure-filled cave. She loved her playmates, especially a little boy named Christopher, and they tumbled like puppies. She came home chattering happily each afternoon with scraped knees, an empty lunchbox, and new ideas. By November she was sounding out and recognizing printed words. Her much-loved teacher Miss Sally, who never made me feel awkward seated in a parent-teacher conference alone, told me that Lark was one of the smartest children in the class, the best reader. *Oh, Dean.*

Grandma Olivia's transition back to work was a seamless and productive one. The gratified owner, thrilled by her return, immediately increased her salary by a third and then offered to sell the shop to her for a fair price. My parents were considering it. Grandpa Hank was so crazy about Lark he often dropped by the school on his lunch hour. Since Lark and I had moved into our own place, it had been our habit to walk back for late lunch at the brownstone after Sunday mass. A couple of times a month we had my parents over for dinner at our tiny place. And one night a week, Lark and I took our laundry over and visited with them while the clothes washed and tumbled dry.

Determined that Lark wouldn't be a picky eater, I devoted myself to learning to cook well. I pored over *The Joy of Cooking* until the pages were smudged with chocolate fingerprints, splotched with oil and tomato sauce. Lark's favorite meal was croque monsieur with a flavorful ham—the owner of the corner deli loved giving her samples—and Gruyère cheese. She ate spears of fresh asparagus like french fries.

One apple crisp of a fall afternoon when Lark was in first grade, my little girl, swinging her Care Bears lunchbox and kicking at acorns, rooted me in my tracks on the sidewalk. "Why don't I have a daddy?"

"Oh, sweetie, well …" She'd rendered me effectually speechless. My thoughts made concentric circles around the question. *Oh shit. Why didn't I prepare myself for this?* I dug deep for a casual tone and willed my legs to walk on. "You do have a dad, darling."

"Well, who is it? Where is he?" She looked up at me, her light brow furrowed, one red ribbon trailing from a pigtail.

Stalling for time, I looked for a place to sit down. There were a couple of benches around the corner in the pocket park close to our apartment that Lark had named the Little Park.

"Let's go sit in the Little Park. It's such a pretty afternoon," I said brightly. A woman with an enormous blue Great Dane whom we recognized approached and diverted Lark for the moment. Lark stopped and spoke, eye to eye, to smoky, silk-coated Wellington.

Lark was aware that a couple of her school friends didn't live with their fathers, so I thought she might be able to understand our lifestyle. Reaching the park, we settled ourselves on a bench in the slanting sun. I retied the ribbon and kissed her soundly on the head. "Lark, darling," I said carefully, "you do have a father. Everyone has a father. But you know sometimes fathers don't live with their families. Rebecca's father lives in Connecticut, right?"

The child looked at me from Dean's clear gray eyes. "Why not, Mama?" she asked.

"Well, sometimes mamas and daddies decide not to live together, and sometimes mamas and their little girls or little boys live together."

She seemed to chew on my words for a minute. "Who *is* my daddy, Mama?" my God-sweet girl asked again.

"Your daddy," I said, plowing ahead with a sangfroid I didn't feel, "is a wonderful man named Dean Falconer. He … lives in Virginia." I paused, remembering I had read not to give a child more information of a delicate nature than what she asked.

"Can he come see us?" she asked as a squirrel jumped to the seat of the bench across from us. Bristled tail twitching, it stood on its hind legs and begged for a treat. We laughed, and I took my daughter's hands in mine.

My throat felt clogged with grief. "Well, darling ..." I looked into her eyes. "I haven't seen your daddy since we were in college together. But we loved each other very much then." Lark swung her legs back and forth at the edge of the bench, scuffing at uneven brick with the toes of her sneakers.

"Does Dean love me?"

My heart on the verge of imploding, I looked across the park at the traffic, the tourists in yellow taxis, the cars with families inside. I struggled to compose myself and a careful answer. "I'm sure he does, sweetheart, but he has another family now. And we have a family too, Grandma and Grandpa, who love us more than anything in the whole world. Right, Lark Bird?"

"Right, Mama Robin." She smiled a little smile and snuggled against my side.

Holding her close, I offered a silent prayer of thanks. The conversation seemed to have gone well and appeased Lark. *At least for now*, I reminded myself. I wondered how long she would be content with my answers.

It was getting chilly. "Let's go see about some dinner," I said as Lark picked up three acorns and put them in the pocket of her denim jacket.

I unlocked our door, dropped my keys on the table, and opened the electric bill with a thumbnail. Lark scooted off to feed her pet goldfish, Georgie. I smiled at an airmail envelope and set it aside. I would savor that one later with a glass of scotch. And I had to call my mom and tell her what had happened with Lark.

As I turned on the lamps, I thought about how much I loved our little home. Since that first hectic year, I'd papered the kitchen in a cheerful yellow geometric pattern and put up crisp white café curtains. I'd had the old, worn green kitchen linoleum ripped up and replaced with a classic black-and-white square pattern. I stuck my finger in the soil of the glossy jade that spilled like a weeping willow on the table by the front window. It needed water. "Lark, please come water the jade." I opened the pantry, thinking about what to make for dinner. Lark chattered to the plant as she watered it with the little brass can. "You have such a green thumb," I said with a smile and pulled out a can of tomatoes.

She looked at her hand. "A green thumb! That's hilarious, Mama."

I laughed at her vocabulary and wistfully thought about how not that long ago she had said "fumb." I explained the idiom as Lark set the table with our pretty, old, mismatched dishes, the ones that had spoken to me in a village thrift shop. I displayed a few special ones on a wooden shelf on the wall. I liked to wonder about the families who had eaten from them. "Who did the pink one belong to?" I asked Lark now.

She traced the flowers on the plate with a finger. "I think it belonged to a little girl. Named Rosie … with curly black hair and a little dog named Tippy."

Later that night, Lark and I snuggled in her bed to read. We took turns reading pages. As Lark read, I regarded her sweet room. The alphabet poster I'd bought in Paris hung above the bed. We'd found a dusty old gumball machine at a junk shop for six dollars.

I'd had it made into a bedside lamp with a smart paper shade and had filled it with gumballs. On Saturdays, I allowed Lark to insert coins from her allowance for a special treat. An impressive dollhouse that Grandpa Hank had constructed from a kit squatted in one corner, little dolls strewn around it like confetti. "Mama, it's your turn!" Lark said.

I took my turn, and then, as she read again, I glanced at Georgie swimming back and forth in his bowl on the bookcase, where books competed for space on the narrow shelves. Often they spilled to the floor with a slither or thump and annoyed Lark. One day, I'd heard her utter, "Dammit!" I'd been shocked but tickled. I reminded myself where she'd heard the word in the first place. I was happy that books were Lark's favorite belongings, her treasures.

"Time to say your prayers, love," I said, marking the place as we finished a chapter. Lark blessed the two of us, her grandparents, Georgie and Atticus, Christopher and another friend Lindsay, and her teacher Mrs. Parker.

"Close the closet door, Mama," Lark reminded me. The apartment had only one closet (in my room), so I'd found a small, pretty armoire for Lark's room. One Sunday afternoon we had painted it with birds—highly stylized robins and larks—fat-petaled flowers, and one orange fish in honor of Georgie.

"What's the magic word?" I said.

"Please!"

I kissed her good night, her butter-soft skin and fragrant hair filling my senses, closed the closet door, and turned out the light.

Unbuttoning my blouse, I padded to my room, my oasis. A blue-and-white ceramic lamp softly lit the blue-and-white bedspread and crisp white sheets that welcomed my tired body each night. Stacks of my favorite books sat alongside found objects on bookshelves I had constructed from hardware store two-by-eights and white bricks. With my last raise I'd bought myself a small stereo system with a cassette player. I contemplated the blue-and-yellow braided rug that covered the stained old carpet our chintzy landlady, Mrs. Ratcliff (whom I dubbed Nurse Ratchett), refused to replace. It needed vacuuming. But not tonight.

Lately before sleep took me under its wing, a lusty yearning had begun to bloom in my chest, like an orchid with an open throat. I needed another dimension to my life. I was lonely … for the touch of a man, someone to love and romantically tend me. I had found myself noticing and appraising men on the streets again as I'd promised Tee. And a new awareness had emerged: Dean Falconer had spoiled me for anyone else. Who could possibly be as fine and beautiful and wonderful and sexy and gentle as he?

* * * * *

The firm of Wickersham, Collins, and Adams was growing. The partners hired two junior associates and another paralegal, a young woman just a year older than me, Lindy Corcoran. I hadn't had a girlfriend in New York since Theresa left for Paris. Working closely, our desks adjacent, Lindy and I got to know each other quickly. Lindy was living with her parents in Brooklyn and working to pay off college loans before going to law school. She was tall, with permed brown hair and unremarkable brown eyes, but Lindy was conscientious and quick, with a dry wit that kept me giggling all day. Her high school sweetheart, Michael, was a big macho fireman. Michael, in his uniform as crisp as new currency, grinned at me every day from the photograph on Lindy's desk and reminded me of my aloneness. Lindy and I went to lunch together a couple of days a week. One Thursday, she asked me to go to happy hour with her after work. My parents had urged me to go out, and they were always happy to babysit. I called Mom at Speak Volumes and asked if they were available that night.

Lindy and I were wearing our work suits and heels, but I could slip off my jacket and look nice in my navy-and-red foulard blouse and navy skirt. I unclasped my hair from an updo to fall over my shoulders. The bar was dark and smoky, wall-to-wall with young working people drinking, laughing, and calling to each other across tables and over the music. Lindy ordered a gin and tonic and I my usual scotch and water. Michael came in and sneaked up behind Lindy, grabbing her around the waist. His photograph hadn't prepared me for the sheer size of the guy. He was at least six three and 220 pounds. What a hunk! But Michael wasn't my type. As I looked about the bar, I didn't see many guys who were.

I hopped down from a stool to go to the ladies' room and bumped smack into a guy, spilling my drink down the front of the red tie he'd loosened at his throat. I apologized into his starched shirtfront and dabbed furiously at the tie with my napkin. He took my wrist gently. "It's really okay," he laughed. He introduced himself as Stuart Eskew. When I came out of the restroom, he was waiting for me by the bar, a fresh drink in either hand for both of us. Stuart's softly curling brown hair, smug grin, and sherry-colored eyes were appealing. I invited him back to our table, where Lindy and Michael sat gazing at each other with the concentration of brain surgeons.

Stuart was a tax accountant and three years older than me. He was polite and attentive and told me a couple of truly funny stories. When Lindy and Michael were ready to leave, Stuart gave me a business card, with his home number on the back, and asked me to call him. He was staying on at the bar to meet friends.

I walked out with Lindy and Michael, the cool night refreshing after the smoky bar. "Cute guy, Stuart," Lindy said. "I've seen him around. He's been in there every time we have … right, Mike?"

Two weeks later, I regarded Stuart's card taped to the refrigerator next to Lark's current painting of a dappled cow chewing on vibrant green grass and got up the nerve to call him. First I cleaned the kitchen, the little radio playing softly in its spot next to the toaster, and supervised Lark as she completed her math problems and spelling practice at the kitchen table. "What's AIDS, Mama?"

"Where did you hear about that?"

"On the *radio*; they *just* said it," she said as if I were one marker short of a box.

"Well … it's a disease, a sickness that a few people get where their bodies can't fight off infection like healthy people. It's very rare."

"Oh," she said, satisfied.

We moved to the front room and curled up on the sofa to watch *Family Ties* on TV. Later when Lark was asleep, I poured a Scotch—Dutch courage as Dad called it—and dialed the number on Stuart's card.

"Hello, Stuart? It's Robin Hamilton."

"Robin! Great to hear from you!" I could hear the smile on his face. He asked if I'd like to have dinner with him that Friday night, at PJ Clarke's on Third. I told him I would meet him at the restaurant.

Mom and Dad were babysitting, so I hurried straight home from work that afternoon for a fresh bath. The weather was hot for early June in Manhattan. I pulled on nice jeans and a sleeveless asymmetrical top. I slipped wedged espadrilles on my feet and a gold bracelet on my slender wrist. I stood and took a deep breath before the mirror. *My first date in eight years. How is that possible?*

I entered the rowdy, packed restaurant and found Stuart inside. "Beautiful!" he said. His breath was beery, his color hectic, as he lurched from his seat at the historic bar and tried to pull me into a huge embrace. He had been there awhile.

I planted a hand in the middle of his chest and pushed him gently away. "Are you ready for dinner?" I asked brightly. This guy needed to get some food in his stomach. We ordered draft beers, and I asked for water as well. I suggested we order an appetizer. "I'm famished," I lied. We nibbled on parmesan tater tots, and Stuart seemed to sober up a little. But after smacking down five tots, he downed his beer and signaled the waitress for another. He was talking in an embarrassingly loud voice by then and elbowed his silverware onto the tiled floor with a series of metallic clanks and tings. The southern tourists at the next table, as red as a flock of cardinals in their Arkansas Razorback T-shirts, were staring openly. When Stuart remarked what a brick house I was, I'd had enough.

I was on my feet and dropped my napkin to the table. "I should call my babysitter." Stuart looked at me quizzically. "Yes," I said, "I have a seven-year-old daughter at home." In the bar, I slipped into the battered phone booth Ray Milland had used in the movie *The Lost Weekend. How ironic,* I thought, pissed and disappointed I'd wasted the evening on a loser. I called Mom and told her I was on my way. I stalked back to the table and stood looking down at the buffoon. "I have to go."

Stuart was midway through his next beer. "Do you wanna try this again tomorrow night?" he asked, oblivious and slurring his words.

"Definitely not," I said and poured the rest of my water into his lap. I left him sitting there staring at the widening spot on his crotch, his big mouth agape.

I met Bill Simon one rainy Friday afternoon at the diner around the corner from the office. I had finished a contract and dashed over for a late lunch. It was gross and humid out, so I'd left my suit jacket at the office. I twisted my damp hair up into a topknot. My pink sleeveless blouse clung to my back and torso like spider silk. I ordered a chef's salad and wiped my neck and arms with a paper napkin. As I drank deeply from my glass of iced water, I noticed a man being seated in the next booth.

We looked up from our lunches and looked directly at each other. After the second time he smiled at me, after the third I returned his smile, and after the fourth we laughed together. "This is pretty awkward," he said. "May I join you?"

Surprising myself, I said, "Sure, but I have to be back at work"—I consulted my watch—"in fifteen minutes."

Bill's deep, pansy-blue eyes lit up when he smiled. He was in the neighborhood of truly handsome but a couple of blocks away. I appraised his dark-blue suit. *A banker,* I thought. Bill was indeed an investment banker and articulate and intelligent. He asked how often I came to the diner. We figured out that it was equidistant from our offices, and I agreed to meet him there again on Monday at twelve thirty.

Over the weekend I was determined not to get optimistic. At least I was sure Bill wouldn't get sloppy drunk at lunchtime. On Monday, he was waiting outside the diner smiling broadly. But as we walked through the door together, I noticed he was short. With me in my three-inch pumps, he wasn't as tall as I. Tee and I liked tall guys. *What difference does that make?* I asked myself, annoyed. *He's a nice guy.* And Bill was as impressive as he was the first time. *Two for two,* I thought. I told Bill about Lark. Bill was thirty-one and divorced, with a nine-year-old daughter of his own. *Hmmm ... that could be neat,* I thought. He asked me to go to the movies with him the next night.

My thoughts returned to Bill the next day at work, and I looked forward to the date. We stood in line to see a movie with Goldie Hawn and Chevy Chase. "You look beautiful tonight," Bill said. It had been so long since I'd heard those words from a guy. And I could tell he wasn't just coming on to me. The movie was good; we laughed at Chase's pratfalls and shared a box of popcorn. But as I watched the screen, I felt Bill's eyes on my profile.

"What is it?" I asked, finally turning to him. "Aren't you watching the movie?"

"I'd rather watch you," he said dreamily. It was a bit off-putting. Bill stared at me at intervals throughout the movie. "You have the perfect profile," he murmured, "the perfect nose." The staring was getting creepy.

After the show, I let him convince me to walk to a piano bar a couple of doors down for a drink. Afterward when he walked with me to hail a taxi, he leaned in to kiss me. But as his lips touched mine, I couldn't stand the intimacy. An old checker cab was trundling slowly down the block. I stuck my hand up as if someone had asked for volunteers to accompany Mel Gibson on a cruise. "Thank you for the evening," I said as the taxi screeched to the curb, and I jumped into the backseat.

Undaunted, Bill called as we sped away, "I'll be in touch!"

I stared ahead at the battered partition, the cracks in the glass mended with tape and pressed my fingers to my lips. No one had kissed them since Dean had. *Dean's lips. His lovely kiss.* I closed my eyes and almost managed to suppress a great gulping sob. "You okay, miss?" the driver asked in dubious English. The bloodshot eyes that appraised me from the rearview mirror had seen their share of misery.

I looked dully out at the rain that had begun to fall and wash the grime from the streets. "Fine."

Bill called me for another date, but I made excuses, saying I would call him another time. There would be no other time.

A month later, I was shopping at Macy's with Lark for new school clothes. Her pants and skirts were getting too short. *She'll be tall like her father,* I thought. Lark was getting opinionated about what she would wear. It was maddening but funny to see her becoming a person with her own ideas. It was my lucky day, though, and we found several cute outfits that pleased us both.

"Mama, I'm going to be in third grade!" Lark exclaimed, bouncing up and down on her toes as we headed down the escalator to lunch. Her birthday was a little over a week away. She was having her first party with friends at my parents' house, so that the kids could spread out and into the back garden.

"I know, darling." I smiled and squeezed her hand. We had a special squeeze: one of us would squeeze the other's hand three times, I—love—you, and the other would squeeze back four times, I—love—you—too. Grinning up at me, Lark squeezed back.

I smiled and glanced to my left. On the up escalator I saw a familiar face and recognized my old college friend Nick. Almost at the top, he must have felt my gaze and looked back at me. "Robin Hamilton!" he called. "I'll be right down; stay there!"

"Who is *that*, Mama?" Lark asked.

"It's an old friend … who went to college with Tante Tee and me. His name is Nick."

As he stepped off the escalator, I said, "Nick! How are you?"

"Fine! How are you? It's been a while!" We stepped forward to hug. Nick had the same easy grin and rangy, loose-limbed way of moving—a man entirely comfortable in his own skin. "Nick, this is my daughter, Lark," I said smiling. Wide-eyed, he stuck out a long-fingered hand to shake hers.

Lark said, "How do you do, Nick?"

He grinned, enchanted with her precocious manners. "It's nice to meet you, Lark. You're a *doll*, and I like your name."

"My whole name is Laurel Olivia Hamilton," she said.

Nick and I chatted for a few minutes. He had stayed in New York City and worked in advertising. He lived in a Soho loft not far from NYU.

"So you're a married lady, Robin."

"Uh … no."

Lark tugged at my hand and said, "Excuse me, Mama, but I'm soooo hungry. Can we go eat now, please?" Nick laughed softly.

I said to Nick, "Will you call me? I'd *love* to catch up." I pulled a pen from my purse and scratched my number and the words "I'm single" on Nick's paper shopping bag. We parted ways.

The next Friday, Nick called. "I would've called you sooner, but I couldn't find that damned bag. I had to paw to the bottom of the trash can like a raccoon to find it." I laughed at him.

We planned to meet for lunch the next day. I couldn't wait to see Nick, to catch up and talk about old times. My mother said they would be happy to have Lark spend the day with them. She and Dad were going to take her to the park. I dressed in a floral sundress and sandals, my hair loose and flowing.

Nick and I met at Gatsby's, where the owner placed a fresh white daisy in a vase on each table—a charming nod to Jay's girl—and were seated at a corner table. I regarded my friend across the table. Nick was more appealing now than ever. He reminded me a little of Jackson Browne with glasses, his shiny brown hair shorter but still shaggy. That day he wore jeans, a gray NYU T-shirt, and running shoes. "Robin, you're as good lookin' as ever," he said. "I can't believe you're a mother." We ordered lunch, and I told him the story of my time at Georgetown, the Eagles concert, and Dean … the whole thing. Nick listened sympathetically. He had dated a girl for four years and wanted to marry her, but she had broken up with him a scant three months ago. Finishing the meal, I asked Nick if he wanted to walk awhile. We still had seven years to catch up on.

It was a beautiful late-August afternoon, the back of the summer broken. We strolled down Bleecker Street and around

campus. We stopped to get ice cream cones and wandered over
to Washington Square Park, where we found an empty bench in
the shade. We talked about Theresa. I told Nick the story of the
blackout. "That's right," he said. "I was in Ithaca that summer.
Man, I can't believe what you guys went through." I told him I
remembered wishing he were there that dreadful night. "I wish I
had been, honey." Nick reached over and wiped ice cream from my
chin with a thumb. "How is Theresa now?" I told him about my
trip to help Tee and Laurent in Paris and then about how Theresa
had traveled to surprise me when Lark was born.

Then Nick told me he couldn't believe I had never contacted
Dean. He pushed up his glasses, the lenses very clear, and looked
into my eyes. "Robin, I can't imagine having a daughter ... and not
knowing it. She'd be ... well ... family."

As though by cinematographic trick Nick's face seemed to
become Dean's, just for an instant. I heard the words he had
spoken again, in Dean's voice. I felt my face drain of color. The
skirts had been lifted from my careful house-of-cards defenses for
keeping my daughter a secret, brutally exposed. I sat staring at
Nick. My parents had never approved of how I'd handled the truth,
nor had Theresa. Hearing the opinion of a trusted friend, his male
point of view, I saw other implications with clarity: not only had I
deprived Dean of his child, but I'd also deprived Dean's mother of
her grandchild, and my child of the other half of her family.

"Rob, are you okay, honey?" Nick was concerned. Suddenly it
was vitally important to make someone understand why I'd never
told Dean the truth.

"Nick, I want you to know that I've struggled with this thing … this huge *dilemma* … ever since I found out I was pregnant."

A gaggle of NYU students, an orientation group, passed through, the giddy teens playful, noisy. I saw that the afternoon light had changed and thought to look at my watch. It was ten minutes after five. I needed to call my mother. "Let's go to my place, Robin. We can talk there," Nick said. He put a comforting arm around my shoulders. "C'mon, you can call your mother and check on Lark."

Stopping at a crosswalk, I gathered my tumultuous thoughts and looked up at Nick. "Things like this happen in families all the time, don't they?" I asked, yet another juicy rationalization from the Robin Hamilton collection.

He looked at me and said simply, "They do."

We stepped off the curb, and I looked at him again. "Nick, I *will* do it. I'll find the right time to tell Dean. I will." We turned a corner and stepped around a legless man on a grate. I began to cry.

"Shhh, honey, it's okay; we're almost home." We were at Nick's building. He shepherded me inside and toward the elevator.

"Nick," I began again. But an older couple entered the building and followed us into the battered old elevator talking about their good-for-nothing son. Inside the apartment Nick led me to his sofa. I was still sniffling. "Do you judge me for what I've done, Nick?" I asked plaintively.

"I don't judge you," he said kindly. "You know the right thing to do. The timing will come to you." He held me then, rocking me back and forth until my tears were spent.

"Nick, what have I done without you all these years?" I said against his tear-wet T-shirt.

"All will be well, Robin." And after a moment, he asked, "Are you hungry? There's a good Chinese place on Prince that delivers."

"That sounds good. I haven't had Chinese in forever. Maybe a little later?"

"Sure. Do you want to call your mother now?"

I picked up the phone on the end table and dialed my parents' number. Nick went to the refrigerator and pulled out a bottle of white wine. He held it aloft, questioning me with his eyes. As my mother answered, I gave him a big thumbs-up.

"Are you enjoying yourself, darling? Tell Nick hello. Everything is fine here. We're playing a game of Clue. Lark called Miss Scarlett as usual. And Dad's going to grill hamburgers in a little while." She was quiet for a moment. "Robin, why don't you take the night for yourself and pick Lark up in the morning? We'd love to have her spend the night with us."

Nick had left the room, and I could hear water running. "Okay, Mom, I might do that. Thank you. I'll call you in the morning. Love you."

"I love you too, darling."

And I hung up. When Nick appeared, I excused myself to freshen up as well.

When I returned, Nick had moved back to the sofa, his lanky arms spread across the back, two big glasses of wine on an iron-and-glass table in front of it. "What kind of music are you into these days, Robin?"

"Surprise me," I said. Nick had a super-nice sound system. He put on a Sting CD. "I love Sting!" I said, pleased. "And aren't CDs cool? They're like little doll records." Nick laughed.

"Do you still have your old albums?" I asked.

"What do you think?" He smirked. "Me, part with my albums?"

I picked up my glass and wandered around looking at the loft. Nick had done well for himself. Really just one big room, the place suited him. Like him, it was spare and comfortable. Movie and music posters, some like ones we had in college but now handsomely framed, were artfully arranged on one huge wall. I complimented Nick on his decor. He explained that his former girlfriend Natalie was a decorator. The kitchen area boasted a massive, rustic and knotty, polished wood counter. "This counter is fantastic, Nick; the wood is *beautiful*. What is it?" I asked, running my hand along its length.

"Cypress. You know it's the wood Noah used to build the ark." He grinned. "I cleaned up. I hoped you would come over."

I sat in a chair near the sofa and smiled at a lush brown bearskin rug. Nick and I talked about our album collections and the way technology had changed the music world. I told Nick that I had been in Paris when I'd learned that the Eagles had broken up. He had been bummed about it too. Then he asked, "Robin, do you still get high? I mean, I know you're a mother now and everything."

"I haven't since I found out I was pregnant with Lark," I said thoughtfully and then grinned.

"Well, I still do occasionally, *and* I just *happen* to have a couple of nice joints right now," he said with a wolfish leer. "Can I corrupt you tonight and sully your perfect record?"

"I'm going for it." I grinned again, feeling young and excited and cool.

I'd forgotten how good it felt to drift and find everything absolutely hilarious. And then we were hungry. Nick called to have the food delivered and poured the last of the bottle into our glasses. I was glad I didn't have to go and pick up Lark. In fact, this night was kind of a "lark." It was crazy and pretty wonderful.

We ate shrimp with snow peas and sesame chicken, ferrying bites between the container and our mouths with wooden chopsticks, talking and laughing. I told Nick about my apartment. Nick talked of the traveling he'd done. Then he put on another CD, an old one, Steely Dan's *Aja*.

I told him I didn't have to go and pick up Lark, and he replied, "Well, all right! Let's open another bottle of wine. The night is young, and so are we!" There was a singular sweetness to Nick's smile as he said, "I can't believe you're really here!" He spoke then of Natalie and their breakup, and I told him about the two guys I'd dated, making him laugh some more. The incidents were funny in retrospect.

We were on the sofa now at either end. Nick slipped off my sandals and began to rub my feet. I actually began to purr; it had been so long since I'd had that kind of attention from a man. I drifted in a tranquil bubble. The revelation that afternoon had been cathartic for me. I felt especially close to Nick now, grateful for his support and for how he hadn't judged me. I felt sexy, as I hadn't in a very long time. I righted myself and slid down the couch and next to him. I took off his glasses. Nick was perfectly still. "Robin?" he whispered. I leaned over and planted a light kiss on each of his eyelids. "Robin?" he said again. "What are you doing, honey?"

I looked into his sweet eyes and slowly said, "Nick, I haven't had sex in eight years. Can't you tell when a girl wants to get laid?"

"Are you sure?" I thought he trembled a little. I placed a hand on his thigh. "I'll be right back," he said. He was back in a flash with protection. I pulled him down to the rug. As Steely Dan sang, "Aja, when all my dime dancin' is through, I run to you," we kissed and undressed each other slowly. The rug felt exotic and warm against my skin. Even as toasted as I was, it was curious seeing Nick naked after all this time. He was even rangier that he looked in clothes. But Nick was extraordinarily pleased with *my* body. "I can't believe this is happening. Robin Hamilton in the raw," he breathed. "Gorgeous … you're so gorgeous." I giggled some more and trailed my fingers down his concave belly.

It was a sweet joining, light and playful. When it was over, Nick reached for a throw, covering us lightly, and we slept there until morning. When I awoke, the scent of fresh coffee in my nostrils, Nick was in the kitchen. I crawled around picking up my clothes, slipped into them, and padded to the kitchen. He stood, eating last night's rice from a container, in jeans and a clean white T-shirt. He hugged me and kissed my forehead, a brotherly kiss.

"Thank you, Nick," I said warmly. "It was a wonderful night … all of it."

He looked at me for a long moment. "It won't happen again, will it, Robin?" he said. It was not a question.

"I don't think so," I said slowly, peering up at him. "But can we be best friends?"

"Absolutely." He nodded firmly. "I make a mean cup of joe. Want some?"

My head was beginning to ache. I moved over to sit at the counter, grimacing. "Please, and a couple of aspirins if you have them."

Nick walked me downstairs and to the street. "Let's sit with this awhile and then get together again … as friends," I said, smiling at him in the early sun. "I would like for Lark to spend some time with a really good man."

"She's a doll. I would love that," he said. And with that I left to go and retrieve my daughter.

Lark loved every minute of her birthday. Five friends from school attended, bringing bright, pretty packages. Atticus retreated to safety under my parents' bed, only the tip of his broad carrot tail sticking out from under the dust ruffle. The Roths and a couple of other neighbors joined us. Lindy popped in to meet Lark and my family and brought Lark the first of the Barbie dolls she would collect. Lindy's fireman had presented her with a small diamond ring, and they were getting married at Christmastime. There were balloons and party hats, and the children played vintage games like pin the tail on the donkey and musical chairs with little prizes. We had refreshments and cake and ice cream at a pretty table Mom had arranged in the garden. Lark was adorable, a polite and gracious hostess. I stood at the periphery, grateful for the new video camera that hid my face. The tears I blinked back tasted bittersweet. I was proud of my child and knew Dean would have been too. Lark was eight years old. It had been almost nine years since Dean and I had been together. I was nearly thirty years old. Dad put his arm around my shoulders and asked, "You okay, sweet pea?"

"I'm okay, Dad," I answered, squeezing him in return. And I knew that I was.

CHAPTER

15

Lark

1996–1998

My mother was making me crazy. At sixteen I knew everything, and she knew nothing. And she was constantly on my case.

My clothes: "Lark, that dress is cute, but it's way too short."

My diet: "Lark, all those Pringles will make your face break out."

My time: "Lark, your curfew is eleven o'clock. It is now eleven oh three!"

My music: "Lark, that grungy Nirvana business *again*? Please turn it *down*!"

My friends: "Lark, is Jeanne smoking cigarettes? I thought I smelled smoke on her yesterday." Or "I don't want you riding with Christopher until he has more driving experience."

Ad nauseam. The things she said made me itch to respond like a hornet. At least I wore a uniform to school—a tartan skirt and vest—and didn't have to argue with her every morning about what I put on my body. When I started ninth grade, my grandfather offered to send me to the school my mom went to, Miss Pruitt's. Mom was making more money by then as well, and we'd moved to a larger apartment closer to the school. I missed the cozy place we'd lived in since I was two, but the new place was really nice. We finally had our own washer and dryer and an elevator. The building even had a doorman, an old Hispanic guy named Romeo. He was cool and always joked around with me, calling me his Juliet. It was neat that I could walk to and from school by myself and not have to have a watchdog, although Mom would have probably preferred that I did. I made straight As, and my friends were perfectly nice girls and guys, so why the constant scrutiny? If Robin and my father were together, there might be a kind of buffer or mediator between the two of us. Maybe Mom wouldn't have to hyperfocus on me all the time. She didn't even have a boyfriend.

My friends were always saying how beautiful my mother was. She was certainly prettier than the other mothers; a few of them were strictly Hagsville. And she didn't try to dress and talk like a teenager; I had to give her points for that.

I asked her once when I was younger if I looked like my father. She had turned to me, her mouth a surprised O, and then gotten this faraway look in her eyes. "You have his gold hair, the angles of his face, and his beautiful gray eyes." She smiled, but the smile never reached her eyes. "And his narrow feet … with that little sliver of baby toenail." I hated my pinky toenails. They were a bitch to paint and always looked crappy. But at least I had Mom's figure. My friends said I had the best boobs and tiny waist of anyone.

It was *obvious* that my mother had had sex with my father without being married ("No shit, Lark," said Jeanne), so why was it such a big deal for me to be guarded like some paragon of virtue? I babysat for a family in the neighborhood, and who was to know if my latest boy toy Asher came over after I put the kids to bed?

"You will not make the same mistakes I did!" Mom said adamantly, raising her voice during one of our fights.

"So I was a mistake?" I yelled, outraged. That had been a bad one. Even as I ran to my room in tears and slammed the door so that it rocked on its hinges, I knew better. I heard Mom crying through the vent in the floor but was too mad to go to her. I knew she adored me, and I adored her right back. Why did it have to be so hard?

Once at my grandparents' I eavesdropped on her and Grandma Liv in the kitchen. I'd been watching an old movie in the study with Grandpa Hank and his new puppy Blondie, the dog curled like a skein of yarn in my lap. Poor arthritic old Atticus had died two years before. "Grandpa," I had said when I'd held the new puppy for the first time, "you can't name her *Blondie*; that was Hitler's dog's name." But as the dog had grown, she'd become blonder, almost white atop her fluffy head, and the name fit her. She was a sweet dog, more even-tempered than Atticus had been.

Grandpa had said he was naming her after some old comic strip character anyway.

I went downstairs in my sock feet to get a soda but stopped short and tucked into the alcove by the kitchen door when I heard the conversation.

Mom: "I don't know, Mother." She sounded exasperated.

Grandma: "Robin, Dean has a right to know. Have you considered his legal rights?"

Mom: "But after thirteen years? There are statutes of limitations on those things."

Grandma: "If only you had let him know before she was born …"

Mom: "*Mother!* We've been over this a hundred times. You know I was only trying to *protect* Dean. He was going through hell at the time."

Grandma: "I know. I'm sorry, darling. You can't worry about the timing now. But if you get in touch with—"

At that moment Blondie came up behind me, licked the back of my knee, and scared the shit out of me. I jumped two feet and stumbled against a planter with a loud ka-clunk. The talk stopped. The silly dog's tail was wagging three-quarter time, her version of a delighted smile. I scooped the dog up and breezed into the kitchen. "Oww, I stubbed my toe," I said, limping toward the refrigerator. My heart beat like a wild thing.

I poured my soda and obliquely saw them exchange a look, and then Grandma asked me what Grandpa wanted to do about dinner. They didn't seem to suspect anything, and Mom never said anything to me about it. But I was freaking out. *My father doesn't know about me? Is that what they meant?* I could hardly sleep for a couple of nights, no off switch for the thoughts that spiraled through the darkness. I knew my father's name was Dean, but I couldn't remember the last name. And he lived in Virginia … I thought that was right. I had snooped around trying to find my birth certificate before, but Mom must have locked it away. Could I find him myself? How could I without a last name? Did Mom intend to tell me at some point?

For a while I asked myself if it really mattered. I had a family who loved me, but still … it was there. I felt confused, hurt, and betrayed. But by whom? Mom? Or my father? Or both of them? It was something I would wrestle with for a long time.

My uncle Nick taught me to drive a car when I was sixteen. He wasn't really my uncle but my mom's good friend from college. He was a cool guy, with a hip loft in Soho and a bangin' car, a red Porsche 911. Nick took me to the movies and ice-skating a lot when I was younger. Like Mom, Nick had never married. The two of them were close. He came to our holiday gatherings, even at my grandparents' house.

With my August birthday, I'd just turned seventeen when I began my senior year of high school. My friends and I were totally amped and called ourselves the seniors of '97 in seventh heaven. My boyfriend of six months Louis' school and mine were in a consortium, so we went to dances together and saw each other during the school days sometimes too. Jeanne and I had been best friends for five years and still slept over at each other's apartments. Good grades came pretty effortlessly to me, but Jeanne had to study. When we started looking at colleges, we agreed we wanted to go away for school and room together. My Tante Tee and Mom had been roommates, and they were still tight even though Tee lived in Paris.

Louis was set on Columbia and begged me to stay in New York. I felt bad about leaving him behind, but Jeanne said, "Look, you wanna do Guiltapalooza, fine, but I'm done with the high school scene." Jeanne had no qualms about dropping her boyfriend, Jason.

So we applied to Boston University, American and Georgetown in DC, and Duke down south in North Carolina. We also applied at NYU, even though we really didn't want to stay in New York.

In the end we were both accepted at BU. Mom was excited and happy for me, but I knew how much she would miss me. I told Jeanne I bet Mom had breathed a sigh of relief that I wouldn't be going to Georgetown—probably too much history for her there.

Our senior prom was the first Saturday in May and hosted by a Miss Pruitt's board member out on Long Island at a mansion with a name, Emerald Point. Louis, Jeanne, Jason, and I were going together. Robin was spazzing about me riding out there and back late at night with Jason at the wheel. "Darling, we can rent a car to take you all," she said.

"Mom, chill! We'll be fine. Jason's a good driver. I promise I'll be home in time for curfew." She had halfheartedly extended my curfew until one o'clock for the special events.

Mom went with Jeanne and me to shop for dresses. At Bergdorf's I chose a sleeveless coral chiffon dress with a scoop neck. I liked the way the wispy chiffon layers swished against my ankles when I walked. "You look very elegant, Lark," Mom said, smiling. Jeanne found an aqua taffeta with a ruched, fitted bodice and big, puffy sleeves. It looked really pretty with her blue eyes.

"You two will be the belles of the ball." Mom grinned the evening of the prom as we dressed at my apartment.

"Thanks, Mom," I said. I felt like a fairy princess in that ethereal dress, but it was too embarrassing to say out loud.

My mother extended a palm to me. In it was her pair of diamond stud earrings. "Would you like to wear these on your special night?" She smiled her loving smile.

"Mom ... *thank* you!" I hugged her. As I pushed the posts through my lobes, Romeo buzzed the apartment.

When the guys came up, Mom took pictures and hovered anxiously in the doorway as we left, calling, "Have fun and be careful!" I felt kind of sorry for her standing there all by herself.

It was super dark in the burbs, but when we found the address, the magnificence of the place blew us away. Jason drove through towering iron gates emblazoned with the gold initials EP. The place, lit by a dozen floodlights, was enormous, rising astonishingly from the hill on which it was planted. "It's the freaking Emerald *City*!" Jeanne breathed. I had to agree. We entered the vast foyer and were greeted by our headmistress, Mrs. Prudhon, and some board members and teachers. My French teacher, Madame Quinn, exclaimed over my dress, *"Tu est belle, Alouette,"* and hugged me. About twenty couples were there, stunned and blinking in the golden light of elaborate chandeliers: five- and six-foot stalagmites in formal wear.

At the end of the great hall, a rock band was warming up with the Goo Goo Dolls' "Eyes Wide Open." We hit the dance floor before finding a table. My beautiful dress moved alluringly as Louis and I danced. As he held me during the slow songs, I liked the feel of his starched tux shirt against my chest. Long tables were laden with flowers, crystal punch bowls, and tiers of an amazing array of refreshments: my favorite petit fours, cookies with the school seal piped on top, nuts and candies, sandwich rolls with ham and roast beef, glazed meatballs in chafing dishes, vegetables and dip, and enough fruit and cheese to feed an African village. We found our table and attacked the food on our plates during the band break.

The party was over at midnight. We thanked our hosts and moved down the sweep of drive, Jeanne and I still dancing and singing the Stone Temple Pilots' "Big Bang Baby." We felt like Cinderellas leaving the ball before our coach (Jason's dad's Peugeot) turned into a pumpkin. The car hugged the curves of the road as if it was on rails through a rising, swirling fog.

"Slow down, Jase," Jeanne said tightly from the passenger seat. She clutched the overhead passenger strap in her right hand.

"I'm doing the speed limit, babe." Jason leaned over the wheel, straining to see the lines on the road.

Louis and I had been fooling around a little in the back. I felt one of Mom's earrings slip down the front of my dress and bounce into my lap. Reaching around Louis's arm for it, I knocked it to the floorboard. "Wait, my mom's earring." I released the buckle of my seat belt to reach for it on the floor, my fingertips blindly grazing the mat. I pinched the solitaire between two fingers. "Got it!"

That was the precise moment a majestic buck materialized from the mist directly in front of the car. The others screamed as Jason stomped the brake and swerved to avoid the deer, hitting the edge of a culvert. My eyes shut tightly with the impact, and I felt myself catapulted up and over. The lark was flying.

I awoke in stages. Once, I opened my eyes but, feeling the sting of bright light, closed them again. Then hazy images shimmered as though I peered through the gauzy fabric of my skirt. My mouth and throat felt as parched as July pavement. I tried to speak but only swallowed painfully and closed my heavy lids again. Another time, my vision clearer, I could make out people in the periphery. *Mom? Grandma? Uncle Nick?* But my head didn't seem to want to move. I heard my mother's stricken voice. "Lark darling, can you hear me? Lark?" A cool, soft hand smoothed my forehead, and I drifted some more.

Another time, Grandpa said, "Lark, you're all right now, sweet pea. Will you wake up for me?" I opened my eyes against a dreadful pounding in my head.

"Where is it?" I croaked disoriented, my throat ravaged. "What happened?"

"You were in an accident, darling … on the way home from the prom, but you're all right now," my mom said. *Mama*. She was crying.

"My head … my head hurts so *bad*," I moaned. I tried to look around me. I was in a hospital room. Grandma and Grandpa were there. I saw Nick and Mrs. Roth behind them. Everybody looked like hell, Mom a shell of herself, oily hair in a ponytail. I'd never seen my mother with dirty hair my whole life. "Jeanne?" I asked, suddenly frightened.

"Jeanne and Louis and Jason are just fine, darling," Grandma Liv said.

"Your head hit the windshield. You've been asleep for three days, Lark," Grandpa Hank said and gently kissed my right eyebrow. "Good thing you have a hard head."

"Asleep for three days," I parroted, incredulous. "My head?" I tried to raise my arm, but it felt as if it was pinned beneath a heavy object. Grandpa told me my head had broken the windshield. I had lost so much blood before the ambulance had arrived that I'd needed a transfusion in the ER. That freaked me out. I didn't want to know any more.

On the room's long windowsill three balloons floated above a flower arrangement flanked on either side by a host of greeting cards, my grandmother's favorite handbag, and my grandfather's gray rain hat. "Just lie still and rest, darling. Just rest now," Mom soothed. She smiled, but her eyes looked wrecked.

When I awoke again, it was late afternoon, the sun through the blinds striping one wall that held a painting of Jesus and children. Jesus's face was luminous. Mom and Grandpa sat talking quietly on the sofa, one of those ugly plastic hospital ones. "What day is it?" I asked.

Mom bounded to my side. "It's Wednesday, baby. How do you feel? Are you hungry?"

"Yes," I said and realized I was starving. "I want a cheeseburger."

Grandpa laughed his big froggy laugh. "A cheeseburger you shall have. Fries? I'll be back in a flash." He moved toward the door.

"Grandpa, have I told you how much I love you?" I managed.

"And I you, sweet pea," he said smiling. The door snicked closed softly behind him.

A nurse named Carla came in, bringing me an icy cup of Sprite and another pain pill. She deftly changed the bag on my IV. Carla, who was really skinny and pretty like Ally McBeal on TV, said brightly, "The doctor says you should be able to go home the day after tomorrow." She nodded at Mom and slipped out again, shoes squeaking on the waxed floor.

"Oh, Mama …" I hadn't called her Mama in a very long time. "I'm so sorry about all this."

"Darling, we are just very thankful you're going to be all right. It could have been so much worse. God has a plan for your life," she said and took my hand.

"I love you, Mama Robin," I whispered as another nurse strode in to check my vitals. Mom squeezed my hand three times. I squeezed back four.

The next afternoon after school was out, Jeanne, Louis, and Jason came to visit. Louis was shaken and pale and bearing a chocolate milkshake. Jason's left arm was in a cast. Jeanne's face was bruised, a bandage on her chin. We all cried a little bit as we spoke of the accident. I sipped the shake, the best I've tasted to this day, while they took turns reading the funny get-well-soon cards to me.

I ended up taking my final exams from home but was able to attend graduation with the others a week later. I was awarded both the senior English and French awards. As I moved the tassel on my mortarboard at the ceremony, I thought, *I'm going to college!* In the audience Mom's and my grandparents' faces were suffused with pride. With them were Dr. and Mrs. Roth, Uncle Nick, Tante Tee, and Uncle Laurent, who my friends all thought looked like a movie star. After the ceremony my family went to lunch at Tavern on the Green. My mother presented me with a small pair of diamond stud earrings of my own. I opened an envelope, a gift from the Pelletiers. Inside was a round-trip ticket to Paris and a check for $5,000—"To save for a rainy day," Tante Tee said with a wink.

CHAPTER

⌒

16

Robin

1998–2012

The days surrounding Lark's accident were the absolute worst
of my life as a parent. I received the call from the state police
at 2:20 that ghastly early morning after the prom. My child,
critically injured, had been taken to the hospital; there were no
further details at the moment. Almost literally blinded with fear
and anguish, I called my father and asked him to meet me there.
He insisted on picking me up. I was pacing up and down in front
of the building, a raincoat over my pajamas, a pair of slip-ons on
my feet. A miserable Romeo attempted to calm me and bring me
inside to wait. *Why is he staring at my feet?* I thought at one point. I
looked down and saw the shoes were not from a matched pair. Dad
drove breaking every NYC traffic law, jaw tightly clenched, one
hand a death grip on the wheel, the other atop my hand.

The young emergency room doctor who smelled of Clearasil
would not let me in to see Lark. Dad almost had to physically

restrain me from blasting past security and into the room. My daughter could not, would not die. Mom arrived by taxi, and the three of us spent agonizing minutes praying and pacing until the doctor approached. He removed the mask from his acne-scarred face. "Mrs. Hamilton," he said, "your daughter has sustained a significant head injury. She lost just enough blood at the scene that we need an immediate transfusion. Do—"

"Take mine," I blurted. *What is Lark's blood type? I knew it when she was born.* Then I remembered with a flash of lucidity. "No, wait, my daughter's blood type is B negative and I'm B positive."

"What is your husband's type? Is he here?" The doctor appraised our group.

Dean. Why isn't he here? Why do I have to do this by myself? I thought with an irrational flare of anger. "Her father is not in my life," I said evenly.

Dad spoke up, a placating hand on my arm. "Her grandmother is B negative."

At the same time Mom, her face a bone-colored oval framed by messy hair, stepped forward, her hand raised as if she were about to take an oath. "Yes. Let me do it," she said.

The staff took Mom back immediately. Dad and I were left to wait again. "If Lark dies, I will die myself," I said to him at one point.

"Lark will not die, at least not now, and neither will you," he said sternly. "We are going to hang on for the next minute and then the next hour … as long as it takes … until we know something."

"I should notify her father … but under these circumstances? After all this time? What have I done?" I asked him, practically wringing my hands. I began to sob. His face blasted, he patted me absentmindedly.

Another hour went by. Mom reappeared. "Any word?" she asked, looking anxiously from Dad to me.

"Not yet," Dad said shortly.

Mom was pressing cotton batting to the inside of one elbow and sipping from a small plastic cup of orange juice. I moved to embrace her. "Oh, Mama, thank you. Are you okay?" *Mama. When's the last time I called her that?*

"I'm fine, darling, and Lark will be too." She smiled briefly.

Another hour passed as the three of us sat slumped and hollow-eyed on a bench covered in hideous orange vinyl. The doctor walked toward us again. I was on my feet at once and searching his eyes. "Your daughter is stable and resting comfortably but still unconscious. We're running more tests now. Lark's a strong, healthy young woman, and I expect her to be all right," he said. "We'll give you another update as soon as we can."

"Thank you, Doctor," the three of us breathed in unison.

All through the interminable day we waited. I called Theresa in Paris, catching her as she was leaving her office. I told her not to come, that I would keep her abreast. At 3:20 we received word that the brain scans had predicted no permanent damage. It was just a matter of time before Lark reawakened. She was moved to a private room and monitored closely. Nick joined me when Mom and Dad went home to rest, but I would not leave the chair beside Lark's bed. He sat silently and did paperwork, a solid and soothing presence. From time to time I drifted off, jerking awake when my head fell to one side or the other. Nick tucked a pillow behind my head, and I slept for two hours.

As Lark began coming around the second day, we all maintained a bedside vigil. When at last she spoke, I begin to cry scalding tears, my knees almost buckling with relief and gratitude.

In the following months it was clear that my daughter had moved beyond her disdainful teenage years and become a loving and gracious young woman. She spent ten days in Paris with Tee and Laurent and came back enriched, with a palpable new maturity. Lark and I spent a great deal of time together before we made the drive to Boston, enjoying shopping for clothes and dorm items together. We were two birds of a feather once more, our relationship renewed and stronger than before.

Driving back to New York alone three days later, I was forced to reevaluate my life. I had achieved my goal of making myself indispensable to the team at work, and I enjoyed my collegial relationships with Lindy and the partners, but the work no longer provided the challenge I needed now that Lark had flown the nest.

My nights were long, with no one to share my home. And I was uncherished, lonelier than when I had been young and without a man's arms to hold me. Nick had been a faithful friend to me and to Lark, and I was grateful for his agreeable company, but I needed a romantic relationship. Often Dean Falconer, who hadn't aged beyond twenty-five in my mind, made cameo appearances in my dreams.

I fantasized about the life he must lead. I decided to place the call.

One evening after work, I sorted through the mail—my credit card bill, a decorating magazine, and a glossy postcard addressed to Lark that of course I read—and poured myself a glass of wine. I thoughtfully regarded my solitary apartment. I slipped my new iPhone from my purse and sat down with it at the kitchen table. I smoothed a lone place mat with the flat of my hand and, once again, called the number in Virginia.

A woman answered, the cadence of her voice Hispanic, "Falconer residence."

"May I speak with Dean Falconer, please?" I asked. My heart threatened to choke off my air supply.

"Mr. Falconer is not here at the moment. Would you like to leave a message?"

"I'm an old friend ... Robin," I said inanely, as if anyone would know me. "With whom am I speaking, please?"

"I'm Rosa," the woman answered kindly, "Mrs. Falconer's caregiver." *His wife was ill.* "Would you like to leave a message?" Rosa asked.

"No … No. I'm sorry." I tried to corral my wild-mustang thoughts. "There's no message. I'll call another time. Thank you," I said dully and pushed the end button.

I began to cry … for Dean, for his wife. Were there children? For myself. For Lark. For all that had been lost for such a terribly long time. As a slogging fatigue crept over me, I laid my head on folded arms. When I awoke, the kitchen was fully dark. My neck stiff, I felt as though I had been pummeled. I put my glass in the dishwasher and walked through the house and up the stairs to my bed. I was weary to the bone of thinking about my responsibility for the truth. My efforts to try and square things had met with nothing but a series of emotionally charged obstacles. Maybe later. I fell asleep in my clothes on top of my covers and slept for ten hours.

A week later I met Greg Faircloth at a dinner party at the home of one of the partners. He was a very tall, handsome radio show host, and his deep velvet voice and crooked smile left me weak-kneed. Greg was thoughtful and intelligent and, after the third date, a skillful lover. He always had tickets to the best shows and sporting events. We had fun together, but after almost a year, he made it clear that he was not a fan of commitment. When I found out he was still hung up on his first love, a woman from Tennessee named Debbie, Greg and I went our separate ways amicably and without rancor. I moved on.

I wanted to be married, to share my life with someone. I became restless and bored and abhorred that in myself. Then one day it came to me; I could return to law school. It wasn't too late. Once again I talked it over with Dad. It would be two more years of hard work, but Dad was keen on the idea and insisted on paying my tuition. "We would have paid for it the first time, and we'll do it now. Besides," he said with a grin, "my motives are entirely selfish. I want to bring you on board with John and me."

With the money I'd saved through the years, I could afford to work only part-time. Stephen Adams agreed to allow me to stay on in that capacity, sharing the position with a new paralegal named Khaled. It was settled almost too easily. Lark and Tee were excited for me and became my cheerleaders from afar. We e-mailed often. And via Skype sessions, Tee and I were able to "see" each other frequently after more than thirty years of letters and brief phone calls.

A few months into my studies, I noticed my mother repeating herself in conversation. One day she called me Lark and not in the way you do when your mind is busy and full of the people in your life, where you correct yourself with a laugh and "Where is my mind?" Another time, I asked where she and Dad had had dinner the night before. "I don't know," she said, a perplexed look on her face.

A few days later I called Dad at his office and asked if he had noticed anything amiss with Mom.

"Rob, we need to talk," he said with a fifty-pound sigh. We met the next afternoon for coffee. He reported similar anecdotes and voiced his growing concern. We agreed to wait and watch.

But Mom's short-term memory continued to deteriorate. She was often confused, her eyes wide, fearful. Scattered around the house was a collection of sticky notes scrawled with the things Mom wanted to remember—the types of birds in her garden, how to use the microwave, Lark's name and Boston University. Mom's once lovely, round penmanship became jagged, her sentence structure like that of a third grader. With burgeoning dread we suspected Alzheimer's disease. Then the owner of Speak Volumes called my father. Things had been slipping through the cracks at the shop, and Mom's sweet and loyal assistants had been covering for her. Dad gently convinced Mom to take some time off from work and rest. She would not be going back.

Dad took her for a neurological evaluation; the report was grim. The doctor confirmed that Mom was in the early-mid stages of the disease. A devastated Dad insisted that Mom not be told the result. "Why would you want to know?" he asked me, his eyes agonized and red rimmed. "I don't want your mother to spend the time she has left with that terrible knowledge." I agreed wholeheartedly. And so we kept it from her. It was a suspended time. Again we watched and waited to see where the dread road would lead.

And then one day coming home from the market just down the street, where Mom had shopped for twenty years, she got lost. Miraculously, Anita Roth was walking home and saw her standing as motionless as a fire hydrant on a busy corner, hordes of people brushing past her in both directions. Anita took her old friend's hand and walked her home. She stayed with her until Dad came home from the office.

Fearing for Mom's safety, Dad and I quickly looked for someone to stay with her during the day. Uncommonly kind

Sharron, a friend of Lindy's who had lost her husband and was looking for work, agreed to take the job and became part of the family. We introduced Sharron to Mom, and the two hit it off right away. Sharron was a godsend. I don't know what Dad and I would've done without her equanimity, humor, and affection for my mother.

When Lark came home for the holidays that year, she could hardly bear to be in her grandmother's presence. "It hurts so much, Mom. I'm afraid I'll burst into tears." We carried the ache inside us like a malignancy.

The arrangement with Sharron worked for almost a year, and then Mom needed more than help with bathing and dressing. She was no longer able to climb the stairs to her bedroom and became increasingly agitated and on occasion even combative with Sharron and Dad. She forgot my name and one day introduced me to Anita as her sister. Other relationships grayed and blurred in her mind. She no longer remembered anything about my life, not even my childhood, and that hurt me to the marrow of my bones.

I had read that it was most difficult for the spouse of an Alzheimer's victim to face the hurdle of placing him or her in a nursing home, and I struggled to help Dad see beyond the denial he felt. We found a facility that specialized in the care of Alzheimer's patients and took Mom there on a Monday morning. I decorated her room with a few of her special things—an Asian lamp, a pretty mirrored tray on which she kept her toiletries, and a few botanical prints on the wall—while an attendant took her on a tour. Mom was placidly sitting in front of a bingo board when we slipped out, though her hands remained like a pair of oven mitts in her lap. In the empty brownstone afterward, I held my father as he wept. "How can I live here after all these years without your mother?" he sobbed.

Dad visited Mom every evening, and Anita and I each went two days a week. The staff reported that Mom had adjusted well. Her contentment was the most important thing to us. For a time we lived in a shell of quiescence.

Then Mom became incontinent and was put into adult diapers. She loathed the papery feel against her skin. Next she lost her appetite, and her weight plummeted. And then my lovely genteel mother began to curse and snipe at other residents. She was placed on medication that helped with the hostility but left her with a flat affect and unable to sustain a conversation.

It was one of the worst times of my life. I dreaded going to the nursing home. I spaced my visits farther apart and limited the time that I spent with my mother. The guilt I felt threatened to consume me. One Saturday afternoon, I walked into her room with a vase of her favorite white peonies, a smile pasted across my face, and a stench hit me with the force of a tsunami. Mom had been nattering at the hated diaper again, and trying to hide the unspeakable evidence, she had smeared it around the room. There were unholy brown stripes of shit across her bedsheet and the little French chair and swaths of it down one wall—like a mad decorator trying out paint samples. Transfixed, I saw that the dark stuff was lodged beneath her too-long fingernails. I dropped the bouquet and fled, sour acid rising in my throat, and pushed through the double doors to take in great breaths of fresh air. The nurses had seen my exodus; I knew they would follow up on Mom. And so, God help me, it was the last time I saw my mother.

I stayed away a week, two, unable to face going back. And then it was too late. Dad received the call about three o'clock one morning and promptly called me. Olivia Courtwright Hamilton had passed away in her sleep. I knew she was already in heaven. The next days were blessed with an outpouring of affection from friends who had loved her. The good women of St. Michael's Parish kept us hugged and fed. It was a terrible relief.

At my most vulnerable following my mother's death, lonesome to the point of floor-walking insomnia, I astonished Nick one cold, cold night after we'd been to a movie by inviting him to my bed. He had begun seeing an editor named Tonya, and I'm afraid I derailed that relationship in my need for succor. Nick's and my lovemaking was as it had been years before, as freeing as slipping into a happy childhood dream. We both knew the affair was temporary, and we got it out of our systems after a month. Although I wanted to be, I wasn't in love with Nick.

A year later, I graduated from law school with my doctor of jurisprudence degree, eighteen years after I had first begun. I jumped on the bar exam and passed with a comfortable margin. I was an attorney with all rights and privileges. My father and John Hicks took me to the Four Seasons for an exquisite dinner and fine champagne. They offered me a partnership with the firm. We were Hamilton, Hicks, and Hamilton. I relished the new role and began working with my own clients excited about buying their first homes.

Shortly thereafter, Lark graduated with honors from Boston University with a master's degree in education. Teaching was the noblest of professions in my mind, and I was so proud of Lark and all she had accomplished. She would make a wonderful teacher. Lark returned to New York and lived with me for a couple of fun months before finding a plum first position in a charter school for the arts and moving into an apartment with another new teacher at her school.

The bottom fell out of John Hicks's world. Our elegant and conservative friend was devastated when his wife, Linda, in love with another man, told him she was leaving after forty years of marriage. John's humiliation was complete when he learned that not only was the man much younger than Linda but also an ex-con, a professional poker-playing stud who wore gold chains around his neck.

Two years later, Dad blew all of our minds by announcing his plan to retire and move to the Outer Banks of North Carolina. One of his clients was selling her summer home there. He hadn't even discussed it with me. "My bones are tired of the New York winters," he said over lunch one day. As I looked at my father, I saw that he was thin. He looked tired and old for seventy-five. He asked if I would take the brownstone. "I would love for the house to stay in the family. And your mother would be happy with that."

The full circle feel of the idea compelled me. An excited and grateful Lark took my apartment. All the pieces came together smoothly, as though orchestrated by Shostakovich. The evening before the movers arrived, I helped my father pack the things he would carry by car. Blondie, restless and confused, paced and sniffed at boxes. I poured a couple of neat scotches, and we sat down at the dining table Dad would take to the beach. *What wonderful times we had with Mom around this table*, I thought.

My dad was concerned about me. He scooped Blondie up, stroking her fur. "Robin, I worry about you being alone here and lonely. Would you get married if the right guy came along?"

"I do get lonely, Dad," I said, propping a foot on a box. "My life is pretty full again, but if I met the right man, I'd definitely consider it. Funny the way life turns out, huh? I never dreamed I would be an old maid."

He laughed. "If you could only see from my perspective how young you still are. It's all relative, sweet pea. Your mother and I were so happy … We always wanted you to be as happy in love as we were. It's so sad the way things turned out between you and Dean." He pulled pensively at his scotch. "And Lark. She and Ben have been together for what? Three years? I wish they'd hurry up and tie the knot. What are they waiting for?"

"I know. It must be Ben's travel. They love each other, but I'm not sure Lark wants a part-time mate." Blondie nudged me with her leathery black nose. I reached to scratch behind her ears. "I'm going to miss this mutt."

My thoughts crept to Dean again. "You know, Dad, sometimes I think over the years Dean became … an abstraction for me. An idea. A symbol of love. Maybe that made it easier for me to live the lie."

"I guess so, Rob." We sipped at our drinks in silence.

"What a morose pair we are! Let's talk about your new house!" I said, brightening for my father. "I can't wait to see it. You'll be walking on the beach every morning while I'm slaving away at the firm."

"But I'll be thinking of you," he said and rose to kiss my forehead. "And I want you to get your first visit on your calendar."

Five years Dad's junior, John Hicks stayed on at the firm. We hired another attorney, a young whippersnapper named Morgan Jordan whom we lured away from a helter-skelter two-year stint with the DA's office. Morgan became an integral part of the practice. Her superior technology skills helped take the firm into the twenty-first century.

Dad's contemporary home in North Carolina with walls of glass and sweeping view of the Atlantic was breathtaking. Dad relished being able to sit on his deck and watch Blondie run the beach, darting and barking at the leaping and slapping surf. The timeless sea helped to heal his grief. He met Nancy Bronson, a Carolina native who was close to his age, and they clicked immediately. Nancy loved to dance—ballroom, salsa and samba, and even the Carolina shag—and taught Dad to enjoy it. He lost the haggard look, his life revitalized. I liked Nancy and was grateful for her vivacious presence in my father's life. The Outer Banks became the perfect getaway for Lark and me on long weekends. Lark enjoyed extended school vacations there. Theresa even came from France and stayed with us there for a month one happy, lazy summer.

And then there was the sanctuary of my home in New York City. I padded about the uneven, old wood flooring and imagined my bare feet as the roots that anchored me to the place where I had been born and reared, laughed and cried, where I had loved and been loved. I kept many of Mom's old special pieces, hoping that Lark would want them for herself one day. Combining them with the pieces I'd collected over the years, I created a charming, eclectic space.

The only new things I purchased were a large, comfy sectional and heavy, antique dining table that had once graced the dining room of a monastery. Charmed by its history, I loved running my palm across the indentations near the edges worn by a century of elbows and forearms. I kept the top of the treasure shining and fragrant with lavender polish. Sleeping in the master bedroom had taken some getting used to. The room was steeped in memories of my mother. I spent the first nights downstairs on the sofa. But I had the room freshly painted and decorated it much as I had my bedroom in Lark's and my first little place, a restful blue and white, with white cutwork linens and matelassé spread. The space soon became my own. I cut back the garden foliage that, as if mourning for my mother's gentle care, had grown scraggly, almost obscuring the kitchen window. Abundant sunlight made the room inviting and cheerful again. I felt my mother's spirit as I cooked.

One late February evening while the wind probed and rattled the shutters of the brownstone, I read online that the Eagles had produced *The History of the Eagles* in two parts. The premiere would be on cable that Friday night. Excited, I called Tee, wishing we could watch it together. I called Lark and asked if she would come and watch it with me. We hadn't had a mother-daughter night in a while.

I worked until six on Friday and took a taxi home. The weather was so damned cold. I took off my skirt and pumps and pulled on a pair of jeans. I had bought our favorite truffle cheese and a couple of bottles of wine that Lark and I both liked. With Ben out of town I might persuade Lark to spend the night. It would be fun, a slumber party.

Lark rang the bell at a quarter to seven. I couldn't believe she had walked over in the cold. She got herself settled while I pulled the snacks together. I was still in the kitchen when the show began. Lark called me to come and look at a girl she said looked like me. I laughed to myself: we girls all looked alike in those days-- the hairstyle, the outfits we wore. But as I ferried the tray to the coffee table I was thunderstruck. The producer had included footage from the Hotel California tour. The scenes looked eerily as though they'd been filmed at the DC concert.

And then I saw myself. And *Dean*. My heart slammed against my ribcage.

I sat in stunned reverie, Lark beside me suddenly looking so much like her father my heart squeezed with ineffable sadness, with regret. All the rationalizations with which I'd built my careful house of cards shimmered before me.

I wanted to tell Lark. Now. Maybe it wasn't too late for Lark and Dean. It was time to embrace the truth.

Damn the consequences.

CHAPTER

17

Lark

2013

My stomach clenched like a fist. Convinced my mother had some big revelation to make, I asked again, "Who?" I sounded like a petulant owl. I saw that I still clutched the remote and pressed the mute button.

"My darling daughter, that is your *father*, Dean Thompson Falconer," she said evenly, at once altering the course of our lives.

I looked back at the screen and saw that it was true. I stared at the young man frozen in time. *So much younger than I am now*, I mused, and a range of emotions washed over me. I watched him smile and sway to the music. Hot, salt tears began to flow down my cheeks, tears of loss, of grief, but through them I smiled and uttered little laughs of amazement. A spark of hope ignited in me like good, dry tinder.

The expression on the young Robin Hamilton's motionless face was a look I'd never seen before. I found that I had moved closer to the television on my knees and turned back.

At last the words came past my teeth. "Why, Mom? What happened to you two?" My mother turned and pulled a couple of afghans from the sofa. She moved to sit with me, and we faced each other before the hearth. As she told me the story, her gaze was clear and direct. Occasionally she prodded at the snickering logs with Grandpa Hank's iron poker.

She told me about the night she'd met Dean Falconer at the concert she and Tee had attended in DC. Mercifully, she gave me what had to have been a PG version of the first weekend they had spent together. She spoke of falling in love with Dean at first sight, and he with her. As the old Courtwright clock ticked away the hours from the mantle, she told me the whole of it, the glorious and tragic story leading to my birth. As she looked from my face to the fire, I saw the pain she'd suffered again and again. She had wanted to tell Dean about me many times, but revelations had stopped her like road-closed signs on desolate highways. When she'd learned that Dean was getting married, it had been as though she'd suffered a small death. And finally as she told me again how much I meant to her, all the pieces of our lives came together. I thought I should feel betrayed. I thought I should feel anger. But woman-to-woman, I found I understood my mother, the bittersweet choices she had made. All I felt was a gessoed peace. By tacit agreement we hauled the afghans over us and slept.

"How do you want us to go about this?" Mom asked the next morning with a smile. She blew across the surface of a nutty

226

Peruvian coffee Ben had brought from his last trip. We sat in the kitchen nibbling toast, the photograph of her and Dean Falconer, the only one she ever had, on the table before us. I regarded the two again. They looked as if they'd just won the New York State lottery.

"Will you call him, Mom?" I asked. "It should be you. And I want to know every word he says. Promise."

"Every word, darling, I promise." She flashed a grin over the "Best Mom" mug I had given her in seventh grade. "I'll take notes."

CHAPTER
18

Robin

2013

I cleaned up the kitchen and gathered the afghans and pillows from the living room floor where they lay tangled from the night before. I thought about all that had transpired and summoned courage. I had no sense of what Dean would say when I called him, but something told me that unlike my former ill-fated attempts, this time Dean himself would answer the phone.

I sat at the monks' table with my cell and the dog-eared notebook paper with the address and number penned in Dean's hand so many years ago. I'd kept his letters along with the single photograph of us and Lark's birth certificate folded and tucked into the false bottom of my jewelry box.

Taking a last deep breath, I dialed the number. Dean's unmistakable voice, though deeper and more resonant with maturity, answered, "Hello?" on the second ring. How many hundred times had I heard that voice in my fantasies?

"Dean, this is Robin Hamilton calling from New York City," I said in my best lawyer's voice.

I heard a sharp intake of breath and then silence. Then he said, "*Robin*? What … Are … you all right?"

"I'm fine, Dean. It's just time … I got in touch with you." The words drifted like mail through a slot onto a carpet runner.

Finally he said, "After … thirty-four *years*?"

"Dean, it's best that I speak with you in private. Do you need to call me back another time?" I heard the scraping of chair legs on a floor. *Yes, I guess you'd better sit down*, I thought.

"No. Yes. I mean it's okay; I'm alone," he said. And then after a moment, he said, "I was married. But my wife … Victoria … died of ovarian cancer in 1985. We were married just five years."

"I'm so sorry, Dean," I replied, meaning it. My thoughts did a 180: *What about the caregiver I spoke to, what, four years ago now?* "I actually tried to call you several years ago. I spoke with a woman who said she was Mrs. Falconer's caregiver. I assumed she was there for your wife. Was it your mother?" I asked quietly. I heard a dog barking on his end and tried to picture Dean in the house at Villeneuve.

"Oh, that must have been when Mom fell off her horse and broke her leg. She's fine, by the way. Strong and healthy. She made a complete recovery from the breakdown when ... after my father died."

"I'm so glad, Dean. That's wonderful."

"Victoria ... my wife ... was four months pregnant when they found the cancer. She lost the baby ... a girl ... and Victoria died just three months later."

"Oh, Dean," I said, tears scalding the back of my throat. I rose to get a Kleenex and sat heavily back down. "And you never remarried?"

"No," he said shortly. "I just never had the ... impulse again."

"Oh," I said lamely and softly blew my nose.

"It's surreal talking with you," he said then. "What about you, are you married?"

I checked my emotions and swallowed. "No. I *never* married." The pivotal moment was at hand; my segue had come. "But I have a daughter ... an incredible daughter." I paused and took a deep breath. "She's thirty-three years old."

"*Thirty-three!* Incredible. Robin Hamilton with a thirty-three-year-old kid," he marveled. I waited while Dean did the math. And then he knew. "Is she ... *mine?*" he asked, his voice rising on the last word.

I realized I'd been holding my breath and let it out slowly. "She is." I clung to the answer as if it were a life preserver. Dean's choking sobs sounded as though from far below the surface of deep water. I would wait; I would give him time.

He cleared his throat, his voice husky, raw. "Good God! Why, Robin? Why didn't you tell me?"

I closed my eyes and grasped for the words to explain the last three and a half decades. I'd rehearsed them a dozen times, but they seemed to have flown from my head like birds from a shaken tree. Then with sudden clarity I saw myself in my little studio apartment in DC, heartsick, morning sick, and frightened. I began to speak as that Robin. I described the first days after I found his letter under the door when I had drifted in a transitory bubble of shock and disbelief. I explained how through the years I'd waited until I thought it was the right time and how it never seemed to be.

Dean listened in deafening silence. Finally, he heaved a ponderous sigh. "Robin, I'm sorry. This is just too much. Too much of a shock to deal with right now. I don't ..." I heard the scrape of the chair again. "I can't ... I have to go." And he hung up the phone.

I stared at my phone until the screen went to black, anguished I had hurt him so profoundly and swamped with uncertainty. I'd been foolish not to expect a visceral reaction from Dean. Had all the years that I'd held the secret close to me in the dark desensitized me? *Of course* Dean would need time. *Of course* he would need to absorb the shock, wrap his head around it.

I rose heavily to my feet to shower and dress. I called Lark to see if she wanted to meet for lunch. An hour later we shrugged from our coats at Cappomaggi's, where the comfort food was rich and substantial. In a quiet corner booth over hearty bowls of minestrone and buttery garlic bread, I relayed the conversation I'd had with her father. Lark's face was very still. "Darling, I just know," I said, placing my hands over my heart, "that Dean ... your father ... is a thoroughly good man. He's had a *terrible* shock today, but I *know* he'll come around."

"I hope so, Mom," Lark sighed, hands cradling a cup of hot tea. She tried on a little smile for me, but her clear gray eyes were replete with unspoken questions.

"My number's on his caller ID now." I winked at my daughter. "That will be our juju."

CHAPTER

19

Lark

2013

I found myself standing in the market before a plundered
display of Valentine cards with no memory of walking the familiar
route. Thoughts of my father and of Ben whirled and tumbled
like socks in a dryer that would have to be sorted. Poor Dean.
Not only had he lost his first love, my mother, without a trace, but
then his young wife had died. I knew enough psychology from
the two years of sessions with Dr. Rike—ironically therapy I'd
needed from growing up fatherless and believing he didn't know of
my existence—to realize how profoundly the news that had come
out of the blue must have affected *him*. I plucked a loaf of Ezekiel
bread from the rack.

Someone had said, "The truth will set you free, but first it
will make you miserable." The revelation had been difficult for all
three of us. But would it prove ultimately freeing? Organic apples
and bananas and Greek yogurt fell into my basket. If only Dean

and I had met when I was a little girl. Was it possible to forge a relationship now? Would we want to? I wanted so much to know this man from whom I'd inherited my gray eyes, my pinky toes, and the planes of my face. What sort of man *was he*? To hear Mom tell it, when he was twenty-four, Dean was God's gift to the planet—friendly, loving, talented, loyal—an *actual* Eagle Scout. But Mom hadn't seen the man in more than three decades. How might life have changed him?

And then there was Ben. Just two days ago I'd been consumed with thoughts of our relationship. Ben traveled constantly. We had talked of a life spent together only in nebulous terms. But I knew I wanted to have at least one baby before my eggs began waving microscopic white flags. Absently, I swept brown rice and quinoa from the shelf.

I didn't want my children placing moist and sticky kisses on a framed photograph of their father at bedtime, Ben in South America, in Manizales or Cuzco. I wanted a real home, one like my mother's, a home filled with carefully chosen, well-loved pieces, a home that rang with the music and clutter of family. While my little place on West Eighty-Sixth could be generously described by an ambitious real estate agent as "cozy," Ben's apartment was no more suitable, a studio impersonally furnished by IKEA, a functional place to crash.

Two days ago, I'd made the decision to talk with Ben about my feelings this weekend, perhaps even issuing him an ultimatum. But as I squeezed avocados as unyielding as river rocks, I thought about what I taught my students: we must study the past in order to inform the future. Perhaps my root system should be exposed and inspected before I could wholly cultivate my future.

Queuing up at the register, a litany of questions eddied about my head like a vortex. What about Dean and my mother? Could a thirty-five-year-old love be rekindled? Since the big revelation, there had been a new look in my mother's eyes, a different rhythm to her breathing. Had the hope of love come to roost in her heart? What would it do to her gentle soul if it didn't work out this time?

On the sidewalk, a text alert sounded. I fumbled with my bags. Mom: "I've heard back from Dean. He's calling me at 8:00 tonight. Love you, darling."

It was time to rock and roll.

CHAPTER

20

Robin

2013

A bee in my bonnet, I pulled out an Eagles' album, dusted it with a sleeve, and put it on to play as I cleaned my house from top to bottom. It had been a long time since I'd listened to albums, but they connected me with the past, and the Eagles felt like good karma today. I would never erase from my phone the voice mail I'd received while at mass that morning: "Robin, this is Dean. I'm sorry about last night. I'm ready to talk now. I will try you tonight after eight. Until then."

I popped a frozen entrée in the microwave and picked at it from a tray before the fire, watching the news as though the anchor spoke in some unknown tongue. At 7:50, I turned off a Cary Grant and Irene Dunne movie and peered out the front shutters at the street. The warm front had shown up, and a chiming rain had begun to fall. I stoked the fire and sat on the sofa, surprised by the balloon of calm in which I seemed to float. At 8:05 the phone rang in my lap: the 434 area code. *Here goes everything.* "Hel-lo?" I answered brightly.

"Robin? It's Dean. Listen, I'm sorry about yesterday. You … pulled the rug out from under me to put it mildly. I needed some time. Time to try to get my head around this thing."

"Dean, it is okay. Really. I totally understand," I said.

"I've had one day to take this in … while you've had the thirty-year home-field advantage." He was calm, his voice more like the old Dean's. "I've had some … I guess righteous indignation going … I had a right to know, Robin. No matter what was going on in my life back then, you should have told me."

"I know," I said miserably. "I was so young. I thought I was protecting you. When I look back on it, it's easier to see what I should've done … the times I could've told you." We were silent again.

"All this time I had a daughter … I still can't believe it," he marveled. Then as if it were just occurring to him he said, "I don't even know her name."

"Her name is Lark," I said, warmth pouring over me like spilled honey. "It's her nickname. I named her Laurel Olivia, after your mother and mine." A jagged sigh from Dean was followed by the liquid sound of tears. I continued, "She was such a happy baby that one day my father said she was as happy as a lark, and the name just stuck."

Dean sniffed deeply and cleared his throat. "Lark." The name was a sonnet on his lips. "I like it. Did you … does she have my last name?" he asked expectantly. I told Dean his name was listed on the birth certificate as the father but that her legal name was Hamilton.

"So you lived with your parents?" Dean asked. I told him about how I had come back to my parents' home in the beginning.

"I'm just so damned sorry for us both, Robin." His words were suffused with disappointment. I heard him crying softly again. "For it all … for all that we missed. I don't …" His voice caught, and I heard the devastation he felt. "After thirty years … my whole adult life … it shouldn't matter, but it does. I'm … stunned by how hurt I feel."

"I know."

"I loved you, Robin," he said evenly. "If only I had known about the baby then … I would've asked you to marry me right away."

"You don't regret your marriage, Dean?"

"No. I don't know … It was a long time ago. She was my next-door neighbor. My years with Victoria were good. We had a nice life. I feel disloyal to her memory … telling you … that things between her and me were never like they were between you and me … but it's true. Maybe you only get to love that way once … with that … passion." My heart soared and shimmered above his words.

241

Now a youthful and energetic seventy-nine, Dean's mother enjoyed a full life and lived alone in the main house. Dean had designed and built a new house for himself on the property. He worked as an architect with an office in Charlottesville, designing homes for clients in the central Virginia area.

And then it was my turn. "I worked as a paralegal after I dropped out of law school … for *years*. Then, believe it or not, I went back to law school ten years ago."

"That's fantastic. Congratulations." he said warmly.

I spoke of my mother's illness and death, of becoming partners with my dad, and of his move to North Carolina. Dean talked of his sisters and how well their lives had turned out. We were quiet then, each of us lost in our own thoughts. And then he said, "Robin, I was thinking last night about when I left you that first time … after my father died, after that first weekend we were together. The Eagles' concert weekend. Remember?"

"Of course I do. I was devastated. But do you remember that I forgave you?"

"Yeah. You did. And those months in DC were …" He fell silent.

"Yeah, they were." Those memories were drawn in indelible ink. I wondered if Dean was seeing as I was the two of us in each other's arms.

"Dean," I said very slowly, "I need to ask you to forgive me now. For keeping the knowledge of Lark from you."

Everything depended on his answer. My fingers gripped the phone like a life preserver. Finally he sighed again. "I do. I forgive you, Robin. It must have been very difficult for you. I know that."

"But I got a wonderful daughter out of the deal," I said smiling into the phone. "I want you to know her too, Dean." My eyes slid to Lark's picture on the mantle. "She belongs to you as much as me. I realize that now."

"Ah, Rob. It seems we were both so caught up in emotions ... we made some irreparable ... misjudgments ... didn't we?" He paused. "It's terrible doing this over the phone," he said, echoing my thoughts. "I want to see you." My heart leaped again. "I want to meet our daughter. There's so much more I need to know. Do you think you could catch me up on the last thirty-five years?"

"I'll give it the old college try." I laughed a little. "No pun intended." Then I added, "Can we take a break? I really need to pee."

Dean laughed his old laugh. "So do I. So call you back in ten?"

"Okay, my cell's almost dead. I'll plug it in. Bye." I snared my power cord from my briefcase and plugged it in behind the sofa, smiling tremulously to myself. Before the phone rang, I put another log on the fire and poured myself a glass of Pinot Gris.

I took a deep breath and answered on the third ring. I heard the clinking of ice in a glass on Dean's end. "What are *you* drinking?"

"Scotch," he laughed.

"I'm a scotch drinker too. But I opened a nice wine for this ... for tonight."

I told Dean about his daughter. "Lark's a third-grade schoolteacher *and* a yoga instructor. She's not married but has a boyfriend of three years, Ben Holland. He's a terrific guy; you'd like him."

Before I knew it, the old clock was striking one, the wine at low tide in the bottle. I eased myself down to lie on the sofa and pulled an afghan over me. I tried to picture Dean doing the same on his end. "Robin, we have to make this happen. There's an AIA, American Institute of Architects, Convention in New York next month, late March. Would that be a good time to see you both?"

"Yes, of course," I said, scanning my mind's calendar. *That's only four weeks away!*

"I haven't asked ... but does *she* want to meet *me*?" He sounded diffident now.

I smiled. "She's *dying* to meet you. She made me promise to tell her everything you said tonight." And then incredibly, I began to yawn. The emotion had exhausted me.

"Could you and I meet first? I'd like to take you to dinner. We could talk face-to-face ... before I meet Lark."

"Of course, Dean. I'd love that." *That's the understatement of my adult life.*

"I think I'm feeling like a nervous father-to-be," he added with a small chuckle.

"I can only imagine how you must feel. I have to say you've taken this really well."

"It's all a big act. You should have seen me when you called yesterday. I was literally shaking. I've been a wreck ever since." He mused, "There's so much I want to know … I don't know where to start." He was quiet a moment and then pragmatic. "I'll call you the day before I get there. It's been a long time, Robin." His voice thickened. "I'm looking forward to seeing you."

"Me too. Talk to you soon. Good night."

I spent the next weeks in a tempest of fevered excitement. I willed myself to compartmentalize the visit so I could focus on work. I talked with my support circle—Tee, my dad, and Nick— asking for their thoughts, advice, and affirmation.

Tee said, "*C'est pas vrai*, Rob, you talked to him? My God, I can't believe you finally did it! What did he say?" And when I had told her the whole of it, she said, "I'm proud of you, Rob. You deserve to be happy. And you deserve a second chance at a life with Dean. The stars just may align for you two after all." I gulped, loving her. Then she burst out, "What are you going to *wear*?" and I snorted with laughter.

My dad said, "I couldn't be happier, sweet pea. It's not too late for Lark to benefit from a relationship with her father. And as for you and Dean, this could be a second chance at a life together. I hope to finally meet this young man."

Nick said, "That's *fantastic*! I'm sure Lark's jumping out of her skin. Dean's a *helluva* lucky guy. Just wait till he sees how gorgeous you still are. The guy will be on his knees. Just be you, and the rest will take care of itself." Nick was happy in those days. He was engaged at last to his girlfriend of the past year, a boho-chic designer named Dakota. I had had dinner with the two of them twice and liked Dakota.

Of course I was wildly curious about what Dean looked like. I tried to envision his face through the lens of one of those age-progression photos on missing-children posters. Then one morning in the office, I remembered the professional networking database LinkedIn. Morgan had created a slick new website for the firm and had shown John and me how to create profiles on LinkedIn. I had done little with my account. Did Dean have one?

I fidgeted, drumming my fingers on my desk, and typed in the password I used for everything, Eagles!77. I logged into the site, navigated to the search box, and typed in Dean Falconer. There was a maddening delay as the page loaded, and then there he was! Dean T. Falconer. My tummy did a funny little flip. I leaned forward in my chair and studied the thumbnail image. First I noticed the wavy gold hair was missing in action. He must have begun to lose his hair and buzzed it short. I could imagine Dean doing that and gave him respect points for it. The only thing worse than a man with a comb-over was a man in a toupee.

But Dean's face! His face and neck had broadened, but his gray eyes were still clear and beautiful even in the tiny photo. Although he smiled a closed-mouth professional smile, I could still see the sexy shape of his lips. The sum of his features amounted to a man who was still very attractive. *Okay, Dean Falconer!* I grinned and glanced furtively up at my open office door. I had a meeting in fifteen minutes.

I navigated to *my* LinkedIn page. What if Dean had looked me up too? What would he think of how *I'd* aged? My coworkers' and my LinkedIn profile pictures had been taken by the photographer who had helped design our website, so the photographs were of good quality, well lit and flattering. At least you couldn't see the full extent of my middle-aged voluptuousness in the headshot. My hair was expensively colored and highlighted. The silk scarf I had worn around my throat for the photo session hid the changes that gravity had wrought there. My color was vibrant, the green of my eyes prominent. *Not too bad overall, old girl.*

I called Theresa. It was six hours later in Paris, but Tee was working late. She asked me to hold as she got up to close her office door. The time difference between us had *always* been annoying and damned inconvenient, so we had long been used to planning our calls. And unlike the early years of the scratchy sound of overseas long distance, we could hear each other as clearly as if we were in the same room.

I told Tee what I'd seen on LinkedIn, about Dean's picture. I waited while she shuffled papers and navigated to the website for her own assessment. "*Mais il est vraiment bel homme.* He's aged well, Rob."

"I know! I'm so excited."

Theresa was quiet for a moment and then said, "Do you see how much Lark looks like him?"

I had been so busy evaluating Dean's appearance I hadn't thought about that. "Wow. Yeah. The eyes … and planes of their cheeks," I said. And then I asked, "But, Theresa, what about me? I weighed about a hundred and twenty pounds the last time Dean saw me!" To my chagrin I was now a size twelve.

"Robin," she said chastising me, "with that hourglass figure of yours?"

"Yeah, but the glass has … expanded. The sands are … passing through and settling in the bottom at an alarming rate," I said ruefully, looking down at the generous hips and thighs in my suit skirt. With my big boobs, I was as curvy as a bag of apples.

"C'mon, Robin. You see the way men look at you," Theresa said. "You know damned well you still look great. And with all the walking you do, you're pretty fit. I'm assuming you don't have halitosis?" I hooted with laughter, and she said, "You have *nothing* to worry about."

Reflecting on our conversation as I stood before the mirror before bed, I thought that on the main Tee had to be right. I had taken scrupulous care of my skin, slathering on moisturizer and sunscreen through all seasons. If the jeans I wore now had a high percentage of spandex in them, it was my secret.

"Mom, come to class tomorrow night," Lark urged the next day. She had been trying to get me to start practicing yoga. "You'll feel so good. Look at my yoga body. Lean thighs are nothing to sneeze at."

"I also have twenty-two years on you, darling daughter," I said archly. But Dean's visit was the impetus I needed to follow her advice. Lark's studio offered beginner-level classes two evenings a week. I began that week and immediately felt better in my own skin.

The evenings also provided a great diversion from long nights of waiting and wondering. I hadn't come right out and told Lark I was still interested in Dean, but she sensed it, and I often caught her smiling an indulgent three-cornered kitten's smile at me. I told her Dean and I planned to have dinner alone the first night, while she was at the studio. "That's probably a good idea," she only said.

Dean would be there in less than two weeks. Lark and I planned for the evening as if it were a state dinner. She and I would cook the simple meal, roast chicken, quinoa, and spring vegetables and a salad dressed with my homemade shallot vinaigrette. For dessert Lark would prepare a strawberry shortcake trifle. I would light a fire in the fireplace if the evening was chilly, and we'd have drinks in the living room before dinner. I splurged on an extra-nice bottle of scotch for Dean and two special wines for chilling, a rich white Burgundy and a Chardonnay from the Jura Mountains of France. My liquor-store guy smiled and waggled his caterpillar eyebrows at the extravagance of my purchase.

Dean called me the night before to give me the name of his hotel, the Hotel Lucerne, which was in walking distance of my home. I thought that my favorite Italian restaurant, Crispo in

Chelsea, would be the perfect place to have dinner. I made a reservation and gave Dean the address, and we agreed to meet there the next night at seven.

And then it was D-day. Dean day. The day we would breach the foreign soil of the future. I took the day off and hit the spa. After a massage, facial, manicure, and pedicure, my skin glowed like a string of cultured pearls. Damn the brown spots on my face and hands—but they were what they were. The week before I had found a little black dress whose price tag didn't make me shudder, with a V-neck and wrap waist in a knit that gently skimmed my curves. My muscles felt more toned and supple from the yoga, and I knew I'd feel good in the dress.

I'd never told my hairdresser Rhonda—a true romantic and single mother herself who was so adept at styling she could simply run her fingers through my hair, gently tugging at this or that strand, and it would look amazing—the story of my past. But today as she applied my base color and shimmery highlights, I regaled her with the whole of it. When I asked for my check, she stunned me. "No charge today. Just all the best, Robin."

At home I brought in the mail, flipped on the foyer lamp, and fairly skimmed up the stairs with my shopping bag. I bathed and slipped into my robe and padded downstairs to pour myself a big glass of wine. I put in a sultry Diana Krall CD that matched my mood and rested for a few minutes.

Finally I appraised myself in the new dress. I felt satisfied. I texted Lark for luck. She was dashing out to the studio. "Love you,

Mom. Have a wonderful evening!" *In twenty-four hours my sweet girl will be with her father for the first time in her life.*

As my heels clicked down my front steps, I noticed a taxi trolling slowly down the block. I hailed it so abruptly I looked as if I were doing the Hitler salute. The driver pulled to the curb right in front of the house. Good omen number one.

But the traffic was heavy, and I arrived at Crispo five minutes late. Stuffing bills to the driver, I stepped out of the cab and stumbled a little in my heels at the curb. Looking up again, I became aware of a tall figure, hands in pockets, silhouetted against the bright facade of the building. Heart pounding, I stepped forward. The figure took a step in my direction and into the light. "Hello, Robin Hamilton," he said in the voice of my dreams.

"Hello, Dean," I said, staring. He was even better looking than I'd thought he would be. In the half light I saw the familiar relief map of his high-planed face, a little broader, the cleft in his chin not as deep as before. Dean's darkened gray eyes locked on mine. His short hair was still blonde, but bristles of gray-white shimmered among the gold. We extended our right hands, but then he grinned and put both arms out to hug me. I stepped into the light embrace of man and memory.

Light-headed as we stepped apart, I heard Dean say, "Ready?" He opened the restaurant door. I remembered his southern gentleman's manners. As we stood together at the hostess stand, our eyes kept sliding to each other's faces. We smiled together again, and I suddenly felt shy. Dean looked handsome and broad shouldered in a dark-navy blazer—the first I'd ever seen him in—over a blue checked button-down shirt, crisp khaki slacks, and tasseled cordovan loafers. The ruddy complexion and deep creases at the corner of his eyes testified to a lifetime of outdoor work and of frequent smiles. He said, "Robin, you look beautiful. I knew you would." My chest filled with a rush of warmth.

"You look wonderful too," I said softly. Dean pulled out my chair for me at the table, and I draped my wrap over the back of my chair. I pulled my hair forward to frame my face and flow over my collarbones. Dean looked around at the warm brick walls studded at intervals with flickering votive candles.

"Nice place," he said.

"This is some of the best Northern Italian food in New York City," I said, tilting my head back to peer at the menu through my bifocals. "I love the pasta with truffle butter, peas, and parmesan," I said, pointing it out to him, "and we *have* to start with the grilled parmesan-crusted asparagus appetizer."

"Do you always wear glasses, Robin?"

"I do. I like them. I started wearing them for distance in my twenties, and now I need them for reading."

"They look very attractive on you."

"Thank you." I smiled, acknowledging the compliment, and then laughed as Dean slipped a hand into his breast pocket and withdrew a pair of tortoise readers of his own. He unfolded them, cleared his throat, and made a big deal out of putting them on. "Would you like to choose a wine for us?" I asked. A large woman at a nearby table shrieked with laughter as her companion loudly described her class reunion. An unobtrusive black-clad young man arrived to pour water into our glasses.

"Sure, let's see … a nice red?" Dean scanned the wine list. He looked sexy in the dark plastic frames. He selected a bottle of Montepulciano d'Abruzzo with black cherry notes and a dry finish that would complement the pasta dishes. I sipped my water and watched him. His beard was heavier than it had been back then, and the darker shadow spread over his jawline. This older version of Dean appeared effortlessly elegant and self-assured.

We ordered roasted kale salads and I the black truffle ricotta ravioli special, Dean the pappardelle and duck ragu. Taking the first sip of wine, I complimented Dean on his choice. He smiled and leaned back in his chair. "I don't know where to start," he said. "There's so much more I want to know. Does Lark look like you? Is she pretty?"

I grinned and said, "She's beautiful. She has my mouth and nose … hands and … figure." I blushed. "But she has your eyes, the planes of your face, your gold hair … and your feet." Dean laughed, rubbing a hand over his scalp, and then slid one loafered foot from under the table, looking down at it for a moment. "She looked so much like you when she was a baby. It haunted me for years," I said, looking into middle distance.

I slipped my cell from my purse and thumbed to find a recent picture of Lark. I handed the phone to Dean. He peered at the photo through his readers. As he studied the face of his daughter for the first time, his throat worked with emotion. Finally he said,

"You're right: she's beautiful." He took a big sip of wine. "Do you have more?" I showed him all I had on the camera roll. He studied the pictures as if he had been handed Jefferson's blueprints for Monticello. "She also looks a lot like my sister Leslie."

"Really?" I said, interested.

He raised his head and smiled at me again. "I can't believe I'm going to meet my daughter, *our* daughter tomorrow night. I hope I sleep. I didn't do so well last night. Are we still having dinner at your house?"

"Walk over about six thirty for a drink? Does that give you enough time after your sessions?"

"Yes, perfect. I should be finished by four." Dean took my hand and squeezed it. Our salads arrived, and we declined the proffered hot bread and olive oil.

"Do you remember the last meal we had together?" I asked him shyly, sipping at my wine.

"Of course," he said right away. "The first big meal you ever cooked." He smiled at the memory. "Roast beef and potatoes. It was delicious, and you looked … gorgeous … in a green dress," he added triumphantly and speared a cherry tomato.

"Wow, very good." I couldn't believe he remembered the dress. The look on his face told me we were both remembering the rest of that night. I flushed and changed the subject. "Do you cook, Dean?"

He refilled our wineglasses. "I've lived alone for twenty-eight years remember, so yes, and I'm pretty good at it actually. My mother taught me a lot, and I watch the Food Network. I like to grill and smoke meat and fish too. I make killer smoked salmon. I use pecan for the wood chips and add a beer to the water. Speaking of smoking," he said, lowering his voice and grinning, "do you ever smoke weed anymore?"

I laughed and said, "Not since I did with you." Then I remembered the night with Nick years ago. "Actually, I did once with a friend from NYU, Nick, who's still a close friend." Dean looked up at me, the unspoken question in his eyes, and I felt compelled to add, "Just a friend. Nick. Actually, he's been a godsend for both Lark and me. He spent time with Lark when she was young; she loves him."

Dean put his elbows on the table, laced his fingers together, and lowered his head to rub his lips across his knuckles. I saw his jaw muscles clench and unclench. I wondered what I had unleashed and sipped at my wine, waiting. After several minutes he said quietly, "I should say I'm glad that Lark's had your friend as a father figure, but I'm surprised by how I feel like I've just been impaled with a fence post." He swore under his breath and then looked at me in apology. I pressed my lips together and nodded, trying to beam understanding from my eyes. "I should have been the one spending time with her," he said.

The server approached smiling cautiously. "Your dinner will be here shortly."

"Thank you," I answered. Dean ordered another bottle of wine. Tipping the rest of the first bottle into our glasses, he asked, "And Lark is close to your father?"

"Oh yes. She and her Grandpa Hank have always been close. Dad is my rock. I couldn't have made it all those years as a single mother without him and Mother."

"I'm so sorry, Robin," he said, his eyes suffused with sadness. "I'd give anything if I could have been there for … both of you."

"I know," I managed and squeezed his arm. The waiter arrived with our entrées then, and we tucked into them in silence, reflecting on the devastating events that had passed through our lives like a natural disaster.

Dean ate several bites of his pasta and moaned with pleasure at the flavor of the duck. "This is seriously good," he said and smiled again. A group of women passed our table on their way out of the restaurant, and I noted two of them noticing Dean. Without a doubt the man was stare worthy.

A mother and teenaged son in a Rolling Stones T-shirt with the big red lips and tongue were being seated at the next table. Regarding them for a moment, Dean said, "I meant to tell you … I told my mother about your call and about Lark. She boo-hooed, Robin, especially when I said that you had named the baby after her."

"Awww, Dean." My eyes stung with tears. "I'm glad she was touched. I would love to meet your mom. I know that she must feel terribly hurt too, about being separated from her grandchild."

"She told me about the time you called when I was engaged to Victoria. I know you tried to tell me about Lark then … but I can see that you wouldn't have felt right telling Mom about Lark without telling me about her first." I nodded sadly in acknowledgement. We returned to our plates and shared a bite of each other's dishes.

I put my hand over Dean's on the white tablecloth. His skin was very warm. He put down his fork and looked at me. I asked, "Can we agree to try not to beat ourselves up anymore about the past? About what we can't change?"

He put his other hand on top of mine. "Yeah," he sighed. When he leaned to kiss my cheek, my head reeled. We had connected emotionally, and the feel of his lips on my skin left me dizzy.

Mopping up sauce from his plate with a last piece of pasta and savoring it for a moment, Dean looked at me again. "Do you date much?" I told him about my few bad dating experiences and about Greg.

"What about you?" I asked. Dean told me that he had dated a few years after Victoria's death and then again recently but hadn't found anyone he wanted to spend his life with. My heart swelled with hope. The waiter appeared then to clear away our plates, and we declined his offer of coffee and dessert. We sipped the last of the wine.

"Thank you, Dean. I enjoyed that so much," I said as he paid the bill.

As we rose to leave, Dean took the wrap from the back of my chair and dropped it over my shoulders like a blessing. As I pulled my hair from under it, he said, "Your hair still looks the same." My mind's eye flashed back to leaning over Dean in my bed, my hair spilling around us. I had to steel myself to walk through the restaurant gracefully.

Outside, I asked casually, "Want to share a cab?" We waited for one to appear, each lost in our own thoughts again, Dean's hands in his pockets. The early spring night had cooled. I pulled my pashmina closer. In the cab, Dean's solid thigh pressed against mine, and electricity leaped between us like lightning between clouds. But we talked of inconsequential things, New York City versus life in a small college town.

I asked Dean to come in for a nightcap. He said he had to get up early to prepare for a presentation the next morning but looked forward to seeing my home the next evening. "Thank you for having dinner with me," he said. "It was terrific."

He leaned in, his eyes on my mouth, but froze there. His eyes moved up to meet mine. Mesmerized, I answered the unspoken question and inclined my face slightly. I closed my eyes as he kissed my lips, a searching kiss. I noticed his scent that I thought I'd forgotten, and another rush of memory rolled over me like so much surf. My hands clung to Dean's elbows as he held my face in his hands. Then he released me and stepped back, nodding once. "See you tomorrow night, Robin Hamilton," he said.

As I turned the key in the lock, I was breathing as heavily as if I'd run back from the restaurant. Dean waved once and moved off down the sidewalk toward his hotel.

I spent the next day at the office preparing contracts, meeting with two young couples closing on their new homes, and watching the clock on my computer as if I were afraid it would steal something from my desk. I left the office at four to join Lark at my house. She had shopped for the ingredients for our meal and was already preparing the chicken for the oven. She looked young and lovely in one of my aprons over a heather-colored sweater and jeans, her hair pulled back from her face in a half ponytail. Excited myself, I hugged her and hurried upstairs to freshen up. I pulled on jeans and chose an emerald-green silk blouse that I knew accentuated my eyes and a creamy cardigan. *This is Lark's night, Robin,* I reminded myself.

Downstairs I helped Lark prepare the salad. The chicken was in the oven, and Lark had chopped the vegetables. I whisked together my special dressing, put it into the refrigerator to chill, and tore radicchio and romaine for the salad. Walking back into the living room, I saw that Lark had set the dining table with a bright blue-and-yellow Provencal tablecloth and napkins. "Where did *those* come from?" I asked, smiling my approval.

"Impulse buy." She grinned. "I saw them in the window at Williams-Sonoma on Fifty-Ninth and couldn't resist. I thought they would look nice for our French meal." She regarded the table. "Doesn't it look spectacular?"

"It looks wonderful." I admired the flowers she had placed in my French white soup tureen. "And what a good idea to pair daisies and lavender. You have a great eye, darling." We set three places with my plain white plates over natural rattan chargers, and Lark added my cobalt water goblets and casual stainless flatware. We stood back admiring our work with the scrutiny of art appraisers.

"My ... father ... is going to be sitting right there," Lark said, her gray eyes large and dark. "Mom, he'll like me, right?" She sounded as she had when she was twelve.

"Oh, Lark, how could he not?" I said hugging her. I looked over her shoulder at the old clock on the mantle. "And he'll be here in precisely nineteen minutes." That sent her scurrying back to the kitchen. The night had turned chilly, so I lit the fire I had laid just in case. I put the bottle of scotch, three glasses, and a plate of the pâté and crackers that Lark had bought on a black tole tray, carried it to the coffee table, and plumped the cushions. I tried to picture Dean in my home. I pushed play on the CD player, and the French soundtrack from the movie *Something's Gotta Give* spilled from the speakers like blown kisses.

The doorbell rang at exactly six thirty, as Lark was pouring water into the goblets. She took a deep breath and whipped off the apron, drying her hands on it. I smiled at her reassuringly. "Do you want me to get the door?" I asked.

"Yes, please!" she said. I opened the door to the handsome, smiling man holding a sheaf of yellow-and-red parrot tulips, as riotous as a parade.

"How beautiful! Thank you."

He stepped inside, smiling nervously, and then noticed Lark standing by the table. "You're Lark," he said evenly and walked toward her. The three of us stood together for a moment, smiling, frozen like a tableau in the Museum of Natural History: *A Family*.

I said simply, "Lark, this is Dean Falconer."

She had been holding her breath and let it out. "Hello, Dean, it's nice to finally meet you."

Dean's eyes were the same polished gray as his daughter's. He extended his hand to her. She extended hers, but instead of shaking it, Dean took it between both of his for a moment, looking down at it and then into her face. Choked with emotion, he said, "My daughter." They stood smiling shyly at each other, looking so much alike that I burst into happy tears. We all laughed in relief, and I swiped at my cheeks. I invited Dean to help himself to a drink and slipped into the kitchen to put the tulips in water. I stood, my back against the counter, hugged myself around the shoulders, and bowed my head. *Thank you, God.*

Dean and Lark were sitting on one section of the sofa, spreading crackers with the pâté. Remarking on their beauty again, I placed the flowers on the coffee table next to the appetizers and settled into the sofa to study Dean. More casual this evening, he was wearing a tweedy brown blazer over a denim shirt. He leaned forward, forearms on his knees, hands clasped loosely together—a posture I still recognized. The swell of belly that pushed against the shirt above his belt heartened me. The few little imperfections

261

I'd noticed only served to make him more attractive. Lustful thoughts were springing up again like spring jonquils. I took off my sweater and laid it over the arm of the sofa.

"Wow, what a nice bottle of scotch," said Dean.

"Well, I splurged … for tonight." I grinned.

"Lucky for me." He poured some of the golden liquid into each glass. We all took a sip, agreeing it was excellent. Dean asked Lark about her work. I excused myself, popped a cracker into my mouth, and returned to the kitchen to put the quinoa on to boil and the vegetables into the oven. When I returned, Dean was telling Lark about his career as an architect as Eartha Kitt belted out "C'est Si Bon." Indeed. It was very good.

When the oven timer signaled the chicken ready, Lark rose to go to the kitchen. Dean and I were alone for the first time. Eyes glistening, he said, "Robin, she's a beauty. So intelligent and poised."

"Yes, she is," I agreed happily.

"Thank you," he said simply, shaking his head in amazement, "for the … incredible job you did raising her." He pulled a monogrammed white handkerchief from his pocket. "I can't imagine … I know how hard you must have worked." He blew his nose quietly and pocketed the handkerchief.

"It was all worth it," I said as Lark reappeared with the platter of golden chicken and placed it on the table. Dean and I watched her movements, deft and economical, graceful. I hopped up to help bring the other dishes to the table, and we sat down to dinner.

"Dean, will you pour the wine?" I asked.

"I'd like to ask a blessing first if I may," he said humbly, looking from Lark to me. We smiled and nodded, touched. Dean bowed his head and began, "Dear Lord, thank you for this delicious meal and the hands that prepared it. Thank you ... for this wonderful young woman, the daughter you gave us, and for bringing us all together. Amen."

"Amen," Lark and I said together.

Dean sniffed, took the wine bottle, and filled our glasses. Raising his glass, he said, "To Robin and Lark." Lark and I smiled, and we all clinked glasses.

Then Lark surprised me by raising her glass again. She added solemnly, "To family."

"To family," Dean and I echoed, eyes bright with tears again.

Louis Armstrong's distinctive falsetto filled the room with "La Vie en Rose" as we began to eat. The simple meal was delicious, Lark's chicken moist and tender. The conversation flowed comfortably, allaying my worries about awkward pauses. I mostly listened quietly, letting Dean and Lark initiate the majority of the conversation, delighting in watching them together. Lark told her father about the accident she had been in senior year of high school and then about her college days. Dean talked about his family. "You have a grandmother and aunts, you know, Lark." He sipped his wine thoughtfully and suddenly said, "I have a great idea." He wiped his mouth with his napkin. "What do you think about coming to Virginia this summer for a couple of weeks? I know you have summers off from teaching, Lark. Could you take some time off, Robin?"

Lark and I looked at each other. She said, "Sure … I would love that actually. I could probably block out my schedule at the studio too."

I took a bite of chicken and chewed it thoughtfully, planning ahead, and then took a sip of water. "I think I could make that work too. I suppose we could hire a temp, an interim paralegal to help John and Morgan. And God knows I have vacation time I haven't taken."

Lark excused herself to fetch the dessert and returned brandishing the prettily presented trifle dish. "That's impressive," Dean said appreciatively. Lark spooned the dessert into my little Italian dessert dishes as Dean continued, "I can't wait for you both to meet my mother and sisters … and see Villeneuve. There are so many things to do and see around Charlottesville too. I can take you to the Shenandoah National Forest—it's gorgeous—and to some world-class vineyards. Believe it or not, there are over fifty in the area." He waggled his glass.

"Really?" I asked, astonished.

"People in Virginia are *serious* about their wines. They say Napa is for auto parts." Lark and I laughed.

"We have wonderful restaurants and all the shopping you could want."

Lark and I sipped at our wine, listening with enjoyment. I winked at her across the table.

"I built my house and a two-bedroom guesthouse behind it. It would be comfortable and private for you. It's nice," he said, sounding like a kid talking about Disneyland.

"Sold," Lark said, spooning berries into her mouth.

"I guess that pretty much settles it," I said.

"What month would you want us? Late August is out for me because of in-service and back-to-school stuff. But June or July would work," Lark said.

Dean had a dab of whipped cream in one corner of his mouth, and I wanted to blot it with my napkin ... or lick it off.

"We could come the second week in June," Lark said. "That would give me time to button everything up at school and then get packed. Mom? Would you be able to work it out then?"

I was astonished at how casually we were planning it all. "I'll talk to John this week about it." I was as excited as they were. That was only about ten weeks away. "This was superb by the way, Lark Bird," I said, taking another bite of my dessert.

Dean grinned, cocking his head at the expression. "Lark Bird?" Lark told him about the nicknames we had given each other when she was a little girl. He was leaning back in his chair enjoying himself. "I love it," he said.

He finished his dessert, scraping at the last of the whipped cream with his spoon. "Yum. Well, between now and June, may I call you both?"

"Sure, and we could Skype," Lark said. "Do you know about Skype, Dean?"

"I know about it but haven't done it. I'm a pretty quick learner though." He grinned.

"I could call you from school and have my kids meet you. They would love it," she said, the idea exciting her. "And you could even tell them what it's like to live on a farm. Most of my kids have never been out of the city."

"Cool. That sounds like fun. Let's do it," Dean said enthusiastically.

I sipped the last of my wine, my heart full again as I watched them. I rose and carried the dishes into the kitchen and spooned some decaf into the French press. Then I carried the pot and three cups into the living room. We talked for a while, enjoying the coffee, and then Dean leaned forward, his hands on his knees and said he had an early flight the next morning and should get going. Lark and I walked him to the door, and as he turned to her, she held out her arms to him. He smiled tremulously, and they embraced for the first time.

"Call you soon, Robin?" he asked me then.

"I'll look forward to it," I said.

"Thank you, for one of the most wonderful evenings I've ever had," Dean said, looking from me to Lark. "The food and drink were superb and the company first rate." As I moved to open the door, he turned to me and pulled me into a brief hug. "Talk to you soon," he said to Lark. He looked at me again and mouthed a silent, "Thank you."

CHAPTER
21

Robin

2013

Lark and I had sat aboard the suffocating commuter jet on
the runway for almost an hour, but we got excited all over again
as the plane finally lifted off. Lark was in a doubly celebratory
mood; school was out, her faculty checkout list complete. "I think a
glass of champagne is in order," she said, fanning her face with an
airsickness bag.

My partner John (who was completely supportive of my
journey) and I had hired Morgan's friend Cory, an NYU law
student, as a summer intern who would help handle the workload
while I was away. I would follow John's parting advice and not
worry about a thing. A flight attendant who looked as if she had a
terminal case of jet lag served us tepid champagne in plastic cups.
"To Villeneuve," Lark said, grinning as she touched her rim to
mine. We grimaced around our first sips of the cheap airline stuff
and wrinkled our noses at each other. *Oh well.*

Lark leaned her seat back and opened a fat, juicy *InStyle* magazine, thumbing pleasurably through pages of a periodical that for a change weren't related to education. I grinned as I watched her begin reading at the back. I always read a magazine from back to front too. I leaned back and breathed deeply, thinking about Dean and the weeks to come. Was this thing completely insane? Six months ago it would have been inconceivable. From time to time I looked over at the glossy pages of stick-figure celebrities in red-carpet attire.

Lark looked up, interrupting my reverie, and caught me off guard. "Dean is attractive for his age, don't you think?" I feigned an offended face at the age remark. "You know what I mean," she said. "You two *have* been flirting, haven't you?"

Indeed, we had been "flirting." Dean and I had talked many times the past few weeks. The last conversation had lasted into the wee hours and had left me loose-boned and wriggling with pleasure under my covers. In physical science, the law of conservation of energy states that energy can never be created or destroyed but is conserved over *time*. The inherent magnetic field that had encompassed Dean and me in 1977 was still powerful. How I loved his southern baritone curling into my ear again.

"Ye-ess, you could say that," I answered Lark with a small smile.

She laughed and squeezed my hand on the armrest. "I'm glad, Mom."

I slipped my earbuds in and queued up my playlist. The attraction wasn't *entirely* physical; Dean and I truly liked one another. As before, we never ran out of things to talk about. We talked of historical events, cultural trends, music, and life events from the three decades we hadn't shared together. Some of those talks were bittersweet, tinged with sadness. Of course now we could talk about Lark. That I would have the pleasure of telling him the story of her childhood—a narration that could literally take the rest of our years—was a small semblance of recompense for all we'd forfeited. My stomach gave a fishlike leap: I would be with him again in a couple of hours. I pushed the play button on the Eagles' latest, *Long Road out of Eden*. At Richmond, Lark and I would rent a car and drive an hour west to Keswick and on to Villeneuve. If the drive was smooth, we should arrive at the farm around four o'clock, in time to freshen up before dinner. Mrs. "Please call me Laurel" Falconer had invited us for dinner at the main house. Dean's sisters and their husbands, who lived in Charlottesville, were driving out to join us. I felt a little nervous at the prospect of their scrutiny, but Dean assured me they would be supportive.

Lark dozed, her mouth slack, and her head fell to my shoulder. *My precious girl.* I reflected on what Lark had told me of her conversations with her father. Getting to know one another, they'd found that some of her affinities reflected Dean's. It brought to mind studies of twins who were separated at birth and met later in life to learn they had taken similar paths. Dean's genes had contributed to Lark's interests and attitudes in seemingly random ways: they had strong aversions to the scent of rosemary and of turmeric, were gifted spellers (each had won a spelling bee in their sixth-grade years), threw up if they saw someone else getting sick, and made an almost identical funny sound when they sneezed.

Lark and Dean had executed the Skype session with her third graders the last week of school. Dean had worked up a special PowerPoint presentation for the children with photographs, painting a picture for them of life on a horse farm. The Q&A period at the end had been lively and funny. Dean had loved it and had been as proud as a gamecock to be introduced as Lark's father. The children had made construction-paper thank-you cards, with drawings of horses and dogs on them, and Lark had mailed them to her father.

Everything I'd witnessed between the two of them had convinced me that Dean would have been the father I'd dreamed. I began to think about the future and what Dean would be like as grandfather to Lark's children. Without a doubt I now knew he would want to be involved in their lives. I closed my eyes and pictured Dean leading a delighted child around on horseback in the sunshine, Lark looking on with contentment from beneath the shade of a great tree, Ben's arm around her waist. A baby a few rows behind us began to shriek, and I laughed to myself. But where did I fit in this fantasy of mine? Would I be there as well? And in what capacity? Lark woke abruptly and stretched, her limbs as supple as a lizard's. "What time is it?" she asked, crinkling her nose and yawning deeply. "Did I really sleep?"

I peered at my watch. "We should be landing in ... twenty-five, no, twenty-seven minutes." I was wearing black leggings, a tunic, my double-strand turquoise necklace, and black flats. Lark was pretty in black shorts, an Indian cotton print blouse, red chandelier earrings, and silver sandals. Dean had asked us to stay until after the Fourth of July celebration, and we had packed accordingly. The airline had zinged us for an extra hundred bucks for overweight bags. Dean had a pool, so Lark had bought a sleek new red suit before we'd left the city. I loathed the thought of making an appearance in a bathing suit, especially in front of Dean. I didn't even own one.

As the plane touched down, Lark and I groped underneath and above, gathering our belongings and grinning like fools with excitement. We headed to baggage claim only to spend fifteen frustrating minutes in line at an understaffed rental car desk. Finally we schlepped our bags in the June heat to a particularly hideous beige Dodge Avenger. So much for arriving in style.

The Central Virginia countryside was beautiful, pastoral: rolling hills and valleys dotted with contented black-and-white cows and sleek horses. The sunlight was more luminous here. It dappled the forest floor through white bark and evergreens. We turned off Richmond Road at Keswick and, according to our GPS device, onto the road that would take us to Villeneuve. Lark and I were enchanted by stately old houses on beautiful farms with a romantic lexicon of names that conjured images of the earth, soil, and trees of the region: Tall Pines, Willow Brook Farm, Fox's Earth. We passed two vineyards, antique shop fronts, and a great old stone church. And at last ... among split rail fences and weather-smoothed rock walls was our destination. A small, white oval sign made of wood and rimmed in gold swung gently from an iron post: Villeneuve, established 1877.

Lark swung the car onto the gray graveled drive bordered by white fences and sprawling oak trees. *So this is Dean's world!* My stomach flipped again. To our left and right as the car crunched along were manicured paddocks of green, green grass bisected at intervals by dark wooden horse jumps. I lowered my window to breathe it in. "Wonder where the horses are," I murmured to Lark. Until then, neither of us had spoken, as if fearing to break some alchemy. We climbed a gentle mound, and there settled elegantly atop the rise was the main house, a gracious and modest old Georgian with twin chimneys. "How lovely!" I breathed.

Lark braked and stared. *"Wow,* right?" The butter-yellow stucco with multipaned windows and black shutters seemed to preen for us in the late-afternoon sun. A columned portico topped with a Chinese Chippendale railing sheltered the small front porch and drew the eye to the glossy black front door flanked by red geraniums in concrete urns. And all around, massive oaks with twisty, gnarled limbs shaded the house. Their leaves shimmered faintly in the summer breeze as Lark veered smoothly around the circular drive and came to a stop. Tandem dogs appeared from around the house. We looked to the door and around but saw no one about. We giggled, debating whether or not the dogs would find a couple of New Yorkers too tough for an afternoon treat.

Then a figure stepped from beneath one of the oaks, raising a hand in greeting, and called to the dogs. My heart inched up my throat as I recognized Dean's face under a University of Virginia ball cap. He was in faded jeans and a T-shirt. From the deep shadows I saw a broad smile stretch itself across his tanned face. Lark and I opened our doors and stepped onto the drive, the jagged gravel as big as eggs. This was not a place for heels. "Welcome to Villeneuve, ladies!" Dean said.

"Dad!" Lark called. Never in her life until that moment had I heard my daughter say the word. The endearment on her lips was palpable and tinged with promise. My nose stung with tears. Dean stepped toward her, and they embraced. The dogs circled, sniffing us out and wagging their broad tails.

"Robin, you're here," Dean said, moving to hug me too. As our bodies touched, I was suffused with the feeling of coming home and something exotic and unexplored at the same time. I felt Lark's eyes on us behind her big Kate Spade sunglasses.

"I know ... I can't believe it." I grinned. "The farm is spectacular, Dean."

"Just wait; Villeneuve's pretty seductive. It will get into your blood." He grinned. My stomach rippled again at the word *seductive*. "These savage beasts are Charlotte," he said, indicating the smaller of the dogs, a chocolate Labrador retriever, "and Hudson." Hearing his name, the great glossy black Lab seemed to grin himself and nudged Dean's leg for a petting.

"Hello, sweeties," I said, bending to pet Charlotte. She bathed my hand with her pink tongue.

Dean said, "Careful, her breath could knock a buzzard off a dead skunk." Lark and I hooted. "Come on in, girls. We'll get your bags to the guesthouse later. Mom can't wait to meet you." We were still giggling as we entered a small, stately foyer hung with colonial-era portraits. Just ahead were stairs of gleaming old wood, a graceful curving bannister. To the right a small dining room seemed stuffed with a great cherry table and chairs, more oils, and handsome English antiques. And to the left was a living room or parlor with deep, comfortable chairs, a great fireplace, and many shelves lined with books that had been read.

From the rear of the house a woman approached. Petite, sturdy, and smiling, with a cap of lustrous gray curls, she said in a cultured southern voice, "Welcome. I'm Laurel Falconer."

Dean said, "Mother, I'd like you to meet Robin Hamilton."

Laurel took my hands in between hers and leaned to kiss my cheek. "Hello, Robin."

"And this is Lark." Dean was grinning like Howdy Doody.

Laurel turned to Lark and held out both arms. "Lark, my beautiful granddaughter. At last." She pulled Lark into a warm embrace and then stood back again and gazed at her, tears darkening her lashes. "You are the image of your aunt Leslie."

"You really are," Dean said happily.

"Really?" Lark replied, pleased.

"You'll meet her tonight … *and* the rest of the family," Laurel said. "Come on, Robin, Lark, you must be parched."

Dean inclined his arm toward the kitchen and then followed me down the hall.

The kitchen was the heart of the old house. Gleaming copper pots and sheaves of dried herbs and flowers hung above a large central island, and everywhere were touches of vibrant color— plaid curtains, art, and family photographs. In the breakfast area a wooden church pew bracketed one wall and served as seating for the rustic farm table, a copse of mismatched wooden chairs on the other side. A pair of comfortable old wing chairs dressed down in a neutral duck fabric sat in one corner. The table between them was scattered with mail, reading glasses, a leather journal, books, and pens, telling me this was where the lady of the house spent most of her time. The large modern windows afforded her a generous view of the rear of the farm. "What a wonderful, cozy room," I said.

Lark and I perched on stools at the island as Laurel pulled a metal pitcher of iced tea from the stainless steel refrigerator. While Lark talked with Laurel about her teaching career, I watched Dean repair his mother's leaky sink sprayer as if he were performing Macbeth in the nude. I downed a second glass of iced tea. Laurel followed my gaze. "Dean's so busy; I have to snare him when I can." She winked at me.

We chatted about the home and its history. Dean told us the house had originally been built in 1877 and had been remodeled three times, twice in the forty years the Falconers had owned it. A powder room and laundry/mudroom had been added off the kitchen, and other structural reinforcements and improvements had been made through the years, all without compromising the integrity of the original house. Dean had designed the flagstone terraces in the backyard for entertaining. Laurel told us that a few of the enormous post oaks around the house were reputed to be at least 270 years old, around since the time "Mr. Jefferson" had been president. "The name of Thomas Jefferson is always spoken with reverence in the Charlottesville area," she said with a grin. "You may know that his home is here. Monticello."

"I'd love to see Monticello," I said.

"I would too," Lark said.

"Dean's a great tour guide," she said smiling at her son. "Now if you girls would like to rest and unpack, we'll have dinner here about seven," Laurel said.

"Thank you, I think we would." I looked to Lark, who nodded her agreement. "We're looking forward to dinner and meeting everyone. Thanks so much for your hospitality, Laurel," I said.

"It is *our* pleasure; we are just thrilled to have you here," she said. "Dean will take you back to the guesthouse. Please let me know if there's anything you need during your stay." Her eyes glistened again as she looked from me to Lark. "I'm looking forward to a nice long visit."

"Another Jeep," I commented to Dean as we walked out to the driveway.

"It's the only make of car I've ever driven; they're good cars. Ride with me, Robin?" Unlike the basic green one I remembered, this model was tricked out with leather, heated seats, a sunroof, and all the extras. Lark followed us in our rental car around the back of the house, and we saw the barn for the first time.

"Where are all the horses?" I asked.

"In the heat of the day they're in the barn, but the help will be turning them out in a few minutes to graze the paddocks. We'll go meet the horses in the morning. My plan is to *ease* you into the saddle." He grinned. About fifty yards back, Dean's home, also Georgian in style, nestled into the landscape of oak and towering pine. "I designed and built my place twenty years ago. I hope you like it," he said shyly.

"Dean," I said, full of pride for him, "you're an architect." Then I felt like a fool. "I mean … you know what I mean." He laughed softly, and I said, "I'm happy that you have the career you wanted and are obviously successful. I knew you had a gift."

"I knew what you meant." He smiled. "Thank you. That means a lot to me." He drove around the side of the house to a parking pad. Lark nosed the awful rental car in next to his Jeep. A large pool surrounded by a black iron fence shimmered in the sunlight between his house and the guesthouse, a low-slung one-story bungalow.

"This is fabulous," I said.

"I'm … so happy you're here," he said, turning to look into my eyes. I wanted so much to kiss him then, but Lark was waiting. Dean opened the door of the guesthouse. One large room, a kitchen/sitting area, was flanked on either side by a bedroom and bath. The space was well appointed but spare.

"This is so nice," Lark said. "We'll be really comfy here."

He left us then, and I watched him walk back to his house. He stopped and appeared to fish something from the pool and then disappeared through french doors at the back of his house. I loved the way the man moved.

Lark was already staking a claim on a room. Each room had a queen-sized bed, a chest of drawers, and a roomy closet with padded hangers. The bathrooms had glassed showers and deep soaking tubs. In the well-stocked kitchen, I discovered that someone had filled the refrigerator with cold wine, beer, bottled water, and fresh fruit. What luxury! It was as welcoming as a four-star bed-and-breakfast cottage.

Lark snared a bottle of water and said she was going to do a half hour of yoga practice. "C'mon, Mom, we've been sitting all day. You'll feel great." Consulting my watch, I saw that she was right. I'd still have an hour afterward to take a soak and dress for the evening.

Freshly stretched, relaxed, and bathed, Lark and I walked to Dean's. "This pool is fab!" Lark said as we skirted it. The gunite bottom was as dark as a deep, still pond, the decking formed of natural stone. It seemed to belong somewhere in the French countryside. I wouldn't have been surprised to find topless sunbathers reclining languidly at its perimeter. We knocked on Dean's back door. He appeared wiping his hands on a bar towel.

"Come in, come in," he said heartily. Most of the downstairs was occupied by one huge living space with a fireplace—large enough to roast a pig in—a group of chairs and sofas at one end, and a long open kitchen at the other. Lark and I exclaimed over the house and Dean's special pieces as we drifted through. Foxhunt prints on the walls and animal-patterned fabrics on the furniture reflected his interests and lifestyle. Dean had striped the white ceilings with dark wood beams.

Glass shelves above a well-equipped wet bar held jewel-toned glassware that Dean had collected during his travels. "What can I get you to drink, ladies?" he asked. I chose a glass of cold sauvignon blanc, and Lark, a craft beer. Lark and Dean talked about the breweries in the area and the one Dean wanted to take her to first. "Let's sit down," he said, indicating a grouping of comfy chairs. "So you're about to meet the sisters." Dean grinned. He prepared us. Interestingly, neither sister had had children. Lark was Laurel's first and only grandchild.

A few minutes before seven we walked the gravel drive and a path through a copse of fragrant pine and cypress to the main house. The dogs barked, announcing the arrival of the others. So Lark and I were introduced to Mary, Leslie, and their husbands, Robert and Warren, in the driveway for the first time. I immediately noticed the uncanny resemblance between Leslie and Lark. "Lark, it's like looking in the mirror … *twenty years ago*," Leslie marveled. Although Leslie colored her hair now, she said that Lark's shade was close to her and Dean's natural color. Leslie's eyes were large and, like Lark's, as gray as moonstones. Both sisters gave us hugs and told us they were happy to finally meet us. Amid the chatter we entered Laurel's house through the back door, and our noses sprang to attention at the spicy smell of meat sauce (sans rosemary for Dean and Lark) and garlic bread.

"Wait till you taste Mom's meat lasagna," Mary said with a grin. "It will make you happy to be alive." Mary was lean and willowy, green-eyed like her mother, with luxuriant red hair, a few shades lighter than Tee's. "Mom, where's the wine?" she called to Laurel, scanning the refrigerator without success.

"It's iced down with the beer in tubs in the mudroom. Y'all help yourselves!" Laurel called, bustling around and sliding on blue gingham oven mitts to take the lasagna out of the oven. "Leslie, dress that salad, please?"

Unaccustomed to large family gatherings and the booming voices of the hearty, back-slapping husbands, Lark seemed a little overwhelmed, as I was. When we assembled at the dining room table, Dean asked a sweet blessing, and everyone tucked into the meal. The conversation was easy, comfortable—if the Falconers were assessing us, it didn't feel that way. We learned that Mary had earned her veterinary degree years before but now worked exclusively with the Falconer animals. Both she and Leslie were responsible for training the horses, readying them to compete in what they termed "three-day events." Several times a year they took the horses to compete in regional and national competitions.

After coffee, everyone helped clear the table and stack the dishwasher and then drifted out to the back terrace. Robert and Dean carried the tub of beer out between them. Warren consulted his Weather Channel app. "Man, it's going to be ninety tomorrow." Dean suggested they all come swimming midafternoon. Warren and Mary said they would bring meat and "fixin's" and grill burgers.

I had been drained by journey and emotion, and my head felt too heavy to hold up, my neck a hollow dandelion stem. "I think I'd like to turn in for the night," I announced.

Dean set his beer can down and was on his feet. "I'll walk you back." His mother and sisters exchanged meaningful looks. Lark said she would stay and visit a while longer.

"Good night then, everyone," I said.

Dean and I walked off down the drive, a voluptuous moon lighting our path. The dogs ambled in our wake. As we reached the tree-lined path again, we were surrounded by fireflies— lightning bugs, Dean called them—their brief flickering like those of match strikes. "We used to catch 'em in jars when we were kids." Dean grinned at my puzzled look. "We used 'em for night-lights, city girl."

Hoots of laughter echoed from the main house. I recognized Lark's musical lilt and smiled thinking of her in the midst of her new family. After a moment Dean said, "They're all pulling for the two of us, you know. If I know my family, there's probably a bet going."

"Oh no!" I said, embarrassed but pleased. Our arms brushed as we walked the uneven ground. When Dean reached for my hand, my arms shivered with contentment. With the country sounds— the drone of cicadas, the wind through the trees, the occasional snort from the barn—I felt I might succumb to a sensory overdose. Sleep would sandbag me soon.

We had come to the pool between Dean's house and the guesthouse. "I'm looking forward to tomorrow," Dean murmured.

"I feel the same way."

"It feels like ... a dream. I can't believe you're really here at Villeneuve." At last he bent his head down to mine. The pads of his fingers were warm on my upper arms as he kissed my lips, once, twice, and again. "Sleep well, Robin Hamilton."

My head had begun to swim. "Yes," I said.

"I'll make breakfast for you and Lark ... about eight?"

"Night, Dean," I mumbled, turning the knob on the guesthouse door.

My last conscious thought when I'd slipped between cool sheets in my underwear was of Dean's kiss. The way our lips fit seamlessly together. The way their fusion seemed to glow like filament wire.

It was not until six o'clock that I woke again to the sounds of Lark—the inveterate early bird—moving about the kitchen, making coffee. I rose refreshed to join my daughter. She'd had fun learning more about the Falconers and was full of information and funny family anecdotes over coffee. She said that Dean had returned to the group after walking me back. "He was actually humming," Lark said grinning. Apparently he had looked sheepish as talk had abruptly died away and the family had regarded him. "Should I speculate about what's happening between the two of you," she asked, "or am I on a need-to-know basis?"

"*I* don't even know what's happening between the two of us," I said, drawing my shoulders up in a high shrug. Then I looked into my daughter's eyes. "But I *can* tell you, my darling, that I am unequivocally in love with Dean. Part of me may have never stopped loving him."

"Oh, Mom, I knew it."

"But I don't know what my loving him will mean … for the future. And I don't know what his feelings for *me* are now, other than …" I took a sip of coffee, fumbling for the word. "Lust." I blushed. "I know you and I don't talk this way … but after all … you *are* thirty-four."

"It's okay, Mom; you're entitled to lust," she said, topping up our mugs from the steaming carafe. "For the record I know that you slept with Nick on occasion too." She grinned.

"Laurel Olivia Hamilton! How did you know *that*?" I asked, truly shocked.

"It wasn't hard to miss the signs," she laughed.

"Well … *that's* certainly in the past. But, Lark, there's something else. I want you to know I've been feeling guilty."

"*Guilty?*" She raised her dark brows.

"Because this summer was supposed to be about you and your father."

"But I'm getting to know the family too at the same time." She smiled. "It … takes the pressure off feeling like I have to forge"— she rotated her hand in the air—"this … perfect relationship with Dad. It feels more *natural* in the context of other family. And

Mom," she said, covering my hand with hers, "I'm glad you love him."

I pulled her into a hug then, my heart brimful, until her phone chimed with a text. "It's Dean," she said with a grin. "Are we hungry?"

"Tell him we'll be right over."

Dean's formerly scrambled-egg breakfast repertoire now included bacon and homemade biscuits with Laurel's strawberry jam. *A man who makes homemade biscuits!* Lark and I ate with gusto, heaping praise on Dean's fuzzy head.

We trooped to the barn. The baying of hounds as we approached made the back of my neck prickle. "Those are just the foxhunting hounds," Dean said. "They're penned behind the barn. They're just *annoying* as hell, the way they howl, but completely harmless." The horses had been let out at dawn and were already back doing their thing in the barn.

"Exactly how *early* do you get up, Dean?" I asked.

He laughed shortly, "Early." The barn's interior was cool and dim, painted a dark green. The first stall was labeled King George. Dean leaned a brown arm on the bottom half of the dutch door. A blowing and snorting began as the horse left off eating hay to plod toward the door. "On the weekends, my barn manager, Billy, and I let them out about six, so we can clean the stalls, but the other days the help are here early. Billy lives in the apartment upstairs," he said, pointing to the ceiling. "You'll meet him next week—he's on vacation right now. Billy's in charge of the whole operation:

the horses, the dogs, and the physical property. We have a small crew that maintains the property. There's Justin, who's been with us since before Dad died, Dillon, and Andi. Dad always gave the help the weekends off, so I've carried on that tradition. They do an awesome job for us."

"*Here's* King George," he said as a large brown head with black mane poked curiously over the door, nostrils quivering in a nicker of greeting.

"He's a beauty. May I pet him?" Lark asked, holding out a tentative hand.

"Pet him up here on the nose, but hold your palm out … flat … and let him smell you first. *Then* you can scratch back here on his neck or high up here on the withers. You *like that*, don't you, George?" he said, stroking the horse. "He needs to get to know your smell."

As we petted King George, I blurted, "I love the way they smell … the whole barn smell. It's so … organic and leathery. Like a *really* expensive handbag." Dean laughed and touched my nose with a finger.

Lark moved toward the next stall. "Kirby," she called, reading the nameplate.

"George and Kirby are my foxhunters, the retired event horses. And across the hall here is one of our older mares, Trolley. She's the one I have in mind for *you* to ride."

"Well, hello, Trolley," I said, turning to regard a pretty chestnut mare with a lighter mane. "She's the one for you to get started on. Trolley's pretty unflappable, what we call a bombproof horse."

"*Bomb*proof?" I said. "That's too funny."

"Her color has always reminded me of your hair color," he said, reaching to slip a hand into my hair. "I've never forgotten it." Then he froze, embarrassed. Lark moved on to the next stall.

Dean stroked my neck with a thumb. Trolley nickered softly to be noticed again. I grinned and reached to let her smell my palm once more, rubbing her nose. I was charmed with the beautiful creature, though her size was a little overwhelming. "When's the first lesson?" I asked.

"Tomorrow morning. Lark!" he called to her down the barn. "The first lesson's tomorrow morning."

"I'm ready," she called. "Are you in, Mom?"

"I'm in if you're in." A great swollen gray tabby stalked into the barn, twitching her tail.

"And who's *this*?" Lark asked, squatting to stroke the length of her back.

"That's Sassy. She's about to have a new litter of kittens. The barn cats keep the vermin at bay. Let's see, there's Sassy ... Voltaire, and Penelope now. You'll see 'em around."

We moved on to the other horses: the resident studs, three-year-old stallions Cavalier and Frankly My Dear; a graceful palomino, Lady; four more chestnut broodmares, Martha, Pandora, Magnolia, and Missy, who was Mary's thirty-four-year-old mare; and a half dozen darling yearlings and untrained young foals. They were all so beautiful I couldn't decide which one I liked best. Mary and Leslie were working with the yearlings, teaching them "manners"—to lead quietly, wait, and stand tied. We stopped to watch awhile. "Which horse will I ride?" Lark asked Dean.

"I'm going to put you on Lady. You'll be a natural … It's in your blood after all," he said grinning and slipped an easy arm around her shoulders as we walked back to the house. Lark's look of transparent pleasure made me so happy.

Later that afternoon, the gang arrived for the pool party. Lark, looking lithe and strong in her new red suit, draped a towel over a chaise and sat to rub sunscreen into her fair skin. Wearing a short black A-line linen dress and wide-brimmed straw hat against the sun, I sat down on the side of the pool and plunged my feet into the cool water. The Falconer women wore summery floral sundresses or shorts over printed swimsuits. In my black, I was a crow in a field of summer flowers. *An albino crow,* I thought wryly, peering down at my arms and legs.

Dean and the other men were in the pool talking and drinking from cans of beer. Dean swam to the deep end and took my ankles. He floated and squinted lazily up at me against the sun. He wore a pair of aqua trunks, his shoulders slightly sunburned, his chest and the tender underside of his throat pale. "Where's your suit, pretty lady?" he asked.

"Bring me a beer, Sister!" Leslie yelled to Mary, who was bending over the ice chest. "It's hotter than the hinges of hell!"

"I didn't bring a suit. The only time I appear in one is on the private beach at my dad's," I said prissily. Then I heard myself. "I just don't feel comfortable in one."

He smiled a lazy-lidded smile. "You're kidding me; your body was made for a bathing suit." His gaze moved over me like oil, settling into my curves.

He still hasn't seen my body, I thought, dubious. Still holding my ankles, he pulled his body closer. He was aroused.

"Dean!" I gasped, quickly scanning the pool to see if anybody was watching. Lark had disappeared into the little pool-house bathroom. The husbands were busy planning a cannonball contest. Laurel and Leslie watched them, smirks on their tanned faces, shaking their heads in a "boys will be boys" way.

"Let's play some volleyball!" Mary called from the pool steps, hands planted on the hips of a vibrant Lilly Pulitzer suit that contrasted with her tan and her big white sunglasses. Dean turned to the group at her words, and the spell broke. Warren and Leslie stretched a net across the expanse of the pool. I saw that Lark was going to play too and rose to take her chair, a better vantage point to watch the game. Laurel pulled up a chair to sit beside me.

"Hi, Laurel," I said. "What a wonderful place you all have here."

"*Are* you having fun? I want you to like it here."

290

"I am. This is so relaxing." I smiled warmly at her.

"You have beautiful skin; you've been smart to stay out of the sun," she said. Her crinkly skin, brown as a berry, was patchy all over with dark spots. We talked quietly amid sprays of water and shouts from the pool. Laurel expressed regret for the years that we all had lost but told me she was grateful that Lark and I had come back into their lives. I retrieved an errant ball and threw it back to Rob. Then I looked at Dean's mother and saw something of his face in hers. It seemed the right time to say what was on my heart. "Laurel, I hope you'll forgive me for not telling you about Lark all those years ago."

She patted my hand. "I learned a long time ago not to dwell on the past. It's a dangerous preoccupation," she mused, gazing across the apron to her granddaughter in the pool. "I live in the present now." She grinned at me then and tipped me a wink. "It looks pretty good from where I sit." We regarded Lark and Dean standing next to each other in the water. They gave each other an exultant high five, laughing. "I don't know when I've seen Dean happier," Laurel said. And after a moment, she said, "Thank you, Robin." I smiled, not trusting my voice, my throat working against tears. Then she put her hands on her leathery knees and pushed herself to her feet. "Would you like a soda or a beer?" I asked for a beer, and she went to the ice chest to retrieve beers for both of us.

The game over, Leslie yelled to her husband, "Warren! We need more beer!" Mary, Dean, and Lark padded over to us laughing and shaking their limbs like big wet dogs.

"That was fun," said Mary, drying her sunglasses on a towel. "Lark, you play well."

"I played a little in high school." Lark smiled, squeezing out her ponytail with both hands.

Hudson and Charlotte had begun barking at something. An elegant Range Rover crunched around the side of Dean's house, nosed into the parking pad next to the Avenger, and beeped its horn twice in greeting. Dean looked up. "James is here!" And to me he said, "He's my partner. You remember my friend James from Georgetown."

"*He's* your *partner*?" I was astonished. I did remember James. The last party Dean and I had attended together—the night our only photograph together had been taken—had been at James's apartment.

"Yep." Dean smiled, looking toward the gate. "I lured him away from the big city fifteen years ago when business took off. He and his wife, Jill, moved down here from DC. James is one talented architect." Dean stood, removing his sunglasses, to greet the couple as they stepped inside amid calls of "James!" and "Jilly!" from the others.

Dean kissed Jill's cheek and ushered the couple over to meet me. "Robin Hamilton, I'd like you to meet Jill Culpepper. And you remember James." We exchanged greetings.

James remembered me and said, "You're just as good lookin' as you were thirty years ago." He hadn't done anything about the quirky gap between his teeth, but it still suited him. The shoulder-length hair I remembered was almost as short as Dean's now.

Jill was plump with masses of blonde hair and a beauty queen smile, and Laurel said, "Jill was a contestant in the Miss Virginia pageant back in the day."

"*Way* back in the day," Jill laughed. I liked her immediately. "Robin, it's nice to know you. I've been hearing about you for the last month. We want to have you and Dean over for dinner."

Across the pool Lark and Leslie were lying on chaises again, deep in conversation, another beer screwed into Leslie's fist. "Lark, come meet my partner and his wife," Dean called.

Jill and James got into the water. I admired Jill's skirted swimsuit. Maybe I could get one like that. Leslie called, "We need music, peeps!" and sashayed, dripping, into the pool house. Dean sat next to me on the side, our feet in the water. Momentarily "Hotel California" began to tumble from the speakers. Leslie reappeared and saucily announced, "Some mood music for Robin and Dean! We *all* know how they met." Leslie abruptly crumpled and fell hard on her bottom, her eyes wide.

"My sister's had one too many," Dean murmured. "Don't pay her any attention." I felt the eyes of the others on us as Laurel swam over.

"Robin, we have to get you a bathing suit. Aren't you burning up?" she asked. I was grateful to her for running interference.

Mary climbed the ladder from the shallow end. "Let's go get the burgers and fixin's," she said, pulling her blushing sister to her feet. "I'm positively ravenous."

Soon the air was infused with the smell of grilling meat. The dogs appeared at the fence hoping to find a soft touch among the guests. Laurel, in a white terry cover-up, flip-flopped to the fence. "Now you pups have already had your dinner. Yes you have," she said to them in baby talk. Dean and I walked over to help with the spread. Mary had made huge dishes of baked potato salad and slaw and a large pan of baked beans. We sat casually around the deck, eating and talking. *It would be fun being part of a big family like this,* I thought and then realized I already was, at least by proxy.

The next morning, my phone chimed with a text message at seven o'clock. I was barely awake. It was Dean. "Morning, sleeping beauty," it read. "Ready for the riding lesson? Would have let you sleep but couldn't wait any longer. Meet me at the barn ASAP."

I grinned and typed, "Be right there." I stretched and kicked aside the covers. I padded through the house to see if Lark was up. She wasn't in her bed.

"Lark Bird?" She wasn't in the bathroom, but all of her gear was. I rolled my eyes. Despite her scrupulous personal care and appearance, Lark had always kept the messiest room, the floor perpetually strewn with clothes and belongings. I had finally given up on making her straighten it when she was in high school. One fewer battle.

Dean had told me to wear jeans for riding and that there was sure to be a pair of one of his sisters' paddock boots to fit me at the barn. I pulled my hair into a ponytail, slid my feet into flip-flops, snared a granola bar from the kitchen and headed for the barn.

Entering the gloom of the barn from the bright sunlight, I blinked and saw my missing daughter stepping from a stall door, pulling an Amazon length of green hose behind her. I stooped to pet Charlotte, who had appeared behind me and nudged my leg. "There's my missing daughter. I *wondered* where you were."

Lark turned, disheveled and thrilled. Hay clung to her water-splashed T-shirt and jeans. She looked about eighteen. "I've been out here since six. I'm doing all the watering this morning." She looked down at herself and laughed. "If Ben could see me now." She disappeared into Lady's stall, and a calico cat, hair standing up on her back like toothbrush bristles, streaked out. "That's Penelope," Lark called to me. "She sleeps in Lady's stall." Hearing our voices, Dean came around the corner. He and I were alone. He stalked hipshot in my direction and pulled me to him by the hips. His eyes were dark with longing. He gave me a thorough kissing as Penelope twined around our legs.

"Excuse me," a lilting female voice said. Stepping back from Dean, my face pinking, I regarded a young girl with curly black hair who was dressed in khaki britches and paddock boots and hauling a bucket of what looked like brown trail mix.

"Robin Hamilton," Dean said, "this is Andi DeFelice. Andi's a student at UVA." I smiled politely. "She boards her horse at

295

Villeneuve in exchange for working sixteen hours a week at the barn."

Cavalier poked his head over his stall door, nickering and bobbing his great head. "Chill, Cav, I'm coming!" Andi called and continued her work.

In the tack room Dean found a pair of Mary's boots that were a good fit for me. Dean settled a black helmet onto my head, bending to kiss my throat as he fastened the clasp. "Let's go get Trolley," he said, "before I end up carrying you into an empty stall."

We walked out to the sunlit corral, Trolley on a lead rope. Mary and Leslie were out in the paddocks working with other horses, so Dean and I were alone. It was as if I were scaling the barn itself trying to get my leg over Trolley's back. "You know what Ian Fleming said," I panted. "'A horse is dangerous at both ends and crafty in the middle.'" Dean chuckled at my discomfiture. Trolley was patient with my attempts, and at last I was in the saddle. I felt exhilarated, though, looking down at my lap, I was sure my round thighs looked repulsive. *Oh, what the hell.* I reached down and stroked Trolley's light-chestnut withers. Dean pulled his phone from his back pocket and took our picture. It would always be one of his favorite photos.

Ten minutes later, I was riding around the corral by myself. By that time Lark had joined us, and with her father's direction, she was comfortably astride Lady in no time. She *was* a natural. Dean leaned against the fence and beamed. Lady tossed her head and pranced, more spirited than Trolley, but that suited me just fine.

That afternoon Laurel taught her granddaughter to can vegetables. Entering her kitchen, I found them in faded aprons, Lark stirring a huge pot of tomatoes: a blonde good witch over a bubbling cauldron. My phone chimed with a text from Dean: "I have a surprise for you. Meet me behind the barn?"

Sure he had something seductive in mind, I felt my pulse speed up. "See you later, gators," I said to Lark and Laurel.

I rounded the corner of the barn almost bumping smack into Leslie leading Cavalier to the paddocks. "Oh … Hi!" I said. I noticed the horse stopped in his tracks as soon as Leslie did. Cav was almost twice as tall as Leslie. I had to marvel at the control Dean's sisters had over the massive creatures.

"Hi, Robin. Listen …" She stopped, looking miserable. "I wanted to apologize about the other day. I was drunk and stupid at the pool. My big brother gave me hell."

"Don't think another thing about it," I said with a smile. "I'm sure I've been drunker and stupider. Are you getting Cav ready for the event?"

"Yep." She smiled gratefully, pulled a hunk of carrot from her pocket, and offered it to the horse. "Thanks, Robin." Leslie and Cav moved out, and she called over her shoulder, "We really *are* glad you're here."

Beyond the corral the object of my desire leaned against an enormous tarp-covered object. "What are you up to?" I asked, walking right up to him and twining my arms around his neck. Dean cradled the back of my head as we stood kissing under the beat of the afternoon sun, the muffled drone of mowers up by the road the only sound. He smelled brothy with sweat, his shirt back damp under my hands. I realized it was the first time I'd ever smelled Dean's body odor, and the cumin-like earthiness of it turned me on. There was little about Dean Falconer that did not.

Then he broke away. "Guess what I have here."

Looking down at his tented jeans front, I laughed throatily, "You mean aside from the obvious?"

"Woman, you are killing me," he groaned. Dean grabbed the heavy tarp with both hands. At the first glimpse of large tires and green paint I knew.

"Dean! You still have the Jeep!" Awestruck, I watched as he unveiled the vehicle like a waiting bride, the Jeep in which I'd fallen in love with him that first weekend in DC. I looked from the man to the machine and began to cry. I sat in the passenger seat running my hands over the upholstery and the dash, and a deluge of memory swamped me. Dean climbed in and gathered me to him. "I can't believe you kept it," I sniffled.

"Believe it or not, it still runs like a top. I use it around the farm. I couldn't bear to part with it."

I looked up at him then. "I'm glad you kept it."

Dean pointed to the key in the ignition. "I still have my lucky roach clip." He grinned, indicating the key chain. I ran my fingers over it, recalling another long-buried memory. "Do you want to go for a spin?" he asked.

"Yeah." I nodded, drying my eyes with the hem of my shirt. We went for a fine ride around the property. When we had covered the Jeep again as if putting a much-loved child to bed, Dean and I walked hand in hand toward the main house. A great rumbling announced a huge silver pickup truck rolling down the gravel drive.

"That is a *big* truck," I said.

"Around here we call that a big-ass truck," he said with a grin. "Billy's back." Charlotte and Hudson rose from their places under the giant oak in the front yard and moved toward the truck their tails wagging like metronomes. Dean raised a hand and watched the truck's approach from beneath the bill of his cap.

Shorter than Dean, solidly built and strong looking, Billy Babbitt stepped from the cab with an empty water bottle in hand. He hauled a bag from the truck bed. "Hey, boss," he said, smiling shyly.

"Robin Hamilton," said Dean, putting his arm around my waist, "this is Billy Babbitt, one of my oldest friends and our farm manager." Billy removed his sunglasses and stepped forward to shake my hand.

"Billy, I'm happy to meet you," I said warmly.

"Likewise." Billy had trouble looking me in the eyes and bent to pet the dogs. I wondered if it was shyness or if his cool reserve spoke of something unnamed.

"When you get settled in, Bill, come over to Mom's. I want you to meet my … our daughter," Dean said, smiling down at me. The two of us went in to see how the canning was going.

* * * * *

The next day Dean and Lark took the first of the father-daughter hikes they would take that summer, up to Crabtree Falls. They came back after seven hours, stinky—concentric rings of sweat at their armpits—but happy companions. A scholar of the nuances of my daughter's moods, I could tell that Lark had been crying. Faint, dried snails' tracks of tears streaked her cheeks. I guessed that father and daughter had had at last the opportunity for a long-needed conversation.

Later that afternoon, the hikers freshly showered, the three of us drove out to Blue Mountain Brewery for dinner. We sat on the terrace under a red umbrella, drinking fancy craft beer and sharing a huge, gooey Mediterranean pizza—the kind where the cheese stretches long from your mouth. Lark and I gazed at the perfect view of the mountains that appeared azure in the slanting sun and indigo in the blooming shadows made by clouds.

As we drove home, the setting sun turned the sky a vivid cobalt streaked with orange. Moved, I watched as the blue slipped from purple to gray before darkness blurred the seam connecting land and sky. My sit bones were painfully sore from riding, and I felt every bump with the Jeep, but I was happier than I'd ever been before. Lark fell asleep so quickly and profoundly that night on the guesthouse sofa that I knew I'd been right: the day with her father had been cathartic. I hoped it had for Dean as well, but I never asked either of them. It appeared they each had made peace with the past.

CHAPTER

22

Robin

2013

The weeks were passing like scenery from a car window. On the third of July, Dean took Lark and me to see his Charlottesville office. The firm resided in a narrow, character-filled, old house, a rabbit warren of rooms, drafty in the winter and hot in the summer. It smelled of tobacco from James's clandestine cigars and of the peppermints that their administrative assistant Divya kept on her desk. The conference table where they met with clients anchored the dining room of the house. The guys had added gas logs to the fireplace there for warmth and ambience.

Dean had completed a big project just before Lark and I arrived and was keeping only one office day for the summer, one of the perks of having a partner, and the firm was running smoothly in James's capable hands.

The forecast promised that Independence Day would be much cooler than the previous days. The evening was letter perfect, even cooler on Carver Mountain, where the family, Billy, James, and Jill gathered for an open-to-the-public picnic and firework event with summer food from local food trucks and plenty of cold beer. At dusk, sitting back against Dean on a quilt and savoring his solid warmth, I gazed at the panoramic view below—the silhouetted small towns amid ridges of night-navy mountains. The rising apricot moon suddenly seemed full of portent. A shiver crept along my arms, but I let it pass unexamined as the fireworks began—red, white, and blue bursts, glowing spidery tendrils against the indigo sky. As the others exclaimed and clapped, Dean took my chin and turned my face to his. From the next blanket, Mary said, "You two! You need to get a room." Lark was having a blast somewhere up ahead in the group drinking beer with Leslie, Rob, and Billy. I could hear her laughter and smiled as I kissed her father.

Minutes later we were gathering up blankets and coolers, giddy and singing all the patriotic songs we knew, laughing as we stumbled over the words. We picked our way through the trees and the other revelers back to the cars, the moonlight our only guide. Then something I heard Mary say sobered me as if I had plunged headlong into a glacier-fed lake. She and Jill were tripping along arm in arm for support in the gloom behind Dean and me. Jill was saying something about how happy James had told her that Dean was, and Mary said evenly, "Thank goodness Robin came along when she did, or we might have ended up with Heather De Hart."

"Oh, God, *Heather*," Jill said.

Who the hell is Heather De Hart? I thought. I glared at Dean.

"What?" he said, laughing in surprise. "What was *that* look for?"

"Nothing," I said. We reached the Jeep, and Lark and Billy hopped in the back to ride back with us. It gave me a few minutes to collect my tortuous thoughts and will myself not to overreact.

At Villeneuve again, Dean and I walked into the pool area. Dean asked if I wanted to take a late swim. "I'll sit this one out," I said and sat down on a chaise longue.

"*Okaaayy*. Then I'll be right back." His handsome face bewildered, he walked to his house. I sat there stewing, prickly, bitchy. When Dean reappeared, he sat silently down on the edge of the pool in his red trunks. Why did he have to look all sexy at this moment? The full moon—that portentous moon—seemed to hover above his right shoulder. "What's all this, Robin?" he asked, annoyed.

"I don't know, Dean. You tell me. Who is Heather De Hart?" I sat unyielding, my arms crossed over my chest.

He whipped his face around to stare at me, astonished. "Where did you hear about Heather?" he asked. I was perversely glad to have shocked him.

"Something I overheard Mary say to Jill tonight … Exactly what she said was that she was glad I came along when I did or they may have ended up with Heather De Hart," I said, defiant and childish.

"Sweetheart, will you come sit over here and let me explain?"

After a moment I moved to sit on the side of the pool, leaving enough space between us for a sumo wrestler. "I told you that first night at ... Crispo ... in New York ... that I had dated someone recently—it was last winter actually—and I also remember telling you that I hadn't found anyone I wanted to spend my life with." Dean raised and lowered his feet in the water; I watched the ripples spread in circles on the water, dreading what he would say next. "It was Heather," he said. "She had a catering business here that everybody used. Robin, I broke it off with her as soon as you called me in February."

"In *February!*" I said.

"Yes!" He was defensive and angry now. "As soon as you and I started talking in February, I knew I wanted to make something happen with you. I was never serious about Heather, and at that point, any ... thoughts of *her* ... flew out of my head." He paused. "But she wanted me to marry her. Everybody knew it."

"Heather," I spat, getting up to pace the pool's apron. The name conjured an image of some wispy blonde waif with enormous blue eyes.

"Robin, you're not being reasonable. I feel like I've been sent to the principal's office. How the hell was I supposed to know you were about to come back into my life?" he demanded. And when I didn't answer, he barked gruffly, "Huh?"

I sat as silent as granite, irrational, unwilling to concede. Dean lowered himself into the water and began swimming laps. After five or six, he was back, running his hands over his face and head.

He rested his arms on the side of the pool, studying me again, his breathing heavy.

"It's not just that I'm more ridiculously jealous than I can believe," I said, continuing my rant. "But you should have told me that you were seeing someone, someone who wanted to marry you!" My voice rose and quavered on the "marry you." I would not cry.

"Shhhh, Robin, I'd rather our daughter not hear this." Lark had disappeared into the guesthouse after the picnic.

"I'd rather her not hear it either ... *and* I think *I've* heard enough myself." I stood and stomped back to the guesthouse, as effectively as I could manage in my flip-flops, and shut the door without turning to see his face. I crept to my room and saw that Lark's door was closed. I hoped she hadn't overheard the ugly conversation. I lay awake most of that night replaying the fight. Burning with righteous indignation and throwing the covers aside, I realized it was humiliation I felt—Heather had wanted to marry Dean, and "everybody knew it." Who was this woman? Had I seen her around? Did she still want Dean? I had to know. But the next morning, my pride and I stayed in the guesthouse when Lark left for the barn. I drank coffee, sulking tiredly.

At ten I received a text from Dean: "Baby, I'm sorry. I should have told you. Will you forgive me?" At eleven he sent the same message again.

This time I typed a terse "Not sure yet," milking my resentment. Dean replied that he was leaving the next morning to see a client in North Carolina and returning the day after that. I replied with a brusque "Have a good trip." He was *leaving* at a time like *this*? I got up and stalked to the closet, hauled my big suitcase from the top shelf, and tweaked my lower back. *Shit!* My eyes filled. I would get myself back to New York City tonight, I would. I had lived without Dean Falconer for thirty-five years. I had a career I had worked assiduously to build. Good riddance to bad rubbish.

My silent rant lasted about five minutes. But I stayed inside the entire day and night for good measure. Lark, sensing that something was afoot, treaded softly around me and spoke little, only remarking as she came in from the barn the next morning, "Dean just left for his trip."

Laurel knocked on the door and invited Lark and me to go to a movie. "I saw in the paper the downtown cinema is showing a revival of *Pretty Woman*. Wouldn't it be fun to see that on the big screen again?" Itching to get out of the house, I said I'd like to go. Laurel gave Lark a conspiratorial wink. *What was that about?* I thought as my daughter chimed in, "Let's go to dinner too. Leslie told me about a French place, Petit Pois, that she likes."

Billy saddled Trolley for me, and I rode for a while, feeling bummed that Dean had gone away while we were at odds. I wondered if Lark and I should stay in Virginia. I handed the mare off to an obliging Andi for grooming and went in to shower. The three of us had delicious dinners of mushroom risotto; trout with green beans, almonds, and brown butter; and glasses of creamy Virginia viognier. But Julia Roberts's on-screen fairy tale left me feeling sulky and timorous, as if I were coming down with something: Would the tale of Robin and Dean have a happy ending? We stepped onto the lamp-lit cobblestoned mall again afterward, and Laurel spotted a friend. She waved her over to introduce us. Lark was introduced as "my granddaughter, Lark," while I was "Lark's mother, Robin." I felt the woman's eyes appraise me and shrank from the unspoken question that leaped and lingered there.

Though the forecast called for a summer storm, I walked to the barn the next afternoon to see Trolley. Billy was hauling hay from the back of his truck to the barn. Lately, he had been even quieter than usual, introspective. "How are you, Billy?" I asked.

"I'm good," he answered shortly, but his smile didn't reach his eyes. The storm was beginning to brew, the slate sky roiling. The horses grew restless and nickered as warm gusts blew through the barn and raised the dust.

We heard the familiar sound of the Jeep's engine before we saw it. My heart flipped over, concern for Billy momentarily forgotten. In that moment I knew I could no more live without Dean Falconer again than without physical nourishment. The first drops of rain spattered the dusty ground like bacon grease on a stove. Charlotte, whose broad tail had been thumping against my legs, cantered out to meet the Jeep. Billy and I walked out accompanied by Hudson, who had emerged from his favorite spot under Billy's truck.

Smiling tentatively in my direction, Dean stepped down onto the gravel drive and then turned to fish the back of the Jeep for an umbrella. "Welcome back, boss," Billy said. Then he seemed to sniff out the tension that stretched like a partition between Dean and me and said, "I'll catch you later, man." He called to the dogs, "Come on, pups," and limped back to the barn. The limp had become more pronounced, I noted. Dean raised the umbrella over us, and we stood facing each other alone.

"Hello, Dean." I flinched as a great boom of thunder crashed at the heels of a flash of light from the west.

"Hello, Robin," he said, his mouth twisting. "Let's take cover. Want to ride back to the house with me?"

"Sure," I said, nonchalant. We got into the Jeep, and Dean put the car in reverse and his hand behind my headrest to look back. The familiar smell of his skin in the warm, rain-spattered shirtsleeve caught me by surprise. I closed my eyes. We drove the two hundred yards in silence. Dean parked the Jeep and turned off the engine.

I spoke first, my heart an undigested bolus behind my breastbone. "Dean, first, I'm embarrassed that everyone knew about Heather but me, and second, how do you know she's over you?"

Dean rubbed his eyes tiredly and looked at me. "I won't lie to you. Heather was supremely pissed when I broke it off with her. I'm considered ... a catch ... at least around here." I raised my eyebrows at him. "Well, it's true," he said. "I saw her one more time after that in April."

In April? I opened my mouth to object, but he jumped right back in. "I ran into her at the farmers' market one Saturday morning and bought her a lemonade. We talked for a few minutes,

308

and she told me she was moving north to Middleburg to be close to her folks. Her parents run an old inn and train foxhunting dogs. *That's* how I know she's over me. Heather's long gone."

"Well," I said, slightly mollified, "I just wish you had told me about her, before I heard it from someone else."

"I regret that. I was thoughtless ... It was a stupid error in judgment."

"But, Dean ... I've had this in the back of my mind: Are you absolutely certain you're not interested in me simply because I'm the mother of your child? Sometimes I worry that I'm just ... part of a package deal. If that's the case, *please* tell me the truth right now." My eyes implored him as great drops battered against the roof and made opaque the expanse of windshield.

Dean unhooked his seatbelt and opened the door. "Let me change clothes, and I'll pick you up with the big umbrella when the storm passes. It's time I showed you something."

An hour later the two of us walked to the barn beneath the umbrella. A light rain continued to fall. The farm looked crazily green. Dean led the way to Kirby's stall. The horse was busily chomping forage in the corner. "Stay here; I'll be right back," he said to me and entered the stall. I waited in stillness, inhaling the scent of dampened hay and animal. Dean's voice floated over the stall door. "When I was a kid, I made a secret hiding place here. It was my horse Wahoo's stall then." I heard the screech of wood against wood and the sound of something sliding. Dean sneezed once, twice, and reappeared with a cobwebbed and dusty old shoe

309

box. He wiped his nose with his shirt sleeve. Derelict masking tape strapped the box's lid to its bottom. Across the top in black marker DEAN's was written in his hand. Dean blew across the box and sat down on a tack box. Mesmerized, I watched as dust motes drifted in the dim light. "Sit here with me?" he asked. "When I knew I couldn't find you and had to … move on … I packed you away in this box." My pulse quickened as Dean pulled away at the strips of tape.

He lifted the top, and a spindly daddy longlegs scrabbled from its depths. "Ooooh!" I started as he flicked it away. In the box were envelopes from my old pink-and-green floral-bordered stationary. My throat began to ache with an ineffable sadness. One at a time Dean handed me the funny little cards I'd sent to cheer him and the scrap of notebook paper with my name and phone number in DC. He removed the letters, the deeply emotional ones I had written when only I had known I was pregnant with his child. "I read them a dozen times," he said. I scanned the letters, penned in my careful, youthful handwriting, through the bright sheen of tears. His hands in the box again, Dean untangled a tinkling item and held the St. Thomas medal aloft. A sob escaped me as I took the necklace and wound it around my hand, peering at the inscription. Dean reached inside once more and lifted the photograph of the two of us—the twin to mine—and his Eagles' concert ticket stub from the bottom. Dean's lashes were dark with tears as he said, "These were all I had of you; I couldn't part with them … but I didn't want anyone else to see them either." I gulped, nodding my head. "Robin, I was in love with you when we were … kids, before we ever even thought about having a child." He took my face in his hands, the box across his knees. "I'm in love with the woman you are now, with *you and only you.*" I smiled at him with trembling lips and closed my eyes. "Look at me, Robin. Don't you know you're the girl for me?"

"Yes. I do know. I love you so, Dean," I answered in a wash of love, forgiveness, and hope. He held me then. Outside the rain had stopped, and light once more filtered through the boards of the barn.

That weekend, the whole family gathered at Nelson Mountain Vineyard for an afternoon of relaxation. The staff was pouring twelve wines for the afternoon's tasting, and by the time we had sampled the sweeter wines, we were all feeling merry. We took bottles of chilled summer rosé out to the terrace where comfortable rump-sprung furniture waited, the hazy blues and greens of the mountains a breathtaking backdrop. "How beautiful is this?" I exclaimed, utterly charmed. I gazed down at a small, picturesque lake, a battered yellow rowboat bobbing at its edge.

Languorous, Mary said, "Robin, you wouldn't believe how gorgeous it will be here in October. The vines will be tinged with fall color—red, purple, gold. You just want to hold the swollen grapes in your hand like …"

"Ba-by!" Rob grinned. "How 'bout coming over here to sit with me?" We all laughed.

I knew I would have to come back to Virginia in the fall when the trees would burnish the mountainsides in jewellike colors and see the vines for myself. And the farm. Villeneuve would be ablaze in the autumn. What would it be like when Lark and I went back to New York? Would the summer haunt my days? I looked about at the family I was coming to know. Mary and Leslie had become dear, spontaneously affectionate with Lark and me. Robert and Warren were what Anita Roth would call *menschen*: honorable, good guys you knew you could rely on. And Laurel. Dean's mother's sweet ways had begun to patch the tear in my heart torn by my own mother's death. It was hard to believe the spirited and sturdy woman I knew had once been institutionalized for depression. Before we left that afternoon, Leslie asked a staff member to take a picture of the whole tipsy group of us, Dean and me front and center.

The next morning, Dean made a run into town. Lark and I did a yoga practice. My daughter was pleased with my progress. My warrior poses and sun salutations were much steadier, my balance improving. Over lunch at Laurel's, Dean asked me to take a trail ride with him that evening. He and Lark had taken a long ride together, and now it was my turn.

When it was cool enough to be comfortable for the horses, we saddled Trolley and Dean's aristocratic Kirby and headed out, a picnic of cheese and sausage, a baguette, fruit, and a bottle of Pinot Noir in a canvas tote secured to Kirby's saddle. Dean urged the horses down the road and through the back woods of the farm. Trolley, shoes clopping over the rocky places, followed Kirby through the narrower trails at a comfortable pace. I felt authentic and pleased with my appearance wearing new britches, riding boots, and a smart helmet that Leslie and Mary had bought for me. Charlotte and Hudson trotted along behind until they grew tired and turned back for home.

When we reached the summit, I was captivated by the view below. I could just make out the doll-sized gray gambrel roof of the barn. Its copper weather vane winked like a flame through the trees at Villeneuve. We dismounted, tied the horses off, and spread out an old wedding ring quilt made by Dean's grandmother Helen. We peeled off our boots and reclined, deeply inhaling the clean air. Dean poured us some wine. It wasn't long before we were making out. At once, Dean sat up, his breath fast in his throat. "Robin, there is nothing in the world I would like more right now than to make love to you, here in this perfect place, but I need to talk with you about something." Grimacing, he tucked his shirttail in. I sat up and crossed my legs in lotus position, curious.

He began, "I've thought of at least a half dozen ways to say this."

My thoughts spiraled crazily. Did he want to take a step back? Had things been happening too fast between us? Could I have misread all the neon signs? I gazed at him mildly though my heart inched toward my throat. Dean's eyes penetrated mine. I could see the tiny flecks of blue around the gray.

"I never wanted to lose you when you left DC … and then all the years I spent alone. It was a miracle when you came into my life again. And you gave me a daughter." He paused, choked with emotion. "I don't want to lose you again. I know it's only been a month. But I love you more than I've ever loved anyone on this earth."

My chest filled with suppressed sobs of hope.

"I want you to be my wife. I want you to live with me here at Villeneuve. Robin, will you marry me?"

Tears flowed as my entire being flooded with happiness. Looking into the eyes of the man that I adored, I breathed, "Yes. Only yes."

Dean dug into the pocket of his jeans and withdrew a tiny black box. Opening its hinged edge, he carefully removed a ring. The oblique rays of early-evening sunlight captured the brilliant flash of gems. "Dean," I breathed, "it's exquisite." He smiled shyly at me and slid the gold ring onto my finger. "I couldn't love you or the ring more," I said, gazing at the two-carat, emerald-cut diamond, surrounded by about a dozen luminous emeralds. Something stirred in my memory.

Dean asked, "Do you recognize the diamond, sweetheart?"

"No," I said slowly. Then, "Yes … I do, I think." I looked at him questioningly.

What he said next left me speechless: "It's your mother's diamond." He told me then about his covert mission. I sat gaping at him as if he were channeling Scheherazade. He had met my father, quite literally for the first time, in Raleigh and spent an evening with him. A week earlier he had asked an ecstatic Hank for my hand by telephone, and my dad had brought my mother's wedding ring to Raleigh. Unbeknownst to me, my dad had kept my mother's diamond with the hope that Lark or I would one day wear it. In the years after Mom's death, I had never thought to ask him about it. With my father's blessing and the ring in pocket,

Dean had sought a Charlottesville jeweler, who had extricated the diamond from its original setting and created a new piece, adding jewels "the color of my eyes" around it.

"So *that's* where you went," I said softly. "Oh, Dean, I'm sorr—"

He placed a finger over my lips and smiled and then kissed my hands, cheeks, forehead, and lips. We began to laugh, kissing and kissing. Finally he said, "There's more." I searched his face. What more could there be? "Robin, I want to give you the wedding ... *and* the wedding *night* that you should've had, that *we* should have had, all those years ago." He paused. "Let's wait to make love on that night." Dean looked down at his hands. "What can I say? I've become a very traditional man. It just seems the right thing."

Dean and I were living another lifetime. After so many years, it would almost be like making love for the first time. I found that I loved the idea.

"That being said, can we get married tomorrow?" he deadpanned. I hooted, and we were off in a fit of cackling.

When we got ourselves under control, we spread the picnic. As Dean sliced the sausage on the diagonal, he asked, "What sort of wedding would you like, sweetheart?" I pensively chewed a piece of creamy Havarti, and a vision passed before my eyes: a small outdoor wedding at Villeneuve. Perhaps I would walk from Laurel's house down the steps to him in the sheltering of one of the great oaks. We sat facing each other, finishing the meal and the wine, and talked of plans until the sun dipped low, darkening the blues of the mountains.

We mounted the horses again and moved along the narrow wooded corridor that rose steeply above the farm. As Trolley and I bumped down the trail, my eyes slid to the beautiful ring on my finger over and over again. My thoughts leapfrogged over themselves. *When? Can I get ready for a wedding from Villeneuve? Will I stay here until the wedding? And what about my home? My practice? Lark needs to get back to New York for teacher in-service and the start of school.* It was all too much to get my head around.

At the barn we handed the horses off to Billy. He listened to our news as dispassionately as if watching a grocery clerk scan his purchases. We walked hand in hand to Laurel's to share the news with her and Lark. Dean asked, "What the hell's wrong with Billy?"

"I've noticed too! He seems depressed to me. You know him better than anyone. Does he get like that?"

"I've never noticed him acting depressed, and he's been my manager for thirty-five years." We had come to the main house and, without consultation, sat down on the terrace. Dean continued, his brow furrowed, "I wasn't around after Billy had his accident in seventy-six. I was at UVA and then in DC. I don't really know what he was like then. But when I came home again and asked him to manage the farm, he was really happy. He loves this place. When Victoria died ... and when Mrs. Babbitt died, Billy was pretty resilient."

"Talk to him, sweetheart," I said. "See if you can find out what's going on."

We stepped through Laurel's mudroom, and I realized how I had come to love the old house, its idiosyncratic creaks and groans, its smells of lemon-oil polish and old wool. Lark and Laurel were sitting in the wing chairs in the kitchen watching the news, sipping from mugs of tea. We shared our news with them and showed them the ring that of course they already knew about. Laurel cried, her eyes shining, "Oh, Robin, it's stunning! And your mother's diamond. Aren't you thrilled, honey?"

"I am!" I said, my heart filling again. "I can't wait for Dad to see the finished piece." I loved that he and Dean had been coconspirators.

Lark grinned, her eyes polished pewter. "Well played, Dad." And to me, she said, "Mom, it's gorgeous and so unique."

I couldn't wait to call my dad and show Leslie and Mary the ring … and Theresa! I had to call Tee! We had talked a couple of times that summer. Now she needed an immediate update.

I woke the next morning with a goofy grin on my face. Dean and I were engaged! I walked outside in my robe and saw Dean and Billy getting into the Jeep. I knew Dean must be taking Billy somewhere to talk and wondered where they were headed. They waved as they pulled out. After a yoga practice I dressed and went to the barn to see Mary and Leslie. They were working with a beautiful yearling they had named Mercury in the corral. "Hot damn!" Leslie said, sliding her sunglasses up into her hair. She removed her leather gloves to examine the ring. "It's fabulous! Dean pulled it off," she said to her sister. "Were you surprised?"

"It's fabulous," said Mary. "We're so happy for you both." And then she cried, "Sister hug!" swooping Leslie and me in her arms.

"Welcome to the family," they said together, and we all laughed.

Lark and I went into town to shop for groceries and dog food. When we returned, the Jeep was still missing from its parking spot. About three o'clock, Dean tapped on my door. "Just hold me," he said, his voice hollow. Over the next hour, Dean told me what he had learned from Billy. The two had driven over to their former high school baseball field and had sat on the bleachers in the sun and watched the kids play. At one point Billy had said to Dean, "You know, before Robin came along, I felt like you and I were in the same boat. Man, I haven't had a girlfriend since … Becky Park and I broke up … senior year of high school." Dean had looked at him in surprise. "I mean, sure, I've had *women*," Billy had said with a shrug, "but I've never had anyone … that *loved* me … like Robin loves you. Now here you are getting married." Dean's heart had ached at Billy's naked expression of despair. "I'm sorry, man. I just feel left out … you know? How will I ever have what you have? I'm lonely, Dean."

Dean said he felt terrible. He'd been so wrapped up in me and in Lark that he hadn't really thought about Billy this summer.

"How could you have known?" I asked.

"I should have. He considers me his best friend. I feel like shit."

"Look at me, Dean," I said. "Billy considers you his best friend because you *have* been to him. You turned his life around when you brought him to Villeneuve. He's just going to have to sort this out. Why does he think it's too late for him to find love?"

"I don't know … the short-term memory stuff and the limp, I guess."

"His little memory glitches wouldn't be a deal breaker, and the limp? A woman couldn't love Billy because of a limp?" I said nonplussed. "He's a good-looking man, a talented man, a thoroughly nice man!"

"Maybe you should tell him that," Dean said, kissing me on the nose and smiling for the first time. "I tried to build him up this afternoon, but you sound much more convincing."

"I will. When we get back from the honeymoon, we are going to find somebody to fix him up with."

"Yes, ma'am," Dean said and pulled me into his lap.

We chose a wedding date of August 10, a Saturday morning, four days before Lark began teacher in-service. She would leave for New York the day after the wedding. Dean wanted to go to Paris for the honeymoon; he had never been. I would stay in Virginia until the wedding and after the honeymoon would return to New York long enough to attend to the details of relocating my life. I spent hours on the phone with my excited father, and with John Hicks, discussing what we would do with our practice. John was nearing retirement age, and my leaving would present immediate problems for him, but it couldn't be helped.

One night after Dean and I had been to Jill and James's for dinner, I tossed and turned, uncomfortably warm though I wore only a short cotton gown. I had had too much wine and knew what I needed was a huge glass of water. I padded to the kitchen thinking of the fun we'd had that night. How fun it would be to do couples things with the Culpeppers after Dean and I were married. Drifting back to my room, I stood at the window, looking for the moon, and drank deeply from the glass. A bright gibbous moon hung low in the sky and spotlighted the roof of the main house. I became aware of what looked like an enormous swarm of gnats in the air. Curious, I stepped outside onto the concrete of the pool's apron, cool now with the night, and saw more of the swarm gathering. And I knew with a prickling chill up the base of my neck that it was smoke before I smelled it. *Laurel wouldn't be burning her fireplace in the summertime. Or in the middle of the night.* I shook my head to clear it.

The air was now filling with flickers of ash—the gnats I had seen—and then I could see the red glow of flames at the roofline on the back corner of the main house. *"Dean!"* I screamed, running for his house and banging through the door. "The main house is on fire!"

Lark came out of the guesthouse in short pajamas. "Mom?" she cried, alarmed. Dean stumbled through the door pulling a pair of jeans up his hips. "Lark! Call 911!" he yelled. The two of us ran in bare feet through the grass.

"Mom!" Dean screamed, sprinting ahead of me. He reached the back terrace, overturning two chairs with a series of loud, metallic clangs and burst through the back door. I glanced up and saw Laurel's startled face framed by her upstairs bedroom window. I could hear Dean screaming to his mother as he made his way through the house.

"Oh my God," I said as Lark caught up with me, her phone clutched in her hand. I watched as Laurel, who appeared to be sleepwalking, turned slowly from the window. Lark and I stood clinging to each other and blubbering. "Are they on the way?" I asked her desperately, my heart trip-hammering in my chest.

"They said six to eight minutes," Lark sobbed. I began to pray.

Dean, half-carrying his mother, stumbled from the back door, and the two tumbled onto the terrace in a heap, coughing and gagging, their eyes streaming. "Robin! Get back!" Dean shouted. He got up again and pulled Laurel across the terrace and onto the grass where Lark and I waited in dismay.

The windows at the corner of Dean's boyhood room exploded with a roaring flash. Shattered shards of glass flew several feet and showered the ground below. Lark and I could feel the heat from where we stood. We turned as we heard trudging footfalls from the direction of the barn and something heavy slithering across the grass. A wild-haired Billy Babbitt tugged the big hose behind him, the surge of water making a stream through which his bare feet slogged toward the house. *Billy!* I looked from the man back to the blown-out windows, where shadows of flames now leaped and danced. I imagined Dean's old mattress ablaze. Dean ran to Billy, and together they aimed the hose at the windows.

From the main road then we heard the thin yowling of sirens. Relief suffused me, and I turned to Laurel and Lark. Laurel's hair was an untidy gray nimbus around her pale face, her open mouth a rictus of incredulity. Her body trembled in her long nightgown. *She's in shock.* "Lark, run and get your grandmother a blanket," I yelled. I led Laurel to a safer distance and lay her down in the grass. I sat on the damp ground and cradled her head in my lap. Lark reappeared with two blankets, and we covered Dean's mother.

Big Hudson paced up and down, whining at the commotion and pawing at the ground. We could hear the horses moving in the barn, alarmed and restless, the mares whinnying loudly. Billy and Dean were slipping and sliding in the fallen glass as they grappled with the hose, but they halted and turned as the emergency vehicles screamed down the drive. "Charlotte …" Laurel moaned, trying to sit up. "She nudged me awake. Is she still in the house?" *Little Charlotte!*

Lark and I dragged our eyes to the open back door through which smoke now rushed. The dog appeared like an apparition. She limped down the steps, her eyes bloody and crazed. Foam flecked her muzzle. We watched in impotent horror as the dog staggered across the terrace, a great spate of diarrhea spattering the brick. As Lark ran to her, Dean screamed, "Get back, Lark!" Lark dragged Charlotte by the collar to where we sat, stricken and paralyzed. Lark curled her body around the animal whose sides heaved with laboring breaths, her tears falling on the dog's sooty fur. The firefighters tumbled from the truck and yelled for Dean and Billy to get out of the way. In moments torrential blasts of water were arcing through the air. I ran to meet Dean. His hands and feet were cut and bloody, his eyes dazed. He pulled me into a tight embrace for a moment and then moved to Lark and his mother on the grass.

The fire was out, and the sun began to rise. Early pale-yellow light filtered through the great oaks, the dew on the grass like tears the night wept. The firemen stomped into the house in their dirty boots, one with an axe in his hand. "Oh, Lord, what are they going to do to my house?" Laurel moaned. As we waited for the crew to reappear, we appraised ourselves. Billy had a gash down one cheek that needed tending. Both men were soaked to the bone and bled from their feet. Bright poppies of their blood bloomed across our grass-stained nightgowns. Lark hurried back to Dean's to get a first aid kit, and we bandaged the men in the dawn. The firemen tromped back out onto the terrace, their faces calm. Billy's efforts with the hose had slowed the conflagration until the firefighters had arrived to quench the remaining blaze before it could spread to the rest of the house. But smoke had escaped through the door and vents, and heavy soot limed the upstairs. Capricious old wiring was most likely the cause of the blaze; the upstairs of the house hadn't been remodeled in many years. With the windows blown out and gaping, their frames blackened, the corner of the house looked like the shell of a war-torn building. The flames had licked onto the roof, and a large swath of it had burned away.

As Lark and I walked Laurel to Dean's house, Dean and Billy surveyed the wreckage. The room was a dripping black cube, the stench of melted plastic and fabric unbelievable. In some spots one of the firemen had gashed through the walls to the outside wall with his axe to make sure embers did not smolder there. The next day a professional cleaning crew came, and Dean and Billy went into town to pick up enormous scrubbers—air-cleaning filters—and installed them throughout the house. We heard the low roar of the scrubbers day and night, but they took care of the lingering charred odor in a week's time. Laurel moved in with Dean until the house and roof could be repaired. "I always did want to redo that room," she wryly said. Charlotte lay quietly on Dean's den floor, her head on her paws, her red-streaked eyes drowsy for a couple of days, healing herself the way animals do, and made a full recovery.

One afternoon Dean, Lark and I finally visited Monticello. The docent who led our tour was a fount of information on the life of Thomas Jefferson. Dean's appreciation for Jefferson's architectural genius enhanced the experience for us. Lark and I loved seeing Jefferson's inventions, the fine antiques and portraits in the home. That evening Dean and I prepared a dinner of smoked salmon and Caesar salad for Lark and Laurel. After the meal I told them I had a surprise. "We're due for a good surprise," Laurel said as I dashed back to the guesthouse. In my packing for the summer I had included the first volumes of the photograph albums from Lark's childhood.

Lark said, "Uh oh, here we go," but with good humor. Mother and son sat, their heads together, as Dean opened the leather album.

The first picture was of two-day-old Lark in the sweet little gown with pink embroidered rosebuds. I remembered propping her on my hospital bed pillow as my father took the photo. "That was taken just before we brought her home from the hospital," I said.

Dean looked at me and then at the picture for a moment, and a closed sign settled over his handsome features. He stood and walked from the room.

"He just needs a minute," Laurel said, looking after her son and nodding once. I rose and stepped around the corner into the living area where Dean stood, looking out the broad expanse of window at his farm. I wrapped my arms around him and lay my head between his shoulder blades. He turned to me and put his arms around me, his cheek atop my head.

"I just felt this crushing ... regret ... remorse ... when I saw that picture. That incredible baby girl ... that was *mine* ... I should have been there. I should have been the one holding the damned camera."

"I know, sweetheart," I said. We stood that way for several moments. Dean seemed to draw strength from our embrace. I heard the vacuum seal of the refrigerator door opening, a cabinet door closing, the sighing of cork pulled from a bottle, the murmur of voices.

"I can't believe how tiny she was, and already so pretty," he said. "I bet I could've held her in one hand." He stretched out a palm and cupped it. I told him about the day in the hospital I had unwrapped Lark from her little gown to examine her and had discovered the feet and toes the image of his own.

"I'd like to think I would've been a good father. You did it all by yourself ... I still can't wrap my head around that."

325

"I had lots of help from my parents," I reminded him. "You'll be there for her the rest of your life, darling." I smiled, kissing his cheek. "And she loves you, you know."

"I do know," he said and smiled a little. "Let's get back. I want to see the rest of the pictures. But I may need some Kleenex."

Laurel handed Dean and me glasses of steel-aged Chardonnay, and we returned to the album. I knew in time Dean would make his peace with the past. "It's such a gift to see these," Laurel said. "And, Lark, I still can't get over how much you look like Leslie, even then. We need to show her these."

"Oh no, the naked ones," Lark said, cringing as they flipped a page. "Mom, that was just *wrong*."

"Everybody takes those pictures of their babies," Laurel said. "I have a couple of your father in fact," she added impishly.

"Uh, let's not go there," Dean said.

I laughed. "I would *love* to see Dean's pictures sometime, Laurel."

"Well, remind me to dig them out for you, honey." I flashed a victorious grin in Dean's direction.

The next day Lark, Leslie, Mary, and I escaped the clamor of the construction crew working to repair the house (Laurel insisted she stay and supervise) and drove to Richmond in search of a wedding dress. At the fancy bridal salon Leslie recommended, a woman discreetly regarded my figure and directed us away from the strapless gowns to a collection of dresses for the mature bride. "The *old* bride," I said, wrinkling my nose. "I may end up looking like the Queen Mum."

Leslie laughed and linked my arm with hers. "You are going to look *fabulous* and *sophisticated*." The salon owner seated the four of us in Louis Quatorze chairs, and an associate brought a tray of champagne in flutes. The first gown they brought out was undeniably dowdy, beige with horizontal pleats. Horizontal pleats! The second was an elegant ivory lace, but the big bow on the behind was out of the question. The third selection knocked us out. Leslie, Mary, and Lark said I had to try it on immediately.

I reappeared grinning and sent the trio into rhapsodies of approval. Tinged with the palest shade of apricot, a color so subtle it sneaked up on you, the gown was made of exquisite, finely wrought Burano lace layered on organza. The softly scooped neckline and modest short sleeves flattered my figure. And the way the A-line skirt flowed so softly and easily about my hips and thighs … It was the one. "It was *made* for you, Robin," Mary said smiling, her champagne flute raised in a toast.

"You have to wear your hair up, so the lace in the back will show," said Leslie.

The price of the dress made me feel as though I'd put a cake in the oven and forgotten to add the sugar, with company coming. But my sweet father had insisted on paying for the dress and the flowers. "Indulge the old man," he had said. "I've been waiting for this for decades."

Late that afternoon, Dean and I sat by the pool talking about the wedding. We both wanted it to be intimate—just family and our closest friends—and we wanted to honor the people who meant most to us. I had already asked Tee to be matron of honor. Dean said he had thought he would ask James to be best man but asked me what I thought about him choosing Billy instead. I reflected on Billy's recent feelings. "I think it's perfect ... In fact, it's *completely* brill!" He grinned and grabbed his phone to text Billy and ask him to come to the pool. Billy and Hudson strode across the grass from the barn. Billy looked sheepish as he came through the gate in his work clothes.

"Our hero!" I called to him, pretending to swoon. Laurel and I had been teasing him with the title since the night of the fire.

Billy smiled diffidently. "What's up, boss?" he asked Dean.

"Mr. Babbitt," said Dean expansively, "have a seat. We're about to have this wedding, and I need a best man. If you're free, I'd like *you* to do it."

Billy sat back against the chair and grinned his old easy grin. "Honored to, man."

I jumped up and hugged him. "I'm taking you handsome guys into town tomorrow for new suits!"

The next day we met at a men's store where we found a pair of elegantly cut gray suits and ties. "How come you get to see me in my suit and I don't get to see you in your dress?" Dean asked.

"It's traditional. Remember tradition?" I asked saucy and grinning.

That night Dean and I invited Lark and Billy to go to Blue Mountain Brewery with us for dinner. Billy was sun burnished and attractive in a plaid madras shirt and khakis. Dean and I observed Billy's interactions with women. Shy, away from his milieu of the farm, he was definitely rusty. But in the following days we noticed that Billy seemed happier, his limp less obvious again. We vowed to include him in our plans more often.

I turned my attention to a dress for Theresa. A cool aqua would be a lovely summer color and flattering for her high color. I called her with the assignment of finding a dress in Paris. *What a hardship.*

Lark had had a perpetual smile on her lips since Ben had booked his travel itinerary for the wedding. He was due to arrive two days before. Lark couldn't wait for Ben and Dean to meet.

The mother of the groom was in a fevered ecstasy of plans for flowers, a minister, a caterer, musicians, and a photographer. I was happy for her to take the lead on those details, for she knew the area resources. Laurel, Dean, and I put together the small guest list one night after dinner, and the sisters helped me send out simple invitations.

Dean and I went into town for blood tests, simple gold wedding bands, and a late lunch date. We were usually up late at night, looking at online information on Paris hotels, transportation, and excursions. After Victoria had died, Dean had made trips to

Germany and Czechoslovakia and later to Italy and Greece, but he had always believed Paris to be a gap in his architectural education. Of course I was thrilled. This time I would be visiting the City of Light for a purely happy reason. Theresa was ecstatic. "I hoped you'd come here, *cherie*!" she exclaimed. "I'm going to find the perfect little *intime* hotel—a little jewel box—for you and Dean!" I laughed with pleasure at her perpetual enthusiasm. Theresa and Laurent would fly over for the wedding, and afterward the four of us would fly to Paris together. The hotel Theresa found seemed perfect and was near their apartment building on the boulevard Saint-Germain. Dean and I booked it immediately. We were ready for a wedding.

CHAPTER

23

Robin

2013

The beautiful people arrived. After a week's visit with Colleen in Chicago, Theresa and Laurent made it to Villeneuve the day before the wedding. Tee stepped from the rental car looking impossibly young and svelte in tight jeans, a black T-shirt, and big glam sunglasses. I ran to swoop her up in a hug. Laurent, immaculate as always, launched his frame from the rental smiling broadly.

The Pelletiers and Dean and I sat around Laurel's kitchen island drinking iced tea. Theresa, hands darting like barn swallows, described the hotel she had found for Dean and me. I felt butterflies the size of kites in my stomach at the thought of leaving for Paris after the wedding. Dean asked Laurent about what architectural attractions he should see in Paris in addition to the obvious. From his artist's perspective, Laurent described *les incontournables*—the must-sees. Laurent in turn asked Dean about running a horse farm. I saw they would become friends as they walked out for a tour, Dean smiling proudly. No one could believe the lovely main house had been devastated by fire just weeks before.

Lark had been sitting on the stoop with her laptop since Ben had called from Richmond. Tee and I walked out to join her. As Ben's rental car rolled up the drive, Lark was on her feet. Before Ben could turn off the engine, she was in his lap. "They haven't seen each other in a month," I said to Tee with a grin.

"Jeunes amoureux," she sighed as we slipped back into the house. "Ben's as beautiful as Lark!" she whispered.

Lark brought Ben in to meet her grandmother just as Dean and Laurent returned to the house. "Hey, Robin!" Ben said, pulling me into a hug. I regarded the pair with pleasure as Lark made the introductions. With Lark's light features, the two made a striking couple, a chiaroscuro. I mentally crossed my fingers hoping the wedding would put Ben and Lark in the marrying mood. They would make such beautiful babies. Lark's eyes seemed lit from within as she introduced Ben to her father. My chest felt as effervescent as if I'd inhaled champagne bubbles.

The rest of that day Lark and Ben disappeared a few times. Tee and I speculated they were finding places to make love. "Don't make me think about that," Dean said with a moue of distaste. "She's my baby girl!"

When my father and Anita Roth arrived late in the afternoon, I was awash with familial completion, perfection. My jean pockets were full of mascara-smeared tissues. That evening, we had a lovely rehearsal dinner at nearby Keswick Hall with family and friends. Seeing Laurent for the first time, Mary, Leslie, and Jill were agog. I thought Theresa looked a bit smug as she held his arm. Billy, as best man, made a simple but eloquent and poignant toast to the bride and groom. It meant so much to Dean and me after our friend's confession a few weeks back.

Back at Villeneuve by nine thirty, we were all too keyed up to go to bed. Laurel, Billy, Dean, Laurent, and Dad sat drinking wine in Dean's living room. Laurent was staying the night at Dean's house along with my father. Ben would sleep at Billy's apartment over the barn. Lark and Ben said they were going for a walk, to more than one set of raised brows and amused twitching of mouths. Theresa and I went to relax in the guesthouse. It had been a long time since one of our sleepovers and a chance to really talk.

When I walked over to kiss Dean good night, he and Ben were sitting by the pool drinking beer, talking about baseball teams and the pennant races. The two had hit it off right away. Lark sat on the end of Ben's chaise longue watching them, her face incandescent.

Theresa and I got ready for bed. Lark's room was still dark. She and Ben had disappeared again. Tee and I finally reclined on my bed in our pajamas, glasses of scotch in hand as we'd done so many times before. Tee said, "Rob, Dean has aged *well*. He's *très* sexy!"

I grinned like the Cheshire cat. "We're waiting for our wedding night to make love. It was Dean's idea."

Tee's eyes widened over the rim of her glass. "You're kidding me," she finally said.

"Nope, and I'm convinced it's going to be ... well worth the wait. He was so sweet about wanting to give me the wedding we should have had and a proper wedding night."

"Rob ... you're killing me," she said, dipping to wipe her eyes on the hem of my pillowcase. She smiled then and pulled me into a hug. "Let's see that fabulous ring again." Tee rocked my hand like a cradle so that the stones captured the lamplight. "*Olivia's diamond*," she said, shaking her head with wonder.

"But, Tee," I fretted after a moment, "Dean hasn't seen me naked. Things are a lot ... you know looser and *bobblier* than they used to be."

Theresa snorted with laughter. "Rob, the man practically worships you. Do you really think he's going to be thinking about that in the heat of the moment?"

"I don't know!" Theresa was still as slender as a girl, her champagne-glass B cups fairly perky. My DD cups were definitely on a downward trend.

"Well, he won't. He'll have his hands full, and I do mean full!" she teased.

I hooted with chagrin, choking a little on my Scotch. "What if I'm too set in my ways from living alone my entire adult life?" I whined.

"Robin, stop it! This is your miracle. I'm not going to feed your paranoia. It's going to be fine. This is your fairy tale ending, *cherie.* You're going to be married. To *Dean Falconer.*"

We heard the front door open and close softly. We looked at each other and giggled. The conversation turned to other things: Tee's mother, my dad, my thoughts for wrapping up my New York life, Lark and Ben, and Theresa's career—she was spending more and more time at the gallery and was thinking about leaving the magazine for good. Then drowsy, our glasses empty, we hugged good night and crawled beneath the covers. Theresa wriggled into her customary stomach-sleeping position, and I onto my side. After a moment I said into the darkness, "I love you, Tee."

And she murmured through layers of linen and down, "Love you too, baby. Forever and always."

It rained the next morning, which everyone insisted was good luck for brides. About nine thirty, the dogs barked the arrival of John Hicks, who had traveled from New York on the red-eye. And less than an hour before the ceremony, the sun made its appearance. Those working outside stopped what they were doing to stand and look upward. The swath of beautiful colors that arched across the sky was a brilliant reminder of God's grace in Dean's and my lives. As the trees dripped away the remnant of the rain, the catering team had the chairs for the ceremony and the lunch-reception tables and chairs set up in the paddock with the symmetry of a chorus line. Laurel had insisted I be secluded in her house with Tee and my father until time for the ceremony. Peering out the front windows, I watched Dean's mother, still in work pants and clogs and clearly in her element, directing the florist to wire the lush white peonies and trailing English ivy to the makeshift altar and along the aisle I would walk. She called to Charlotte and Hudson, who seemed to be supervising it all, and tied great white bows to their collars.

Lark came in to see me and slipped a hand into mine. She murmured, "You look perfect, Mom." She squeezed my hand three times. I squeezed her back four and smiled into her eyes. Laurel came back inside to get dressed and shooed us from the windows.

With just a few minutes to go, Dad took me aside. "I am so glad you have your mother's ring," he said, looking down at the engagement ring. "And soon you'll have a wedding band to wear forever."

Tears stung my nose. "Thank you, Dad. I love you." I kissed his cheek, fragrant with vetiver, and then, as if orchestrated, Theresa appeared to hand me my bouquet. The peony-and-rose combination smelled like heaven must.

"Are you ready, Rob?" she asked.

We heard our cue—the violin and guitar strains of Pachelbel's Canon in D. Laurel, clutching a hankie, blew us a kiss and stepped out to proceed to the front row and sit with the rest of the family. Dad gulped and offered me his arm. I took it, full of love for him. I knew he was thinking of my mother. Stepping into the sunshine, we moved down the steps to the sibilant sound of appreciative whispers. Theresa followed, graceful in exquisite aqua lace.

My eyes sought Dean's face at the altar next to the minister and Billy. I gazed at him all the way down the aisle, and he at me. Our traditional ceremony began. When the minister asked, "Who gives this woman to be married to this man?" my father solemnly said, "Her mother and I do." We both sniffled as he kissed my cheek before taking his seat beside Laurel. I handed my bouquet to Lark in the front row next to Ben. The guests spoke a collective *"Aww"* as Dean leaned to kiss his daughter.

I turned to him then, gorgeous and distinguished in the gray suit that matched his eyes. We fought to keep our composure as we exchanged vows and rings. When the minister pronounced us husband and wife, Dean kissed me lingeringly, amid applause and laughter. As he pulled back, I tossed my head, and for the first time he noticed the little silver bird earrings, darkened with age. He murmured in my ear, "The robins. You kept them." He kissed me again, and we turned to the congregation as Mr. and Mrs. Dean Thompson Falconer.

We moved en masse into the paddock, where tables waited under shady oaks for a lunch reception. From beneath one of the great trees, a string quartet spilled the music of Mozart. Later, sated with delicious food and wine, I leaned against the back of my chair and gazed languidly around at family and our closest friends. Dean, holding my hand, was chatting with Billy on his right side. Lark was feeding Ben bites of wedding cake. I watched as she wiped crumbs from his chin and leaned to kiss his laughing mouth. How I wanted them to be as happy as Dean and I were. Those two would get it right the first time.

To Ben's right my dad sat talking with elegant, silver-tressed Anita Roth. What memories the two shared from their years as neighbors in New York. And how they had loved my mother. Dad leaned back in his chair, relaxed and happy in a dark-navy suit, a white rose in his lapel. He had gained weight in the last year, but it suited him.

Beside Anita, James was whispering something in Jill's ear. She giggled and sipped from her glass of champagne: a ripe peach in a silk wrap dress and chunky gold necklace. And I was astonished to see that across the table my mother-in-law was flirting with an attentive John Hicks on her left. It seemed that anything was possible on this day. Regal in an aqua silk suit that accentuated her sun-browned décolletage, she fingered the lustrous pearls at her throat and swung one crossed leg up and down. Her shoe actually dangled from her toe! John appeared to be teasing her about something.

On my other side sat my darling Tee. She and her splendid Frenchman were kissing, and as I looked down, I saw that one of his large hands cupped her bottom, not much bigger than a skein of wool. I remembered they had celebrated their thirty-fifth wedding anniversary that spring. *Ahh, love,* I thought contentedly. Dean turned back to me. "Sweetheart, how are you? Happy?"

A sphere is the easiest shape for nature to assume: a bubble, a planet, a drop of water. Our journey of love had come full circle— assuming a sphere of profound wholeness. "Happier than I ever imagined," I answered.

He kissed my neck and murmured, "How would you like to go on a honeymoon with me, pretty girl?"

"I'm all yours," I whispered.

Dean tapped his water goblet with his spoon and stood. "Fill your glasses," he instructed everyone. He thanked our guests for their love and support on our special day as we had rehearsed. And then he surprised me.

"In eighteen seventy-seven my paternal grandparents established a new settlement in Virginia, and they named it Villeneuve." He looked at his mother and smiled. "My mother came to Villeneuve as a bride. She and my father were always happy." He grinned and looked at his sisters. "They raised two daughters and a fine, upstanding son." Everyone tittered, and Leslie hooted.

Dean looked down at me then. "In *nineteen* seventy-seven, one hundred years after Villeneuve was established, I met the love of my life Robin Courtwright Hamilton. Coincidence?" He reached down and took my hand. "I was happy here all my life, but I've never been as happy as I am at this moment. I'm sure my grandparents would be pleased to know that another bride will make her home at Villeneuve." He reached to pick up his glass. "To my beautiful bride, Robin Hamilton Falconer." Everyone stood.

"Hear, hear," the men chanted. And at once we were surrounded with hugs and kisses. Dean and I went back to our separate quarters to dress for the trip to Paris. We had a five o'clock plane to catch from Richmond. Theresa giggled at my excitement. I was practically vibrating with it as we skinned out of our wedding finery and dressed in comfortable travel wear, me back into my dark New York clothes for Paris. We assembled at the Pelletiers' rental car with the family.

Dean and I turned to Lark. I realized that all summer she'd seemed very young, almost girlish in the uncharted territory of her father's presence, but since Ben had arrived, our daughter had again become the sophisticated and sexy woman I knew. The three of us, now a family in the truest sense of the word, had a private moment together.

Two hours later Dean and I were seat belted in aboard the jet for Paris. Across the aisle from Theresa and Laurent we toasted our happiness with good champagne (Laurent was an endless reservoir of resources). The flight attendants to whom Theresa told our story were charmed and then especially attentive. Dean and I snuggled under a blanket together for the nine-hour flight. While walking the aisles to stretch our legs once, he murmured, "Hey, green-eyed lady, want to join the mile-high club?"

I laughed and elbowed him. "We've waited this long; I'm not about to do it for the first time in a gross public toilet!"

Laurent drove us to our hotel as the sun rose over Paris, the early sky a rosy pink. Tee was curled like a tawny kitten in the passenger seat, her pink mouth slack. We would meet up with them later for a late lunch. Dean had made reservations for us at the Ritz Hotel.

Dean and I entered the lobby of the small Hotel Juliette St. Germain replete with nineteenth-century furnishings and art. Laurent, acquainted with the owner, had known we would be pampered there. Although it was very early, Monsieur le Patron himself emerged to greet us. Dean registered us as Mr. and Mrs. Dean Thompson Falconer while I suppressed the goofy grin that tugged at the corners of my mouth and managed a decorous expression.

The luxuries waiting in our suite were assaults on already overstimulated senses. First we were met with the heady scent of a great bouquet of fresh flowers—peonies, roses, and stock. The attached card read "Theresa and Laurent Pelletier." "Oh, from Tee; how lovely!" I said. "Oh my gosh," we then said at the same time as we found *two* bathrooms—his and hers— a Jacuzzi large enough for water polo in between. In the bedroom, the king-sized bed was turned down. Luxe white toweling robes lay across it, their arms crossed as if daring us to hurry up and get it on. Slippers peeked from beneath the dust ruffle. "Whatever happened to your water bed?" I asked, thinking of where we had first made love.

"The water bed!" Dean laughed. "It sprang a leak ... *before* I could get rid of it. The landlord was *pissed*."

On one of the pillows was a white box wrapped with pale blue ribbon. My curiosity piqued, I wondered, *What* more *could there be?* Atop layers of blue tissue nestled another little card, this one handwritten by Theresa: "He'll howl like a wolf. Love, Tee."

"Tee!" I hooted, tucking the note in my pocket. "I better open this by myself," I said to Dean. He went into his bathroom chuckling softly. I unfolded a length of silky fabric from its tissue nest: an exquisite emerald green lace peignoir—the most beautiful piece of lingerie I'd ever seen. Dean and I had spoken of jumping into the shower together as soon as we arrived, but as I held the peignoir against me, I found that I wanted to come to him fresh and glowing from the shower in the delicate robe. I pushed it back into the box as Dean reemerged.

As I showered, I was flooded with gratitude and at last desire. Hastily drying my hair, I slipped the peignoir over my skin. My heart suddenly feeling as if it had left the building, I opened the door.

Dean lay on one elbow in the great bed under sumptuous Egyptian cotton, his face flushed with longing. I approached the bed and stood before him. He gulped and uttered, "Robin," as he scanned my body in the filmy robe. Mesmerized, he peeled the covers back. I saw that he was gloriously naked and quite ready for me. I let the peignoir drop to the floor with a whisper and shook my hair to sweep my shoulders. I moved into his embrace.

"Madame Falconer," he said huskily. "That body … your body has *always* looked like it was carved … to adorn the pillar of a palace."

Tears prickled at my lashes. "Oh, Dean … I love you so."

As we kissed deeply, our hands explored each other again as if blind and reading texts of braille. We made our first married love. I heard sounds like mourning doves on the zinc roof above and realized they were coming from me. And then the urgency came crashing in; thirty-five years of waiting to join together again rose on a tide that took us far, far down. Our cries rose as if in homage to the one who had created love just for us. Finally sweetly sated with each other, our lassitude from the wedding and jet lag complete, we slept entwined until twelve thirty. Dean made love to me again, tantalizingly slowly this time.

We found it was time to get ready for our lunch with Tee and Laurent and reluctantly rose to dress. Blinking like night creatures as we stepped into the early-afternoon sunlight, we were like any married couple on holiday. Almost. I wondered how many other pairs could possibly share a history like ours. My heart seemed weightless as we strolled hand in hand in one of the world's most beautiful cities. Theresa and Laurent met us in front of their building, Tee beaming at us. "Did you rest well?" she teased. Already late, we hopped quickly into Laurent's sedan, and he aimed it for the Ritz.

The hotel was magnificent; even the ladies' room was opulent. "Tee, have you seen that bathroom?" I hissed. Lunch was as beautiful as it was delicious. On my third glass of champagne I quoted Hemmingway: "When I dream of afterlife in heaven, the action always takes place in the Paris Ritz."

"Hear, hear." Dean grinned, raising his glass. We laughed a great deal and shared bites from each other's plates of delicacies: poached sole and artichokes; glazed sea bass and grapefruit peas; lobster salad with lemon balm and baby lettuces; and fragrant French bread and butter. Dean and I spooned poached peaches in pink champagne with raspberry glacé into each other's mouths and sealed the bites with little kisses.

That evening, Dean and I stayed in and ordered a light room service dinner. We soaked in the great tub and made love with exuberance. At fleeting illusory moments I saw glimpses of Dean's young face. I know I slept that night, but my heart stayed awake.

I awoke before Dean did that morning and turned to see his head on the next pillow. *We're married*! I thought with a rush of deliciousness. I could wake up in the mornings with Dean Falconer for the rest of my life. Dean lay on his back breathing softly. The sunlight that filtered through sheers at the windows revealed his stubble of blond and silver whiskers. Abruptly the alarm on his phone sounded from the bedside chest, and he shot out an arm to silence it. He turned to look at me, and unadulterated happiness registered in his eyes. "Good morning, wife," he said, stroking my hair.

An hour later we grabbed croissants and cups of café crème to go and hurried to the Metro. We strolled the streets of bohemian Montmartre. And on a guided tour of Sacré-Coeur, I thought Dean's eyes would tumble out of their sockets. We had a leisurely lunch with glasses of summer rosé at a little bistro and took a boat cruise along the Seine. That night, we walked to the Pelletiers' for a scrumptious dinner deftly prepared by Madame Heloise. "*Allons-y*," Laurent said. He held his fork aloft and grinned at Dean. We tucked into the meal. Dean closed his eyes and moaned with pleasure with his first bite of Heloise's goat cheese, caramelized onion, and tomato tart. This was followed by bacon-wrapped figs, salad greens, and for dessert chocolate tartlets with candied grapefruit peel. It was a blessing to be in Tee and Laurent's home again, this time with a healthy and whole Theresa *and* my very own dream husband.

On a couple of days Dean and I made no plans at all, finding that we only wanted to wander and discover. Once on a bridge arching the river, a jazz band with saxophone and cello materialized. A rotund little man in a red jacket accompanied them with aplomb on a tiny console piano mounted on a child's wagon axle. On other bridges we were intrigued by hundreds of combination locks, like the ones on high school lockers, fastened to the metalwork. A Japanese man being walked by a slobbery mastiff told us that couples sealed their love by placing locks on the bridge.

Later at Laurent's gallery, Dean fell in love with Laurent's work. His architect's eye appreciated the precision with which Laurent depicted homes, buildings, and cathedrals. On two soggy days, Dean and I explored the Louvre and the Musée D'Orsay. One fine day, the sky vivid and blue again, we ambled through the Tuileries Gardens and ate lunch al fresco at a small café under the chestnut trees. On our last day I wanted to take Dean to the Luxembourg Gardens I had loved with Theresa those years ago. We packed a picnic although the sky was leaden. And the park was just as enchanting as I remembered.

Theresa and Laurent drove us to the airport that evening. We had a drink in a bar before boarding, talking of plans for the two to come and spend time with us the next summer, at Villeneuve and the Outer Banks. Finally, Theresa and I faced each other arms outstretched and shared a long, bittersweet embrace.

* * * *

As our Jeep crunched down the oak-lined drive at Villeneuve again, my heart soared. I would no longer sleep in the guesthouse:

that night I would share Dean's bed as his bride. Smiling, I reached for his hand and squeezed it three times. "Are you sharing that with *me* now?" he asked happily and squeezed mine back four.

We passed Billy in the paddock and waved to him. He smiled and raised his hat in salute. We climbed out of the Jeep to pet the ecstatic dogs. Laurel was happy to see us and anxious to hear about the trip. Typically thoughtful, she was busy preparing dinner for us. I saw the colorful postcard I'd sent from Montmartre posted on her refrigerator door. She asked about a huge parcel that had arrived from Paris. "I had the man prop it against your back door under the awning. I've been dying to know what it is." Dean and I looked at each other and shrugged. We had no clue. The little gifts we'd bought for family and friends had been carefully tucked into our carry-on bags in case our luggage was lost. Laurel said she would bring dinner over later, and we invited her to stay and eat with us. Dean brought the box—whose torn return address was unreadable—inside. We would shower and take a nap before dinner and open the parcel with Laurel after dinner.

We ate our fill of delicious pasta primavera and spoke of what we had done and seen in Paris. I gave Laurel the elegant little silver clock we had found in the Marais for her dressing table. We took our coffee into the living room and regarded the curious package. Inside was a wooden crate that Dean had to use tools to pry open. Incredulous, we stared at the painting of the Paris Opera House Dean had most admired at Laurent's gallery. I translated the note scrawled in Laurent's heavy back-slant script: "May you be ever joyful in your marriage. Theresa and Laurent." Overwhelmed, and although it was late in Paris, Dean called Laurent immediately to thank him.

Dean propped the painting against our mantle, and we stood admiring it again, toasting our happiness with glasses of good Virginia Cabernet Franc.

My mind turned to the business I had to take care of in Manhattan. After Dean and I unpacked and rested for a few days, I flew to New York to meet my father. Dad had offered to come and help me supervise the packing and moving of the furniture I wasn't selling. We would hold an estate sale with Anita's help and put the brownstone on the market.

I met with John again about the sale of my share of the firm. He was seriously considering retiring and leaving the city. Extraordinarily, he was interested in courting my mother-in-law! I learned that John had stayed on at Villeneuve an extra couple of days after the wedding getting to know Laurel and a spark had been set alight between them. Why had Laurel not told us? Dean and I had some romantic investigating to do.

Later in the week I met Nick for lunch at PJ Clarke's. Despite our intimate history there had never been any awkwardness between us. I had invited Nick to the wedding, but he and Dakota were expecting their first baby in two weeks. "I'm finally going to be a father," Nick said with a grin, as smug as if he'd invented fatherhood himself. "But I'll be seventy-four and decrepit when she graduates high school."

Burning the candle at both ends, I was able to take care of most of the details of relocating with Dad's and Anita's help. The unresolved loose ends would have to be handled long distance. I was exhausted and ready to get back to Dean.

The day after I returned to the farm the huge orange moving van trundled down the gravel drive. Charlotte and Hudson ran in front of it as if it were their job to herald its arrival. After the movers left, Dean and Billy indulged me by moving some of the furniture again to suit me. The panoply of pieces and the memories they evoked provided an eclectic and interesting look and feel to our home. We loved the monks' table in its new setting, and my family clock looked perfect atop Dean's rough-hewn mantle. What wouldn't fit went to the guesthouse to complete its furnishings. Neither of us could wait for Lark to come and visit.

It was time for Dean to return to work. I unpacked boxes and settled my belongings. I had the wedding photos and pictures we had taken over the summer handsomely framed and placed them about the house. Most days I took time to ride Trolley. Mary taught me how to rise to a trot and to bathe and groom the horse myself after a ride. I enjoyed shopping and lunches in town with my mother and sisters-in-law and learned my way around Dean's kitchen, mingling my pretty dishes with his plain ones. After doing all his own cooking for so long, Dean loved having dinner prepared for him each night. It became our ritual that Indian summer to have a swim and drink by the pool before dinner. Sometimes we even skinny-dipped and made love in the night-cool water.

I talked with Dean about practicing law again. As full as my life had become, I'd begun to miss my work. Dean and I had thrown around a few ideas. The best was that I would set up an office in Dean and James's building on High Street. Dean approached James with the idea of using a canted room, currently cluttered with ancient files and boxes that neither of them knew what to do with, things that their assistant Divya was dying to throw out. James agreed. "Not only," he'd said with a grin, "will we get that room cleaned up, but having Robin here will give the office an immediate upgrade."

One chilly night in early October Dean and I relaxed on a sofa, reading by the first fire of the season. The dogs lay companionably on the hearthrug—Charlotte's tail giving the intermittent thump, her eyes watchful, and Hudson snoring and occasionally farting in his sleep. Logs of white birch cracked and popped, filling the room with the aroma of wintergreen. I inhaled deeply. "Mmmm, the wood is nice!"

Billy and Laurel had come for dinner that evening for a batch of chili and buttermilk cornbread muffins. Billy had been palpably nervous. His first date with his old high school friend Margo, whom he had run into at Trader Joe's, was coming up that weekend. "Man, she's still *hot* for fifty!" he had told Dean confidentially, but of course Dean had told me. Laurel and I were proud of him for asking Margo out and had good-naturedly coached and teased him about it throughout dinner. I presented Billy with a good-looking new denim button-down shirt, just for luck.

My telephone rang, interrupting my reading of the *New York Times*. It was Lark. "Darling!" I said after one ring. My eyes fell on a black-and-white photograph in a pretty silver frame on Dean's end table, a laughing Lark at a vineyard that summer.

Lark and I exchanged chitchat, and then she asked, "Mom, is Dad there with you? Will you put me on speaker?" With a flicker of excitement, I told Dean what I was doing.

He put his book aside. "Larkster!" he called.

"How are you, Dad? I miss you. Mom, Dad, Ben's here with me. We have news."

"Hi, guys," Ben said. I could hear a smile on his handsome face.

"Hi, Ben, darling! How are you?" I called.

"Mr. Holland!" said Dean.

Lark interrupted, "Ben has a new job."

"Well, that's great! What will you be doing?" I asked.

Ben said, "It's a new gig with Coloma actually—director of sustainability."

Lark's voice was buoyant. "He'll be working from New York!"

"That's wonderful news!"

"Congratulations, Ben," Dean said warmly and asked him more about the job.

Ben told us what the position entailed and then stopped. "Listen, folks, Lark is about to burst."

I heard Lark laugh, the fumbling of the phone, the sound of a kiss. "Well," Lark said, "how would you guys like to be part of another wedding soon … like in two weeks?"

Stunned, Dean and I looked at each other and stammered, *"Really?"* I said, "It's about time!" and Dean added, "In *two weeks?*" Lark and Ben laughed at us.

Lark said, "But there's more … It seems I'm going to have a baby." I let out a whoop of joy, jarring Dean, who blinked and then grinned as if he'd learned he'd inherited the Palace of Versailles. They told us of their plan for a simple wedding. They wanted to be married at Dad's house on the beach on Lark's fall break from school. She would continue to teach until the baby was born in April. We ended the conversation telling them we loved them, foolish grins plastered on our faces.

Dean's face was full of wonder as he said, "Well, I'll be damned." He studied the calendar on his phone. Then he looked up at me. "How can I be a good grandfather when I'm just learning how to be a father?"

"We'll cross that bridge when we come to it." I smiled, rising to let the dogs out the back door. I went to the bookcase where Dean had connected my old turntable. I glanced at the framed photos on the shelves—the beautiful eight-by-ten wedding picture, a five-by-seven photo of me astride Trolley the first time, the grainy little snapshot of Dean and me from 1977, and the picture taken of the whole Falconer clan at the vineyard. I raised the cover on the record player and dropped the needle on the album that had brought us together all those years before. I padded back to my husband and hitched a leg up to straddle his lap. Slowly, I began to unbutton my blouse. Dean waited, brows raised, his eyes darkening to slate.

"What's your pleasure, Grandpa?" I asked.

ABOUT THE AUTHOR

Elizabeth Wafler's passion for a story told with heart led her to write her own fiction. A former elementary school teacher, she lives in the foothills of the Blue Ridge Mountains of Virginia with her husband and Cairn terrier, Mirabelle. The author can often be found at a local farmers' market in search of the perfect heirloom tomato or bouquet of flowers or at one of the area's beautiful vineyards enjoying a glass of Virginia wine. She is currently at work on her second novel, *A Faculty Daughter.*

ACKNOWLEDGEMENTS

Merci bien to Debbie and Greg Ketchum: to Deb for her loving support, even while planning a wedding; and to Greg for his editorial perspicacity and endless reservoir of encouragement.

Thanks are due to the team at AuthorHouse, especially Rob Clarkson and Viola Willis for their availability, enthusiasm and patience.

I owe deep appreciation to my enthusiastic beta readers, Mary Sumner, Anne Chambers, Alice Fitzpatrick and Beth Lofton.

I am grateful to Alice Vargo whose beautiful painting graces the cover of *In Robin's Nest*, and to photographer Kim Veillon for the fetching author photos.

I thank Shelley Payne for educating me on all things horses. She helped me imagine Villeneuve and send it galloping onto the page.

A fond bow is due newlyweds Katie and Ben Fitzpatrick for the sweet engagement ring story.

Special thanks are also due to Theresa Jackson and Mary Tillson, the besties who inspire and keep me laughing, and to lovely Joyce Seibert for her unflinching faith and encouragement.

I am especially grateful for my family. Without my husband Porter's unconditional love and support of *In Robin's Nest* this novel wouldn't have seen the light of day. His keen eye for inaccuracies and help in making Dean's sports analogies work were invaluable. My daughter, Liv, was my cheerleader from afar. It is a truly special moment when your adult child tells you she is proud of you.

This book is a work of fiction. All errors of fact or supposition are mine alone.

December 2015, Keswick, Virginia